If He Hollers, Let Him Go

A NOVEL

Beth Harden

Crawford Books 2015

To my father, Richard
who was there to listen
to my first words
and to my husband, Josh
who will stay to hear my last.

Prologue

An old chest freezer stood in our woodshed with an iron anvil on top. Rust had splayed the hinges. Its lid sprung from a quarter-century of hands opening it up, reaching in, lifting out plucked roasters, bricks of stale banana bread and blueberries hard as marbles. That old appliance was like the life my mother laid out for us. All sentimentality stacked and stored for no good reason. Our history in no sensible order, nothing dated or logically placed. All the important things my mother should have told her only daughter were shelved on ice. And each fall when we pulled the plug and chipped out all the yellowed, frozen condensation and pools of melt that had formed inside, we discovered there was very little left there worth keeping.

My mother's presence was powerful in absentia; not the she was dead or gone. Her body walked around our lives, her time logged in with hours of ironing and mending alteration but she kept her silence. She occasionally told grandiose stories of dead relatives, but with a vision skewed from always looking over her shoulder at the past where things appeared larger than they were. I wanted to know the things she didn't want to talk about. How she dreaded the idea of any us growing taller than her apron ties; and mourned over Polaroids of me and my five brothers standing sprawl-legged over the sprinkler or sitting on the porch floor spread with pages from the Down East American and the contents of the old ribbon candy jar dumped in our laps. Beach pottery, chips of cups and saucers lost in tea parties at sea and washed up on the banks of Frenchman's Bay. Dinner service for the entire population of Gust Harbor, Maine if the flotsam of other people's lives could be held together with thirty-minute epoxy. *I miss my babies. Where have those little people gone?* she'd say, even though we were there squabbling right in front of her.

In the end, my youth left me longing for the big picture, one that expanded far beyond a peek through the fringe of poplars and pines outside my farmhouse dormer. I fully realized the lack at the age of nine when I approached my mother and asked her why black people only lived on television. There was no Sesame Street where we lived. There was Maine and then there were the other forty-nine states. God's country, I'd been told all my life; so I figured I was one of the lucky ones hand-picked to live at the end of the Earth. With pride I stood knee-deep in the dead cold sea water and saluted the summit of Mount Cadillac that loomed out of a liquid horizon. Every so often a beam of blinding light twinkled as the sun glinted off a bumper of another car wending its way up the incline. Tourists, those unfortunate souls whose stay in heaven was held by deposit and booked a year in advance. It all came clear at age sixteen when I was hired as a chamber maid to clean up summer cabins out on Acadia Island. While God's people scrubbed lime stains off toilet bowls and soaked fried clams out of dirty sheets, the unlucky rest of the world played clay tennis and floated on lovely wooden sloops with names like Mary Todd. I asked myself, who would elect to go to paradise from Saturday afternoon to the following Saturday morning at eleven and spend the rest of the fifty-one weeks somewhere else? It wasn't destiny at all; it was a decision. Turned out, God dwelt in Glen Ridge, New Jersey too. I left my pail of Murphy's oil, ammonia and a pile of wet towels sitting on the sticky linoleum floor in Gull Cottage. It took me the rest of my five-hour shift to walk home past the deep green coves and beds of rock beach where the ocean rode high waving kelp and turning sea urchins over on their spineless backs. Miles of *our* land locked up and roped off from people like me. By the time I turned the stretch down the west side of the peninsula, fog had begun to wrap around the outlying islands that bristled like sleeping porcupines. Gulls swirled above the lone lobster boat that had lingered to pull its last traps and was rocking on the swells. In minutes the bay would be swamped in blindness. Nothing but gray that might last for a day, a few weeks or a lifetime. I knew then if I didn't go I too would disappear into unending sameness.

In the mind of my mother Mel, my decision to go to college in Boston was a flagrant rejection of God's good design. Crossing that bridge meant no turning back. She didn't say that, but she didn't have to. Mom turned a cold shoulder to the announcement and went to collect the faded beach towels that had blown clear off the clothesline. My father was beyond grieved. It showed in the drop of his shoulders like the luft and sag in a sail that has lost the tail wind and can no longer lead its craft. He took my hand in his palms worn rough from climbing utility poles and steering an oil truck all over Aroostook County just to keep his family tucked away. Safe from a world that regarded them through the binocular vision of the tower opticals up on Cadillac as merely specks of stubbornness in the way. But Russ Braum understood that his destiny was a choice he had made for the good of others. Just like mine would be. He wrapped me up in the scratch of his wool shirt and squeezed my cheek into a sleeve full of wood smoke, coffee and petroleum.

"Go! Run for your life. I want you to find all of what is waiting out there for you. Just be safe, sweetie."

Sometimes we do what we have to, knowing that it is contrary to what others want. And the people who love us most, even those that have trouble saying so, know it has to happen too. We make false promises and tell true lies, believing that we'll come back after a time and pick up where we left off. But they know differently, those that speak their reservations and those that give us their blessing. Because they are old enough to straddle the full landscape of life – the comings and the goings—like my mother who could only cling to the beginning and my father who sensed the end coming and sent me running towards it.

"The past is never dead. It's not even the past."
William Faulkner

PART ONE

CHAPTER 1
LAWFUL RESTRAINT

A first step into the unit confirms the menu of government-style chicken rationed, baked and floating in vats of grease. Still it's the one day of the month that prisoners actually hurry to the chow hall. A sweet stench of sage ekes through broken glass and permeates the humid atmosphere. The Native American inmates are sweating out their sins in the lodge that was erected hastily in the muddy Rec yard. The entire compound is filled with the musky aroma of lust and longing.

I unclasp the padlock on the counselor's mailbox, and reach in to gather the pile of plaintive stories. Per usual, it is stuffed to overflowing and as soon as the lid is raised, the stack catapults out onto the sticky floor. It takes several long minutes to assemble the strays into a manageable hold and then horror of horrors, stick my hand back into the depths of the box for the rest. Like the Halloween prank where some poor fool reaches through a blind hole in the card table to finger Jell-O made guts, there is always some tangible surprise at the bottom. Regurgitated gum, a porno picture, broken pencil stubs or worse. I manage to slip into the counselor's office undetected where an assortment of written requests awaits my notice. Most of them are drafted on the appropriate form and wedged through the gaps between lintel and hinges. Others are scribbled on cardboard or the back of legal envelopes and come skidding under the jamb. Some are folded in intricate origami shapes or tattooed with flowing script and smiling faces. Each one vies for first read.

I've barely punched the power button on the monitor when Tommy Pisano's mug comes into view. He juts his Neanderthal jaw against the pane and holds the pose. I ignore him. Next he points to the doorknob and snaps his thick fingers impatiently. I avoid eye contact and pull open the desk drawer to rearrange the money slips. My heart rate accelerates. Tommy flits out of view but returns moments later. A dark upside-down halo underscores his bulging eye sockets. This time he leans sideways against the door so there is no mistaking the profile, the shelf-like brow, bald sloping forehead, heavy nose and a sneer that wraps up his jowls like the Grinch who's just realized the depth of conniving evil he is capable of. I hold up a finger, indicating that he needs to wait.

"Aww, c'mon!" comes the muffled protest. Small drops of spittle hit the glass. Though I shouldn't, I give in to the pressure, get up, walk around the desk and release the door just an inch.

"I'm not ready yet," I say, using my boot heel as a door stop, just in case.

"Will I be on the list today?" he demands. Pisano jerks his head back and to the side in a tic-like motion. He forces his bulk into the airless office and stands there, blocking my exit. Advantage inmate. A major trespass in our behavior management class taught at the Academy.

"You have to write me," I repeat.

"You promised you'd see me," he froths.

"Write me and I will," I say calmly. The trick is to hold the voice steady; always fair, firm and consistent especially with people like Tommy who has no control switch. Just an itchy trigger.

"I did write you. Two day ago!" he shouts. I look around him, avoiding his gaze. There's a lopsided New York Yankees logo painted on the cinder block wall behind him. On closer inspection, a preliminary pencil sketch of a pair of red socks bleeds out from under the cheap white acrylic. This place thrives on rivalries. Loyalties are perpetuated or punished.

"I collected all the requests and I didn't see anything with your name on it." It's a risk, I know, to ask him to follow a system that displaces him as top seed at the doorway perch. I take my seat in the mangy, stained office chair that is set in the lowest position. I crank the lever on the side to bring myself back up to adult height.

"I need to make a legal call. It's important." Never mind that he has used up his two allotted calls and an extra off-the-record voicemail to his shrink just four days into the new month.

"You *know* this pisses me off," he slobbers, his arms flinging out to the side. He pulls a visiting application from the bookshelf, flips it over, grabs the inmate pen from his side of the desk and scribbles in large ranting letters: I GOT TO SEE YOU. Then he slides the memo under my desk so it pops up at my feet.

"Mr. Pisano, the longer we stand here debating this, the longer it's going to take me to get to everyone."

"You know I don't like to wait in line with the others! I know myself. Someone's gonna push my buttons and I'm gonna catch another bid out there."

"I'll have the officer call you when I'm ready. Does that work?" I ask.

"I'll be on my bunk," he says in disgust, and is gone. The perspiration from thousands of confined sit-ups has pushed the dew point up a few notches in here. Guys are running in place, doing dips off the window sill and curling up to knees slung over bunk rails. A roomful of big boys held in for a year's worth of recess due to inclement behavior.

To the left of the computer monitor, a metallic burgundy coffee cup has stood obscured in the rush of comers and goers for three days now. I never get more than a sip or two down before the cappuccino is set aside to brew curdled foam. My leather briefcase is a snarl of risk assessment forms, detainer notices and post-it reminders that have dropped out of order and nest in a heap of pens at the bottom. This week's case notes have crimson stains like lip gloss spattered on them. There is little option other than dribbling Greek yogurt and raspberries over the sheaths of paperwork while I type in the quiet just before roll call sets the shift in motion. Once inside the housing unit, there is no stopping the outflow of a need so aching and overwhelming, you can feel it throbbing behind the walls and up the main corridor. Each man spends the night on his bunk with his mind's eye focused on one thing: getting out. As the days boil down into vicious sameness, this distant mark on the calendar becomes a raving obsession. All eyes are fixed on the one egress that leads out to the real world. The fervent prayers of Muslims, Catholics and Native Americans alike begin and end with the same petition. *Allah/ Sweet Mary/ Mother Earth, please get me the fuck out of here.*

The windowless office has absorbed the odor of four hundred damp Nikes. The one ancient desk fan putters to a palsied hum. The copy machine is broken.

"Fuck," I say. I quickly reach under the blinds on the door and tape up today's list in order of priority. One by one, they start lining up outside the door.

"Pardon my language," I add for the benefit of the twenty peeping eyeballs that glare through the slats in the lowered blind. Why I say it, I don't know. *Fuck* is just fine with them.

#

The morning is well underway with few snags in the sequence of men who file in empty-handed and back out with new parole dates, updated money accounts, pending warrants to serve or a care package of dwarfed toothpaste and bars of soap that smell like kerosene. Suddenly, the door flies open crashing its leaden weight against the back of the chair where Mr. Dwyer sits sorting the daily mail.

"I swear to God, I'm gonna beat the fuckin' shit out of you, Mike!" Tommy is in high mania now. Saliva pools in the corner of his dry lips. Sweat clamps the front of his greyed tee shirt. A flame-red rash runs the width of his neck. Dwyer, the B-dorm block worker, whips to his feet and turns to face his bunkie. He says nothing, just hangs his head in the face of this tirade. Tommy's anger has coagulated in visibly extended veins and stringy tendons. It's not the kind of rage built from pumping push-ups but from getting pushed around. A lifetime of it. He continues to seethe, crowding all his ugliness into the other man's space.

"Hold on, Tommy. Not now…" Dwyer stutters with his hands at his side, disarmed. I move between the two men and face the provoker.

"You need to step out, Mr. Pisano!" My right hand is just out of reach of the inmate receiver. If I jiggle it off the hook, then the signal will be sent to Control to send cops running this way.

"This kid is gonna get hisself killed, and it'll be all your fault!" he yells at me, then turns his attention back to the submissive man who keeps mumbling, "C'mon Tommy, c'mon man" over and over.

"I know what you're up to. You sit in here taking up all her time, you fucker!"

"Calm down. He works for me. You know that. I asked him to be in here," I tell Pisano and move closer, creating more space behind me and less room for him to maneuver his fists into striking range.

"Yeah, and what you don't know is, he's been taking the envelopes you give him and selling them to the other guys. Plus you can't trust him with the mail. He's been reading my shit," the bully shouts.

"I just do what I'm told," says the sheepish Irish kid whose complexion has turned the color of week-old groats. His reaction denotes the all-too-familiar frequency of his neighbor's irrational outbursts.

"Just go. I'll meet with you tomorrow," I tell the lesser man and usher him out. The situation is too volatile and the noise is beginning to draw attention from the other inmates.

"Take a seat," I say harshly. Pisano slams his body down into the plastic chair. Instantly, the juice goes out of him like a circuit breaker that's been tripped off.

"Can I call my lawyer now? I wrote you," he says calmly as if nothing out of the ordinary just happened. I pretend the tachycardia in my chest is imaginary and the cold pit of fear in the gut is only the natural pang of a mid-morning blood sugar drop.

"What's the name of your lawyer?" I ask. Pisano beams and pulls out the business card to a Frank Solomon in Dorchester. The win goes in his column today. I dial up the number, wait on the line to identify the law firm and then signal for him to pick up the inmate phone. I quietly replace the receiver and without making any sudden movement, turn back to the computer screen. As client and public defender converse, I pull up the inmate query system, making sure the monitor is tilted away from his line of vision. Inmate number 137113's risk scores come up. Assaultive: 5 Severity of Violence: 5. Mental Health: 5. Paranoid. Suicidal.

"You never call me, man! You told me to cop to this plea and now here I sit...Bullshit! I'm the one doing time here...I can't do shit in here...No programs...I can't get a job. I want you off the case...I'll handle it myself....just get me to trial."

The receiver slams down so hard that a plastic splinter from the cradle flicks on top of the file cabinet. Tommy Pisano stands up, satisfied.

"Thank you," he says politely.

I could very well write him a Class A ticket for Threatening and get him removed from General Population. But Tommy doesn't have the tools to do anything differently. Never has. In primitive fashion, problems are solved by a barrage of flurried fists on chest, spit in his attorney's face and a senseless beat-down of the irritating world that gets in his simple-minded way.

The bell rings for Rec time and the officers reluctantly stand and begin yelling orders. They amp up the decibel level with raunchy jokes, football stats and a general need to out-shout their captives. On Tuesdays, it's bottom tier first. Once the rest of the men are settled in, I start to tour and distribute the mail, hoping selfishly that they're napping with sheets pulled up over their heads and won't notice the paper that comes spiraling onto the floor.

I'm a tier walker by trade with not a stitch of safety net but my own sixth sense. It's a far leap for the long-ago girl from Gust Harbor, Maine. White, wobble-kneed and bursting with life, she was steady on her feet despite learning to walk on slimy kelp and sharp barnacle. Now, it's a gamble. Every day, a jockey for survival on a walkway of concrete. My spotters are lazy and lean up against the desk with menus of double-stuffed pizzas in hand. They wear stately blue and parade around the perimeter with their eyes on the prize of their own fat retirement. Forget about the circus girl who takes center stage, dangling by her gums and guy-wires in a cellblock of two hundred violent men. Even on their wobbly rope, the Wallendas were more likely to fall among friends and survive.

I head first to the upper level that is stale with the overflow of forced heat. The lifers there live in single cells with Muslim prayer rugs angled south to southeast. Cardboard stolen from the kitchen deliveries covers the open toilets when the convicts-turned- converts kneel down to pray. Thirty feet below, bolted tables sport red and black checkerboard squares painted on the cement tops so no one can steal the fun. The young bucks with taut bare chests decorated in tribal ink are loose down there and start up the chorus.

"Miss! Miss! Counselor!" they yell. I keep walking above them, following the numbered cells in a clockwise rotation laid out like a postal route with odd numbers on the left side and evens on the right.

"Did you do what I asked you to do?" someone yells. I indicate with a circling motion of my hand that I intend to keep on track.

"Did you take care of that thing for me?" They keep at it, whining, asking the same questions over and over when the answers are not to their liking. One lap complete, I head down to the next level. Everywhere I go, I'm being watched. Eyes intently peer through gaps between doors. Small shards of mirrors poke out and are angled to see who walks this mile. The self-consciousness has never disappeared; my heightened state of alertness is permanently ingrained. The difference now is the amount of years under my belt. I do not shirk away from discomfort. I apologize to no one. *Don't mistake my kindness for weakness,* a bluff thrown out by men who don't have the strength to make it in here. I'm not ashamed to tell the truth. My kindness is a defect, a weakness grown out of trust, that genetic crack in the female armor that evil men count on and act upon.

A towering Hispanic sporting a knitted skull cap blocks my way. He looks disappointed already.

"Mr. Acevedo. I passed your time sheet on to Records to double-check. They're looking into your question about jail credit." His shoulders relax and a faint grin smoothes out that snarl. It is enough that I know his name, that his question has not been forgotten in the barrage of needs.

"Thank you, Miss Abrams," he says cordially and steps back into his cell to let me pass. I'm headed to get a signature from the pasty twenty-one year old from Gloucester who's been convicted with the rape of his ex-girlfriend. The charges were pressed by her parents when they found out he decided to break up with their slutty daughter. He was subsequently charged and sentenced to ten years with mandatory time. He took it very hard yesterday when I had to tell him he was stipulated to the year-long in-house sex offender treatment program. I left him sniffling and rubbing his acne-covered cheeks after I put him on the phone to his mom despite the directive that prohibits that. Sometimes empathy has to overrule ethics. Now they're rescinding his good time. Seventy-two cell is at the back corner of the middle tier tucked away where the rolling laundry bins for B-block are kept. He's an okay kid who didn't double-check his addition before sleeping with his fifteen-year old seductress. I hate this kind of case. It has injustice stamped all over it. But I need to remind myself, this is why I'm here.

I pull up in front of the cell door. A draft of frigid air is blowing through from the north side. The glass must be broken or they've jimmied makeshift antennae through the small space where the old windows drop in. This corner of the block is dark and devoid of direct sun. Both bunks are empty. The blanket on the top is missing and the mattress bare and free of the usual crowd of GED books and papers. *Was he moved out?* And then I see the limp body partially concealed by the front of the metal bunk and the plastic chair tipped on its side. He's still moving in tiny jerking motions that are powered by reflexes only. The braid of shredded linen sheet around his neck has done its job. A bustle of foam leaks from his nose. I push the button on my body alarm and freeze in place.

"Code purple, "I stutter as the first two guards arrive on the scene. All my training goes out the window. I forget about the glass box on the wall with the cutting tool that could free him. And the incident report I will be required to fill out, the one that will claim the officers did their thirty-minute tours per post order which I will eventually sign to confirm that all protocol was followed and no one is at fault. The banging of multiple levers starts up as the cells are popped open, prisoners pushed back and then locked up. Everyone herded away from the truth.

It all comes rushing back. The movie starts up. Now over twenty-six years old, the film has lost its color and is only a flickering series of black-and-white frames. I close my eyes and put a hand on the railing to steady myself.

"Counselor Abrams. Are you alright?" someone asks. The trusted tier men come to the rescue with wet rags and a small carton of sour orange juice. I feel them lower me to the gritty floor where there are more germs than the number of stars that have passed over this prison in the past eighteen years. Their strong hands touch my skin. Good men with bad choices or bad men with good intentions? Decades ago, these kinds of men had left me for dead. I was the victim, just about that kid's age, noosed, and left out to hang by a system that failed me. It's a movie played in rewind skimming fast over the hard parts. A memoir; a horror story; a frenzied dream flapping madly off its reel in the haste to get back to its beginning.

#

March – 1988

My first thought was that the Rapture must have happened. Jesus had finally made the trip down to meet his children halfway to heaven, gathered his latch-key kids up out of this disappointing world and brought them to the eternal party. But if so, then God had split the Second Coming right down the middle of the long stretch of Barnum Boulevard which opened up like a parade route minus the spectators. All the evangelists apparently had lived on the north side of the street. Once I stepped inside Tap House Spirits to pick out a bottle of ice wine for the night's celebration, two things were readily apparent. Number one, I couldn't afford the specialty beverage I had in mind and secondly, the place was strangely empty. At that time on a Thursday night, happy hour should have been in full swing with freshmen bumping to the Bangles over at Malone's Place. In the ten minutes that it took to browse the shelves, not one customer stepped in the establishment. I paid for the discounted Riesling and walked outside. The parking lot adjacent to Galardi's Market, which was typically thick with frat brothers banging green grocery carts like bumper cars into the fenders of parked sedans, was dead quiet. I gazed at the *Checks Cashed/ Bail Bonds* strip across the way. Restless men collected in shadows under the pharmacy awning. Still too early for trouble, they mimicked and swaggered and shouted instead.

It occurred to me suddenly that it was Spring Break which explained the absence of activity on the academic side of town. People had cleared out in Dodge Darts or on Greyhound buses headed towards Lauderdale; everyone except a twenty-year old over-achiever who cared more about my suma cum laude honors than dangling my breasts over balconies. It was dusk by then, that uncertain hour which was not yet night but well beyond the clarity of day; certainly not a great time to be walking alone up this deserted stretch. I picked up the pace, clutching the bottle that threatened to slip from its paper bag sleeve. If I hadn't been so focused on other things such as Aaron's pending visit and the deadline on my thesis, I'd have remembered to stuff an extra twenty bucks in my pocket to call a cab. The city bus stopped a few blocks back at the intersection of Walden and Highlands Avenue and even if I rattled together the right amount of change, it seemed a contraindication to walk back through dark territory to meet it. I crossed the recess playground of Revere Elementary which sprawled in empty abandon with a few lone tetherball poles that dangled limp rope. On the far side of the fenced lot, modest bungalows and pre-World War II homes started up and ascended in stature and glory as the streets backed farther and farther away from downtown. I kept heading north.

As each subsequent block unfolded in a darker cast of shadow, I checked and double-checked my surroundings. Small details caught my eye. A McDonald's wrapper tailed the foot of a stop sign and one small light blue child's shoe was new to the sidewalk since yesterday. It was times like these I regretted not having my car but off-street parking had proved fatal to my Buick Apollo. Its transaxle had been pinned against the curb by the epileptic neighbor who came roaring out of his garage mid-seizure. I crossed for the last time just south of the Victorian Tudor that was my temporary home. Mrs. Schuster, the next door neighbor, was sitting at her card table on her all-season porch sipping tomato soup while her cross-eyed, urine-colored poodle dug frantic nails against the glass. I lifted a hand in greeting though I wasn't at all sure she could see me looking from the inside out.

I jumped two steps at a time up onto the pressure-treated deck at the back of the house. The tiny plum-colored buds on the Japanese maple had already begun to swell and ripen. It was a balmy March evening full of late winter wind and warm as lamb's breath. The atmosphere was moist and expectant, a perfect climate for couples. The key turned in the dead-bolt and as soon as the door swung inward, I heard the ringing of the wall phone. I jimmied it again to quickly lock the bolt but it resisted, so I yanked the key out and ran to catch the call.

"Hey, Lissa. I was getting worried. I called several times."

"Oh, I didn't mean to be gone that long. I just went to do a few errands. You getting ready to leave?"

"Well, here's the hitch. I've had so many employees call out sick that I need to be on shift and try to recruit some workers," Aaron said hesitantly. He was all too aware of how disappointed I would be. Our opportunities to see one another had dwindled as each of our separate lives picked up momentum and responsibility.

"Oh. Does that mean you can't make it down at all?" I asked tentatively.

"No. My plan is to get everything running smoothly on the first shift production run tomorrow and then I can check out. This means I could probably be there by dinner time tomorrow."

"Well, I wish we had more than twenty-four hours together but I understand. It pisses me off though that people don't consider the effect of their actions on others. Like maybe you had plans, too."

"That's the downside of being the boss. Comes with the job," Aaron said.

"Well, I'll get the bulk of my essay done tonight and get to bed early. Maybe I'll cook up something special for us," I said.

"No chance, sweetie. You'll be rewarded for your patience with a night out."

"Alright. Drive safely on your way down."

"I do love you," Aaron said, followed by an audible sigh of relief. The grocery stock boy turned food manufacturing supervisor was off the hook. There was plenty of time now to chill the wine and beer which I popped onto the top shelf of the refrigerator next to the tray of gouda cheese, half-sours and sliced kielbasa. Food could wait. I'd go change and work for a few hours first. Walking through the Welton's residence was like a trip through a National Geographic magazine. The hallways, study and parlor housed a collection of museum-quality souvenirs from numerous sabbaticals. I loved to float from room to room revering each intricate and valuable object; items like the hand-stitched table tapestries from Calcutta with lavish beading and jeweled embroidery or the Sese grinding bowls from Acra carved into a swirl of safari animals. The hallways were decorated from floor to ceiling with grainy photographs, visual tributes to travels where elephants lolled on their sides in septic rivers spraying joyous loops of water in a heavenly arc over the malnourished backs of their trainers and young women in royal kaleidoscope silk scraping the skin off their heels as they padded dusty miles to a school with no desks or books. The irony of temples besides tents and palaces besieged by peasants. The dichotomy was both cruel and captivating, no different than the families back home living in broken-down Buicks with skinny dogs and shiftless husbands, their women, ugly-mouthed from stringing up wet diapers kid after kid. Their poverty in stark contrast to the Village Improvement Society whose aim it was to clear the unsightly clutter from view as their sloops sailed around the leeward side of the Point.

I headed up the main staircase to my room. The camisole and panties for tomorrow's soiree were already laid out on top of the cedar sweater chest. It mattered little what clothing covered up these delicates. The outer garments would be stripped and flung in a boisterous display of hasty conquest; but from there, the pace always became a ritual of worship. Aaron liked to linger over lingerie tracing fingers on lace straps and elastic hem, pressing down, rubbing inwards, nudging and nuzzling the thin fabrics that prevented him from having me. And when the gorgeous, slow dance ceased and he finally peeked beneath, it was the like the first time, each time, as he gazed fully on the fragrant mysterious folds between my legs. But tonight, I would relax in casual comfort and use my thinking cap instead. I switched off the light and walked back down to the kitchen.

I didn't want to break open the chilled wine so I helped myself to a glass of Northstar merlot from the owner's overstocked collection in the pantry. I hopped back on the IBM computer Dad had donated as a going-off gift. It was no small sacrifice on his part, even with regular overtime. I picked up the thread where I had left off in my analysis of the self-destructive dynamic of Prader -Willi Syndrome, a rare genetic disorder that causes the sufferer to gorge himself to death, if allowed. Charlie Kravit had all the classic signs: the prominent nasal bridge, high narrow forehead, tapered fingers and thickened middle. He'd been my study subject at Mass General's genetic counseling clinic for over sixteen weeks now. This piece of cutting-edge research might just seal my chance of making the leap from a state university to Northeastern, the golden sister school down the way.

#

Two hours later, I was growing weary. I decided to print off this latest version and quit for the night. The green button flashed off and on as the ink cartridge jumped into high gear and began spooling out the eight-by-elevens. Several pages cascaded out of the Hewlett-Packard and onto the wide pine boards. I leaned over almost flush with the floor in order to snag the strays that landed under the desk and then straightened back up with effort. Suddenly, something felt different. The bamboo blinds on the French door brushed ever so slightly against the glass. A fluctuation in the air flow, perhaps? A flicker of a shadow appeared to race across the glass front of the china closet. I spun quickly to my right but the dining room and adjacent parlor were empty. It was just me and Dan Rather whose stone face flickered from the portable Magnavox on the Formica countertop. There was a slight rush of sound like the break of suction, then the full clatter of the storm door as it swung open wildly and hit the iron railing. The little spit of a dog next door started another volley of yapping.

"Shit!" I said. I had neglected to close it tightly. The pin on the hydraulic arm had dropped out a while back and the outside door had to be manually pulled shut or else it would set sail on any stiff breeze. I got up and slid on quiet socks in a little Katarina Witt spin over the icy ceramic tile floor. The dim bulb on the oven hood threw only a faint spotlight on what I had imagined to be a one-woman exhibition. I realized abruptly that I was not alone. It took only one appalling moment to fathom the facts. There were two hungry-looking men who'd just rushed in the back door and were paused, half-panting, trying to get their bearings like insects who alight on a strange surface with antennae aloft. They'd brought cigarette smoke and the odor of fast-food in with them. The distinct smell of the streets. Perhaps they were confused and had walked into the wrong door looking for someone else's party.

"Can I help you?" I asked. The question came out like a digital recording that was both neutral and generic in tone.

"Are your parents home? Anyone else in the house?" snapped the bolder of the two. His eyes were glazed and appeared to tick in circles. His entire demeanor was jumpy. Instantly, my whole affect dimmed and flattened. My survival instincts dictated the modus operandi: Calm is Contagious. I hoped my blasé demeanor would communicate that.

"No. I rent here. This is not my house," I stated in a wooden tone. The threat was perceived and intercepted in the air space between us. In any version of good self defense strategy, the next move should be mine. My mind fell back to military training passed on from a fighter-pilot grandfather. In a crisis, he had told me, revert to the OODA loop: Observe, Orient, Decide and Act. My senses took hold of step one and began making quick visual notations. Two African-American males in their late twenties wearing discolored baseball jerseys and dark sweatshirts. One wore a New York Mets cap that tucked down a rash of short coarse curls. He was of medium height, maybe five-ten or so with little contrast between skin tone and shade of eyes. The other ducked his head away from my detection. Step two: quickly get your bearings. *What tools or means of exit are available?* Before I could act though, a wiry arm laced around my neck from behind. Warm fingers traced the line of my collar bone in an insidious hug that I instantly wanted to throw off. The man wore a leather glove that curled back from a dark wrist revealing chalky skin with a serpent coil of tattoo ink that spelled some sort of name. It was an important clue to decipher, but I couldn't make it out. My eyes were suddenly swimming with panicky tears. The calligraphy morphed into a blur of olive-colored hieroglyphics that defied interpretation.

"You expecting anyone?" asked this third invader. His breath was sour and emitted an acrid smell like the extinguished wick of a candle.

"No," I answered hastily and instantly froze in a pose of compliance. *Now! Use your education!* All those notebook pages of psychological theory could be put into clinical and critical practice. I had the greatest weapon of choice on my side – communication — and its power of persuasion.

"If you're lying, someone will get hurt. Understand?" he hissed. Instantly the rules were clarified. This was no social encounter or case of mistaken address. The three-to-one odds were not comforting.

"Yes, okay. My boyfriend is due here any minute. If you are looking for money, I can give you some cash and you can leave without any hassle. I haven't seen your face. No harm done."

"Better hope he doesn't show," said Suspect # 3. A cold block of fear lodged in my stomach. His breathing was choppy and excitable, coming and going in sharp shallow bursts. The faint aroma of diesel fuel clung to his sweatshirt sleeve. He fidgeted uncomfortably, shifting his weight from foot to foot. One man turned the dead bolt on the door behind him; the other rushed about the room tugging on the curtain pulls, quickly lowering the blinds and fumbling for the dimmer switches. They obviously did not know the footprint of this house but something told me this was not the first time they had dared a brazen invasion of someone else's home. The two followers were now all wild eyes and eager palms reaching for what didn't belong to them. Strange hands pawed over precious objects. One of them let the hand-painted Staffordshire vase slip and it splintered into fragmented halves. How would I explain the mess to the Weltons? Maybe someone from the Paier Art School knew how to do porcelain restoration and could be commissioned for a repair before its owners ever noticed the damage. Their movements were quick and exaggerated as they executed a haphazard sweep of the area. The rash nature of their actions suggested this crime might be an impulsive idea. If so, maybe these thrill-seekers could be spooked or distracted from completing this errant mission.

"The house at the end of the street has a valuable stash of paintings," I suggested meekly. My captor gave no indication that he had heard and continued to clench my neck.

"C'mon," he said, grabbing my elbow and pushing me in the direction of the wall phone. "You're gonna make a call. Tell him something's come up."

Suspect 3 stood anonymously behind me within inches of my ear as I nervously pressed the digits. The signal patched through to the Mitchell home in South Portland, Maine. Someone picked up after the second ring.

"Has Aaron left yet, Mrs. Mitchell?" I asked.

"No, he's right here, honey," she answered cheerfully.

"Can you put him on for a moment, please?"

"Sure Lissa. Hold on a sec." I could hear her bustle towards the far end of the room and call out for her son. When he picked up, my antagonist leaned in closer to listen.

"Hey, there. We need to change the time. Can you hold off until morning before coming down?" I asked. *Don't break down. Don't scream. Stay steady.*

"What? I thought we had already agreed that I would…" I cut him off.

"My sister either has a case of food poisoning or else she's really sick with a virus," I interrupted. "I'm going to take her to the ER now. Who knows how long it will take," I added matter-of-factly. *Don't believe me. Read between the lines. Danger!*

"Lissa? What is…?"

"So I'll see you tomorrow then," I said without waiting for a confirmation.

"Wait, tell me…"

"I love you too. See you then," I said and clicked the receiver back on its cradle. The code had been sent. The non-existent sister was a clue that hopefully would be translated: *Trouble. Call for help. Please hurry!* My tormentor removed a sharp Exacto knife from his pocket and sliced the telephone cord which spooled like disemboweled intestine down the wainscoting.

"Area code 2-0-7. That's long distance. Not in Massachusetts. Jersey, maybe? Either way, we got time. Now, move!"

There was no way to appeal to this young man on a personal basis, no name to put to the face that was also unidentified. All I knew was the superficial color of his skin appeared to be as dark as his heart. *Concentrate now! Step two: Orient.* Two famous African-American men flashed to mind, one who rallied for peace and one who died for preservation. It occurred to me how kind it was that shock numbs perception allowing both mind and body to waltz into a distracted dance of trivial thoughts, but this was no time for meaningless games. My brain was trying to transmit crucial information that could protect me. I took my best guess. My persecutor was from the latter school of politics. Malcolm Little (aka angry Malcolm X) once said, 'Tactics based on morality can only succeed when you are dealing with basically moral people.' That truth was more and more unlikely here. Mr. X pulled me off my heels and escorted me backwards through the pantry area into the dining room.

"Stop, please. I'll cooperate," I begged hoarsely, tugging at his forearm which had cinched higher up near the larynx. His boys rushed ahead. They stopped to regard the computer monitor on the table with the textbooks stacked beside it. One sweep sent the research material skittering onto the Turkish carpet; the second lifted the hardware off its stand and let it drop. There was a rattle inside the casing and the power shorted out. My heart clenched with regret. The gift Dad had given to propel me towards my chosen profession had been laid to waste. This act of wanton destruction seemed to give them specific pleasure and further license to destroy and take from the just- barely-haves.

"Please. Let me go! There are valuables here. I can show you," I suggested.

"Where do they keep the good shit?" he asked impatiently.

"There's a portable safe in the master bedroom closet but I have no idea where the key is. Or if it has a combination." We crossed out into the main foyer in a tangled knot. My attacker motioned to his followers to fan out in front of him. His jaw of sharp stubble was clamped against the side of my neck.

"Which room?"

"Upstairs to the left. The one with the blue and white wallpaper. Let me go, please. You can have anything."

"Show us!" he said, brusquely pushing me ahead of him. I took the stairs cautiously, carefully testing each riser for a crack or creak that might upset the equilibrium of the moment. At the top of the landing, the German cuckoo clock started ratcheting its leaden pine cone weights up the winding chain and the little bird bobbed and cracked open its beak. Seven o'clock. Time noted. Still an eternity before help could arrive. Hopefully Aaron had thought to alert the troopers. A runner of plush green carpeting ran front to back down the center hallway to the master suite. I pointed to the closed door. The co-conspirators bullied the glass door knob and pushed inside. My conjoined criminal pulled us up short.

"Which one is your room?" he hissed. I shook my head. "Which one?" Panic began to well up in my chest. *Step three: Decide.* Was there a way to create a disturbance or slip his grasp? I tightened up my muscles in silent resistance. He detected the slight refusal and applied more pressure to the throat. I couldn't remember if it was better to struggle or go along with the attacker's demands. The rough grapple of his bicep near my windpipe prevented any accumulation of sound. There was no volume behind my attempted cry. I stepped forward and we moved in choppy unison to the room in the south corner of the house. Once inside, he released me with a push forward, flicked on the switch and slammed the door. I rushed to the opposite wall and huddled near the tall wooden wardrobe.

"Come here, Pretty," he said. Our glances locked. We were committed now to some action of great import, both of us key players in a one-act tragedy whose ending had not yet been scripted. I knew I would not depart that room unchanged. As deeply terrified as I was, I determined that I would not walk away from the encounter without leaving some permanent mark on his soul. He looked to be two, maybe three years older than I, though there were generations' worth of skin divots and scars on his face from a genetically-flawed lifestyle handed down to him at birth.

"Can you please let me go now? I have a big family that loves me. Like I'm sure you do, too," I pleaded. His mouth turned into a curdled grin. He moved to the roll top desk where a copy of my senior thesis paper sat in its near-final draft. The electronic version was likely lost in the chaos of looting that appeared to be in full play. I could hear someone ransacking through the rooms below. My antagonist picked up the paper-clipped bundle of printed text and screwed down his brow as he began to intently read it. Halfway down the first page, he looked up and smiled.

"You're brilliant as fuck too, huh?" said Mr. X. He methodically tore ten pages at a time and allowed the tatters to drift in columns onto the hardwood floor. Six months worth of work destroyed in sixty seconds. Mr. X dragged the wooden chair away from the desk and dropped into it, kicking his Timberland boots up onto the pile of folded laundry on top of the sweater chest.

"Take off your clothes!" he said matter-of-factly. "But leave your underwear on." The fear was instant and as sharp as an arctic inhale. This scene was one right out of movies that I had seen before, the kind that sent me flying off the edge of my seat when the female victim cowered with inevitable surrender before her perpetrator. 'Get that bastard,' I'd yell. But now I better understood my doomed sisters' lack of action. My limbs were clotted and sluggish with instant paralysis. I couldn't think clearly. I could hear my brain shouting without any reaction from the body: *Act!* Mr. X was blocking any hope of a run. I swiftly planted myself in front of the nearest corner window, which faced east towards the street, and started banging my fists on the window panes, hoping that Mrs. Schuster was scrubbing her cast iron skillet with a Brillo pad and might chance to look up.

"I'm not playin' here. Get away from the glass!" he ordered sternly.

I ceased the mad scramble and turned back towards him. X had his fist in his pocket and I remembered the blade that had dismembered the line of communication.

"Now strip!"

"Please, I'll write a check from my account. We can go to the ATM. I have at least a few thousand. I could probably get more."

"Do what I say, smart girl." *Shit!* Palpitations railed behind my breastbone. Fight or flight was in full force. I slowly removed the pale yellow raglan blouse and grey leggings and started to fold them, hoping even a slight intermission might halt the torment. Self-consciousness took hold in the half-light that struck the faint stretch marks on my hips, and illuminated each mark and mole that journeyed across my paper-pale skin. For over five years, I had undressed for only one man and that slow disrobing was a willing dance of desire. There in the unforgiving stare of terror, I trembled and shrank back. I was just another helpless, terrified victim. Mr. X came closer. With nimble hands, he ran his fingers around the elastic hem of my bra clasping flesh as he went and unhooked the plum-colored Victoria's Secret, a secret no longer as he tossed the bra into a heap.

"Lie down!" he said. He didn't ask a second time. When I began to struggle furiously against his touch, he used his superior height and weight as leverage and bent me over backwards still flailing, onto the bed pinning each wrist in isolation, and grinned.

"You want to make love with me?" he cooed sarcastically.

"No, no, no," I moaned. Love? The choice of word was a stinging insult in the context of violence. Last chance. *ACT, goddamnit!* I dredged up some saliva and spat into that dangerous smile. He reared backwards and got one hand into his side pocket, grappling for the solid object that banged against my ribs through the fabric. The glint of a blade appeared. I stopped moving and held my breath.

"How 'bout I fuck you instead then?" he hissed.

"Please, don't. It's that time of the month. We can do something else," I begged.

"Okay, you win." He pulled up to a crouching position, reached towards the headboard, shook one foam pillow loose from its cotton pillowcase then dropped back down. He began to kiss me starting and lingering just above the pelvic bone then running his tongue up to my teeth. At the same time his hands played a little parlay with my panties inching them downwards in suggestive increments. His voice softened now that he had the strength of a weapon to speak for him.

"Turn over," he ordered. I prayed that my willingness to work with him would pay off. As I rolled onto my tummy, he reached upwards. I caught the fragrance of my True Religion perfume on the sheath of linen as he slipped it over my head. I began to panic. *I'm going to suffocate.* But the cloth was thin and allowed a small intake of oxygen if I took slow, shallow breaths. *Dear Jesus, help me. If the end of the world is coming, let it come on this street in this house. Now. Lift me on high.* He pulled my hands up over my head and cinched them with what felt like a bathrobe sash. The other end was knotted around the bedpost. Leaning close to my right ear, he whispered.

"Relax now. Trust me."

I felt the mattress spring back as he got up to unlock the door. I lay still praying fervently for a deliverer or a miracle. I knew the other men had entered the room by the soft commotion of multiple feet and a draft of air that seeped in during the exchange. I tensed and waited. I remembered now that it was a 50/50 roll of the dice as far as survival; no matter if one fights back or flees into mental retreat and passively allows fate to have its way. The exposed pores on my bare back tingled with apprehension. An itch kicked up under my shoulder blade. Someone approached the foot of the bed and I heard the telltale pull of a zipper. The bed sank under the weight that was now distributed behind me. I felt a brush against my flanks. Someone grabbed my feet.

I could not tell who the groundbreaker was. The violation was unexpected and excruciating as an erect penis intruded into my buttocks. It was initially repelled by bands of muscle wall but the assault was repeated with more determined thrusts. My entire pelvic region suddenly burst with ungodly pressure. An intense tunneling and tugging sensation radiated deep into the tops of my thighs. Fortunately the entrance and exit were quick and the offender withdrew. *It's over. It's over. You've done it.* They would not get the satisfaction of a single cry out of me. Just as I started to relax with relief, the second onslaught began with a frantic fury. Hands gripped the flesh above my waist and yanked me into position. I endured another onslaught of rapid friction between my legs that transferred the pain from a deep ache to raw stinging. This time I was not so lucky. The attack was prolonged and increasingly more violent as my assailant slowly gathered momentum. I had time to think. Nobody wants to be conscious during such an ordeal. I almost wished they would see the kindness in taking me out now. Moans finally came from the beast that had deeply penetrated my belly. Suddenly, it became a slippery ride and then my mount was gone. I was physically sick to my stomach but swallowed back any regurgitation. I didn't want to aspirate and choke; not after surviving the firing squad. Who was guilty of pulling the trigger? There were three men in the room. Either there had been two live rounds and one blank or one man had shot twice.

The door slammed and X was back by the bedside. He carefully removed the makeshift blindfold, untied my arms and rolled me to a sitting position. My legs wobbled as he yanked me upright. Gravity pulled my abused body off-balance. I was a visible mess with trembling thighs that threatened to give out and sinuses congested with sobs that had flooded them uncontrollably. The other suspects were gone. X wasted no time in pushing me forward into the adjacent bathroom. He opened the Plexiglass door and turned the temperature control lever to the red zone. A bristling spray erupted. On the shower caddy was a lone washcloth. He pulled it off and placed it my hands along with a bar of Irish Spring.

"Scrub off good. I'll be here watching," he announced. A wall of steam built between us but the waves of moisture could not disperse his presence. I placed my feet like a stopper over the drain absorbing the little comfort this meager soak provided. X had appointed himself supervisor of my suffering and ordered me to continue whenever reflex pulled my hand away from the chafed parts. Through the cloud of hot vapor, I caught glimpses of a stubby box cutter slipping in and out of its casing and heard its tiny ticking like a miniature metronome counting down my demise. My motions were feeble and took full concentration.

"More soap. Keep going," he said. *I'm alive. These wounds will heal. The surface ones first. Hang in. You're almost there.* Finally he leaned in and shut off the valve.

"Enough. Get out, Princess!" he said.

"I promise I won't call anyone or report you," I blurted out.

"I know you won't," he mumbled. I stepped out into the chill of the aftermath with hair dripping, nose running and head cowed. It was important to remember details like the raspy tenor of his voice and the scent of him as he came closer. At first he did nothing but make me stand there nude in humiliation like the public display of a hooded POW forced to march through the streets of some foreign country. I grappled with the dire outcome that loomed before me. How did a hostage mentally stay in the game? I had two options. I could fold now and allow the tachycardia of terror to take me out or I could grapple deeper and dredge up something. If not hope, then dignity at least. X snagged a hand towel off the rack and threw it at me.

"Dry yourself off. Tits first. Follow me?" he said. In a Simon Says game of slow sport, he named the parts and I touched them, dabbing, covering every square inch of epidermis in a sick sensual show of his making.

"Slow down!" he hissed. I complied.

"Faster!" I did as I was told.

"Turn around! Now, touch yourself. There!" he indicated. I shook my head vehemently. Game over. "One of us is going to. Either you or me. Your pick," he said. I closed my eyes and gently massaged the bump of flesh below my pubic mound. If I didn't see his perverse manipulation then perhaps I could create a counter-fantasy of my own. I still could control my mind and potentially his. X yanked a black silk nightgown with royal blue piping across the bodice from off the hanging rack on the back of the door. First one limp arm and then the other was lifted and guided through the straps. My body was nothing more than a demented plaything in a twisted Barbie charade.

"Time to go to sleep, lovely," he hummed. My tormentor paraded me back to the bedroom. I ached to be released into the refuge of my 1000-count Egyptian cotton sheets and the quilt's safe shield of down but the bed had been stripped clean. Like a stray mongrel marred by unprovoked beatings, I hesitated, afraid to do the wrong thing and enrage the cruel master. I looked to him for a clue. Do I climb up? X jerked his head towards the floor.

"Gotta say your prayers first," he said. I had no strength to counter his wishes. He lashed me to the bedpost once again but this time in a kneeling position on the floor. Immediately, the risk warning went on high alert. I knew his mind was made up and had been since he first laid a hand on me. What I did at this point in the tragedy might not alter his intentions but I could change who owned the moment.

"I get it, you know," I said suddenly, interrupting the privacy of his disturbing fantasy. "If you have no future, then this is all okay. Might as well take yourself out with a splash."

"What you sayin'?" he asked.

"Martyr, right? Some code you believe in that's worth giving your life up for?"

"Don't be talkin' stupid shit!" he shouted, growing more agitated.

"I mean, in the end you'll be forgotten. Maybe your picture comes up on the news for a few days, a week perhaps, and then when they haul you in, case closed. People always move on to something else."

"Shut the fuck up!" he replied. X had angled my arms so that one elbow was wedged against the bed frame and the other suspended in air. My feet were bound by the same method and shoved back so that I was half-sprawled on my shins, bent in a huddle and posed to petition the Almighty Maker.

"You a Christian?" I asked.

"No, bitch. Why?"

"You better ask forgiveness for your sins. You've broken some cardinal ones. The kind you go to hell for."

"Stop running your mouth!" he said, puzzled.

"Why? Don't you believe in the judgment seat? You might want to figure that out before you get there."

"I don't plan on doin' no dyin'. Now shut your mouth!"

"There are worse things than dying, you know. Like spending your whole life in a prison cell."

"You're gonna do what I say. Close your eyes, count to three and then start prayin'. When you finish, I'll be gone." My torturer crouched down and lifted my chin in his palm. "But before you nod off, take a good look. You're in the presence of a legend."

"Boys want to be legends. Men want to leave legacies," I said. He considered this statement for a moment and then sneered.

"Same difference," he replied.

"An eternity of difference," I stated clearly.

"Eternity, it is." X rose to his feet. "Sweet dreams, lovely. Start counting."

"One....two...three...four..." I mumbled slowly, trying to stretch out the minutes to buy me my life.

"Lights out," he said crisply. The first blow to the top of the forehead elicited an automatic flinch response, that base instinct to protect the command center. My hands jerked against the restraints in a failed attempt to push danger away. There was no time to form a cry before the second blow caught me on the right side of my face and temple with a solid force of wood or metal that produced an earthy, organic odor in my nostrils. The smell of blood. My mind began to disengage and float away from the physical parameters that held it. On came a lapse of velvety blackness like a glitch of blank video. There was an extended pause and then I was back in the presence of near-death standing guard above me. His footwear was chalked with the ruin of the streets. One pant leg dragging, buckling, folding in on itself. Man's clothing on a jittery boy. Both strikes to the head acted as primitive shots of anesthesia numbing any further sensation on the surface. My body tucked and sagged involuntarily. Blood spattered in a curious trail like an unstrung necklace across the floor. One cheek was crowding up into view distorting all vision. A warm flush radiated down the right side of my neck. Sleep was descending; I couldn't hold it off any longer. I needed to say something important before I went. But my brain ignored the periods and punctuation marks carefully put in place causing the sentences to buckle up over the tail end of the one in front of it. A fifty car pile-up of reckless words.

"Over the bridge...trust me....back up...." I stammered. The gears were slipping now. I was coasting in neutral, rolling backwards away from those that loved me. The one racing down the dark Interstate to find me and the others whispering grace with my name in it. I started a mental write of my obituary: "...*survived by never-to-be husband Aaron Mitchell, parents Russ and Mel Braum and five brothers.*" My family would be sitting down to steaming chicken pot pie and a second helping of warm conversation when the phone rings to tell them. After tonight the number of chairs arranged around the table will be odd, eight minus one. Bubbles bloomed and collapsed at the corner of my mouth as I blew them all faraway kisses.

CHAPTER 2
STAY ALERT, STAY ALIVE

First there was nothing and then there was light. I realized this only after awareness came like a peek through a dusty window blind. I felt like I had had been created or re-created over again. I was conscious enough to realize that a vast nothingness had existed just before that moment. I couldn't know the size or depth of it; just that it was there.

#

I tried again to open the left eye wider by wrinkling my brow but nothing happened. I squeezed the muscles of the lid itself but it remained in place. Perhaps it would clear like the grogginess after a daytime nap when a latent dream leaves one disconcerted and wondering if it is Monday morning or a Saturday afternoon. There was no preceding dream, just relentless darkness that threatened to roll back over me if I didn't rouse up and stay vigilant. Either way, it must be time to get up. Time for class. *Hurry, get your ass out of bed!* The message went out loud and clear. Strangely, I could see it jump from purposed thought into action. The nerve impulse recorded its urgency and leapt to life racing out from the control center. *You're gonna be late. Move it!* but the signal weakened and then fizzled right before crossing the gap. Both my arms remained inert and my legs were disconnected, deadened and weighted down. *Was I trapped somewhere?* Terror ripped through my mind dragging with it my greatest childhood fear of being abducted. The very thought of it used to keep me awake in a house of sleeping people. It was the sheer dread of strangers propping an extension ladder against the house and scaling two stories up to my bedroom window to steal me out from under my sleeping parents. Being kidnapped and buried in an underground coffin alive but only able to draw a sliver of oxygen through a straw that just barely pierced ground level while the world at large rolled along like nothing ever happened. The school bus would bump along with intermittent stops and starts like a jitter bug on the pond with its hinged door flapping open at the end of my drive. I imagined the exasperation of the driver at wasting two whole minutes waiting for absolutely no one. A few of my friends might notice the empty desk in home room and figure it was the stomach flu, but I'd be completely forgotten by noon as they raced out to play four-square. I couldn't bear the tragedy of never saying goodbye and leaving my loved ones in a dark sphere of mystery like Dorothy Gayle's Auntie Em who's stuck calling out to her from inside the magician's globe but can't see her beloved niece weeping right on top of her.

At this very moment, my parents wouldn't know to miss me or begin to wonder where I was; not until our weekly phone call came and went with no answer on my end. My body began to tremble with an acute sensation of loss and a desperate longing to be found. I envisioned my mother tucking the flat sheet into neat hospital corners on my empty bed, rolling up the collection of china animals into newsprint and packing them in cartons labeled with scrawled magic marker: *Save for Elise.* And where was my father? He must be out on the Turnpike north of Bangor with a sack of forbidden danish drifting under his seat, anxious to unroll the hose and nozzle at the next customer stop and tell them all about his only daughter. You know, the aspiring medical psychologist who would heal a universe of unsettled minds.

I could shout loud enough to catch the ear of a passerby who might investigate the curious sound like the pitiful mewing of an orphan kitten that had fallen inside the drain pipe. Perhaps it might locate one random stranger good enough to detour from his own self-absorbed mission to rescue someone else's stray, who'd dirty up his slacks and drop down to dig me out of this avalanche. The vowels and consonants assembled in the right order ready to take a gunpowder launch up from my diaphragm, but nothing happened. The starting gun jammed; the warning flare fizzled. I could feel something like rigid pipe between my front teeth. The object extended beyond the back of tongue and downwards. Its inflexible presence could be felt if I clenched my jaw and tightened the muscles of my neck. Panic rolled over me. I was suffocating slowly. I tried to reach for the apparatus and yank it from my mouth, but my hands stayed in place. I'm going to die, I said to myself. *So be it. Let's make this fast and painless.* What a cruel reversal this was since someone or something had just lifted me from the deadness of no memory into resurrected life.

But then it occurred to me. I was breathing whether I wanted to or not. A mechanically-induced surge of oxygen filled my lungs and lifted my chest followed by a subtle dip in pressure and a subsequent drop of my ribcage. I stopped struggling and tried to relax into the rhythm. *What did I have control of?* Like a battle sergeant, I took inventory of whatever resources were still available after the dust of the explosion had cleared. The casualties were many. I ran through the roster.

Sight: compromised and only at thirty percent. The right eye was either blind or refused to operate. I had partial vision in my "good" eye, which now seemed better able to sort contrasts. Shadows were slowly pulling into shapes. Still it was terribly dark with only the faint shine of either the moon or weak sunlight coming from behind me. I allowed that one eye to wander freely trying to locate an edge, a border, anything that would delineate a clean margin. Somewhere to start.

And what about hearing, the last sense to go before someone succumbs to the coroner's caseload? Mine was keen. There had to be a fish tank nearby. I could hear the flushing of water though a filter and the carbonation of bubbles rising through hydrogen molecules. In the quiet pauses between the click and hiss of a pump of some kind, I sorted out other sounds. A quick tempo beeping from what appeared to be a standing pole on my right and another series of alarms that sounded at intervals a few feet above and slightly behind my head. Farther out on the circumference, I could detect a droning white noise of competing television sets. People bickered on a faraway sit-com. Female voices were exchanged back and forth. A shrill laugh was followed by a male baritone. I began sorting the footsteps. The fast shuffle on soft soles versus a quick rapping of heels. By the number and length of steps, it appeared to be a long busy hallway. Why was no one coming in here? More time elapsed. I heard a waste can rattle, a siren of some kind and then a toilet flush.

I couldn't define taste or smell. The dryness in my mouth was excruciating and the pipe pressing down on my tongue caused a vague medicinal taste. I wondered if I was hungry or if I'd been fed. Worry began creeping through my veins. How could I chew or drink? I suddenly realized how dehydrated I felt and how horribly thirsty I was. *Calm down, calm down. Move on.* What did I have to work with? I couldn't feel anything. It was more a sense that I was supported on something soft and cushioned. My body rocked from side to side on gentle swells as it had when I was a leggy, big-toothed girl warming on the spine of the summer raft as it swayed in the outgoing tide. I let the image lull me into a false peace which was a welcome distraction from the horrifying thought that was rising on the cognitive horizon; but it came on anyway lifting fully into view. *Was I paralyzed?* At that possibility, I lost any grip on rational thinking and anxiety took over. It throttled in my chest and churned in my stomach. Nausea swelled in my abdomen threatening to rise up and spew out any sense of order or calm. I caught hold of a tatter of sanity and reeled it in. If I allowed myself to get so worked up that I vomited, there was nowhere for the food and bile to go. No way I could do anything but lay here and choke on my own fluids. I tried to concentrate on the metronome of breaths again. In, out. In, out. In, out.

Then it started up, that slight feeling of apprehension like something was about to occur, something I couldn't identify but should avoid. It loomed into a growing, giant-size sense of dread. An inner voice tried to tell me to look up and get out but too late! What I had failed to take into account was that innate sixth sense, the one always jaded by the handful of other faculties. What had taken root and was keenly working was the irrefutable power of one's invisible hunch. It had been there brooding under the surface all along. Something horrible was going to happen. Was happening…

"Trust me."

"Sweet dreams, lovely."

"Eternity it is."

It hailed its arrival with a deafening announcement of sheer fright that ripped through the silence and locked its clammy hands on my heart. I fought to scream. That audible instinct to ward off evil, the most basic of all survival instincts failed me now as it had then when utter terror caused instant paralysis and left me powerless. *Leave me the fuck alone!* My feet jerked spasmodically and my restrained hands yanked against their tethers. An alarm went off. A commotion of bodies converged running from east and west. They'd finally found me.

"It's a seizure. Look there. See! The eyelid fluttering, the hands curled up. Like palsy. Push 2cc's of Diazepam stat. Give it five minutes and we'll dose again."

I tried to explain and tell them they were wrong but the explanation was blanketed in a fog so deep I couldn't imagine wading out to retrieve the verbs and nouns that were sinking into the frigid deep.

#

Sometime later, I regained partial consciousness. Over in the corner of the room, people were huddled together in serious discussion. At first glance, they were only generic figures. Sexless, ageless and nameless. There were three of them, one smaller than the others. Their heads were bent in somber deliberation and they spoke in low tones that were barely perceptible. There seemed to be some discord among them like they couldn't agree on what to do next or which direction to take. The train of awareness departed and I was left behind.

#

I was back again. Time had assumed a new method of measurement that was free of numbers, defined now by the angle of the beam it allowed to wash white and wax pale on the wall in front of me. I could sense the lengthening and shortening of shadow like on a sun dial. All I knew was that time had passed over, passed on and passed by. My three guardians, whether angels or demons, had made no move to leave. I knew they were there by the noise of their movements. They shuffled paper bags and shifted the mismatched arrangement of chairs by dragging them on squealing feet. They stood to look at their watches, rearranged their magazines and took turns filling paper cups with tap water from the stainless steel sink. Occasionally one would leave the room but was never gone long. Objects began to pull into recognizable forms: a soap dispenser on the wall, a plastic container with a hinged lid that had snapped shut on a limp hospital gown hanging half in and half out. A small television set on a swivel arm that reflected a picture of a young woman strapped to a bed looking up at a television set on a swivel arm. Was this a movie in a movie or something like déjà vu? The Droste effect of repeating images in descending size all within the same frame or like M.C. Escher, one hand drawing the hand that was drawing it. Past creating the future? The present imitating the past? My mind wheeled with the magnitude of the struggle before it shut down.

#

Awake again, this time with better clarity. I knew now that the gliding shapes that came and went were nurses who had to lift up the IV bags and squeeze their plump rear-ends around the spectator group that apologized for getting in the way, but didn't budge their positions or interrupt their watch. The shapes on the sill were jackets or sweaters thrown there in haste and the surface on which they lay was an industrial-size radiator that billowed dry heat. When these folks were ready to leave, their outer jackets would be nicely warmed. But for what season? The buds on the maple. Last I recall they were turgid with fertile seed. And what of these spectators? What drove them to huddle at the site of my misery? Money? Curiosity? Were they those that preyed off calamity like jackals on the fringe of a future corpse. Suddenly the screen went black. I could no longer see. I automatically switched the channel to the one with sound only.

"Why do we have to assign blame? It's nobody's fault. This is the shit that happens because the world is random and evil."

"If you knew that to be true, then why did you encourage her to go? To a city, no less!"

"Because we are stewards of the gifts given to us. That includes our children. We keep them for a time but we don't own them. It is our job to send them off when they are ready."

"Well, who said she was ready?"

"She did. And she didn't have to. You could tell it was time."

"So, we take the word of a child as our guidepost. I mean she'd barely been out of Maine and then we send our daughter out to the wolves of this world?"

"Your focus is skewed. You've got the finger pointed at the wrong parties. We are not to blame. The ones at fault are the fuckers who did this and they will pay down to the last penny and inch of their lives."

"But you heard them. The police said there was no forced entry. We must not have done our job properly. She should have known about trusting strangers and making sure the doors were always locked. She wasn't mature enough or didn't have the street sense to know how dangerous a place it was."

"Yes, she is a trusting soul and that may be a downfall of hers but I wouldn't want to change that quality in her. Why are we questioning the best in her and not believing the absolute worst in others? I should have been there. If I hadn't gotten a late start, I would have been."

"Don't even go down that road. No one is more worthy than you. If you hadn't called the cops and they found her as quickly as they did, we wouldn't even be standing here having this discussion."

Like songs drifting through walls with the faintest beat or shred of lyric, they stirred a memory. I recognized them now, the three observers keeping watch. I knew them by their voices. My mother Mel's cheery but incessant warble as she prattled on from room to room regardless if there was an audience or not and the timber of my father Russ's tenor as he read the Herald out loud, his voice lowered to protect us from stories about booby traps and napalm jelly. And finally I made out the gentle earnest rhythm of young Aaron who once told me, 'You're not the first girl I would notice in a room full of strangers, but you're definitely the one that would keep my attention the longest.' A sing-song of comfort that cradled my subconscious. I struggled to connect wishes to words and bleat out a plea to my family to be patient. I was there on the cusp of climbing out of this confinement and linking arms with them in a riotous circle dance of celebration. I tried to break the inertia of my extremities and rattle the bed rails to make them look. I could hear them even if I could not see the past fully.

#

"Look at me! Lissa. Open your eyes again."

I startled awake with heart racing. A man was leaning near my head. His breath, too close. Not enough oxygen for both. Suddenly one pupil opened its refractory lens involuntarily and recognition flooded the good eye. *Daddy.* The parched lips could only form a pucker around the tube and were blowing and puffing like a wounded fish. My father caught the gesture and reached for the call bell that was clipped to the bed sheet at the head of the hospital bed. Within minutes, a woman in lavender was at his elbow.

"How's she doing?" she asked.

"She's awake, Patti. I swear to God, she tried to say my name."

"Let's see what's going on, Mr. Braum. If you can please step to the foot of the bed. Thank you," said the middle aged nurse with frosted hair and sweet eyes. "Do you know where you are, honey?"

Nothing came to mind.

"You are at Beth Israel Hospital in the ICU. Do you understand me?"

asked my father.

"She can hear us, but I'm not sure she comprehends what we're saying. She won't remember it in any case. It's likely just another reflexive grimace. The kind that we've seen randomly cross her face since admission. It can be disconcerting when the patient's eyes are open, but it doesn't mean she's with us."

She drew closer to the bedside, leaned in and shielded my face from the fluorescent light with her hand. The right eye blinked and the pupil strayed to look at the periphery. Patti retracted her hand and pushed the call button. Within a matter of seconds, two other nurses had congregated at the bedside. One held my chin steady while the other targeted a laser beam at the iris of the violet eyeball that could be seen under a partially-closed lid. My gaze turned involuntarily away from the irritating source. I wrestled to open my mouth. Cracked lips pressed together and then parted again.

"Here, honey. Just let it melt. There you go," she said as she lifted a small ice chip on a spoon and gently dabbed the dehydrated skin. I rolled my lips back and forth to draw the moisture deeper into my mouth.

"I'm going to straighten out this tubing. Just relax, okay. This might feel a little funny." Something bit and clung to my bottom lip. Freezer burn.

"Are you in any pain, sweetie?" she asked. I nodded.

"Squeeze my hand, honey." A huge smile spread across her face along with an audible exhale of released worry near the foot of the bed. "I'll give some paper to your Dad and you can write down what you want to say, okay? Here, Mr. Braum, you hold the pad. I'm going to go call the doctors."

On the third attempt, I was able to pinch the barrel of the pen between two fingers and began scrawling a bulleted list of questions. *What happened to me? How long have I been here? How hurt am I?* My father withdrew the tablet of paper and searched it intently. On it was a jagged line of erratic blips, written arrhythmia, and a heart attack of scratches that ultimately took a beeline off the page. He had no idea what I was trying to say. When Patti returned, she saw the dilemma and had the aide run and get a large laminated poster from the nurse's station. On it were pictures of a blanket, a plate of spaghetti, a thermometer, and a house. My arm jerked from the shoulder rotating on its socket like a mechanical crane and dropped a dead hand on one of the neat little squares.

"Home?" she asked gently. "Go home?" I nodded.

"In due time, that's the goal. Let's get you cleaned up. You seem a bit sweaty this morning. Dr. Dominic is on his way."

She left the room but her place was quickly filled by another in scrubs who was all too eager to discuss the startling new development of the traumatic brain injury patient she had been following for the past five weeks to anyone within earshot. It appeared that Braum, Lissa in Bay 3 was going to disprove the dire prognosis of her Glasgow Coma Scale and survive.

"Oh, my sweet Lord! I knew it. I just knew it. It's nothing but a miracle," sobbed my mother who had stepped up out of the dark and was hovering by the bed rail. Shock blanched her face and she covered her mouth with the back of a hand wrinkled like a map of intersecting roads. She looked as though she had crawled on hands and knees down the entire three thousand miles of coastline to be here. Her chestnut bun was lop-sided, her deep brown eyes brimming. Dad stood off to the side in a humble reverent pose until his wife had seen her fill and then he stepped up and put a hand on my brow.

"My brave, brave girl," he said softly. "I am so sorry."

These were my people, the ones I belonged with and to. I wanted this loving barrel-chested man, who had stood next to me on the quarry ledge until my courage was high enough and then had lifted me up on his shoulders to launch me into the deep pool, to do what he had done then. When I dropped with arms splayed and mouth wide open so that the force of water drove up my nostrils, he had jumped right in alongside and ferried me to safety. There was no scolding for failing to listen to his instructions. He offered only comfort in the form of a dry towel and a fierce "oh, such a brave girl" hug.

"The anaesthesiologist and attending are on their way in. If all goes well, we'll be able to get her off the ventilator shortly. That will really help speed up the recovery and lower the risk of further infections. I need to ask you to leave while the respiratory team does what they have to do. We need to keep her sedated for the procedure," said Patti in a perfunctory staff voice. I saw them waver for a tense second. I wanted to never lose sight of them again, but Mr. and Mrs. Braum obediently headed out of the room with my mother clutching her sheepskin coat like a security blanket. My father hung back at the threshold of the sliding door.

"Be strong, baby girl," he said with an audible sob. The suede straps that held the breathing tube from shifting in the larynx prevented any expression but a hollow slack- jawed stare. My parents were ushered out to the ICU waiting room while the respiratory team performed the uncomfortable process to extubate me off the ventilator. What greeted my clearing consciousness was an initial retching gasp and subsequent eruption of fluids that followed the vile deflated bulb that had anchored the pipe in place. I lay quietly as they took the blood gas readings. One respiratory tech stood watch on the monitors while another swabbed my mouth out with a foam brush. They explained all the hardware in place as they worked. The left nostril was still a port of entry for the feeding tube which dribbled thin porridge into the small intestine. The nasogastric tube on the right was still pumping bile up out of an angry stomach. But for the first time in twenty-six days, I was free from the suffocating hose. Five weeks I didn't know existed. When the male aide had finished sponging me off, brushing my hair and repositioning me, the desk nurse called out to the waiting room and invited the family back for the long-awaited reunion. They came quickly, all three of them.

"How are you feeling?" Dad asked. All eyes were on me waiting to hear that voice, the essence of the person that had departed weeks before. The Propofol had been dialed down as I was weaned off it but my veins still felt thick with that soup.

"Back," I rasped. No one was prepared for the mechanical-sounding reverberations that rattled up from the damaged voice box. That couldn't be me speaking.

"Your back hurts?" asked my father. I shook my head and tried to clear the rust out of my throat but the flap at the rear didn't seem to work properly. Saliva was pooling up and there was no way to swallow. I started to drown.

"She's choking. For God sakes, someone help her!" shouted my mother in a panic.

"She's okay, Mrs. Braum. Trust me. Lissa, honey. I'm going to suction you." I heard the sinister sound as the cannula of oxygen reversed its draw and a vacuum of air left my lungs. "Go ahead and cough now." She patiently caught the mucus in a paper towel beneath my chin and then dabbed at the gobs of spit that had leaked down my neck. I mustered up strength for another try.

"Back to base…."

"What are you saying, honey? Back to the basement?" Mom turned to her husband for guidance. "She isn't making any sense."

"Back home, you mean? Yes, that's the plan. But you have some healing to do first," my father said gently.

"Back to basic," I insisted.

"Don't let this alarm you. It is very normal for someone who has been intubated as long as your daughter has to have speech difficulties. And there is such a thing known as ICU delirium. That's when someone has been in a sleeping state for so long they lose track of the time cycle. The body has no idea whether it's night or day. Their natural clock is totally off. And we have the effects of some potent medications involved. She's on a constant drip of Dilaudid."

"The morphine, you mean?" asked my father. They were talking around me, speaking loudly, slowing down the syllables as if I was hard-of-hearing.

"Yes, it has a very strong narcotic effect," replied Nurse Hunt. She turned back to her patient. "Try again, darling."

I trained my working pupil on my father's face.

"Can you get me back to baseline?" I asked clear as a bell, but he looked just as perplexed and cast a hopeful look to find someone to help in the translation. Then he leaned in and kissed the side of my cheek.

"Why is one apple red and one dead?" I repeated. *What was so hard about that?* I was looking straight at the pulsometer with its tiny blinking beam clipped to the finger on my right hand. The other hand had no light. The beacon was off.

"Don't worry. We'll get this right," he said, smiling. He patted the faded blue hospital gown with tiny barking dogs that shrouded the top of my left thigh. It was one of the few places he could locate that was free of needles, tape, tubes or restraints.

"Pack up!" I commanded. The voice was louder than it needed to be. An order barked out of the brain of a madwoman.

"As soon as you are ready, dear. But you've got some work to do yet," he said gently. Goddamn it, had I missed the class? That paper was on the desk right beside the computer. All anyone had to do was just hand it in. *If you want something done, best to do it yourself.* I just needed to get my bearings and the layout of this prison. Get to my route of escape, the elevator.

"Give me directions," I insisted. Nurse Hunt turned an apologetic glance towards my parents.

"Why don't you bring Aaron in? He may strike a familiar chord with her," she suggested. My father nodded his agreement and quickly left the room. An intercom blazed to life. Nurse Hunt was needed in Bay 4. She took off in a hurry leaving nothing but the space between us. My mother stood for a few moments awkwardly clasping and unclasping her knotted hands, uncertain how to begin to build a bridge to reach me from where she stood. She looked like she wanted to tell me something.

'No one knows how to take care of someone better than her own mother," Mom said out loud. Feeling useful seemed to energize her movements with some purpose. She got busy pulling through the drawers of supplies near the sink. Things were sliding around in there and the noise created echoes. She located some paper towels and antiseptic spray and began sanitizing any hard surface within reach. Then she folded the extra knit blanket, tucked in the sheet corner and straightened the scatter of reading materials on the chair. Next she took wash cloths from the clean linen supply cart, wet them thoroughly in lukewarm running water at the sink and pressed them sporadically on my chin, my cheek and the side of my neck. She worked efficiently with precise movements that were a product of caring for so many for so long.

"Talk to your daughter. Familiar voices may help orient her," urged the aide who had stepped in to check the monitors. My mother nodded and cleared her throat.

"Lissa, did you know this is a thirty-thousand dollar bed you're lying on? It is filled with water and fluctuates so that your weight is constantly repositioned. It's good for your circulation and will keep pressure sores from starting up."

She kept dabbing and chattering nonsense. Suddenly a flash of memory blinked into live action on my mind's monitor. Some methodical whore's bath, a patronizing preliminary to lull me into a false sense of security. *Trust me*, he had said.

"Fuck off!" I shouted in a shredded snarl. My foot flailed to life breaking the grip of the Velcro cuff and loosening the felt boot that dropped onto the floor. An emaciated leg had taken the place of the healthy muscular limb that had once been mine. My mother was clearly hurt when another kick caught her in the upper abdomen and she pulled back, bewildered. The bed alarm went off. Several people stepped into the room just out of my line of sight.

"I don't know what I did. I was just cleaning her up. I don't believe I hurt her," said my mother, thinking she was out of earshot.

"I'm sure it's just a reaction related to the trauma," whispered Nurse Hunt who had come to turn off the alarm. They each noticed my glare of agitation and took it to mean that all the crowding and hovering was making me claustrophobic. In deference to my comfort level, they stepped back a few paces.

"Did they find any money?" I asked. Ultimately I'd be the one to answer for any losses.

"Shhhh. Rest your mind now, Lissa," said someone on my left. Instant recognition came over me without even having to look. Patti encouraged Aaron to come around to my 'good' side and there he stood, at least what I could see of him with his peeks of coarse curly hair, blue eyes and faint reddish goatee. He seemed unsure whether or not to try to and engage the hollow disinterest in the sutured eye socket on the right or keep fully focused on the one good eye that blinked back.

"Bad?" I croaked.

"No babe, this hospital is one of the finest in the country. These people know what's best for you. Trust me. I would never mislead you."

I wanted him to reach around the battery of equipment to hold and hug me with a million compliments. He remained distant though, scanning the monitors for signs of encouragement when he thought I had looked away. My vision was clear enough to register grave concern in the creases on his brow and there was something else there. Was it guilt or regret? I almost felt sorry for the guy; what with his girlfriend broken to the point of disfigurement and swaddled in gauze dressings, stitched to keep tissue intact and plasma in circulation and addled as shit in the brain. He could do better.

"Pretty?" I croaked. *Why wouldn't those goddamn words do as they were told?*

"Who loves you more than anyone on earth? I will be here for you," he said reassuringly. I rotated my neck a few degrees in his direction and regarded him cautiously out of the corner of one eye.

"Don't know that," I said, growing more powerful in my pronunciation. He was shaken and didn't know how to respond.

"Why would you think any differently? How can you say that?" he asked, stricken.

"Gonna bag me up," I stated clearly and cohesively. A full sentence.

Five words strung on a clothesline.

"Who, honey?" asked my mother. They were all trying to dodge any direct mention of 'the incident' that no one wanted to talk about. I dipped my head in the direction of the nurse who was now charting in the file.

"Oh no, Lissa. All these wonderful people have been working for weeks to save your life. It wouldn't make any sense that they'd want to hurt you now. It's the drugs talking, that's all," she said dramatically. I shook my head as forcefully as I could although my skull was surrounded with pillowed support that kept movement to a minimum. I needed to tell them they were all wrong. When night came, they'd start bricking up the wall again with me on the far side and whichever third-shift bitch it was that had snuck up fast enough to club me in the head once, then twice more before anyone was looking; she'd be back, too. The maintenance man who emptied the trash, he knew, but he spoke Polish and couldn't tell anyone. Anyway, no one could be trusted with secrets this deep and dark.

I started to fight the restraints. What they saw in my eyes was not a visceral response to a tactile trigger but the frightening realization that though they were standing right in front of me, the most familiar faces on the planet, I could not connect them with any live emotions. Guilt, shame, embarrassment and rage were all floating around in my system like free radicals attaching their poison to each and any cell that opened the door and let them in. *Open the door. Let them in.* The thought came to me like a confession. I had done it to myself; left the door unlocked and allowed evil in. It was all my fault.

"Get the fuck out!" I started shouting. Nurse Hunt was instantly up near the arterial line in my neck reaching for the series of plastic tubes that brushed my collarbone like frozen braids. She snapped a cap off one, inserted a needle and pushed. Paradise came rolling in on an unabated red tide.

They say there are three things that no one can take away from a person: education, experience and memories but it simply isn't true. Three men had charged into my life and looted it of normalcy. My world was now divided. Twice. There was the before and after; and the sooner or later of immutable destiny. Suddenly I knew the answer to my own question. There was no getting back to baseline; no going back to where I had come from. If I was to find my way out, it had to be forward towards a frightening new future.

#

June 2014

The sign above the mainline door leaves no room for personal interpretation. It is a sobering slap in the face to the sheepish cadets who see it for the first time and pull up short to consider the ominous greeting. The groggy double-shifters pay it no heed and push on past. In their veteran minds, what is going to happen will happen with or without caffeine. It always gives me momentary pause if only for a few lean seconds, enough to wonder why a smart girl with promise hadn't just chosen the comfort of a cubicle job where the inspiration placard might be a patsy motivational phrase like: 'Choose a job you love and you will never have to work a day in your life.' Instead we are warned daily that our lives depend upon our vigilance. We are not here to love our job; we are here to love our lives enough to do our job well. It is us against them. When you report for duty on prison property, there are only two colors: blue and tan. Nothing in between.

I circumvent the metal detector and scan the opaque shield of the glass bubble to see who's on shift. The shadowy figure with generic features purposely delays getting up from his seat. He might as well be a body double for every other guard with the colorless eyes, shaved head and swarthy frame. I rattle the heavy door once, twice in quick succession. Finally I kick it hard with the heel of my boot. The audible echo of impatience would be a flagrant breach of etiquette anywhere else but rudeness is a way of life here. It's first come, first serve. Eventually he swings to his feet and pops the door. I slide my chit in the slot. As it turns out, it is a friendly face behind the glass today.

"Number eighty-eight," I say, exaggerating the diction of each digit as I bend my head downward and try to deflect my raised voice through the horizontal opening.

"Hey, Miss A! You know how it's done around here," the officer says with a grin.

"How's that?" I say. The body alarm slides out on the stainless steel tray.

"You're moving much too fast for a Monday. You gotta pace yourself. Build up nice and slow. It's only the first day of the week. Save some for tomorrow and then hit your stride on Wednesday. By midweek, you level off and then it's all downhill from there. Didn't anyone at the Academy teach you that?"

"Not my style," I laugh. "Take care, Stanley!"

I punch in the code to deactivate the lock on the key box, pull key set #35, and slam the metal door shut hard, rattling it to make sure that it is latched tight. Convinced that the alarm has been disarmed, I snap the keys onto the belt clip. Though I've never been one to be impressed with the swagger of authority, there is something powerful about the swish and bustle of keys at the hip. The door buzzes and I am set loose into a world that is both run on time and run out of time. It is a kingdom of counts and codes: the code of silence, the code of brotherhood, and the multi-colored codes barked over the signal radios to send a stampede of adrenaline into the fray. It is all about counting, every man tallied in place shift after shift, each one knowing in his sleep the exact number of digits that will equal time served or time remaining. It's an unholy and unsynchronized calculation decreasing years down to months down to days until that final moment of release. The date set for a parole hearing sits in front of them like a chisel and a wedge poised over a granite headstone waiting to etch its indelible mark. It's either the day they are born or die. Staff is equally as fixated on the moment when they are released into the freedom of retirement, that moment of rebirth when they are propelled out of this grimy tunnel into the fresh air of new life. How you doing, buddy? shouts a fellow member of Local 448. In two hundred and seventy-nine days, I'll be a helluva lot better, echoes the answer. Time ticks down in a clicking microcosm of numbers. Brave men count on each other for protection, for respect, and for the chance to walk out with more than they came in with; disappointed to discover that for most, they are less a human being on the far side of that gate.

#

The plastic wrap didn't do shit to keep out the overnight freeze. The thin film has bubbled and puckered with condensation and pulled away from the metal frame where the Scotch tape did little to hold it. It's certainly not worth getting a Class A ticket for. Chulo rouses up from his single-cell bunk and steps on the cinder block floor. The temperature is that of a tomb. He slept in his boxers and sweats with two mealy blankets tucked under his feet. The advantage of being a convict over a prisoner is the perspective, the ability to average out the extremes of ungodly heat and humidity with bone-numbing cold. If calculated over a continuum of twenty-two years, his conclusion is that the climate in Southern New England is temperate and survivable.

I watch his routine from the privacy of my office. He does his grips off the table edge and tucks in his tans. Count is underway and then the block will be released to the chow hall. Chulo gathers up the stack of class lists that he carefully arranged by unit the night before so that his steps can be efficiently exacted in a sweep around the massive concrete floor plan of this fifty-year old penitentiary. Anyone with half a child's brain can see how nonsensical it is to flip a sheet of paper into the hands of the same apathetic officer each morning knowing that he will lose it, or claim to have, by the time the school call sounds. But an inmate who holds the privilege of a clerk position in the school wing does as instructed whether or not common sense tells him otherwise. And Chulo's no dummy. Killing time as a clerical in the Education Department gets him out of the mayhem of the blocks; even better is the known fact that it is almost all female staff up there. Getting paid in scenery is an added benefit on top of the one-dollar and twenty-five-cents a day wage; plus the windows drop open on ancient hinges to allow a bulk of farm breeze into the building. Along with fresh air however come the free-wheeling mud wasps and yellow jackets who take full advantage of screen-less openings and sweep up to the moldy twenty-foot ceiling to begin the arduous chore of nesting in the light filaments. Guys who are Medical 3's because of bee-sting allergies are sent to this facility since it is a closed compound with indoor tier rec. But the bees don't discriminate among the increased configurations of razor wire and persist on invading the place. It is not uncommon to hear grown men shrieking like grammar school kids and hopping up on rickety desks at the sight of an insect.

Though his original assignment was to move chairs, erase chalkboards and to step and fetch an oscillating fan or a VHS player from the storage pile in the staff restroom, Chulo has gradually branched out. His expertise at picking up typing skills finally granted him use of a secure computer in the business education class to help draft up resumes for the vocational grads. That privilege affords him more movement, increased access to other inmates and a chance to rub elbows with the educators here. He is regarded as a trustworthy reliable inmate and given looser rein as a result. It didn't take Chulo long to notice that the three staff members who run programs are hard-pressed for time with only a half-hour between end of roll call and start of class. During that short span of twenty minutes, curriculum materials need to be copied, housing assignments checked against the computerized housing locator, and a series of sally-ports and sliding gates maneuvered around. He quickly volunteered to be the runner for us as well. Why not? It's the same lap around the perimeter of the pods whether it's four lists or one. He does it for the teachers because they want to do less work; but he does it for me because I am trying to do more.

Chulo knows I am neither a rookie nor a push-over. A quiet strength of will keeps me squarely on the right side of the boundary markers. But unlike most of the other female staff, I allow the inmates to creep ever so close to my personal space without shooing them back to their bunks, figuring I can better manage what is visible and within earshot. If you spook these guys or shut them down, they take cover and run their games from the far corner of the cube. It's dangerous practice to appear disinterested or distant. And it works for him. Having a woman within reach is a rare treat in a male facility. Story has it that the females Chulo ran with in his early years were street chicks and hood rats all playing for his money and tagging along on his reputation. But when he caught his case, they all scattered and ran. Not a one was sending him money or signing in at visiting hours. In his eyes, I represent all the women he had forfeited in his life. The mother who migrated back to Puerto Rico the day her oldest son was sentenced to thirty-four years for dropping two bodies, the sister who struck his name from her rosary list and the holy Madonna who had seen his sins and withheld her absolution. Once his conviction was sealed, they all fled and left him. For decades, his fiercesome reputation has buoyed his iconic standing among his boys but Chulo dismisses all that hype and attention. He has something far more valuable than notoriety in hand now. It's a prize that he does not want to jeopardize. Chulo is supremely grateful because I view him as something he has longed to be from the moment his fate was stamped in blood. I see him as a simple and ordinary man.

Chulo stands off to the side of the metal detector waiting patiently underneath the oversized clock. His feigned snarl lets me know I am two minutes late. He dips his head respectfully and falls into stride beside me as I walk the corridor towards the far end. Since counselors are not part of the educational union, the school personnel reluctantly granted me use of the unclaimed classroom at the rear. The walls there are the color of dead seawater in the advance of a northeaster. The chalk board at the back of the room had been painted over with rocket ships, misguided meteors and a lop-sided Saturn on its ear. The mural was likely done about the time Apollo 8 was thrusting off its launch pad. A wall of windows faces east which promises a warming as the sun rises above the chapel wing. Depending on the season, the room is either insufferably hot or unbearably frigid. There is no tempering the extreme fluctuations. Air-conditioning was not in the budget for this space and since the room backs up to the northerly winds, whatever miniscule amount of heat creeps through the barriers of dust, mold and rodent nests never makes a spit of difference. I like to believe it builds character; although it is difficult to convince a dozen men in threadbare tee shirts that it is worth the shivers. The indigent are hardest hit. With no funds to purchase kicks or boots, they slide around in shower shoes with no socks.

"You need anything copied?" asks Chulo. His eyebrows are raised in striking arches that made him look perpetually skeptical. I leaf quickly through the pile.

"Well, it's possible I'm short one," I reply. "I want to make sure I have enough hand-outs for tomorrow's discussion."

"No worry. I got you!" Chulo reaches for the document and purposely grazes my knuckles. He winks and sets off down the corridor to the secretary's office. His charisma has worked on her too. I set my briefcase down and decide to re-order the desks that seem to have scattered overnight. Across the barren yard stands the gatehouse and just beyond it, the entrance sign to the prison. The stark purpose of this structure is cloaked in more user-friendly terms as a *Correctional Institution*. It's a warm handshake to throw public perception off the track like a pack of simple-minded bloodhounds hot on the wrong scent. More accurately, it is a house of confusion, chaos and constant clamor and one that is haunted by birds like an Alfred Hitchcock film. A stray turkey with a running start and a stiff wing has cleared the corner fencing and now drifts around the perimeter looking for an escape. Black crows leer and hop sideways over the coils of razor wire that snake across the roof line like jagged Slinkys. In the foreground, placid Canada geese toddle about unabashedly nipping for grass shoots. This time of year with the earth hard as brittle and pocked with dried boot heels, pickings are slim. Tar-green droppings deck the paved walkways, a fitting gift to the inmates that tread these lines every day and track the mess of the world behind them.

The cement housing units once sported a coat of proud military gray, but the winds have worn down the paint on the northern walls to the shade of lint. Not much grows here. Even in the height of summer, the prison grounds will remain barren and sprout little more than a Styrofoam cup or pen barrel. The changes are almost imperceptible from the passing of the golden-eyed orb of August moon to the clipped lunar crescents of winter that dodge and peek above a charcoal smudge of tree line. Once in a blue moon, something happens to interrupt the endless hours of monotony and boredom - a moment of sheer terror or unspeakable joy. Otherwise, there is the unavoidable acceptance that nothing will be different by sun-up.

#

"That's guy's a real shitbag. You know what he's in for?" asks Hastings. He leans over my shoulder and peers at the name at the top of the class list. He scans the profile photo that accompanies it with disgust. I shake my head.

"No clue," I answer in a neutral tone.

"Don't you want to know?" he asks.

"No. I never look at the master file before I run my group."

"It's in your best interest to learn what kind of crap these guys have done. You gotta know what you're up against." Hastings has been on the tiers for over fifteen years and has cultivated his own peculiar crop of bitterness, a blend of civility and realism.

"I don't want it to color the way I do my job. I give the same service to each, regardless. What they choose to do with it is their call," I respond diplomatically.

"He diddled a little kid," sneers Hastings. I shrug and show no sign that his comment registered with me. I have my own general cataloguing system in play. For example, the persistent young bucks that whine, manipulate and loudly voice their discontent are almost guaranteed to return over and again, skid-bidding from one drug and burglary charge to another despite the resources they soak in. They are a wearisome challenge. Or the middle-aged guys with infrequent requests who have been down a long time and are rarely seen in my office. They keep to themselves quietly reading on their bunks and usually carry the fading stigma of one rash act of extreme violence perpetrated in the impulse of late adolescence. They are no trouble to manage. And then there is the group of sheepish older Caucasians who are typically overweight and sport thick-framed eyeglasses. These men refuse to speak in group and will not keep any legal paperwork in their trunks for fear of being found out. They are sex offenders, the bottom rung, lepers of a harsh caste system that is brutally intolerant of those that deviate off-track to pillage the pre-pubescent. All things considered, murderers seem to be my client of choice these days.

"But that's just good safety practice. These guys are capable of flipping at any time," Hastings says. He stands at attention as if he's still in boot camp.

"Don't worry. Counselors are the good guys. Not like you," I tease, winking.

"Well for your information, there was a counselor here before your time that got pelted with batteries. They broke her cheekbone."

"And I bet it was no random accident. These guys know exactly who they are after."

"Are you saying she asked for it, Elise?" Hastings looks around to see if any prisoner is near enough to hear his gaffe in using my first name.

"I'm just hoping if anything bad ever happens in here, the inmates will be my allies not my enemies. I'm banking on that."

"That guy's a maggot, regardless."

"He's decent enough to deal with," I conclude. My expression clearly lets him know I don't condone criminal behaviour, but we are not the courts, nor are we appointed to be judges. Their sentence has already been determined and the punishment exacted in daily increments. It is not for us to heap further misery on the guilty and potentially rupture this already precarious peace.

"That's right, Abrams. You're young yet. You still believe you can change the world," Hastings jokes. His respect for my dedication is tempered by what he perceives as a glaring flaw of misguided empathy.

"Least I'm not a bitter bastard like you. Yet," I tease. Class is due to start in ten minutes and the list of participants still need to be walked up and handed in to Main Control.

"I've got to hustle and get going," I say.

"Do your homework, rookie," says Hastings. As I turn to gather up the copies of today's handouts, he softens. "Hey, let me walk you down."

"Sure," I reply. I know this about Hastings. He is awed by the breed of woman that can navigate the military culture of law enforcement and still maintain the gentleness of a feminine and knowing spirit. There are plenty of broads in the system who have rubbed up against the friction of negativity long enough to grow callous skin and chafed hearts, but not this girl. He sees me as someone who carries herself with the refined gait of a thoroughbred that steps carefully, judiciously distributing its weight on delicate hocks. To him, I am a filly that is either prone to injury or recovering from one; someone not easily herded off course but one who could be spooked into a mad retreating gallop by the slightest wrong move. He has told me how he feels; not just once but on numerous occasions with bubbling praise over my most unusual eyes of light lavender with fractured streaks of black like the marbles he dropped into the smooth grooves of his Mancala board. And he has spouted excessive admiration for the waves of dark chestnut hair that resist barrettes and clips. Though the administrative dress code dictates that hair be cut or held above the collar, I have given up trying and just let the knot of loosely-corralled strands tumble down my back. Because I am so pale, people assume I am sickly or have a natural born fragility to my constitution. I am the type of woman men feel an urge to protect; but unfortunately, one who does not need them.

I accept his offer if only for the safety factor. Hastings has a super-hero mystique about him with his fastidiously-developed triceps that strain the fabric of his tactical jersey to maximum torque. His torso is cut into perfect grids and like an action figure his height is disproportionate to his cranium. He has a serious face and sports wire-rimmed glasses that might tempt some people to mistake him for a computer tech or an accountant, but the stereotype ends there. His towering trunk of a body takes bystanders on a roadmap of muscle that derails into ham-size calves tucked neatly into a pair of black sniper military boots. He is an intimidating if not handsome specter, especially on a dead- run to extract a resistant inmate. We head out into the corridor, two mismatched colleagues that merge into the main thoroughfare of mass movement. Down by the gym, my friend suddenly detours to the left.

"Have a sparkling day!" he calls out. "Be safe out there!"

I lift a hand in a mocking salute and continue down past Medical, Commissary, and the Religious Services areas. These offices are all part of a network of little hives hidden in a honeycomb architecture of closed doors and immobile plate-glass. When mass movement is underway, swarms of bodies try to force their way into these sealed chambers.

"Hey Miss A! What up?"

"Mornin' counselor."

"Ms. Abrams. Can I just ask you about…?"

But before I can even acknowledge them, the men are brushed off and waved on by the rovers who view them as nothing but insistent pests. I walk faster, trying to project confidence, setting my eyes just above the heads of the prisoners who amble down the yellow line, nodding at each but connecting to none. Suddenly all passage is blocked by several lieutenants who use their rank and size to flag foot traffic to a halt. They wave me into the nearest open door, which turns out to be access to the admitting unit. Four members of the outside clearance work crew are suited up in their designated orange vests and are seated on a wooden bench trying on random boots.

"What size you wear, buddy?" asks Property Officer Packer.

"Eleven," replies an older convict who looks like he's been sucking up the dust and gravel of the Bay State since before the original colony charter was written.

"Let's see…" says the officer as he scours the numbered shelves. "Well, nine and a half is your lucky number today," he says and thumps down some battered steel toes on the counter. Suddenly the radio call for a lockdown comes through and now the frustrated workers are trapped in here as well. The Department of Transportation vans will have to turn back without them. This means a loss of a whole day's pay, which is the equivalent of two soups and a honey bun. These are the inconveniences that become routine for those on both sides of this hazardous duty life.

"Stand back now!" orders Officer Packer. "No one's going anywhere." The metallic shudder of moving gates begins as they bump down the ancient tracks. From the bowels of the building comes the throttle of pounding feet and chaotic shouts. The K-9 dogs take up the chorus and shrill barking echoes down the hallway. Even on its most uneventful day, the atmosphere is charged with noise amped up on the throttle of unleashed testosterone, the driving energy on both sides of the bars. Power, and the struggle to take it back. A slew of uniformed guards converge on the mainline from every direction: the officer's mess, the john and the visiting room. Some cross-fit champions close the gap in a few bounds; while others in less good shape waddle in a power-walk with radios slapping against their flabby thighs. Despite the pissing contests and flagrant competition among custody clan, when shit hits the fan they move as a choreographed team on a united mission. *I've got your back* is their pledge of allegiance in action. The group runs en masse down towards the scene of the disturbance. Under these circumstances, counselors head straight to the hall keeper's desk to await instructions.

Inner control has activated the alarm and effectively closed off the four spokes that point like a compass to the far corners of the facility. North to the ticket block, south to the industries wing; each direction leading to an eventual dead-end. The inmates are herded back several paces from the gates and mill about expectantly. To them, a lock-down means that someone in their midst has dared to step out of line or step off the yellow line of obedience that runs down the center and has brought welcome disruption to the monotony of routine.

"Back up! Get the fuck back!" yell the rovers as each unit is safely secured and the stragglers are corralled away from the area.

"Hey, Packer! What's going on?" I ask. The portly officer shrugs.

"Some kind of fight. Hold on…" The radio on his belt buzzes with instructions dispatched from Main Control and he turns his attention to the signals. "Yep, Code Blue." The response time is noticeably slower if it is an inmate-on-inmate assault; the thinking being, let the two bastards exhaust themselves and get in a few good shots before breaking it up. It is custody's passive-aggressive way to settle past peeves.

"No wait! Now it's a Code Orange," announces Packer. Suddenly the entire place erupts into high gear. Staff is taught to be always on alert and ever vigilant. The moment one props a foot against a wall, drops his glance or turns her back might just be that one time the poor fool wakes up to find his or her skull turned into a cracked mosaic.

"Abrams, hang here with me. Grab the camera!" he shouts over the static of radio shatter. I allow the adrenaline of the moment to force my training to the forefront. While my brain instantly comprehends that there is no negotiation room in an edict built on safety-first protocol, there's always that split-second of hesitation. The momentary doubt is an involuntary by-product of my traumatic past. *Follow the last order given.* The lieutenant made that clear from the very first day at the Academy. So rather than run towards the fray as all cadets and counselors are trained to do, I sprint to the captain's office as instructed and return with the hand-held video recorder.

The explosion of decibels swiftly settles into a lull of uneasy silence. A stretcher with a lone defibrillator aboard races by with two frantic nurses pushing hard. I power up the camcorder and catch a grainy splice of the action as the medical team reappears with an officer strapped to a rolling gurney. Apparently he was caught up in the melee and took several hits to the chest and neck. Following close on its heels, an RN in scrubs pushes an empty wheelchair behind its intended occupant who refuses to use it and chooses instead to parade proudly down the corridor with hands cuffed and elbows in an escort position. A crimson wrap of sodden gauze is temporarily holding his face together. I train the lens on their movements as they make their way to the door of the hospital unit. There they are met by a battalion of guards with another video recorder in tow that will document the reception inmate #88463 will receive behind closed doors, unless it is inadvertently turned off.

The clock ticks off long minutes while we wait for the 'all clear' announcement. I settle my back up against the concrete wall, glad that I thought to tuck a water bottle in my briefcase. This prison was built a half-century earlier, its interior walls and window frames painted the same battleship-grey that coated the lockers and radiators of my grammar school and made me sea sick back then. I peer out through the squares of stationary glass to the far end of the concrete recreation yard. There is a baseball diamond surrounded by an impressive display of effulgent barbed wire four rolls deep, one for every risk level. It is the home field of the maximum-security team. The fallow ground was turned over to Bay State Officials by some old farmer who buckled under the pressure, threshed down his cow corn and handed over the deed. It's doubtful he knew his heirloom holdings would be cultivated for sport and carved up not by cleats but by government-issued boots on the feet of violent base runners. A few hundred yards beyond the last outpost is a cul-de-sac of modest homes with their backs turned to this eyesore of a tax drain. A thin line of wispy cypress trees provides a visual screen of sorts. I watch a young middle-school girl roll sand under her sneakers as the school bus slowly shuttles its way through the flickering breaks in the trees. I was that girl once, kicking gravel pebbles into the culvert, tossing sidelong glances at the lustful boys who reached over the barricade of seat-back to pull my ponytail or press gum into my braid. A little girl who had no idea that the lurid reach of evil was only a lawn-span away, one hurdle over a gatepost; and that it would arrive only a few short years later, walking right up the flagstone path to leave its bloody calling card. I wish I could warn that neighborhood kid to choose her seat wisely, to be wary of slick boys whose address of residence could just as easily change to 612 Kennedy Drive, Hazen Correctional Facility overnight. That precious little preteen might just end up emotionally homeless and permanently camped out in confusion, afraid to lay her head back on a pillow and close off sight for fear she'd wake back up to a world that no longer recognized her. Just like me.

"Keep to the side!" repeats the line of officers along the right hand wall as staff is finally given right of way. The stench of ammonia begins to seep through the facility. Word ripples out quickly. Hall worker Ruiz raced up to a rival King who was waiting in the med line and sliced his brow from hairline to jawbone rupturing his eyeball with a fisted razor. A swath of blood still staggers in bursts down the length of the corridor marking the victim's retreat like a Hansel and Gretel trail for the cleaning crew to follow.

In the wake of the ordeal, I feel that all-too frequent loss of equilibrium, the immediate sensation that the earth's geologic plates have shifted underfoot and threaten to tip me over backwards. When I have to act, I do so with the objectivity and cool composure that this profession requires. The amygdala, an almond-shaped trigger in the brain, does its job of sensing threats and sending out the alarm, but up in the pre-frontal cortex, operations are less efficient. The control switch is broken. The declination from this high point of arousal will be an uncontrollable and bumpy ride back down. I walk slowly towards my office intending to eat the oatmeal that must have cooled to the viscosity of wallpaper paste by now. An elderly black inmate with white stubble on both chin and cheeks is down on his knees swabbing up plasma with a spill kit. He bobs his head in deference to the female that approaches.

"You drive safely now, ma'am," he says amicably. He's been in here so long he's lost sense of the sun's direction or any tell of time.

"Hey, Mr. Davenport. Look up! It's a good a day in the making." I gesture to the stationery skylights that grant a geometric peek at the azure morning sky.

"Every day's a good day in the land of the living," he says in a hushed prayer-like voice. Is it institutional sanity or pure blind faith that makes a man squeeze this rasher of positive wisdom out of such mayhem? I think of the unnamed felon whose sight has been cut away. With nothing but a blood red horizon in view, he bit down hard on his pain and refused to give up the ghost or the name of his nemesis. If he ever does return, it will be as a man. But there is irrefutable truth in this elder's prescription of gratitude. I am living proof of it.

"See you tomorrow," I say to the kneeling patriarch.

"Lord willin' and the crick don't rise," replies the old man without looking up.

CHAPTER 3
THE WAY LIFE SHOULD BE

I am nervous before the start of every new class. It doesn't make logical sense but by nature, anxiety is half-rooted in the hysterical. The feeling is reminiscent of the age-old dread of walking in a short skirt past a leering crew of construction workers, that same self-conscious swallow when vulgar thoughts start careening through their brains and erupt as whistles on lusty lips. When I started this job, my initial strategy was to stay seated behind the desk. It was a coward's attempt to conceal my femininity behind the battered, monstrous piece of metal furniture; but after awhile, I felt stifled in my delivery. So I decided to stand periodically, even daring myself to approach the rank and file that sat dead-still with hands out for their homework assignments. Finally, I came out of my careful cocoon altogether, snagged a nub of chalk and took my place at the blackboard. No doubt the dozen pairs of eyeballs were still busy scanning rump, thighs and breasts each time I turned to scribble important concepts or challenge them to define words that were likely brand new additions to their vocabulary. Eventually, it didn't matter if they were perusing my body parts. There's no quelling the natural desires of men constrained to celibacy. There were no winners or losers in this peeping match. I get to see them at their absolute worst, stripped down, shower-less, stinking of cheap detergent and stale socks. The playing field had been leveled.

Today, the classroom is as swampy as a Roman bath house and likely there are as many infectious germs brooding on the worn surfaces of the mix-and-match chairs. Several squares of thin glass are cracked or missing altogether, allowing roaming insects to abscond and surrender at whim.

Flies crawl freely along the halogen tubes in the overhead lighting. The men straggle in sporadically. While it is mandatory for the inmate to be punctual, it all hinges on the arbitrary decision of the officer on duty who may or may not be in the mood for complying on any given day. I watch carefully as each man enters the doorway and sizes up the other occupants in the room before choosing a safe seat. A dozen dynamics are at play in this simple move. Questions race through his mind. Does he owe any other dude money? Is there a rival set represented? Did that guy disrespect him just the other day? Are any of his boys in here? I do my best at flavoring the pot by mixing youth with age and black with white, but there is no sure way to know if the recipe will meld or boil over. It's an imperfect science at best.

"Name?" I ask, as a tall African-American slows his swagger and postures in the center of the dirty floor. He does not look me in the eyes.

"Noble," he replies tightly.

"Last name, I mean."

"I AM," he states loudly. "I am NOBLE I AM." He speaks with unbending pride reminiscent of Alex Haley's television tribe. I straighten up from the attendance sheet to regard him. He is dead serious and the urge to snicker at his bold announcement is quelled in the throats of his inferiors as turns his bulk and glares in their direction.

"Wow! Isn't that also the name of the Old Testament god?" I ask. He gives me a scouring look of dismissal.

"I ain't no Jew," he hisses.

"If he was Hebrew, it would read backwards. It would be *Am I Noble?* Better question," pipes in a balding older gentleman in a wheelchair who has just rounded the door jam and backed into his handicapped slot by the door. He is thin and wiry in frame, his face divided and dominated by a nose that looks as if it was snapped in a spar and has taken a downward plunge at the middle of the bridge before righting itself by tip's end. It engulfs most of the pointed face below his sparkling blue eyes.

"And you are?"

"Mr. Zimmer," he replies cordially.

"Fine. Take a seat, Mr. I AM," I reply. Three other prospective students are already staked out along the far wall. One of them is monkeying with the window latch trying to angle the pane wider and allow more fresh air to dribble in. I wait until the remainder of participants have arrived and arranged themselves in a semi-circle formation around the perimeter. The reticence and distrust is palpable. Although rules require inmates to wear their full tans, I am sympathetic to the unrelenting humidity and allow them to stay in their dingy, short-sleeved tees rather than send them back on a pass to retrieve their over-shirts. The saving grace of this half-century old fortress is the more humane architectural decision which includes apertures that drop on heavy metal hinge to allow open air flow. Unfortunately, this barrack-type design of two-tier blocks prevents little exchange of oxygen outside the cells. I suddenly feel a draft and fasten the top button on my blouse. I read off the next guy with a stab at his last name. The mispronunciation is gently corrected.

"*Ma-green-ee*. Just so's you know," says Serge Magrini.

"My apology. I'm not up to snuff on my Italian," I say. He puffs up a few degrees, swelling his upper torso with some forced pressure on his biceps and pectorals, pleased that I have identified his nationality. Not as easy a task as it sounds since Mr. Magrini has hazel eyes, dark auburn curls and a fair complexion. He's a far cry from any Sicilian stereotype, no flinging arms, loud raucous bellow, stocky frame or swarthy machismo; not yet, anyway.

"If you ask around, I'm known as Pop. The cops and all the kids in here call me that. These days, we're old at fuckin' fifty, you know what I mean? One year from now, my sorry self will be down in the Old-Timer's block," says Serge. *Is he indicating complicity in this generational thing? Do I look his age?*

"It's decent down in the Annex, my man. No young bucks down there to disrupt our reading. We've got the New York Times on the desk every morning. You'll like it," says Zimmer. Serge regards him with a sideways glance. The guy in the wheelchair looks to be about sixty-five or seventy. Silver stubble has crept like underbrush across his Adam's apple, his chin, his cheeks, spreads around the circumference of his chicken neck and on down to the nape of his dirty cotton shirt His knuckles are knobby with rheumatoid arthritis that has likely stiffened the major joints of his skinny hips and sharp knees.

"What you in for, bud?" asks Serge.

"Sales, Manufacture, Possession of Narcotics within 1500 feet of a School," brags the elder man. "Oh yeah, and Assault on an Officer," he adds, beaming. Not a bad resume for a crippled Jew originally from Jefferson City, Long Island.

"Serious? You know how to make that shit?" says Serge.

"Sorry to interrupt. We need to move on. I prefer Serge over Pop if that works for you," I say. The two men comply with my request and settle back in their seats with a subtle nod of alliance. I pick up again from there and check off the remaining students by housing location. By the third session, I'll have their surnames memorized and most of their numbers. My memory is eerie that way, a bizarre talent I acquired A.D. (After Damage); this penchant for recording digits in a photographic flash and then linking the numerals by affixing them with the face that will carry them for life. It's my own little handy identity count, though I've learned to withhold use of numbers when I address them. There's no faster way to alienate a crowd of skeptical customers than to separate them from their pride, be it a formal Christian one on their baptismal certificate or the nickname that is their calling card of the street. Everything rides on that name, their most powerful identifier.

"The rest of you, do me a favor. Just raise a hand or speak up when you are called," I tell them.

"Ortega." Hand up. Number 445601. Registered.

"Bowman." One reluctant finger lifted. Number 453617 is accounted for.

"Euclid."

'Miss, you gotta give me some space. I no good on some days." A wild-eyed jungle man with a romp of unkempt blue-black curls claims this unique moniker.

"Roger that," I say. "Denton?"

"I prefer Dent, Counselor Abrams. Is it Miss or Missus?"

"Counselor is fine," I say. "I bet there's a story behind that one," I say. He grins.

"Willis!"

"Present." A quick peek at a statuesque, dark-skinned man in the far corner.

"Mr. Briggs."

"Gemini, ma'am." Right up front and center. A painted female face with kind eyes.

"Harper." A pause. "Harper?" I repeat.

"People call me The Reverend here, Miss." He's waiting for me to ask why, begging me with a not-so-subtle look to open this can of worms right here and now and see what squirms out. I'm not biting.

"Amen to that," I say.

"Crespo." A stream of Spanish ensues. Lots of "a's" and soft "h's" and a simultaneous "he say" interpretations from the guy across the room.

"No Anglais?" I ask. My South American friend shakes his head vehemently.

"Me? No Espagnol. Maybe, un poco," I say apologetically. That includes a smattering of Spanish terms like *joder* and *conos* caught in drifts from the showers or handed to me by Chulo so I would know if and when the men were discussing me disrespectfully. Another long litany of excitable gibberish ensues. His un-official translator cocks an ear in his direction.

"He say he understand, but not write or speak English."

"Tell him he can stay. Someone in the block can help him with the homework," I say. Chulo will be my tutor on this end of things. One would think that with Spanish fast approaching the majority mark in this country, the State (if truly interested in the betterment of our struggling families) would have thought to issue teaching materials in this tongue. Even Lowe's store is better equipped to guide the bilingual crowd up and down their home improvement aisles. This issue is one the government has chosen to leave to Immigration to unravel if and when they show to scoop up the lost and found.

"Okay, gentlemen. The paper in front of you is a contract which is your commitment to being in this program. It basically talks about the expectations on participation, homework, rules of conduct and…"

"Miss! I shouldn't be in here," someone interrupts. It is the younger Hispanic with bronze skin and a wreath of tangled tattoos wrapping around from the nape to the notch of his neck.

"Hold up," I say. "The first rule is that we speak one at a time, take turns and give each person equal time. Everyone here has something important to offer and we all lose out if we can't hear it. Let's see…" I look around. There are very few free-floating objects in here. Pencils, pointers, rulers, and paper clips are all fodder for sticky fingers to create a clever weapon.

"Here." I reach into my water-stained leather briefcase, pull out a dry-erase marker and lob it like a women's softball in his direction. Startled, his quick hands snag the object.

"We'll follow an old Native American tradition. Whoever holds the 'talking stick' has the floor. The rest of us will show our respect by giving him our full attention," I say. Respect, the mother of all words for those who live life on the streets. It is the ultimate measure of a man. Its antithesis is disrespect and is the flagrant step over the line which causes all manner of riots, stabbings, curb-stompings, shootings and murders on the daily. The bar has just been raised.

"Alright, Mr. Ortega. What were you trying to ask?"

"I don't belong here, Miss. I never put my hands on no woman. I wasn't raised that way," he says emphatically.

"Somehow you were flagged to be put on the list. I don't have your file in front of me but I'm willing to double-check to make sure you were coded properly." This appears to appease disgruntled Denier Number One. I can see him visibly release the hostile lift to his shoulders.

"Me neither," echoes another.

"Mistakes are made sometimes," I admit.

"You'll check it out for me, then?" Ortega asks, hopeful that he'll be able to skate out of this requirement and still play pavement hoops with his shirtless cellies.

"Why don't you stay with us for this first class? I'll look into it and let you know on Thursday?" I reply. I like to make them feel they have some choice in the matter even though they have little to no recourse. Sure, Ortega can refuse to come, but then he loses his good time and potentially forfeits any hope of any early release. If an inmate becomes verbally resistant or irate, I can slap with him with a disciplinary ticket and send the guy packing, but I see no wisdom in emasculating a man in front of his peers when he can be led around to the desired outcome with a circuitous steer.

"Anyone else feel like they shouldn't be in this class?" I ask, surveying the room for raised hands. Three guys nod their heads. "So, let me ask you this. How many of you feel like the system has wrongfully charged or convicted you and that *you* are actually the victim here?" Four more join the affirmative with raised hands. That's all but two. I'm not surprised; everyone in prison is innocent, according to those who can't walk out the doors.

"Statistics show that the majority of domestic violence crimes are committed by male perpetrators against female victims; but we know the cases of women who are abusive towards their men are increasing in number." Their ears perk to attention. One rotund Caucasian in his thirties pulls up out of his slouch. His belly bulges over the table top and rims of perspiration encircle his neckline and ripple in his rolls of flesh. His ginger-colored hair is cropped down to a bristle and splotches of eczema erupt on his cheeks.

"Massachusetts is a woman's state," Dent states with a flourish of saliva spray. There, it's out. It was just a matter of time.

"Let's face it. Women really know how to push your buttons, am I right?" I pose the question in earnest, leaning in towards the crowd. This is the tipping point, the critical juncture where they will either conclude to band against me or relax their guard.

"Counselor Abrams, it must be hard for you to sit here with us and talk about this. Being a female and all." The empathetic speaker has a trill to his voice and large pointed breasts that poke at the thin fabric of his knotted shirt. His eyebrows are plucked to a razor thin sweep, his lips painted and pursed. He is well on his way to converting his last Y chromosome into an X, but the process has stopped short of his groin; otherwise he'd be sitting over in Bardston in a burgundy jumpsuit.

"No, Gemini. I don't take this personally. To me, it isn't about gender. It is simply one human being victimizing or controlling the other. It goes both ways on the spectrum and should be treated the same."

He hesitates with his head cocked to one side, pressing his full lips into a puzzled pout as if he's trying to decide exactly which gender he's going to throw his hat in the ring with; that is, if he had been allowed to keep his jaunty beret which now lies crumpled in a property box in the basement.

"Have any of you gentlemen heard the phrase 'the rule of thumb'? Do you know where that saying came from? Anyone?"

Not one man in the group comes up with a ready definition.

"At least one interpretation is that this was a pre-Colonial guideline that allowed a man to take a stick and beat his wife, his maid, his cook, even his cow for God-sakes, as long as the flogging instrument was no broader than his thumb. I say this because it's important to know our social history in order to gain some perspective on the topic. A hundred years ago in this country, it was a man's world. Women were property along with children and animals, but the roles of the sexes began to change. Anyone know what happened during and after World War II?"

"Lots of sex," says the Rev. It makes me wonder if his self-professed priesthood prohibits that activity. By the looks of his devilish leer, I doubt it.

"The dames went to work in the factories while their men were off to war," says Serge.

"Right. And what do you think happened in many of these homes when the men returned home?"

"The females didn't want to be put back in their place," says Dent.

"Sure. They were making all the decisions, earning paychecks and acting as head of the household. I would imagine that there was a great deal of friction going on behind closed doors. And what big movement took hold in the 60's?" I ask.

"Women's lib," says Zimmer. He's just the right age to have been peering out of his fourth floor walk-up as the bras were tossed from the balconies of the neighboring brownstones.

"My point is the pendulum has swung. At one time, it was all the way over to the one side and then as victim advocates and activists started to holler, it swung in the opposite direction. So now, Mr. Dent, it feels like this great Bay colony is, as you coined it, a woman's state. All a female has to do is lift that phone, cry wolf and the cops are coming to lock someone up. And as we all know, that someone is you guys."

The eleven men who will be my audience for the next eight weeks have just been unknowingly disarmed. The floodgates are open.

After the class is dismissed, the men amble back down the corridor to pass the metal detector sweep. I lock the classroom door and follow on their heels. A group of inmates have just been released from the library and is waiting in line for the officer to check ID's. I hear the terse exchange of heated voices and assume it's a hostile confrontation between inmates, which is more likely to happen when housing units mix. A dozen or more men hug the corridor wall facing the officer's desk and watch intently as a staff member and an offender erupt into a heated confrontation.

"You're done here," bellows Officer Laurence.

"You want a piece of me?" seethes Inmate Watson, a notorious and particularly litigious convict. This little encounter will be yet another coup in his building number of lawsuits that are bulging in the Administrative Remedies file cabinet up at headquarters.

"I've seen your shit for over twelve years now. You may play the game

with others, but I don't give a fuck. I know what you're really made of."
Too late. Officer Laurence has just unknowingly added his name to the
burgeoning legal folder Watson keeps in his foot locker.

"Open up your office," taunts Watson. "Let's go in and settle this man
to man."

"You piece of shit," yells Laurence as he waves briskly to his buddies
for assistance.

"Next time you see your mama, she'll be riding my big black dick,"
shouts Watson as they wrestle him into cuffs.

"My mother would never be seen with a nigger!" Laurence gets in the
last word before Watson is escorted out of the wing. Officer Laurence
whips around and gapes at the snickering spectators. "Okay, men. Let's
move along. This isn't a circus!"

Once the scuffle is over, I feel the worry seep in. Who could blame a
man, now hobbled and cowed, from retaliating with a swift shank to the
ribs or a rampage of terror the next time he is free to do so? But it isn't the
fear for my safety that bothers me. That concern got tossed to the wind as
soon as I stepped into the arena. A certain cavalier attitude is a prerequisite
in those who elect to sign a hazardous duty contract. Like dogs that sense
fear in a person and react with intimidation, weakness is sniffed out and
often snuffed out. *Respect begets respect* was the mantra my training lieutenant
drilled into the minds of the young cadets in my class, a living creed that
navigated him through a quarter-century of dealing with high-risk criminals
without ever putting a hand on his cap-stun gun. Unfortunately most of the
brash rookies only nod in agreement before graduation. As soon as they
take their posts, the recruits are indoctrinated by the surly seasoned officers
into the cynicism that comes from being disappointed and dinged by
human nature and corrupt politics on both sides of the fence. I understand
their distrust of prisoners. It is a game of sorts, a wariness adopted by
competing males. But whenever I witness the ugly spectacle of human
hatred such as this flagrant provocation thrown in the face of an inmate, I
become unnerved by it. I'm terrified to slip back towards doubt. I'm fearful
that I won't be able to sustain the belief that men can change, that good
can somehow traverse the slippery slope of injustice, pitch its flag on the
summit and defy what lies beneath that threatens to shift and erode my
solid footing and throw an avalanche of evil underfoot.

#

The Way Life Should Be, the proud signage beams. True when it comes to the scenery, but ever since the Maine Board of Tourism pitched the massive billboard near Kittery, it was not the way the roads should be. All the way to the Kennebunk rest area, the lanes are thronged by 'rusticators' from New Jersey and New York with half the contents of their garages strapped to their roof racks. Twin his-and-her bicycles with wheels spinning madly in the coastal breeze. Kayaks knife through the air current overhead. Small utility vehicles that had never set rubber off-road waxed to the max and jammed with DVD players and I-Pads, as if Maine didn't have a Best Buy of its own. I decide to dodge all the delays and turn off the interstate, but Route One is even worse. Traffic is traveling thirty miles an hour at top speed. A line of cars brakes to give Joe Schmoe a good gawk at the Godzilla-size lobster that's crawled up over Renny's Roadside shack. Brake lights pump again for the shadowy moose on the hillside, which turns out to be a stack of rotting chairs left to decompose.

The five -hour drive stretches out to seven. I knew this would be the case on a Friday afternoon in July with a fair forecast ahead of us, but there was no point going back home to wait it out. While we are only two-hundred-and fifty miles apart, my family and I might as well be in different time zones. Once I relocated to the greater Boston area, my parents rarely crossed the bridge over to the Portsmouth side. My mother confined her driving to small round-trips to the IGA supermarket and Dad drove for a living, so he was never too gung-ho to jump back in the driver's seat on his free time. His road trips always took him north and west in the opposite direction. It was probably better that way. The world that begins just south of the New Hampshire Liquor Store on Route 95 is not one I could ever picture them in. What I do for a living was more easily accepted when it was an imagined picture in their minds that could be white-washed and edited at will.

The Maine I recognize and claim as my own doesn't show its face until after Augusta. By then, the faint-of-heart have turned off to coastal destinations well before this mile marker. Mostly truckers, hunters and anti-social naturalists continue straight on up towards Orono and Baxter State Park. I take Route 3 which begins its winding crawl through forested hills and the stark open blueberry fields. The socio-economic level plummets by the mile. I typically give no advance warning whenever I go back to our beloved farmhouse. It's a childish little prank aimed at preserving the surprise factor, but a safe bet since there is no risk in arriving to an empty house. Mel Braum's customary habits are as predictable as the tide that crests up over the granite boulders, pulls away and barrels back. Some days the routine is a calm drill; other times, it carries on with a fierce urgency but it never deviates from its prescribed path eroded over years of following the familiar.

I arrive at the midway point of the peninsula a few miles shy of Gust Harbor's eclectic collection of bait shops, banks and bakeries. The hard-packed dirt road comes up all of a sudden, pitching its thin tack through a tight line of pines. I turn in and make my way slowly down the mile-long dead-end. Dale is out cutting brush near his new homestead on the west side of the clearing. The pond where his kids now splash and fight has overflowed its borders with the flood of rain that's been spring up here this year. Snapple Creek, we call it, the tint of fructose-filled iced tea. I turn off the ignition and coast my Altima over to the turn-out where four-wheelers have carved an entrance into the woods. My brilliant Tuscan Red vehicle is hard to conceal and is jarringly out of place. I walk up the gravel drive drinking in the aroma of dank juniper and listening to the underpinnings of the silver poplars that rustle lightly. This is the sweet reward of coming home.

Mom is in the kitchen leaning over a cast iron skillet. A cloud of Crisco and citrus blows out through the screens. She is oiling cabinets and frying potatoes at the same time. Somehow her energy is never diminished by the weather or ordered by logic. She is always busy, always moving, cutting things up or paring things down. Hooked in the rabbit hutch as a baby, my first view was through a grid of tiny wire squares at a woman flapping back and forth to the clothesline. She rocked me in the garden cart as a toddler, bumping the handle up and down with her knees as she snipped brown pansies onto my sleeping head. When the demands of the day loomed too large, Mom put us all out into the dooryard and locked the screen handle. Even in late October with hands as red as boiled lobster claws, we'd be there banging on the door. After long minutes, out came a ration of paper plates with peanut butter sandwiches and a breath of heat before the latch was refastened. It was nothing like neglect. We understood that our mother needed to clear the kitchen of small hands and feet so that she could find order in her home. Not until I was much older, up on a stool by the electric fry pan watching strips of sole brown and curl like pieces of stale bread, did

I read something in her movements. She was doing three things at once, hopping from sink to stove with a ruck of clutter that followed her from left to right and back again. Every task dragged out in its importance until there was more to do than when she started. Large decisions, the things that really mattered, she couldn't face and left unfinished, but the details were worked and reworked, done then overdone like the fish.

"What's for supper?" I announce, having slipped successfully through the shed into the kitchen without disturbing her.

"Lissa! My grown-up baby," she says. 'What a nice surprise!" She turns, pats her hands on her pastry apron and comes to greet me. She is pleased but not overly demonstrative. Some part of her is always half-expecting one of us to wander in with a change of heart and move our cartons of crap back into the upstairs. The only time she is truly content is when the house is crowded with bodies and loud with the incessant banging of piano keys. She thrives on shrieks from the grandkids that have pulled their Huffy bikes up to the window ledge at the pretend drive-thru and ordered crab sandwiches and lemonade, which she hands out to them free of charge.

"Is it a good time for me to come?" I ask tentatively. Stupid question. To her, any time is never good enough.

"Of course! I'm sorry I didn't have time to clean up the guest room or change the sheets. If I had known you were coming, I would have prepared," my mother says apologetically. We both know the ropes. The dust is thick in the rooms she no longer wants to tend to. The memories in there are even thicker.

"It's fine, Mom. I can take care of that. I brought some groceries along," I reply.

"I have plenty here," she says. Plenty of the same, she means. A quart bottle of goat's milk, a container of large curd cottage cheese, last year's bread and butter pickles, pre-sliced sourdough loaf from Larry's Pastry, peanut butter swimming in its own oil and soupy strawberry/ rhubarb compote with a rim of mold on the Mason jar. I come with fresh supplies and will discreetly replace items that have outlived their shelf life by a long shot.

"Would you like to take a walk down at the point?" I ask. The afternoon sun is topping over the trees and is still thinly warm. Mom is not good once it gets on toward evening and the dampness rolls off the water and crimps her arthritic joints. She is pleased with the idea and within minutes, we are both in her Ford Escort with a metal bucket and old beach shoes. Dimming eyes or not, she still navigates the four miles that slope past long meadows to the smooth broth of the Bay without ever really looking at the road. After so many repetitions, she can do it with one palm on the wheel and one good eye on the horizon. When she cruises around the first bend in the dirt road leading away from her property line and spots the sporty car tucked into the trees, she clucks her tongue disapprovingly.

"That must be expensive to maintain," she says. Progress and convenience offend her. I make no response and choose instead to glory in the waning sun. We both know the rules. Small talk welcome; meaningful conversation unnecessary. The town road winds along the eastern side of the peninsula where at its highest crest, the sun burns through the low mist and stuns the viewer. A pair of goats cavorts on top of a rusted El Camino that serves as a feeder. Mr. Thorsen's trailer has sunflowers knocking heavy heads on his roof. The windows are still stapled over with thick plastic from the winter before.

"He's been at Ledgebrook Nursing Center now for a couple years," says Mom. Her truck smells like wet dog and fermented corn. She drives slowly and cautiously scans the sides of the road for a sudden ball or bike to come flying out; but the kids who live here are tucked back in the woods on old logging roads and rarely make it out into the direct sunshine. We pass the old Chapel, the stuffy library and miniscule post office that belongs to the private community that has claimed the Point as their boat launch and cocktail party patio. The signs went up when we were still kids, orders from the Village Improvement Society to *keep off, stay back, don't touch*, though we ignored them by climbing up on the railing of the wharf to jump and drop thirty feet, splitting the water like sharp knives. The summer people were aghast and a bit irritated, but could hardly stop us from scampering back up the ropes like water spiders.

Mom parks near the boathouse. Here the stones give way gently under the wheels of the boat trailers as they back in to dump their crafts.

"Wanna head to the left, down to the inlet?" I ask. It's our favorite walk to where the coastline is broken by a deep cove that dries into beds of salt and clam shells. Once we are out on the rocky beach, Mom and I hunt and peck for the perfect find. Although she is nearing seventy, my mother shows no defining age. Her long, thinning hair is still mostly dark and pinned up with bobby pins. Her body is still strong though osteoporosis has been her companion ever since menopause. She is still handsome, no beautiful with her classic cheekbones and smoldering eyes though her vision on one side is dull from increased optical pressure. Glaucoma is causing a thick film to steal over her vision like the sea fog that hangs above the shallow water closest to the beach. Mom creeps along comfortably in her ratty shoes, boys' jeans and terry cloth beach jacket. One lobsterman is bending over his traps and half straightens up to stare when he spies her, probably mistaking her for a teenager.

There is a new line of flotsam, tangled fishing nets, dry sponges and sea urchins left in the wake of last night's tide. It looks to be a great picking ground today. The two of us seek out our own spots and kneel down to rummage through the pebbles and debris. We are quiet in our search. The minute focus on color, texture and reflection is a religious ritual that requires complete concentration. Long minutes pass in separate solitude.

"I found it!" I shout enthusiastically. I hold up an arc of porcelain with a ruby cottage and a garden painted on it, a shard from an antique serving platter perhaps. I run with my prize and carefully lay it into the plastic bucket. She approves and then grins widely. Out of her side pocket, she produces a porous, round object with a fluted rim in various shades of bleached gray.

"What is it?" I ask, puzzled.

"A whale vertebrae," she replies proudly.

"Crap! You win," I say and embrace her shoulders. It's not a hug per se, not like other people know one to be. That would mean two bodies that lean in and apply a measure of pressure to connect them, even briefly. In our case, it is my arm wrapped around her back and her willingness to stand still for that moment. She winces when I squeeze.

"Oh, I'm sorry. I didn't know you were pain."

"Just in that right shoulder," she answers.

"Is that something new?"

"You know how my arthritis gets in this dampness. I can tell there's a storm coming in," she responds.

"You still going to see the same doctor?" I ask.

"Yes, I go the end of this week. I'll probably need a cortisone shot and that'll do it."

We wander the length of the shoreline until we reach the dead end of soppy muck and stagnant tidal pools. The black flies are as big as moths down here and mosquitoes pester every visible patch of skin. We turn back and walk at a faster pace trying to outdistance them. By the time we reach the car, it's almost obscured by the dusky mist that has wrapped up around the boathouse.

Back at home, we sit with bowls of fresh chowder and homemade popovers as the thick cover of night comes on. Mom lights the Aladdin lamp and the mantle flares to a dim yellow orb though the overhead light switch beckons only a few feet away. I don't question her choices; it is her house. We talk in fragments. In between is thick silence while we ladle soup and squeeze honey on our biscuits. After we have covered the cursory checklist of siblings and their spouses, she turns to me with the secret she's been saving up.

"Aaron has moved back to Maine. He came to see us two weeks ago," she announces matter-of-factly. I had heard through my brothers that my former boyfriend had come East in a U-Haul with a load of furniture and had driven straight to our farmhouse, his first stop since Columbus Ohio; and had lifted each of them off their feet even though not one brother weighed less than one- hundred-seventy-five pounds.

"Yes, I know that," I reply. "I heard he's moving his family back into his parents' property down on Dory Road."

"What an excellent young man he is! So supportive, thoughtful. All the qualities of a good husband."

"Right. That's why he's married, I'm sure," I respond flatly, careful to not commit any emotion to this topic.

"I believe he has a couple kids. Teenagers now, I think," she muses.

"Two. Both boys."

"Yes, you're right. He and his wife relocated to the Midwest right after they were married to be near her family. But he was stifling out there. Land-locked in a flat stretch of dust. Poor woman probably didn't know that once a Maine-iac, always a Maine-iac. He was bound to come home." When I keep quiet, she continues. "You should get together. He hasn't changed a bit. When's the last time you saw each other?"

"I can tell you exactly. April of '96. The day of my graduation from the Academy, remember?"

My mother retracts her smile and her mind wanders back, skipping to the pinning ceremony when I stood on the stage with the Commissioner while my comrades saluted me and my father pinned the Class 479 badge on my blouse. She doesn't stop there but continues in reverse, going farther back, skating by the day my college diploma was finally handed out in a drenching Boston rain; still reeling in reverse, she skims around the hearty applause at Gaylord Hospital when I matriculated from the physical therapy madness. The memories spin under her watchful eye until at last, like a roulette wheel, the ball drops into the very slot she picked.

"You two looked like a royal couple that day. The king and queen of Gust Harbor High. And what a glorious party afterwards. Remember your brothers all tailing you two like royal coachmen? You couldn't have asked for a better day. You recall that?"

"Yes, Mom," I say quietly. She stirs her soup in wide arcing circles, banging the stainless steel spoon against the rim on each lap.

"They're hiring caseworkers at Acadia Hospital," she muses. After she throws out the suggestion, she reconsiders her approach. "Do you still like your job?" she asks.

"It's really my passion. So, yes," I answer.

"I worry about you in there with all those criminals."

"Actually, it's probably safer than being out on the street with random people. Inside the prison, we know who the bad guys are. And as we know all too well, worrying about something in advance never prevents it, right?" My mother stands to her feet and pushes in her chair, a signal that she's had her fill of both flounder and fishing for past wishes.

Later in bed, I allow myself to think back. How after returning home as a partial invalid, they all thought they could wish me back together. Aaron in his gentle persistence chose to overlook all the evidence of damage and try to press his love into me over and over. Reassurance that despite the neurological plateau of flattened effect, the tics, lack of coordinated strength, the droop to one lip and a hazy eyeball, I was still his one and only. Inside where no man could go, my mind raged and cooled, flared and flagged with uncontrolled regularity and inside is where my beloved boy Aaron traveled far to reach me and leave a permanent mark of his potent devotion.

My mother is in her room with the light still on. She often lies awake with a book in hand, lights on, one big reel of anxiety all spliced and revolving until the tail end of her thoughts flaps around and around into a frenzied dream. Her slippery King James Bible is still clutched in her hand when I finally get up to shut out the light. As quiet as I try to be switching off the sixty-watt bulb, the tiny noise brings her upright. Like animals of awkward size, she is most comfortable on her feet.

"Go back to sleep, Mom," I say.

"I was just resting," she replies. My mother slips on her reading glasses, picks up the darning needle and the patch of embroidery on the floor and goes to sit in the black rocking chair. On the way back to bed, I gaze over at the closed door at the end of the hallway, the room where I spent months weeping over the boy that we all loved then and love still, wrestling to make the ultimate decision that Aaron deserved to be set free to find a girl like me; like the one I once was when we used to make love in that narrow twin bed while my Mom and Dad were out scratching in the dirt planting potato sets. That room is shuttered now. I have not stepped foot across the threshold since the night I single-handedly packed up my belongings, literally scooping the bras, blouses and jeans with a shaky stone-fisted hand, and hurled them out the busted half-screen into the tiger lilies where my rescuer who was huddled just out of view rushed to press them into his backpack.

#

"Lemme guess. You're white, right?"

My exposed forearm speaks for itself. Pale as a surrender flag in the eyes of the hostile host who watch my every move. The flecks of sun spots are telltale traces of Anglo vulnerability and the bulging pipeline of blue blood swells in knobby veins from wrist to knuckles.

"Uh, yeah," I say with playful sarcasm, pulling my sleeve up higher to give everyone a better view of the obvious. Young Mr. Ortega likes the smirks he gleans from the small huddle of onlookers and knows he is well on his way to making a point. He places both hands down the back of his one-color-fits-all pants and shimmies the elastic waistband lower on his hips.

"And I'll bet you're from the suburbs too, huh?" he says slyly.

"I won't deny that," I say. His movements are fluid, slippery even, as he slides his wiry arms across his state-issued, once-white cotton tee. His overshirt is hanging from his waistband like a flag. The rule states that all inmates must wear their full tans when outside the cell and he knows it full well.

"Tuck in, Mr. Ortega," I state generically. I block the defensiveness that begins to swell in my chest and thicken my vocal cords. Ortega grins and straightens his shoulders. He makes no move to retrieve the missing uniform.

"You see it too, Miss Abrams. It's obvious. You were destined to do what you're doing. Those were your connects and those connections decided how you would turn out. Like go to college, have a nice house. Get a good-paying job like this one you got now. But me, I grew up in the streets of Santiago de Cuba. Then we moved to Miami. Ever hear of the North River projects? Well, it's the worse piece of shit place with drug addicts and gang-bangers. It's all I knew. Those were my connects. It was decided for me. I had no choice but to end up here."

His eyes fixate on my mine. There is not a single spark of contrast in those ominous orbs, not a pin-prick of light or a shimmer of a conscience. They are as opaque and oily as squid ink that repels and confounds those who wade too close. He shakes back a dark halo of hair netted by a rubber band confiscated from the officer's station. The young ones like him, they wear their disobedience proudly. He has a beautiful face with angular bones, a Romanesque nose and a lift to his lips that invite sport. Despite the bold demeanor and dance, I can imagine the little boy he once was, the youngster who knelt in the Our Lady of Fatima grotto to light a candle of good intent. There in his navy trousers and pressed white dress shirt, his hair creamed into submission, he pledged to take his spot in catechism and his rightful role in the family. Any mother could spot the future in that precious little son especially his own had she not been dope-sick in her own vomit.

Mr. Ortega has a crease of flesh near his temple that puckers and bubbles like a zipper. It is the precise trajectory of a bullet that was meant to inflict deadly silence, but has instead given voice to a fresh brand of brashness. There are things I could tell this young man. Crimes and casualties are not the sole claim of curb communities. Weapons are wielded behind six panel doors and security systems too. Danger dwells in cul-de-sacs where words wound more innocents than those remembered by makeshift shrines erected near the play-yard fences of our cities' streets. I don't say anything. What he doesn't understand is people like me, whites from the suburbs; we wear our scars on the inside.

"There may be some truth in that, but the fact is I don't have to come from the same background as you to care about your success as a fellow human being. And you *do* have a choice. You don't have to cling to what you've been handed. This white, uptight, middle-aged lady from the suburbs can be your new connect. And I can hand you off to other resources, people you don't even know who are out there advocating in your community. You can start to build a new support system from there if you make the decision to leave that life."

Though he waffles for a moment as if he might just sign on to this new religion of rehabilitation, Ortega and I both know that he has no intention of converting. The adrenaline of the streets is thick in his blood. He will go back.

I keep a careful eye trained on the movements of my runner, Mr. Vines. These peer mentors are typically old-time convicts whose good behavior has earned them the coveted job of the counselor's overseer running messages and paperwork up to the lieutenant's office or Control. It is a position of privilege that often graduates to a tendency to become unduly familiar in habits and too comfortable in conversation. It happens gradually over a course of months and week. The client chair is dragged up a little closer and pushed round to the side of the desk, elbows resting on top of the caseload folders. The trusted worker eventually leans into the measured space of safety between until it disappears into thin inches. And then it's the reaching into the drawer to get the stapler and 'I bet your husband and children don't like you working here.' The pause that hopes for a confirmation that yes indeed, she is single. I don't need to tell Vines what to do. He has a sixth sense that tells him when he needs to run interference for his beleaguered boss.

"We're closing up shop," says Vines. "Count time!" He is trim and stately in stance. His complexion is like caramel. He has a broad bridge and open nostrils, full lips that are chalky with chapped skin and a gentle, rhythmic voice that works like a lullaby to soothe hostile nerves. He uses his superior vocabulary to coax and herd the ones who linger behind to promote their own agenda and pester the counselor with the same question they've asked for the past three days running,

"Go on! Miss needs to get out of here," he orders. "I don't know why you all gotta bother this poor lady. You ain't boys when you did your crimes, so quit cryin' and do your time like a man." He turns to me with an ingratiating wink and I know that he is hoping I have a new parole hearing date for him.

"No news today," I tell the proud man who has no remorse for the bad checks he parlayed for years to help with the medical bills when the hospital came after him for payment on his wife's third round of breast cancer treatment. Even the banker whose branch bore the brunt of this siphoning saluted the man for taking care of his dying spouse in the best way he knew how and then turning himself in when she passed.

"I don't know, Counselor," says the young Latino with tight-knit braids. "You must go home with a fuckin' headache every day. Why you want to work this job?" He gathers his workbook and fist pumps Mr. Vines on his way out the door. After they all clear out, I drop into the chair.

No, I don't hail from the barrio or the Bronx. And yes, I am white. This statement is not an apology. In some ways, it makes it all the more amazing. I am here to peddle hope and with that earnest intent, I give them my word. That is the sole tool I bring to this compound of radios and towers and circlets of thorny steel. Behind the grinding bump of the sally port doors that usher in and seal out, it is all I have to defend me.

#

"Okay, who has some words of wisdom to share with us?" I ask. My question goes out to the men who have filed in and taken the same seats as they did last week. For them, this assembly of random souls is a unique configuration but for me, it is a dance that is passed down class to class like a cultural tradition. They believe there is safety in numbers and so the men quickly find allies in the mix, thinking they won't be singled out or targeted if the buddy system is at work. Human nature is predictable when it comes to group dynamics. Over the next two weeks, the personalities will surface. Each man will take his place in a classic tale that's been aired time and again with stand-ins and stand-outs, a variety act that is always entertaining and keeps us on the edge of our seats.

"Anyone?" I repeat. Dead silence, typical for a Monday. They're in bad need of a jumpstart. Amazing what can be lost over two days of idle time.

"The assignment was to describe the impact of your control and abuse on others. It could be a quote, an insight. Something you learned from the reading. And by the way, anything that you offer is in confidence and I trust the rest of you will keep that pledge and not take this back to the blocks. This is your group and I am here to help you guys create a place where it is safe to share."

"Miss A. In our addiction services class, we call that cheese and crackers. The teacher gives us the basics, the crackers. Us guys have to come up with the cheese." Curious analogy but I go with it.

"Why don't you go first, Mr. Dent?" I suggest. "Since you already have our attention."

"Kenny needs to take care of Kenny. If Kenny's got his eyes on getting high, then Kenny cannot love hisself and he certainly can't love anyone else." I doubt third-person Kenny has the capacity to look too far beyond his own simple sphere to extend over-reaching empathy to others.

"Good. Thank you. Anyone else?"

"Jesus loves you…but everyone else thinks you're an asshole." I can't contain the smile that breaks out despite the seriousness of the topic at hand. "Okay, but if I said that to you, Serge, what would be your reaction?"

"Nuthin'. Cuz I *know* I'm an asshole."

"I appreciate your honesty, Mr. Magrini. Extra points for that."

The dark-haired kid in the front row still has not looked up or spoken once. His tangled mob of curls falls across his face and he keeps his head averted. I check the roster.

"Mr. Bowman, do you have anything for us?" He shakes his head. At least it's a sign that he's listening. "I'll give you a little more time to come up with something brilliant." A hand goes up over to my right.

"Yes, Mr. Willis. Please." He must be about forty or so, a striking black man with a composure that belies a rare inner peace. Likely he's a Muslim that has made a pact with his Mohammed. Willis is an imposing physical presence but his posture and manner tell me that humility has found a foothold in his life.

"When I first came in, I thought like a boy. I woke up angry every day and I let that anger pull me out of character. But as I've matured, I realized that it is on me. Blame is anger focused outward; guilt is anger turned in on one's self. I needed to own up to my choices. So I learned to fall back and do the time, not fight it. I brought this on myself. We need to think like men now."

"Wonderful. Thanks for sharing," I say, impressed. "Research says that anger is often a substitute for another emotion. In other words, it is a symptom of something else. So when we lash out and abuse others, what could be the hidden cause behind that, do you think?"

"Stress?" guesses a white guy who has slipped into the classroom and taken a seat on my left. It's not uncommon to have stragglers who, when a program is announced, take the chance and press their block officer to let them out. And despite movement policy that prohibits anyone to be released outside their housing unit without a pass or a name on a list, some of them make it undetected to the door of my room. I'll deal with him later. It takes me a moment to register that it is Tommy Pisano in the flesh despite his paranoia and social phobia. I nod in hearty agreement.

"Depression?" offers Euclid. I smile with approval.

"Fear," says an anonymous contributor. I spin around with my arms extended.

"Yes, who said that?" The guy from Guatemala who claims to have twenty-seven kids and speak no English sheepishly lifts his hand.

"Gold star, Crespo! As we now know, abuse is all about control, and those that abuse others are often afraid. Of what, do you think?"

"Losing control. Losing everything," says Zimmer.

"Fuck that. If you ain't in control of yourself, then you're a pussy," seethes a baritone voice. The others flick glances at one another and then at me, waiting for a reaction.

"Mr. Noble, you are free to express yourselves without censorship, but not if your choice of words offends anyone in here and that word offends me." I turn back to Crespo. "Go on…" But before he can speak, Noble interrupts again.

"Listen, my niggas, if anyone disrespects you, you gotta put your hands on them. Guy or broad, no difference."

"Does anyone take offense to this?" I ask.

"I do," says Mr. Zimmer, perhaps the lone Jew in a prison of twenty-three hundred men. "Maybe you could say Ninjas instead." The group laughs in unison, all except Serge, the Italian from New York who is iconic to anyone within the Department. He's outlasted the average retiree by a good ten years in accumulated time and he's only in his early fifties. His ties to the Persico family are well-known and inmates give him wide berth. Serge is getting perturbed. He folds his hairy arms across his chest and locks eyes with Mr. I AM, who is not in the habit of falling back.

"He's pissin' me off right now," hisses Serge. He's talking to me but looking at Noble. "I'm trying hard not to do what I normally do when I'm angry. I'm tellin' myself, maybe this guy's got a problem. I gotta try and be patient with his shit."

"I hear you, my brother," says Rev. "I study vocabulary in my cell. My father and I used to challenge each other with a chosen word of the day. I do that in here still. Each morning, I shout it out to the block. Just before breakfast. Like for example, this morning. It came to me overnight in a divine dream and I announced, Guys, the word today is *tolerance*. There's no coincidence or random chance here. This is the word we need to hear in this class today. I used to be ignorant and self-serving. Everyone else irritated me with their childishness but God gave me the gift of speech and has impressed it upon me to speak to you today. It's pride, my son that governs ..."

"Shut the fuck up," says Noble.

"I get it. The hostility I'm seeing. The devil doesn't like the truth. I speak for all of us when I tell you..." and another ten-minute sermon threatens to ensue before I can wrench the conversation back to topic.

"Aren't we supposed to be using the talking stick?" asks Dent. "Maybe others have something they want to say."

"If the others don't have the balls to speak up, then fuck 'em," says Noble.

"Anyone else want to add anything?" I ask.

"So what, now you think your shit's more important than our shit?" Serge shouts. He's risen to his feet and stepped his six-foot-two inch height a few paces out into the middle of the classroom. He is genuinely trying to control his anger, but a half-century of living on impulse is not an easy thing to tame. Noble pushes his desk away and stands up. He has a bellowing voice but is much shorter in stature. The disparity between the two alpha males is more noticeable now that they are staring one another down.

"Mr. Magrini, you need to please back off," I state firmly. My thumb is on the red button of my body alarm. If this escalates one more notch, I'll press it. Serge turns his head to acknowledge my request and relaxes his stance.

"I'll see you out at Rec. I'll deal with you there," he mumbles to Noble before returning to his desk. I could easily throw them both out of the class but these are the kind of guys that need this program the most. The process of purging can get ugly.

"Thank you, both," I say sincerely. The men settle back into a cautious peace. "Now, consider this. If you control your partner, you are threatening these following things. I'll call them the three S's. Her…Safety." I scribble on the board. "Her Self-determination or the ability to make choices. And finally, you take away her Satisfaction. Look at these concepts in a different way. When we abuse others, we jeopardize their ultimate safety, or life. We take away their choices, which is their liberty. And we destroy their quality of life, or happiness. So what do we have here?"

"Life, liberty and the pursuit of happiness," Dent announces.

"And where do those ideas come from?" I ask.

"The Constitution?" guesses Willis.

"Good guess. You're very close," I say encouragingly.

"The Gettysburg Address?" volunteers Serge. I do not want to curb his contributions. Accuracy is not as important here as authenticity.

"Good answer, Serge. You're very close. Think Fourth of July," I suggest.

"The Declaration of Independence," Crespo says. Ironically Mr. San Salvador is the one guy who is not a natural-born citizen but actually knows something about our American history. Likely he's studying for citizenship or his GED.

"Do you recall its most famous phrase?" I query. He shakes his head.

"Okay, here it is. You all ready?" I ask. The men politely tolerate my enthusiasm though their glazed stare communicates a larger wish to get this over with. 'We hold these truths to be self-evident. That all men are created equal, that they are endowed by their Creator with certain unalienable Rights, that among these are life, liberty and the pursuit of happiness. So let me break it down for you. What this is saying is that we know that ALL men, including women, children, immigrants, people of color and different gender preferences are created equal. We all are guaranteed these same human rights. If any of us abuse or control another, we are taking away that person's right to be independent. Does this make sense?" I ask.

To my great surprise and delight, it is one of those moments that bless an educator's heart. I can actually see enlightenment radiate inside cerebral bulbs that have been dimmed by drugs or defective genes. Most of these men are addicts and are by necessity self-centered, manipulative people that only exist to get what they need. Other people in their lives serve that one clear purpose. Suddenly, it occurs to some of them that in their drive to feed their own twisted hunger, they have trampled over others.

"So that could mean calling them names or not giving them the money they need and shit like that?" asks Dent.

"Yes, abuse is a pattern of coercive control over another person's will with the purpose of beating him or her down to where they submit to yours. And by whatever means necessary. What does coercion mean, anyway?" I ask. They know this one, since it has relevance to the world they operate in.

"Force," says Euclid. He looks downright diabolical. This man is bright as they come. Too bad his genius has only been acknowledged for criminal implications.

"Never thought of it that way. I guess I am guilty then," Dent admits.

"In what respect? Guilty of what?" I ask.

"Do I have to pick just one thing? Balls!" he grumbles. "Hold on." He pauses and rubs the red bristle on his double chin. "Okay, here's one. So, I was in the shop working on a customer's car, right? I've got the whole engine pulled apart and the transmission suspended up in the air when the bitch comes driving up nagging at me. 'When's my husband's car gonna be ready? You said five o'clock,' she says. And I ignore her so I can get the thing tuned up and she keeps yapping so I tell her I'm closed and start lowering the bay. She jumps back into her car real quick and pulls it forward so the sensor on the door stops it automatically, and then she sits there laying on the horn until I come down off the lift and pay attention to her."

"So, she was trying to get a reaction out of you."

"Yep. Broads always know how to push my buttons," Dent replies.

"And did it work?"

"Sure as shit did. I unhitched the transmission and threw it right through the windshield of her car. I said, 'Here give this to your fucking boyfriend.'" The other men snicker and grin.

"And who was this woman to you?" I ask.

"My fourth wife. Well, soon to be ex if I can get out and finalize this divorce. I'm trying to get married," he announces proudly. How this paunchy, less-than-hygienic guy has wooed multiple women is a mystery. "My new baby mama is expecting in two months, so I need to get out and take care of my kids."

"How many children do you have, Mr. Dent?"

"Eleven," he says proudly, rubbing his state-issued lenses on his filthy shirt. I'm thinking he'd make great sport on Jerry Springer with five women rampaging on the set to get a swing at him. But then I take stock of his violent tendencies and dismiss that thought.

"Have you ever taken a domestic violence class before?"

"Yeah, once before. It was held in the basement of a community center and the chick running it bugged out and told me to leave cuz I was too disruptive. She talked to me like I was some kind of dumb-ass so I told her, 'Bitch, who's the stupid one? Here you are locked in room with sixteen violent men. How fuckin' bright is that?' and I picked up my chair and threw it at her. I didn't pass," he said, sounding genuinely disappointed.

The second bell rings, the mandatory dismissal for all inmates in the school unit. Dent lurches up out of his seat but his belly snags under the tabletop. He tugs hard and the desk lifts then slams down on wobbly feet, freeing him. The others hang back and allow him his moment. He has a bit more swagger than he did an hour ago. His confessions have earned him some clout among his peers and a good chest bump from Noble.

"You know how bitches get," Dent says with a wink.

CHAPTER 4
BOYS TO MEN

A sub-contracted hazmat team has cordoned off the entire school unit with plastic, tape and orange traffic cones. It's hardly a surprise to learn that asbestos has been drifting down on all of us for years. Splattering on the concrete floor when thunderstorms open up and rain leaks in streams into the cavernous hallways. Twenty years down the road, we'll all be filing claims with infomercial attorneys such as Jacobs, Jacobs and Kirschbaum for contracting mesothelioma. They'll probably turn us away saying, 'Hey you're the suckers who signed up for hazardous duty.' As a result of the decontamination project, class has been re-routed to the old package room at the far end of the south corridor. The principal has granted permission for us to borrow chairs from his wing and wheel them down on a heavy cart. He offers a few of his workers to help with the move, but Chulo insists on taking charge of setting up shop in our temporary quarters.

The morning started off rough. A confiscated stinger forced a cease of operations and then a facility lockdown. Since hot water can be used as a weapon, the faucets in the common areas eke out only lukewarm dribble. The inmates can order instant coffee through commissary but there's minimal comfort in sipping piss-poor caffeine in see-through plastic cups. The more mechanically-inclined prisoners know how to rig up two wires lifted out of someone's TV or headphones and secretly plug them into an outlet when the officers are busy taking bets on the Patriots. The electrical current will heat up the liquid when the homemade stinger unit is dropped into a cup. I can't blame these guys for not wanting to eat cold soup, but when an all-thumbs crook takes a stab at it, it can short out the circuits for an entire housing unit, which in today's case happened to be the food workers block. Counselors were summoned to the kitchen to fill in so feeding would not be interrupted. Three hours of sweat shop labor followed. Here's the drill. On go the latex gloves and the hair net. Steam tables are pulled into two long lines facing one another and the assembly begins. The doggie-dish container begins its mad journey with a slap of watery baked beans dumped out of #10 cans into hotel pans. Pass fast. Add two slabs of mystery meat we think is slimy bologna. Pass. Two slices of wheat-less, tasteless bread. Pass. A scoop of purple, corn-syrup jelly and another knob of oily peanut butter. Pass. A bag of chips. Pass. One spork. Slam shut. Stack. Repeat process. After the first hundred, the temperature in the room has noticeably elevated as the Blodgett convection ovens heat up for afternoon chow. Sweat pools down the spine and the dream team begins to malfunction. Spoonfuls of beans spatter on the floor. Bread is flung and misses the tray completely. The line comes to a halt.

"Hey, do you think the gentlemen would prefer to have the crusts trimmed off their sandwiches?"

"Fuck you, Slater," chimes in the harried kitchen crew. But the humor breaks the impasse and the line starts up again. There's camaraderie in this chore as nurses, teachers and counselors all work side by side. Once the meals are stacked, taped and labeled for delivery, we roll the Cambro units to the respective blocks. A plastic garbage bag is knotted to the crates of jungle juice that are pulled along behind. By the time the food and beverage arrives at the customer's door, half the drinks have tipped over and spilled. The cutting-edge architect who designed this prison in the mid-fifties never thought about door-to-door delivery to two-thousand caged customers. The newer facilities have traps that drop open so trays can be handed in horizontally. Not here. I always find myself apologizing profusely as the container is tipped vertically and crushed through the square opening. Molasses and watery barbecue sauce dribble down the doors and onto the floor.

Now here I am sticky and over-heated walking alongside a rolling palette of chairs, trying to regain my composure. Chulo manhandles the cart to our designated space and angles it into position as I unlock the door. The room serves multiple purposes but has no real function, doubling as a secret break room, a place to sort incoming packages and a dumping ground for broken furniture. Empty cartons are stacked in one corner. Several old Dunkin Donuts coffee cups are on the table. Chulo senses my discouragement and goes into action. For someone who was removed from the real world at nineteen years of age, he has very strong organizational skills and knows how to step up with initiative. He procures antibacterial spray and paper towels from the cart and starts washing down the tables and chairs, methodically scrubbing away any invisible contaminants.

"I know what goes on in here. This stuff is dirty," he warns. I reach to lift a blue plastic chair from the stack but Chulo hustles over.

"I got you. I got you," he says, and will not let me do what he perceives as a man's work; or more correctly stated, a male inmate's job. While he is arranging the chairs, I begin to sort out the homework and handouts. The sterile room has no accoutrements and the acoustics are horrible. Every sound echoes painfully. The din from the adjoining blocks is muffled but provides a relentless backdrop of competing noise. Chulo pulls the door closed. I note that there is a telephone in the corner and two rovers stationed in the hallway.

"I bet your family worries about you working here," he says. It's a neutral statement set out as bait. I let the ambiguity lie there.

"Nothing to worry about," I reply. He smiles.

"We all talk in here. That's what we do, like a bunch of girls. And I know you've got their respect, Miss A, but there's always a knucklehead or two that will fuck things up. You gotta be tough with these guys. Send a message if you have to."

"I haven't had any problem," I say. When Chulo turns his back to scrub down the table top, I go over and release the door knob so that the door is once again ajar.

"I hear you but like I said, guys talk. The simplest thing, like you speaking to one guy after class or giving him extra help, and next you know he's telling everyone that you like him and he's in with you, you know?"

"Are you referring to anyone in particular?" I ask.

"Listen, I've straightened out a couple dudes who got the wrong thoughts in their head with you being a female and all. You treat us fair like human beings, but some of these guys are crazy and interpret what they want."

"I certainly can't control their thoughts."

"No, but I'm just sayin' to be mindful." He has something or someone in mind. After a year of working in close proximity, we have learned to read each other well. If Chulo had not chosen to gun down two rival gang members, he could really have excelled in life. Even with English as his second language, he is articulate and has a good bead on people. He claims that comes from studying human nature at its worst for over twenty-two years.

"So, who should I watch?" I ask point-blank.

"That Willis dude. I see him in your class and he's a smart guy. He talks a good talk, but I hear him back in the block on the phone to his people. Be careful is all I'm sayin'."

"I think you're wrong about him. Maybe there's a little testosterone quarrel going on here."

"I look out for you because I like you. I've never been able to talk to a woman like I can with you."

"That's because you haven't been around a woman for two decades. Anything looks good at this point," I tease.

"Miss A, I'm serious. The other counselors are alright but they're like girlie-girls and look down on us. Some are straight-up bitches. Everyone can see that you are real and don't judge us. But that kindness can be twisted in the wrong guy's mind." I start wiping the dry erase board with a rag but the permanent marker does not come off.

"You have some of that spray I can use?" I ask. He comes over with the bottle and a clean cloth and playfully dabs at my cheek with it.

"You've got some food or something on you." The touch is a trespass. I react by dropping my eyes and scanning my shirt for stains.

"We had to stand chow today," I say apologetically as a way of an explanation.

"You're blushing. I can see it. Why you be blushing?" he laughs.

"I'm not blushing. I'm sweating," I reply.

"But you looked away. Why, Miss A?"

"You're seeing things, Mr. Diaz. Let's get this finished up." I can sense that he is taking his time and is certainly in no hurry to get back to Cell # 318. Chulo pulls a Polaroid out of the elastic waistline of his pants and holds it out.

"Have I ever shown you this?" he asks. It's a photograph of a young Latino man with long hair, vintage nineteen-eighties or so, dressed in a silky blue graduation gown and holding a diploma aloft.

"Yes, I've seen this before. It was taken when you received your GED. In 1992, wasn't it?" I say. He nods proudly. Since then, he has accumulated an increasing stack of certificates in computer repair, culinary arts and most recently, as a certified nurse's aide and hospice worker.

"How can you not be cocky about that?" I say. It's his turn to flush now. After all, he's Chulo, the rooster.

"I'd like for you to see me someday outside of here. Who I really am, you know? Your kids and husband or boyfriend or whatever, they don't need to worry. We could have some fun over drinks and shoot the crap, you know, like regular people do. I told Mr. Snyder and Mr. Hastings the same thing. Would you do it?"

"Meet up with friends after work? I do it all the time," I respond generically.

"Hey, maybe you can be my ride outta here," he jokes.

"What year will that be?"

"2026."

"I'll put it on my calendar," I say. He does a little Puerto-Rican salsa right then and there with a grin as innocent as a schoolyard boy. I shake my head. When he sashays up closer, my stance straightens but I certainly do not anticipate the embrace that he places around my waist, then slides up to my shoulders. It is firm and close. I can only imagine what this must feel like to a man who has been without a woman for all but one year of his adult life. I stiffen up immediately.

"Just this once," he whispers. "Just one hug." I decide it's wisest and safest to placate him and so I reach around and give him a brotherly pat with both hands on his back, then step backwards.

"We're done here," I announce and walk out of the room ahead of him. We maintain some benign banter as we wheel the cart back up to the warehouse, but I can't decipher what he's thinking. He's always had my best interests at the forefront and has faithfully acted to protect me from harm. One hug is all. After everything he's done to make my job easier, it would be suicide to rat him out. And that's just not what people do in here, least not the strong ones.

#

A car is making its way down the gravel drive. I hold my breath. About halfway down the two-hundred yard road, drivers usually spy the private property sign, realize that they have mistaken this for a state park entrance and use the shorn circle of grass near the cedar gate as a turnaround. But after a slight pause, this vehicle keeps coming. Though it is close to the dinner hour, it is still plenty light and soon the bumper of a big Ford pick-up glints through the maples at the second bend. I have three guns placed at planned lookout spots throughout the house. One 20-gauge sits in the front coat closet with a box of pheasant shell in the hat basket beside it. The loaded .22 automatic rifle rests comfortably with the safety on in the blanket chest by the second-story dormer and my pistol nests in a basket of photo albums near the bed. I watch and wait with my thumb hovering over speed dial. I chose this cape for this one factor alone. Location, location, location. Next to nothing and near no one.

It is a lie, what I told Chulo about getting together with co-workers all the time, a bluff to throw him off track. I keep close to home by choice. They say in life that ninety percent is what happens to us; the other ten percent is how we respond to it, and that we cannot worry about what we can't control. I don't know if it was Mark Twain or Woody Allen or Joan Rivers who made that up, but I have sweetened the odds in my favor. Here in a remote stretch of farmland just south of Brigham and thirty-eight miles from my workplace, I have created a rural alcove as my domain. There is no name on the mailbox, no listing in the yellow pages, no approaching stranger that can't be spotted by Rio, Brindy or Vera, my free-roaming police dogs. Every night is a three-dog night in my bedroom where the trio of scouts circles my bed, ever on alert. I hear the call go up now, the shepherds barking wildly as they tail the truck like wolves running down a slow calf. The driver parks the rig and steps out undeterred by the canine frenzy at his feet. With both a sigh of relief and a register of surprise, I see it is Hastings out of uniform in a short-sleeve linen shirt and camel-colored slacks. He waves as I swing open the door.

"What the hell...?" I call out.

"Hey girl. Thought you might like to accompany me for dinner. You haven't eaten yet, have you?" he asks brightly. I shake my head. I'm barefoot in a batik sundress with not a blush of make-up on. A snap of my fingers sends the dogs to their bellies in the grass. My fingers and palms are stained blood-red.

"I've been weeding the strawberries and am pretty settled in now. Plus I'm filthy," I say self-consciously. A fact easily observed on bare legs caked to the shins with dried mud. Red flares from nettles pepper my arms.

"Well, that works out perfectly because I brought the dinner here. Go take a shower and I'll pour us some wine," he replies. I start to protest but this is Hastings, my close friend and not a person who is easily swayed in negotiations. I back in to the cool interior and he follows. When I return in twenty minutes, the meal is spread on a faded bedspread under the red maple. How perfectly adolescent and sweet! A cloud of jasmine emanates from my wet hair and my skin radiates after a fierce exfoliation with lemon sea salt. I scoot onto the blanket beside him.

"How is it you're free on a Saturday night? Aren't there soccer games or things to grill or a lawn to mow?" I ask, taking the plastic goblet of Riesling. "Thank you," I add.

"There always is, but I had to get out of there."

"I'm sorry. Are things in a rough patch again?" I ask. Hastings (aka James outside of work, though I can't classify him by any other name) leans back and takes in the phenomenal view from this hillside. The acres of agriculture roll back from the main road. Geese are gathered in dark clots debating whether to scrounge for sprouted seed or look for a good launching pad. Seems the seasonal clocks are all off. Sparrows sang all through the deep winter when the persistence of sun teased the thermometer to stay above freezing. The flocks congregated way back in November as usual, but never came to a consensus about the departure time or flight pattern and have stayed huddled in Norfolk Valley ever since.

"You have no idea. It's not a spell or a stage. It's like living with a child. A totally immature and anxious one. Allyson needs me for stability and to make all the decisions and keep things running smoothly. She can't do shit for herself, but she's worse than the girls. She gets so stressed by life that she always trying to control everything. Problem is she doesn't have a clue to what she's doing."

"Is she still on her medication?" I ask. A seed pod falls from the catalpa tree and lands in the tub of potato salad. I lift it out and toss it to the tree line. He shakes his head.

"Well, what can I do to help you?" I ask with genuine concern.

"Not a thing but this. I feel calm around you. Things make more sense. I love my kids but I swear to God I can't take her theatrics anymore. She went into a downspin this morning and started sobbing that she wasn't worth the food she ate. Her self-esteem is shaky and she is so needy.

Complains that I am never home when I'm working double shifts to keep her happy and forgive me Christ, there's days like today that I'd rather be in a shithole prison that at home." He turns towards me and props his frame up on one steady elbow. "Elise, do you think love is only for a time and a season?"

"That's a trick question. I can tell," I say. "I believe in soul mates that are meant to be together. And if you are lucky enough to find that person, there is no desire to be with another."

"So, you've found yours?" he asks. I nod.

"Then why are you alone?" he asks, dismayed.

"Sometimes circumstances prevent that relationship in the physical realm. But in the parallel universe where our minds and hearts dwell we are together. Always."

"Sounds like bullshit to me. You deserve to have the experience of being loved in the present. We all do! Who is this lucky guy?" he asks.

"You silly man! No one you know. A friend from back home." James looks at me quizzically and then decides not to pursue that line of questioning.

"So basically, you're in love with an invisible man. Well, I can see one significant benefit with that arrangement. It sure eliminates a lot of arguments," he teases. I slap him warmly on the shoulder. The sun settles behind the horizon and the coolness of evening creeps up from the dank earth. I allow James to vent, fall silent and vent again. Another glass of wine for both and we wander off onto other topics - books and hiking and philosophy and nutrition and politics and pretty soon the creep of dew has dampened the ground cover. This isn't the first time he has thought to try to kiss me, but it is the first time I have allowed him to linger and find a rhythm with my tongue. James stands to his feet, takes my hand and pulls me up. I lean down to gather up our leftovers.

"Leave it. I'll come back for them," he says firmly.

I should not have been surprised then when he leads me past the den and straight back towards the bedroom. At any point, I am free to pull up short or turn back. When he lifts me up onto the bed in a kneeling position, I hesitate.

"James, this is not what your marriage needs," I say in a firm voice.

"This is exactly what I need. Will you let me love you, Elise? You can't really prevent it because I already do. And have." I smile and cup his handsome, yearning face in my palms.

"Yes, but you can love me from afar and not cause harm to anyone else," I suggest. But all he has heard is the one-word affirmation. He deftly peels the sundress off over my head and then pulls me against him. His hands run along my back in massaging pulses over ribs and shoulder blades and collar bone. They wander through the hair that has tumbled in a wet sheath down my back. And then he pushes back to undress himself while maintaining unwavering eye contact. It isn't until he has lowered himself on top of me that he asks again.

"Is it alright?"

I can't convincingly say yes or no. I have no ready answer but I find my hands reaching up and pulling him downwards. I've never felt the hard weight of such a powerful man before and though my lungs are hard pressed to expand, he rests there only a moment before his urges take him on a crawl down the length of me. 'Beautiful. Amazing,' he whispers at each stop along the way. And then he is quiet as he stops to worship at the most sacred of thrones and suddenly I am the one that is vocal, crying out in a howl that these rafters have never heard. Not once, but again and still he lingers between my thighs kissing and nuzzling me. I squirm to relieve the intensity that is somewhere on the spectrum between pleasure and pain. He senses the shift and climbs back up to hover over me face to face.

"I love you," he says as he exacts a slow entrance, pushing deeper and deeper. It is a tight fit that he explores carefully and then in faster repetitions. When he reaches his climax, his entire frame stiffens and he erupts in an alien moan. The dogs startle in the living room and begin scratching at the closed door. After several shudders, he releases and relaxes on top of me but does not withdraw. My legs are shaking uncontrollably and tears come spinning out of nowhere. I hold him tightly and run my hands over his perspiring skin. I tangle my fingertips in his coarse hair and kiss his forehead.

"*Hold me. Hold me,*" I moan over and over…….

I wake instantly, jerking my head up. A pinching pain shoots up the side of my neck. A small trail of drool has crept from the corner of my mouth and left a circle of residue on the throw pillow. The sensation of culminated pleasure still ebbs between my legs. I am on the couch alone with the reading light still ablaze and my worn copy of *Lolita* splayed page akimbo on the floor. The rocking sensation is nothing more than Rio kicking the couch in spasms of sleep. I jump up to check. There is no pick-up trick, no dewy blanket or picnic leftovers with an ant invasion. I am mystified and embarrassed by the source of my pleasure. Dreams like this are for adolescent boys. Though he is a virile specimen, James is a friend and I don't consciously have a sexual interest in him. I swore to myself long ago that if I could no longer attach emotion to sex, than I would forfeit the pretense of making love altogether. That way, nobody else was involved in the eventual disappointment of hastily pulling on underwear and pants in an awkward attempt to cover up an empty soul. The handful of men I had taken to bed years after my ordeal remained just a few and then became none. It was a part of my life that had people known about it; they would have likely judged me rather than pitied me. The messed-up middle that resembled an erratic pattern of emotional starts and stops that I diagnosed as my own peculiar brand of A.D.D. or affection disconnect disorder.

For years after the attack, my body was buried along with my memory. When I finally rose up out of the tomb of amnesia, I didn't lust because I couldn't love. I was stuck in this limbo of loneliness unless I made some quick concessions, so I turned to what was more easily mastered. In much the same way I had determined to bring my dexterity of hands and feet back, I threw my focus into building up my libido. Sex was something I could do well and something others wanted, an act that required no telling of past history, no spelling out of future goals or matching up common interests. I could unleash a store of emotion in a howling, writhing wrestling match and then disengage into an indifferent sense of being in neutral. Men loved this non-committal un-coupling. We each pulled apart fulfilled. Him, lolling on my batik bedspread with a limp penis slick with victory knowing he could zipper up and be gone. Whether or not they called the next night, the following week or never again, it didn't matter because it had nothing at all to do with them. I was using the one working part of me that elicited pleasure in others to keep people near enough to remind me that I still had a place among the functional living. Men were attracted to the seemingly docile woman who excused their trespasses, ignored their bad habits and asked no hard questions. They interpreted my quiet tolerance as the sign of a forgiving, centered soul. A few very seriously wanted to marry and start a family and begged me to consent. I didn't tell them my fallopian tubes had been welded and fused into free-standing pipe lengths. The ovaries that caused such unwieldy sweeps of self-destructive depression each month had been relieved of their duty. I was not ever going to conceive. And even worse, I was sentenced to the lifelong solitary curse of only ever being able to love once. When proposed to, as I was on several occasions, I patted these gracious men's hands and promised to think about it and then I shipped out. If their hearts were broken, I never stayed on to witness it. There was nothing I could offer them in the way of repair.

Because of one man's ruthless folly, they all had to pay

#

Gemini reminds me of those hairless cats that often win the ugliest pet contests. Sphinxes, the sleek-bodied, bald headed ones with arched back and hips always dancing sideways. He is striking with his emerald green Asian-shaped eyes, thin dark eyebrow arches penciled in a pose of constant surprise, Botox-inspired cheeks or possibly implants. His skin is taut and shiny with abundant estrogen. His most prominent feature is the glossy smile he directs at everyone and anyone. Gemini loves to volunteer for any little thing and will parade on the balls of his feet, nearly rubbing his flanks on anyone within petting reach. He is a cagey feline among a pack of dogs, some of which loathe homosexuals. Others tolerate him with generic respect and look the other way for fear they might be accused of showing interest in the partially-confusing and not-quite- transgendered person.

Today, Gemini has volunteered to tell his story. He is from the Bushwick section of Brooklyn where as a child of six or seven, he had to hop over puddles of cat piss, garbage and blunts to get to the stoop of his grandmother's three-decker brownstone. She was an old Puerto Rican woman that did nothing but cook and clean. She swept each landing, every stair, and waxed the faux-brick linoleum in all three kitchens. She buffed the banister railings and reached up under the raised window to spray ammonia on the pigeon shit so she could see the Chrysler building shining brightly through the haze. Her place was the showpiece in a block of crack dives and dens of iniquity filled with rubbish and whores. That's where Gemini's mother spent her days and nights smoking rocks unless she was called in to work. Her employer was his half French Creole/half Dominican father, a run-about who sold women for pocket money and usually came around once every couple of weeks to check on his sons. More like give them all an ass-whooping for what they may or may not have done in his absence and then crash drunk on the couch for a few days. Once he was gone, Gemini's grandmother would wipe up any trace of him and they would go back to their normal routine.

She could keep the streets out of her house but she could not keep her grandkids from straying out to the streets. One by one they left and it was always back to the two of them, herself and Gemini left to the washing and cleaning and cooking and watching re-runs of Falcon Crest or Dynasty. But it was no Cinderella-in-the-making story. Gemini was a pretty boy and he soon learned his street value courting men curbside. He bought nice women's clothing from boutiques on the Lower East Side and had his face done at Bloomingdale's. Lots of men loved Gemini; many more loved having sex with him. He was a commodity that brought out ugly competitiveness in the dime-a-dozen female prostitutes that roamed that block. Eventually, Gemini settled into a steady relationship with a fashionable urbanite named Darwin who bought him flowers, jewelry and trips to Turks & Caicos and Curaçao. But Darwin also played with women. Gemini seethed with jealousy and fretted since his femininity was only window dressing. He ultimately made the big decision to undergo psychiatric therapy and begin hormone treatment so that he could become what his inner chemistry had always told him was. And then one day, Gemini was standing on the balcony of the rent they both shared near Washington Park when Darwin told him that he was leaving to marry a Brazilian woman who was pregnant with his child. Gemini was completely devastated, crawled on his hands and knees, wept until his mascara stained the carpet and when his emotional tantrum did nothing to stop his departing lover, he blacked out with grief. The next thing he knew he was looking down at Darwin whose face had turned blue from the pressure around his throat. Strangulation, such an awful-sounding word for something that was intended to be a bitch slap and then a forgiving hug. Twenty-eight years. Gemini hadn't even heard the sentence the judge handed down because he was sobbing so hard. Three-quarters of that time had already whiled away in the company of men and in the center of attention once again, sought after either for a beating or a blow-job.

"So that's the story of my life," he concludes with a brandish of a flamboyant wave.

"I am impressed by your resilience," I say. "Strength of character," I add hastily for the benefit of those among the group who are still reading at a fifth grade level. "Okay, now I'm curious. What became off the issue you shared with us last week? Were you able to get an opportunity to address it?"

"Oh yes. So here's my issue for any of you that don't remember," he says. There's a tease of sarcasm and reproach in the way he addresses others. As if he half hopes that they will beg him for an encore and he can once again, jump and throw his arms around his big breasts in feigned modesty. Just in case anyone was absent, he repeats it for maximum effect.

"Every time we get in the shower, these guys come in that are not one of *us*. Or else, they purposely walk by so they can see in. One inmate in particular is constantly lingering there and I know it's just so he can stare at my breasts. They gave us our own separate time in the bathroom for a reason. Just so this kind of voyeurism won't happen." In fairness, I would be hard-pressed not to gape at his monstrous, swinging rack but to solve any remote chance of a false claim of blatant misconduct, I avert my eyes whenever I pass by the steaming shower area and stand clear of the comings and goings-on in there.

We're straying out on a precarious perch now. Most of the men in prison will claim to hate homos and refuse to be housed with them. There have been death threats against the transgendered inmates and a rumble of a targeted attack against their section of the block. His issue has been an ongoing and problematic one in my unit. Heterosexual men who claim they are "'straight to the gate" courting the transgendered and homosexual inmates whose lifestyle was solidly determined before they came to jail. Prison rape is an altogether different animal and one that is minutely managed. Gone are the days when staff turned a blind eye to the practice of alpha convicts dominating subordinates or exacting punishment by sexual assault. When inmates who were victimized in such a way were ignored, it was par for the course. Counselors and captains scrutinize the housing cards to determine the matchups in the double cells. Size difference, nature of crime, mental health issues and race. Anything that might put one person at the mercy of another. The admitted homosexuals are now housed on one side of the lower tier, some single-celled so they won't frolic with one another. Consensual sex is still a violation that brings discipline, but with the overcrowding and guys sleeping in temporary 'canoes' on the gym floor, the Department can't place them all in single occupancy.

"So, inmate…" Gemini starts.

"Leave names out, please," I interrupt.

"Sorry, Miss Abrams. So, this one guy has been hassling me. He calls out from the upper tier every time I'm out for Rec and says lewd things. He's threatened to beat me up if I don't do certain things with him. He's basically stalking me."

Like me, the other men hope he will limit his details. They respect Gemini but not his predilection for penises.

"So, I wrote the warden and the lieutenants and even the Commissioner and not one of the mucky-mucks in Administration answered my grievance. I took the advice of this group and Miss Abrams, which was to address the individual in an assertive way that would cause no harm or offend him, but that would get my point across. So I took this big bad self of mine over to his cell when his door was popped open and he was getting ready to go to the gym. He had his shirt off and was standing there in his boxers, so I hoped he was feeling kind of vulnerable. I did just what you said, Miss A and I confronted him directly and Sweet Mother of God, it worked. He's backed right off."

"Wonderful. That's a great example of good healthy conflict resolution. If you don't mind me asking, can you tell us how you how you worded your approach?" I ask.

"Oh, certainly!" Gemini is on stage now and takes front and center. He cocks his head, purses his painted lips, puts one hand on a jaunty hip and the other up in front of him with the pointer finger extended and circles it near his face.

"I said, does I has to take a shit so ya can lick it?" He looks to me for approval. The rest of the group is amused. A few of the guys have their heads down on the desk and are enjoying a genuine laugh.

"Well, that might not have been the exact words I would have chosen, but whatever works I say. Good for you!" I reply. I can't translate this phrase into any equivalent in uptight white dialect but I get the gist of it.

#

The boys are all off-track this morning and pre-occupied with the fact that some unemployed schlub has won the largest jackpot payout in the history of the Lottery, over five hundred and ninety million dollars, for the second time. This get-rich-overnight idea has fueled the imagination of this something-for-nothing crowd.

"I'd buy a Jaguar," Dent brags.

"No way. I'd go one better. A Bugatti or a Ferrari," boasts Bowman.

"Guys. Are we ready?" I ask. They continue their side conversations without interruption. Clearly it's going to be difficult to steer them back towards the planned material. . Maybe I can get creative and work the wayward dialogue into a meaningful lesson. What matters most to these guys is money and some of them have had more cabbage in their hands than the best Wall Street financier. I mean leafy green Grover Clevelands, stacks of them as evidenced in Facebook photos confiscated from envelopes in their lockers. In some ways, I can't blame them for a lack of appetite when a minimum wage warehouse job at Kohl's distribution center is the best carrot we can dangle. Their income is tax-free and disposable. They must laugh at my sniveling but at least I can sleep at night knowing the State Comptroller will be signing my next check and every two weeks thereafter. And while I'm slumbering away peacefully, a nocturnal war wages on to hold on to the profits. Drug money can easily blow away.

"Have you all heard the saying: Time is Money?" I ask. The circle of glistening foreheads and dull eyes stare back in motionless inattention. All the buzz and pre-class chatter has dissipated into instant apathy.

"Anyone?" Zimmer and Serge finally cave in and nod in unison.

"Do you believe that time and money are alike?" I repeat. Worse than pulling teeth; this is like teasing fleas from a poodle.

"Sure, our time is worth something," answers Dent.

"So if you think about it, there are two things you can do with money. The first is waste it and the second is invest it. It's quite simple really. If you spend it, you lose it. When you invest into something, the intent is to build up more. Now, let's look at time in the same way. You can sit here and waste it or you can invest it and come away more of a person than you were when you started."

"Here's new math for you" Rev chimes in, before anyone else can pipe up. "I say, that if you are not adding positive things to your life, then you are taking away from it."

"Same principle expressed in a different way," I concur. I should know by now if I don't shut him down, an inch of inspiration will drag out to a country mile of melodrama. But it's too late, he's off and running at the mouth

"Gentlemen, my good brothers. I was once like you are now. Skeptical.

Indifferent to change, but God got a hold of my heart and showed me my gift." Rev looks at Bowman. "You, my young friend, remind me of myself as a boy." His expression communicates compassion but there is an insincere ring to his voice. "I too was resistant, bitter, and unyielding. But now I am a man and…"

"Excuse me, Mr. Preacher?" I interject. Serge gets up abruptly, aligns his chair with the Rev and both men swivel their desks at a diagonal to face the younger guys at an angle of advantage. Apparently some bonding has taken place between them. They've assumed the superior posture of wise men lording over the others from their hypothetical pulpit. I've seen guys like them before, the ones who believe the mantra of their own voice is music in everyone else's ears. Zimmer is probably a good fifteen years their senior, but he's been dismissed from the power equation because of his perceived disability and obvious ethnicity. Jews just don't cut the mustard behind bars.

"Hold on a minute, Miss A, if you don't mind. I just want to finish my point." He turns back to young Bowman. "Son, I see that the dark one still has a hold on your spirit. We can't think like boys any longer. We must be men. I can share the wisdom I have learned in my time…"

Our non-verbal student in the front row has shown no sign that he's been addressed or antagonized by the ingratiating bully. Until now, as Bowman slowly uncoils from his reticent crouch and rises to his feet, gradually locking his gangly kneecaps into an upright position.

"Wait. Hold up! Everyone be quiet! What's this?" I say, smiling. "Please…I know something brilliant is brewing in there." It's unclear whether his silence to date is due to a language barrier, self-consciousness or plain old garden-variety indifference. The surly young man with acne awkwardly drops his head. His glasses have slipped down off the bridge of his nose and are cocked to one side. His fine dark hair hangs piecemeal about his face and an unmanicured growth of chin hair has long outgrown the confines of a goatee and spread out along the tendons in his thin neck. It appears that he detests shaving cream and soap as much as he loathes the company of strangers.

"Boys demand respect; men command respect," he says slowly and deliberately before abruptly sitting back down. Whatever prompted him to offer this spontaneous truism seems to have fizzled as quickly as it flared. Bowman drops back into his chair in a crumpled heap.

"Fabulous!" I say with an exuberant flourish of my hands. "I knew something special was just waiting to come out at the right time. Still waters run deep, you know what I mean, gentlemen?" But no, of course they don't. The other members of the group are just as impressed as I am that the mute has finally spoken.

"And since you've brought that up, what is the difference between those two words? They sound similar but are very different. How do you define command versus demand?" Before Rev can command the stage, Mr. I Am jumps to his feet.

"If one of you all disrespects me, I will put my hands on you," Noble says matter-of-factly.

"So, which is that? Command or demand?" I ask. The fact that he has hung in this group without any confrontations as long as he has is a testament to acquired patience or a med change.

"I don't fuckin know," he says.

Willis leans forward and lifts a strong arm skywards. The sleeve of his tans cannot possibly reach the maximum length of his limb. The wrinkled garment drops back from his powerful palm. Patches of vitiligo mottle his wrist and weave a glaring crochet-like pattern of reverse freckles down his forearm. The eerie collage gives the effect of bleached sperm swimming blindly through random blotches of dark ink.

"Your thoughts?" I ask. In another circle, perhaps a schoolyard gang, comments might have been made by the gawking pairs of eyeballs that have never seen a birthmark of serpentine dimensions. Maybe when he was a younger kid and defenseless to the taunts but not here. Here he is given a platform of respect.

"When someone demands respect, they are taking it from another. In other words, they are basically saying, 'Give it to me.' But when a man commands respect, others freely give it to him based on the way he conducts himself," Willis says. His demeanor has the louder voice.

"Beautifully done!" I say. "And let me add that this change from boy to man has nothing to do with age in years. It is a mental transformation. You can be sixty years old and still be a boy or a twelve- year old who has already become that man. Agree or disagree?" I pose the question to the circle of males who are a sum total of half-men and misguided boys.

"In God's eyes, we are all children. Each a boy in need of a father. Those of us who have made the leap to maturity can speak to the rest of you," says Rev. "We can demonstrate what respect should look like and those who have yet to grasp it can look to their elders as spiritual examples."

"Hey man, no offense, but I wouldn't look to you for shit. You're an arrogant hypocrite. Religion is nothing without sacrifice. What the hell have you done in here but swindle people out of ramen noodles and Jolly Ranchers?" says Zimmer.

"I'm not talking to you, old man," snipes Rev. Zimmer places both hands on the arms of his wheelchair and springs excitably up off the seat. He takes a few solid steps in the direction of the speaker and lifts an accusing finger at him.

"Why don't you man up and join the rest of us? Who died and made you king over us? I'm sick and tired of hearing how much you love your wife of twenty years who's dying of cancer. And how you've stood by her when we know you're a cheating shitbag. Your kids are going to bed without a daddy just like ours. You sleep with a thousand other dudes no different than the rest of us. And worse, you dragged your old lady out of a car because she owed you a lousy sixty bucks. I've heard you on the phone bitching her out. You're a goddamn hypocrite!"

"Hold up, guys!" I shout, raising my voice to counter the increasing hostility in the room. "Do I need to call the officer down and get you all tossed out?"

"I'm not going to stay and try to minister to people who can't accept the truth," pouts Rev. He folds his arms across his chest and tries to convict them all with a withering look of reproach.

"The truth is, you're a prick," Zimmer fires back. The class erupts with a few Amen's and high-fives. The Rev is unable to maintain his composure.

"I don't have to stay and listen to this. Pearls before swine," he says.

"You do have to stay unless I deem otherwise," I state. "But I think it's a good idea if you take a nice little time-out right now." I scribble off a hasty pass and hand it to him. Rev is stunned that I have the audacity to choose him as the scapegoat here.

"What about him? He started it," he blurts.

"He's not your concern," I say. "Now go, please," I add sternly. He is the crestfallen boy whose ego has been held up on shaky props of insecurity. A tantrum is foaming up underneath his skin.

"Just so you know you're losing a valuable resource. I'm here out the goodness of my heart. I don't have to care. It's not like…."

"You're here for the same reason we all are. For making bad choices," replies Bowman.

"Well, it's your loss," he shouts in a pathetic wail, his voice trailing off into a pitchy, childish squeak.

"It's only for today. You're welcome to come back tomorrow," I say. Narcissists are never in the wrong, never on the giving end of an apology. He must save face at all costs.

"I wash my hands of you," he spits, but his venom falls short of its mark. Zimmer is not a bit flustered by the attack and smiles benevolently. He stands in all his glory in a yellowed wife-beater tank shirt that bumps and sags over a scrawny chest of white hair. Some religious medallion dangles near his navel on a chain that is many links too long. He puffs up what little sinew and muscle he can and struts a fancy moonwalk across the floor.

"Shit! My lawyer would be yelling at me right now. I better get back in that bitch," he says. Zimmer scrambles into his faithful wheelchair and resumes the pose of an invalid. "Not good for the lawsuit we got filed." Though no one asks, he's quick to fill the lengthy pause with an explanation, eager to separate himself from the legal beagle inmates who spend their library time deep in the volumes of General Statute reference books and file litigation as often as they swap soups for services. Their cases against Department of Correction jam the volumes of pages on the judicial website. "I jumped off one of the State vans when I was on an Outside Clearance crew and crushed all my disks into powder," he adds, winking. "I'm not saying I'm any saint, Miss Abrams. But I always took my time to go down to the Children's Hospital and buy the cancer kids stuffed animals and shit. Yeah, I got money by illegal means, swindling insurance companies and Big Pharma, but I would never steal from a regular person. I have a heart. I see myself as a kind of modern-day Robin Hood."

It's getting harder and harder these days to make out the bad guys from the good ones.

#

I know I shouldn't bring work home. Among other things, I can come up with two very logical reasons. First is the confidentiality issue should a page flutter out of my satchel onto the parking lot where visitors walk; and secondly, it would piss off every other state employee that doesn't do his job at work, let alone outside of it. But how can I ask these damaged men to take up a pen and spill out old wounds in no less than five hundred words and then dump these confessions in a cluttered 'to be shredded' carton? Every single moment of paid time is already taken up with babysitting the basic needs of this helpless menagerie. It's like one huge dysfunctional day care. That's why I squirrel the journal entries into a folder and discreetly walk them out through the sally port. Other people have kids with soccer games and dance recitals and spouses to quarrel with. My evenings are spent drinking wine and weeding through the written overgrowth of perennial filth. The names change, but the games are the same.

I pull the first essay out of my briefcase. The author forgot to put his name on the paper, but I recognize the handwriting. Terran Willis is very prolific when it scribbling out detailed journal entries, like those one would expect from a young female who loves to pour out her heart on flowery pages of flowing penmanship. These girlish confessions surprised me at first, coming as they were from a brawling, brooding man, but they appeared faithfully and with unfaltering candor. This type of transparency is risky, especially in the company of boisterous men who think nothing of trampling sensitive issues underfoot and ferreting out snitches. He's dared to do it, share street secrets with staff and not only that but the incongruent whisperings of a black inner-city man to a white woman. The assignment handed out yesterday asked the men to reflect on this question: *How did I get to this point?* The response he's turned over to me approaches the length of a novelette, or at least, an amplified short story. The tale chronicled here is instantly revealing and riveting. I concentrate on the narrative with growing intrigue. It reads like a gritty, truer-than-fiction memoir that Oprah might have launched on her must-read list. The details are dirty and somewhat disturbing, but the plot is graphically clear.

The girl said he reached up under her skirt. She claimed he put his finger in her vagina. The boy who she blamed was nine years old. None of the other four teenagers either denied or confirmed this; they probably had encouraged him on a dare. Off record, they let the accusation stand. They were not allowed to testify because they were all minors. The accused however was taken to trial and without a court stenographer in residence, was charged with illicit contact with a minor and remanded to a juvenile treatment facility. While waiting for a bed to open up in a facility, they kept this boy in state custody. Nine long months later, he was taken to Athens, Georgia where he celebrated his tenth, eleventh and twelfth birthdays. His mother, frantic with worry and fueled with rage, fought the system at every move. The wheels of the machine continued to roll, totally unconcerned with the woman who kept throwing herself across its dirty rails. Before her boy disembarked at the Boston's South Station three years later, Berea Willis suffered a major coronary and dropped dead at the corner of Rambler Road and Centre Street just as the city bus was approaching. Young Terran was taken in by an aunt who slept all day and worked third shift emptying the bed pans of dementia patients. As bright as he was, which was determined by achievement and IQ tests, Terran Willis scored way behind his peers on the Mastery Test and was socially stunted. He stepped out into his newfound freedom with a label big as day flapping behind him, the unwelcome sign of Sex Offender pitched out in front of his every move. He couldn't work because of it; he couldn't sign a lease because of it. The only place where his hidden brand made no matter was in jail and Willis became of legal age there on a bid for possession of narcotics. Back on the streets, he upped his game and returned to prison to celebrate legal drinking age on a robbery sentence. He was good at running game, doing time, winning respect and so he mastered the art of being a criminal over the next fourteen years, most of which he spent behind bars. He never challenged the judges or the many sentences he received.

But through it all, he never stopped giving voice to being railroaded as a little black kid at the mercy of four white adolescents. Based on their flimsy tattle-telling, his life had been ruined. He wanted one thing only. He cried out for that sex treatment score to be removed since he swore up and down that in no way was he guilty of premeditating or perpetrating a sexual crime. For Christ-sakes, he didn't even know what a vagina was at that age. All appeals had been heard; all grievances denied. He was re-arrested for his failure to register the few times he had been discharged. Willis was denied opportunities for early release because of these two scarlet letters: S.O. Sex Offender. Through his writing, Willis eloquently connected the dots that mapped a steady progression of rage. Now decades later, the wrath had mellowed into a steady pain that motivated him towards meditation and dialogue. He still took up the struggle every day, but resorted to the Bible as his two-edged sword and tried with the word of truth to cut through conscience. Still he had run into deaf ears, even though he had taken his plea all the way up to the Commissioner and the office of the Governor.

It's undoubtedly a tragic tale, true or not. It's difficult to know. These guys leach lies out every pore. Any solid truth is diluted with deceit and so much bullshit that what's left is a standing pool of watered down waste. It's a toss of a coin. True or false, or some combination of the two? I put down the homework paper and my red pen. There is nothing I can say in a few short notations that could address the length and breadth of the horrific treatment this boy had been subjected to. My stomach feels queasy. The dogs sense the unease and press closer, eager to take a walk. I decide to get in a good stroll and let the fresh air dissolve the sorrow I feel.

"Come on. Who wants to go outside?" I call out. The dogs jump and skitter to the door. The four of us head out on a brisk pace down the dirt lane. I try to dismiss the thought of this kid being set up, laughed off and screwed over. In a neurotic twist of conscience, it makes me feel ashamed to share the same demographic category as the little white bitch that took him down. But I mean it's not my problem. We all have our back stories and reasons for straying off the straight and narrow. Although, I'll admit this is a SNAFU of epic proportions. Situation Normal All Fucked Up. I know it well. I'm a card-carrying lifetime member of this crowd. Okay, fine. When Monday rolls around, I will delve a little deeper into this case.

CHAPTER 5
JAMMED UP

Phone calls at night, the solitary jarring ring that erupts out of clear calm. These are the ones that alarm us, calls that come from people accustomed to making them. Emergency room residents or police dispatchers who know how to regulate their tone of voice in order to do the difficult job of dispensing bad news before all hell breaks loose on the other end. Much like the call Detective Hughes made to 17 Casco Lane in the deep of the night, the one that sent Mom lurching to the toilet bowl and my Dad in long-johns straight to his set of car keys. And another just a few short years later, one that left me soaking in a lukewarm bath for three hours, stunned, tracing the face of my father over and over until the lone candle burned to a nub and wax dripped and congealed down the sides of the claw foot tub like blood-red tears. But this was a run-of-the-mill ring in the safe shine of daylight and without any hesitation, I rush to greet my brother's voice.

"Hey, little girl," Dale says softly. We have a good laugh over a few off-color stories from work. He worries about his sister. He's seen the television shows, Lock-Up and Oz, and like most normal folk, shudders at the sight of crude shanks made from clip boards and metal rods off filing cabinets. At the same time, Dale understands the irony of human nature and he knows by experience that life is hard. Anyone who can brave the unrelenting winters and deep economic recession with hands in icy ocean water for as many years as he has understands that gruff humor can be a lifesaver. We chat about the price of lobsters and oil. My brother is typically brief and not much of a talker, but today he makes a grand effort to keep a surface conversation going.

"So, hey! I wanted to give you an update," he says, finally getting around to the real reason he called.

"On what?"

"Mom," he says, mildly irritated.

"Oh, I'd almost forgotten. That was weeks ago. I figured no news is good news, right? Yes, of course I want to hear."

"The X-ray was inconclusive, so she went in for a CT-scan."

"What did it show? Does she have rheumatoid arthritis in that shoulder?" I say. He hesitates before clearing his throat and continuing.

"The news is not good, Elise," Dale announces.

"What news?" My mother always played that little game. *What do you want first, the good news or the bad news?* "Give me the bad news first," I implore.

"There's no easy way to say it. Mom has lung cancer."

What? This woman who's never smoked or drank more than a half bottle of hard cider on the fourth of July? The one who treats her own soil with fermented compost, stocks her cold pantry with compote and pickled cukes and everything rinsed pure in the cold Maine rain? Her? It just can't be.

"Dale, stop! C'mon, don't…"

"Elise, I wouldn't joke about something like this."

"So, why the pain? And what's the plan? Does she need help? Do you want me to come up?" I babble, asking questions before he can answer, filling up the pauses with sound bytes so he can't replace them with something I can't handle.

"Lissa. The cancer has already spread to her bones, specifically her shoulder and hips which is the cause of the pain. They are recommending chemo to halt any further progression. Maybe a clinical trial of something, but Mom wants to think over her options."

"What's the good news?" I ask hopefully.

"She is in healthy fighting spirits," he says.

"Can I talk to her?" I ask.

"She's not in a mood for conversation right now. I think she just needs to process the facts and consider all her options. You understand. I'll tell her we've talked and you're on board to help in any way she needs, okay?"

"Yes, oh yes. Tell her I love her, will you? Please?" I can hear the same crack in his voice that seems to have overtaken mine, as if our vocal cords are losing their charge and can no longer be trusted to flap open and shut on steady command. The volume has grown flimsy. It is time to hang up

"Update me as soon as you can. Promise?" I ask.

"Of course I will," answers Dale. Something in my gut stops me from believing him. There is no telling how long they've all known, but what is suddenly clear is that it's far longer than I have by a long shot. This pronouncement is not news to them. It's been simmering in silence for many weeks in a conspiracy kissed with kindness. It's a reckless business though, playing God without the omniscience he has to pull it off. Mom herself is the architect behind the construction of this lifelong filter to bad news. The things we can't or shouldn't have to handle are kept out, but it's only so long before the windbreak's resistance powders like old plaster. When that happens, the incoming force of truth hits us twice as hard, and along with it comes the burl of resentment at having been held back for so long.

After we hang up, I sit in the dark and try to imagine what it is like to be told that your death is on the radar, somewhere in the scope and range of the mortal eye, waving under a microscope lens. I believe in miracles; in fact, I am one. But I only know about my own death in retrospect, after I had passed over and by it and woke to watch it fade away in my rear-view. I never saw it coming, only going away.

I don't want to go to work tomorrow. I can't be Delilah to hundreds of whining, needy men that have brought their stinking problems on themselves when this one righteous, stalwart soul has been forced to suffer needlessly and asks not a thing of anyone but her own private God. *Assholes! Why can't one of these guilty bastards be taken? Who's going to notice the empty slab of cardboard and dirty rolled-up sleeping bag that's missing if one crack addict begs off this earth?* I feel guilty for thinking such things. And I know full well that any spiritual quest for fairness would keep me up long after Elijah's lamp of eternal oil finally snuffed out. There is nothing to be solved in looking for logic. This is where the giants of faith were at their best, lost in the wilderness, crawling with locusts or teetering on the walls of a city that threatened to tumble down. I could follow suit like the martyrs and cry out. Or just plain cry.

Sleep doesn't come that night. The super moon claims the entire sky with its prizewinning power throwing flood lights on the corn fields, the rustle of deer meadow and the crooked line of dying spruce on the horizon.

It creeps closer than it should, barring any comforting darkness from descending on this hill, this homestead, or this heart.

#

Class is dismissed. Chulo immediately steps in and starts to rearrange the desks back into a neat semi-circle. Any stray hand-outs are collected and placed in the file cabinet. He erases the board, too quickly, before I have a chance to tell him that I had intended to keep that day's wisdom to review on the next.

"You good?" he asks, as he always does at the beginning of the class when he hovers nearby hoping I'll be short on copies or need pencil stubs sharpened, and again at the close of the group. His presence is a regimented warning bell, a faithful alarm that reminds the men who are exchanging gum in the corner to snap to and get out. The inmates are supposed to leave en masse back to their blocks, but there are always a few who linger behind to ask questions. I'm patient to a point. Most of the counselors dismissed them long ago and routinely give them the brush-off, but it is our job to be the conduit to the outside world. We are the information highway that has access to the answers whether they come in English or Ebonics, Spanish or sign language. In one way or another, directly or indirectly, whether it's stammered or shouted, all the requests boil down to the same basic question: When is my time to go? Each man desperately hopes he can get his hands on the get-out-of-jail-sooner card he believes we have the power to offer him. Chulo warned me. 'These fuckers just want to get up close to a female,' he had said. It's their chance to inhale the scent of a woman and jiggle in their pants later on. *Back the fuck off is the* message his five-foot-six posture communicates as he stands between me and the door and stares them down. It's not his size that deters them. The two tears inked below his left eye tell them more than enough about the bodies he gunned down on a city sidewalk. The men move on and give preferential treatment to the more infamous convict.

"So, whatcha talk about today, Miss A?" Chulo asks. He turns back to face the board, "Sympathy, compassion and empathy," he reads, slowly enunciating the words that he's poised to wash from the board. He's always conscious of not grouping himself with the others, and chooses to ask questions with a third-person kind of curiosity under the guise of taking wisdom back to the blocks for the younger guys who might need it.

"You know the difference between them?" I ask. I continue to collect up the paperwork and count the returned pencils.

"Sort of," he says. His English has suddenly dwindled a bit. His brain is fumbling to come up with the equivalent in his native language.

"They are all good words derived from the same Latin origin: the root word 'pathos' for feeling. The first one, sympathy is a feeling *for* others in their trials. Then compassion. Think of it this way. We don't have to know the people or countries who are suffering but there is a community of unspoken feeling for their hardships, like the recent tornadoes in Oklahoma or the Boston bombing. We all can guess what it must feel like to go through these tragedies. And then this final one, the prize quality we should all strive for. Empathy, feeling *with* someone. In other words, standing in his Jordans and knowing fully what is going on with the man because we've been there before. You know what I mean?"

"Yes ma'am," Chulo replies. "I have empathy for you dealing with these guys because I live with these dudes twenty-four seven." Some people are born with inordinate amounts of empathy; others can through self-discipline acquire a knack for it and then there are those like Chulo who simply don't have it and don't claim to. I look up suddenly. Inmate Willis stands in front of the desk with a tattered envelope in hand.

"Oh shoot! That's right," I say. I had promised him I would put through that legal call he requested. His block counselor Wolfe is notoriously thorny and rude. In the veteran staffer's defense, two tours as a gun runner on a boat in the Mekong followed by another nineteen being bombarded by a different kind of crafty enemy has taught him how to defend himself with a crust of sarcasm. His favorite weapon is the word "no." Problem is, inmates have legal right to speak to their attorneys twice a month and preventing that discourse can lead to lawsuits.

"Take a seat. I will put the call through for you, but afterwards, I want to ask you about your case. What you wrote," I say. Chulo has his back towards us and is making busy work jiggling the handles on the windows to make sure they are fully secured.

"Hey Chulo, would you mind giving us privacy? Mr. Willis needs to speak to his attorney," I say politely. My Hispanic helper is reluctant to go. His shoulders stiffen and he starts to protest, but then thinks better of disobeying a staff member and grudgingly gathers up his folder of resumes and hesitates by the door. He nods at the shelves to the left of the teacher's desk.

"I put a little something there for you. Don't forget to take it," he mumbles. I yank out the drawer that rattles on its ancient track. Another Styrofoam container containing peach crisp or vanilla pudding with ground-up graham cracker dust is tucked inside. Though I've told him repeatedly that I can't accept these, he brings the offerings anyway and abandons them within reach, knowing I won't leave them there for others to access. He's caught me in a quandary with Willis as an observer.

"Take that back, please. You know the rules," I say, more briskly than I intended but Chulo knows better than anyone else that setting a precedent is a dangerous move. Sending a strong message is the language that the institutionalized understand. His hazel eyes flash with indignant rejection.

"Nothing personal, Diaz," I add, intending to soften the refusal but he is furthered angered by the use of his surname. He grabs the dessert and stalks off. I've learned to brush off these upsets and volatile mood changes a long time ago.

"Go ahead, Mr. Willis. I'm sorry for the interruption."

"It's all true, ma'am," he replies.

"Where does all this stand right now?"

"They are trying to force me to take Sex Offender treatment, which is a year-long program. If I refuse, they'll take my earned good time away and deny my parole. But I am not going to accept treatment for something I have no need of. Allowing that is admitting guilt to something I didn't do. Miss Abrams, I never touched that girl in a sexual way or forced myself on any other female; so how can I in good conscience put my name on a register of perverts? I wouldn't do it, so they jailed me twice for refusing. I've been fighting this battle for over twenty years. No one in the Department of Correction or the courts will listen because if they do, they will be forced to admit to their errors. I have all the documents. They never charged me with that crime. Everything was nolled. They knew they had nothing on me. Miss Abrams, they took me to a room in the basement of the court house with no court reporter present so there are no transcripts. All I need is to get the copy of the Judge's transcript. They cleared me from any wrongdoing with this girl."

"Then what charge did they hold you on?" I ask.

"Tampering with a witness, but all I did was call this girl and ask her to tell the truth. The phone call is recorded. They have it in their hands. I didn't threaten her and I didn't touch her inappropriately. Period!"

Per self-report, ninety- five percent of sentenced offenders are innocent or at worst, someone who was in the wrong company or in the wrong place at the wrong time or was wrongfully fingered as the suspect. The other five percent are the guys who are proud of what they've done and wave it like a banner. After awhile, all the posturing and campaigning for proclaimed innocence is little more than white noise, a low-grade buzzing in the ears from relentless pests. It's not surprising that Mr. Willis's personal crusade has been dumped in the bucket full of general complaints and shoved aside.

"And you were how old?" I ask, incredulously.

"Nine. Miss, if anyone should be held accountable, it should be the other kids who were older than I was. Doesn't anyone question what they were doing with a little kid like me and no grown-ups around? Shouldn't they hold some responsibility?"

"And you've talked with the therapist here who runs that group?" I ask.

"I wrote him, but because of my Sex Treatment score, they're forcing me to participate in that program. I've written appeals to all of them: the Deputy Warden, the Warden and the Commissioner. Nobody wants to question a wrong and try to un-do it."

"So, where are we placing this call to?" I ask. The abrupt change in subject seems to diffuse his focus. Willis reaches into the slack pocket of his uniform pants and pulls out a pencil stub and small flip pad. The pen is not one from our Commissary. It's sleek-barreled, shiny gold with a monogram of some sort on its barrel. Swiped from a teacher's desk?

"Juvenile Court in Dorchester," he answers.

"Do you have the number with you?" I ask. Willis recites it from memory. I patch the call in to the clerk's office, verify that I have connected with the criminal division, and then indicate that he should pick up the other line. I step out into the hallway. Inmates are allowed private conversations with their legal counsel but they must remain in full view of staff when doing so. A closed door could lead to trouble in the form of false accusations, lawsuits, stolen supplies or vandalism. Willis leans into the conversation with his head in one hand, one knee jiggling nervously up and down as he is put through a series of automated prompts. He taps the keys on the phone. The clock is ticking off the minutes, two of the allotted ten have already been burned and still no live person to answer his question. Chulo appears at the far end of the hallway and hesitates for a moment in the band of sunlight spinning down through the pentangle of ceiling glass. I give him a cursory everything-is-fine smile and he ducks into a distant classroom. Willis suddenly straightens up in his seat and clears his throat. It looks as though his passionate plea to the public defender's office has an audience on the other end. He nods in earnest and rephrases his request. I can hear him spelling out my last name. Suddenly he looks up, slightly panicked and scans the top of the desk but doesn't dare touch any of the papers lying there. He waves me in.

"Miss, what's the number here?" The clerk said she'll send it to your attention." I quickly scribble the number of the fax machine in the office with my title on a sticky note and he relays it to the harried paralegal that is trying her best to foist this guy off on someone else. Finally he puts the receiver down and sighs.

"She said she'll send it to you. I appreciate your help, Miss Abrams. You're the only one who has taken the time to hear me out."

"Well, I'm very interested in what's fair and right. Mistakes are made, even within the justice system. It's worth making sure that things were handled properly. Would you trust me with those over the weekend? I'd like to review what you have." Willis eagerly hands me his personal folder of legal paperwork and rises to his feet.

"I apologize for getting so emotional and taking up your time. I know you're a busy woman, but this is my life here."

"I said I would be objective in looking at your situation. If we don't have our word, then we have nothing. I'll give it a look over the weekend and see you on Monday."

"Have a blessed day," Willis replies. He picks up his homework folder and heads out the door. In the process, he accidentally bangs shoulders with the cocky Hispanic school clerk who's just rushed past him into the classroom. The two men regard one another coolly.

"What's up, bro?" Willis mumbles. There's a quick bump-and-pump greeting exchanged and Willis is on his way. Chulo closes the door in the wake of the big man's departure and watches the retreating figure warily.

"I told you to be careful with him," he warns. He waits for an ensuing explanation. Suddenly, a little trip-switch flips in my head. *How dare he assume to correct or coach me?*

"Mr. Diaz. I've been doing this for a long time. I don't need you to tell me how to handle myself or do my job."

I gather up my water bottle, papers and eject the ancient HBO video, *Battered* from the player. Though dated, it is powerful stuff. The victims portrayed are real-life survivors of horrific trauma. It's plain as day on the disfigured face of Hedda Nessbaum who was systematically beaten by her well-heeled lover. And the mother of two who was bludgeoned with a shotgun by her ex-boyfriend out on an eight-hour furlough from prison. Same with the young Hispanic mother whose five daughters tried to intervene when her estranged husband stabbed her repeatedly in the abdomen as she showered and then staggered out of the bathroom to collapse on the linoleum floor in front of them. On the way to hospital, this brave woman prays that she won't die before she knows what it's like to be happy. 'It's a messed up way to go,' she says, her eyes sad and hollow, having never yet held the faint flicker of a smile. And more powerful still is the seven-year old stuttering daughter with the shell-shocked stare when she calmly tells the interviewer she wants to grow up to be a police man so she can stop people like her own father. It gets them in the gut each time. After the credits skip by, the men shake their heads in disbelief at the brutality and whisper, 'Jesus, that's so fucked up' at the sight of broken eye sockets and a healthy thigh filleted of its skin. No one says anything. The television needs to get rolled back into the staff bathroom and locked up. I place my belongings on the bottom tray and start to maneuver the clumsy cart.

"I got you," says Chulo, his hand brushing mine as he takes over navigation. *Is it an apology of sorts?* I escort him down the short hallway and unlock the door. He positions the electronic antique back in its space. On the way out of the unit, he keeps stride with me though usually he sets our pace at a leisurely stroll back along the mainline towards Inner Control. I can understand why he is in no hurry to get back to the unit where he is only Inmate # 100417. Out here, he is the man of the hour, the prince of the pipeline where he gets his due recognition.

"I'll see you tomorrow. Thanks for your help," I say, as the rolling gate ratchets back enough for me to squeeze through. It quickly reverses direction and we are closed off from one another. Chulo stands for a moment in his brand-new, brushed suede work boots and pressed bleach-white shirt with a hopeful look on a boyish face that hasn't seen more than an hour's daily ration of UV rays in the past twenty-two years. He looks barely a day older than his first mug shot on File #1. I adjust the bag strapped to my shoulder enough to lift my hand in a small wave. He grins widely and does a little bantam strut before the hall keeper orders him to keep moving.

#

Roll call. Seven-thirty a.m. sharp! Come rain, snow, sleet or hail. It's adult attendance with grown-up consequences: tardy on three occasions and you're written up. The officers lug in giant thermal lunch bags and gallon jugs of drinking water, squeeze through the narrow row, knocking over chairs and sweeping papers off the table top before solemnly taking their seats. Nobody stoops to right the chairs or pick up the mess. One day is no different than the next. It's the same wooden walk down the aisle of occupied seats with people already in place counting off the minutes and most of them nursing a hangover or a sour attitude or both. And there's always the one guy running late who shuffles his heavy boots in what appears to be an earnest attempt of getting up the walkway and by the sally-port before the Captain ticks off his shift. Like a classroom full of kids, they claim their same seats like Officer Everett, who for nineteen years, eight months and thirteen days has swung his chair around with his back to the pole, put his head in his hands and fallen asleep and without fail, roused up right in time to mumble when his name is read off. Every other staff person gives that seat berth and allows him that right. The whole contingent is upset and pouts if some newbie mistakenly settles into the wrong chair. A select few claim the non-contact booths along the left hand side of the room, their rear ends perched on the spot where someone's distraught fiancé or momma will be wringing her hands and shedding tears in another hour or so.

At the front end of the visiting room is a raised platform from which the lieutenants make daily announcements and recount any incidents from former shifts. The memos are read. Friday is Tip-a-Cop for Special Olympics. Then a united plea goes out to anyone willing to donate sick time to our ailing brother with a brain tumor. These guys may be stingy in personality, but they will give over and above any lousy tithe when it comes to charity. Maybe it's their way to offset their skepticism and reward the good people in this world. The Lieutenant on duty informs us that Inmate Rodriguez and Inmate Sanchez went at it over living conditions in D-block. Now they are both down in Seg in holding cells, which is the equivalent of complaining about a broken ice machine at the Holiday Inn and ending up at Motel 8 in the heat of summer with a busted air-conditioning unit.

Hastings winks at me from his place two tables over. We usually walk out together and chat for a few. I'm guessing the staff has us down as lovers and so be it. Dysfunctional relationships are the norm in this crowd. Sexual harassment is rampant. Affairs abound on and off-duty. New rumors scuttle through the morose crowd each week and more attention is paid to fodder for their fantasies than the safety protocol being recited up front. We are dismissed.

"Go to work!" yells the Lieutenant in a cursory order. As I pass the podium on my way out, Captain Wittman looks up from his Fantasy Football picks.

"Abrams. Come see me in my office ASAP!" he snaps. This can only spell trouble. The others all cast glances my way and a few make teasing whistles in my direction. It will give them something to ponder while they read the sports section of the Boston Globe. After pulling my keys and body alarm, I head straight down and stand in front of the unmarked entryway which sports a red line dissecting the middle. Off-limits to anyone without invitation. Like Maxwell Smart's series of gates and doors that opened mysteriously as he approached, a metallic click releases the lock and it swings outwards. I step into a room full of lieutenants and captains lounging in chairs and gaping at the television suspended in the corner by ceiling bolts. World Cup action.

"Morning, gentlemen," I say, hesitating to interrupt a good head-butt that's being wildly applauded by the Brazilian crowd

"All the way to the back, Abrams," announces one without looking up. I've never been farther than the first desk and only to deliver official business from incoming investigators. There is a short corridor with a series of small rooms on one side where special business is handled behind closed doors. This is where interrogations are conducted or confidential informants arbitrarily quizzed at their discretion.

"Come in. Take a seat," says Captain Wittman. He seems like a fair man. Three other intelligence officers with dead-pan faces stand off to the side with arms crossed. *What did you do?* I quiz myself. Was it a call placed mistakenly to an unverified law firm? Did I deplete the overstock of unfranked envelopes and hand some out to guys with money on the books? Did I neglect to sign in and out of the block?

"Do you know Inmate Diaz?" asks Captain Wittman. I hesitate for a moment. Who doesn't? There have to be twenty-five guys with the same name in here. "Jorge," he clarifies. Of course, I know him as Chulo.

"Yes, sir!"

"Does he work for you, Counselor?"

"Not in a paid capacity. He is the school clerk and assists many of the teachers with tasks like moving desks or running papers down to the secretary to make copies." I wonder if they are looking to reward him with a privileged job working in the Admin wing. These workers are hand-selected by the brass. "He volunteers with other small tasks," I add.

"Trust me. It's not out of the goodness of his heart," says the Captain. "What has he done for you in particular, Counselor?" he asks. I can see that he has an incident report in front of him. These proceedings are being recorded. My heart picks up speed.

"Erase and wash down the blackboard. Open and close the windows after class. Roll the television cart in and out. Spray down the desks and things like that. He takes the initiative to make our jobs easier."

"In this case, he's made your job a little more difficult."

My best instinct is to act like one would in court. Answer only in the affirmative or negative. Do not offer any unsolicited information. I have no idea what they are going to accuse me of.

"Has he ever given you anything?" he questions. I intend to answer no, but recall the offerings of food and the fan that arrived out of storage by surprise. And when I complained that the clock in the classroom was dead, he donated a little commissary time-keeper that I kept in the drawer. And I can't overlook that motivational poster that popped up out of nowhere and was taped to the wall: *Fail to Plan is a Plan to Fail.*

"Yes, but nothing unapproved and all for use by the group."

"Have you ever given him anything?"

"Nothing!" I answer emphatically. I am certain of that.

"Have you ever had physical contact with him?" he continues. *Are they serious? Shit!* There was that one hug that he sprung on me and I tolerated for a few perplexed seconds. My brain is whizzing now, trying to recall that room. Were there cameras in there? My health insurance and pension ride on this one.

"No." I take a gamble. "Are you implying sexual contact?"

"Yes, ma'am."

"Then no, sir. Absolutely not." I have turned down more than a few propositions from married officers. They know I am not a player. Prude? Maybe. Better-than-thou? Perhaps. Who knows what they think but my reputation should help me here.

"Let me explain why we're here. Inmate Diaz claims that you lured him down to a remote area of the building and made advances towards him. He states he did not report this earlier because he was afraid of reprisal and that he would lose his job."

"Bullshit all." I say. "Sir."

"And he claimed that you were showing favoritism towards him. Giving him things in exchange for certain favors." I feel a spasm coming on in my brain. Adrenaline comes pumping through the pipeline. My hands clench into fists and a cold wave of mental retaliation takes over.

"I definitely did not. I believe my performance evaluations will prove my commitment to professionalism, sir," I state.

'So we did a shakedown of his cell and this is what we found," he adds ceremoniously. He procures the evidence from the manila folder in front of him. There are two pen-and-ink note cards, one of a barn and one of a tabby cat and both drawn by me, brought in and taped to the blank wall of poster paper behind my desk. I hadn't even noticed they were missing. The shift commander then produces a small squeeze bottle of Moonlit Path moisturizing lotion from Bath & Body Works, another accoutrement I kept in the desk drawer to combat the nasty dryness. Lost, I thought, now found.

"Yes, those are mine. He must have taken them from the classroom unbeknownst to me," I say.

"These are what concern us most," states the Captain. He produces copies of hand-written notes and slides them across for me to review. The penmanship is foreign to me.

"I didn't write this for sure," I insist.

"That's not in question. Take your time and read them." It's like the mini Monarch notes on *Fifty Shades*. Lurid descriptions of sexual acts Chulo has fabricated and things he intends to do in positions I'm positive I could not master. These are clearly the private rantings of a man obsessed, a prisoner whose horniness has fomented into full-blown delusions. I sit back and exhale.

"Wow. I don't know what to say. ..."

"I'll say it for you," says the man in charge. My brain has seized up and there is only the soft slushing of sluggish blood in my ears. "The guy's a fucking dirtball. This is not the first time he's tried to jam up one of our own. These maggots will do anything to bring us down."

Suddenly the atmosphere in the room has switched to that of a pep rally. Camaraderie prevails.

"He was hoping to get you fired, but we have a supplemental report from a witness who on one occasion heard him talking about you in the blocks, bragging how he thought he'd got one over on you. His plan was to eventually pressure you to be a duck and bring things in for him. This same C.O. also testified that he has witnessed Diaz stalking you outside the classroom on several occasions and also overheard him attempting to get other staff to give up personal information about you. So, we put a profile on him and he's being transferred to Southern. You won't have to worry about working in the same facility with this creep ever again."

"Thank you, Captain Wittman." My relief is audible to everyone within earshot.

"All I need you to do is write up a narrative statement on what you told me and we'll include it in our disciplinary report. We're going to try and get him on Interfering with Safety and Security and a Contraband B. Advice though, Counselor. Next time you get the feeling that an inmate is getting unduly familiar with you, come to us right away."

"I will. No doubt," I say. I am supremely grateful. It's us against them and us has come through for me. After I am dismissed, I immediately head down to the ticket block where Hastings is on a 5-and-2 post for the next month. He is parked in front of one of the huge standing fans that are meant to circulate air down into the muggy cells, but only serves to create a giant wind tunnel down the middle. I knock on the glass and then kick the door. The inmates are out on Tier Rec and the noise inside the housing block is overpowering. An alert inmate sees me and yells out to Hastings. He comes to the door at a sidewise angle, keeping one eye on the roaming prisoners. The residents of this unit are the bad boys who have gotten badder on the inside. He pops his Folger keys off the key clip on his belt and swings the door open a tight six inches.

"Everything go okay?" he asks.

"Yes, but for a few minutes there, I thought I was getting walked out."

"I told you he was a piece of shit, but I'm glad we snagged him," he replies.

"Thank you, friend" I say gratefully. "I owe you big time." Hastings smiles grandly. This act of chivalry has undoubtedly earned him some good points.

"Then I'll collect on that debt," he says.

"Fine! What'll it cost me?"

"I'm paying," he replies. "You and me, drinks after work. Meet me out at my truck. I'll drive." He states his demands briskly as if he's barking orders at the impatient inmates who are pushing up towards the officer's station, but the slightest twitch of a coming smile and an effervescent sparkle in his eye are not lost on me. He snaps the door shut and herds the troops back away from the front of the block

It's not until I'm back in the solitude of my office that I feel the anger of betrayal bubbling up. *Fuck him! Fuck them!* I am not going to open the door or entertain office hours today. For one man's evil deed, the rest will now pay; just like when some high school jack-ass flooded the sinks in the lavatory and the whole class was sequestered in from recess because of his prank. But most of all, *fuck me!* My instincts are the only really solid tool I have and apparently, they have failed me. I mean, I believed in Chulo. Some shallow part of my ego liked the idea that he saw me as someone special. That sliver of emotional attachment had almost cost me what I had worked so hard for over the past sixteen years. I am hugely disappointed in my failure to listen to veteran wisdom. Chulo's tirade against Willis was what I thought it to be all along, a territorial act or a play for power. No one should be surprised by this. That's how gang-bangers operate. Why did I attribute worth to a worm, knowing his panache at manipulation and extorting favors?

Trust and faith are interlinked; one cannot exist without the other. Because of Chulo's betrayal, my faith in human nature has been diminished, but my trust in two particular men has grown by giant steps. I am happy to be right about Willis and my admiration for James as a true friend has been amped up another notch. The jumpiness in my gut is not related to my near dismissal. It is a peculiar girlish excitement about the prospect of sitting on a bar stool with a married man I know is in love with me.

PART TWO

CHAPTER 6
IN COGNITO

My parents were offended at first, particularly my mother to whom tradition and nomenclature and the passing of ancestral batons meant everything, even if the flimsy roll of paper being handed off was only an embellished pedigree. Lissa was my great-grandmother's nickname extracted from the powerful and proud, Elizabeth, which in Hebrew means *House of God,* the name of queens and also the mother to John the Baptist. My father's people, the Braums, had waded hip-deep in glacier snow through the peaks of the Pyrenees to get to safe haven on Italian soil. People of substance making separate Atlantic crossings in different generations but arriving quite by fate on the same soil in New Sweden, Maine. There I was anointed Elizabeth Cooke Braum and walked tall with the carriage of someone who was often reminded of the team she represented and what was riding on my performance in this life. A country's banner, a kingdom's flag. A name that was stripped from me by men with no honor.

Elizabeth Braum became the poor victim on life support, you know, the one with brain damage. I was an overnight sensation, the infamous poster-child that parents of future co-eds held up as an example of what could go wrong, hoping to scare sense into their wayward daughters. My name was found encrypted into newspaper articles and editorials from 1986 through 1989, or more recently, in quick search engine result if someone Googled 'sodomy,' 'wilding', or 'campus crime.' It was even the lead-off line in a rough-draft obituary penned on the back of the admitting paperwork by a grieving mother and planned as a feature in the Portland Herald; one that was never run as it turned out, but saved instead as proof of a divine miracle.

That girl was buried. Six weeks after arriving at Beth Israel Hospital, Elizabeth Cooke Braum was officially put to rest and effectively disappeared from public record. The cops didn't discourage it. In fact, the Detective who had become a facet in our daily lives applauded the idea. The unidentified third suspect could still be looking for his victim. She was, after all, the single witness and the only one who could put a name to his mug shot. On April 28, 1988, Elise Abrams was born, a greater miracle than Mary's immaculate birth in a barn. This young woman was conceived solely by me and took her first step, albeit on a pair of forearm crutches and with a gait belt, out of Boston City Hall at twenty-three years of age.

Like most of the people I would later come to know, I had my first alias. It took some getting used to. Each time I introduced myself, I had the instant urge to add an apology for not using my real name and an immediate impulse to clarify that the shoulder-length, blunt-cropped hair with its deep opaque shade of brunette was not my chosen style or natural hue. But the fear of discovery is a powerful motivator, and the will to stay alive was soon overshadowed and outplayed by my will to win.

The first step was to re-learn the game.

#

My parents disapproved of the idea from the beginning, but I insisted on it. It was after all the story of my life and near-death. My name was all over it and in it, for God's sakes. If everyone else and their cousin knew the details, then why shouldn't I? While the clarity of my thinking was still under serious medical scrutiny, no proxy or power-of-attorney had been appointed to take my place in the driver's seat so their protests fell flat. So my mother finally acquiesced and agreed to meet Detective Hughes at my Beth Israel bedside. She came for moral support, but really was not braced to offer much since she couldn't bear to look at or listen to anything contained in the confidential document. She stood near the linen supply cart and anxiously picked at her fingernails.

"Relax, Mel," I said. "I've seen worse on Hill Street Blues."

"Honey, it's not like you to show disrespect. I'm your parent," she said cautiously. I gave her the skeptical look an interrogator gives to his suspect under question. Yes, she certainly looked like my mother, but you never can be too sure. She didn't feel like one.

"I'm sorry," I replied, feeling remotely responsible but having nothing to give her but a rote answer. She seemed to soften a bit then and dropped her tense shoulders an inch.

"Why don't you go on down to the cafeteria and get yourself some coffee? I'll be here with your daughter if she has any questions," said the cop who had escorted her to my room. Mel looked at him for one brief second and seemed pleased with his suggestion. She lifted her handbag from the back of the door knob and bowed out. Once she was gone, the policeman pulled a two-page document from his binder, placed it in my good hand and took a seat near the window.

"Take your time," he said.

The police report read like a screenplay to a cop and crook thriller. It was dated and signed into permanent record by a Detective Hughes. Apparently, the homicide investigator was patched on the radio scanner by the city paramedics who had just relinquished any hope of resuscitation and were putting away the defibrillator. The crime scene was fresh, a ripe harvesting ground for forensics. The facts were many.

A twenty-two year old female bound to a bedpost with ligatures so tight they had collapsed any blood flow coming through the radial artery. So tight, the EMT's were unable to cut the knotting without the risk of cutting flesh. The victim's hands were cyanotic; no, worse, a deep, deadened purple and stiffened in severe contracture until the Jaws of Life squad brought in a power hand saw to remove the wooden post and release the tension of the angle. The first blow to the head had opened a superficial laceration, which in the reproduced photo, had donated a generous amount of what looked like acrylic paint spots across the hardwood floor. A random pattern like a puppy that had sliced its paw on a tin can lid and padded about haplessly. The subsequent and repeated trauma to the skull had done the real damage. There were thick distortions to the cranial plates marked by both indented dips and displaced swelling. Subdural hematomas, the fatal variety. Two slashes at crucial junctures by made a shallow sharp: one at the base of the neck just above the left collarbone and a clean slice from lip to ear. When he left her for dead, the perpetrator had neglected to support her head; an act not all that surprising when the intent is to kill. Her body had sagged forward and her head slumped to the right causing an extensive pooling of blood in the orbital socket on one side, In a humane twist of fate, however, it had also opened the airway that was already clogging with fluid, mucus and aggravated tissues and constricted the flow of blood from the near-nick of the internal jugular.

In his notes, the detective stated that he was puzzled. He thought he was coming to identify a body, but when he entered the second floor of the Westerville Victorian, he found a swarm of emergency responders huddled around the girl. The blood pool was indicative of a victim who had bled out. Sexual assault was the assumption but it was hard to tell. Her negligee had been cut and spliced in the haste of examination and her lower abdomen was now cloaked in a blanket. But a once-pretty co-ed? Chances were high. Detective Hughes identified himself and asked the paramedics to step back so they would not disturb the evidence. He was waved to the side as one EMT quickly slid in place on the left side of the victim's chest and relieved his partner who was pumping heavily with persistent compressions. After a final thirty count, Paramedic #1 tipped his ear to her lips and looked down the sunken line of her sternum. Victim Doe had regained a pulse. A flurry of bagging, bracing, pumping and shouting ensued as the ambulance crew slid a spine board underneath her and ran her out the door. The bloodied body was on its way to Beth Israel's trauma unit. At that point, the narrative became sparse and concluded with a dire projection. Detective Hughes did not expect this young woman to survive the night. Likely, the inevitable pronouncement would only be delayed by a few hours of heroics. The offenses were recorded: home invasion, robbery, aggravated assault, unlawful restraint, and was it murder? Detective Hughes had decided to reserve that final charge until daybreak shed some more light on the prognosis. Then the investigator set about doing what law enforcement does best. He searched the premises, connected the dots, dusted for prints, ran some rap sheets, and looked for a motive. It was clear to anyone who had every read true crime stories that his next step was to go pick out the perpetrator from the spooling mass of maggots that seemed to be reproducing at warp speed down on the corner of Temple and Church.

Case number 88-6121759-GA was signed and filed at 11:32 pm on March 17, 1988 at precisely the same moment its doomed protagonist began her slow climb up Jacob's ladder. Thankfully, before she reached the gate of heaven, she was turned back by the angels and ushered out on an escalator ride back down to earth.

#

At the time of the Braum crime, Detective Hughes had over twelve years on the force, five of them already logged in on the major crime squad unit. The inability of the prosecution to put together a case with irrefutable evidence had not deterred his faith in ultimate justice. His instinct was to go forward with a trial and allow the emotional aspect of this case to sway the jurors. A jury box full of a dozen parents would be hard-pressed to keep objectivity at the forefront when the brutal photographs of someone's battered daughter were the first and last things they would see. As many time as Hughes had looked through them, the degree of impact never lessened. The graphic images were permanent like etching plates bitten with acid. Even those marginal souls with half a heart or a middling size brain, the cohort of curb dwellers whose lives were affected by daily violence would blink and turn indifferent to such vicious cruelty. Hughes spent days scouring the neighborhoods and hitting up informants to get someone to turn over something he could use, but the punks in the hood weren't talking.

Hughes respected smart criminals, the kind of crooks that stuffed stolen jewelry in between slabs of steak and stored it in the freezer. But these bad guys were bad at what they did. A blizzard of prints coated the entryway, the door knobs, the light switches, and the array of broken objects on the floor. It wasn't but a matter of days before the cops located the abandoned Corolla in South Boston with the back half burnt and the tag removed. But the same rash immaturity had lit a lousy fire with a single stream of gasoline that had petered out shortly after Carson and Turner had unloaded the artifacts into a waiting van and fled. The prints that were left fully intact on the front compartment of the car were a match to those taken from the house; however, the vehicle was completely free of blood spill. The two young black men were soon tracked down at the Anchor Bar, brought in on a warrant and interrogated for three straight days. No one could crack a criminal quicker than Hughes. It was pure talent the way he groomed his suspects with a sense of brotherly trust, throwing his arm across their shoulders and pulling up a chair on the same side of the table, leaning in to the conversation in a gesture of collusion while he began the tedious task of picking apart their psyches with small inconsistencies that slowly pitted one man against the other. But Hughes had run up against a new opponent. The Bloods had come to town and set up house in the corner of the city where they were particularly active in pushing recruits towards aggressive initiations. It was pretty clear to him that these juveniles were scared shitless of going to prison; but they were even more terrified of what would happen to them should they give up their superior. Hits were called in just as easily on the inside as on the street. Preliminary forensic testing on blood and body fluid samples could not definitively identify the person or persons who had committed the assault. As Detective Hughes had explained to the Braums, DNA testing was in its infant stages. No one had been convicted for rape based on biological evidence alone. While he argued strongly with the D.A., even Hughes had to agree that jailing two was better than letting three go free on a faulty mistrial or a locked jury that was sympathetic to poor urban kids. And he couldn't ignore the element of doubt about the involvement of a third suspect that was certain to be brought up by the state's prosecutors. It was very arguable that this mystery assailant existed only in the tortured mind of the victim; though Hughes didn't believe that for a minute.

The single witness to the crime was the victim whose recollections were faulty and inconsistent. The only other reported testimony that alluded to this mystery man's existence came from the Mrs. Schuster, the next door resident. She had filed her statement the following day and reported that she had been up again during the night due to her busy bladder and noticed the storm door banging in the breeze on the deck side of the adjacent house. The first floor was completely dark. Intermittent flashes of light illuminated the top story and what she believed were people running or dancing, but her cataracts and glaucoma played all kinds of nasty tricks on her eyesight. Just before she closed her swags and turned away, she saw two men come out of the garage level with several plastic garbage bags and load them into that nice college girl's car. She thought it peculiar since the day before was rubbish collection day and the blue containers provided by the city were standing right where they always were, just a few feet from where the car was parked. But then she figured these were college friends of Lissa's (Heavens, how could she forget that nice girl's name) helping to pack up her gear so she could go spend the holiday week with her family, wherever it was they lived again. New Hampshire? Somewhere up north. In the final sentence of her written testimony, Mrs. Schuster swore that right after the blue Toyota with Maine plates, (that was it, Maine) drove away, a third person came out the front door and headed off on foot. No detail on hair color, skin type, height, weight, or build. Good lord, she could barely see to put one fuzzy-slippered foot in front of the other, especially after the sun went down. But she did think it was unusually irresponsible of these young people to leave the door wide open to any passersby, particularly in a cul-de-sac known to primarily house well-heeled University professors; so she took it upon herself to go over, housecoat and all, and latch it shut. A peek in the windows revealed a disarray of messy remnants left behind in the wake of party fun, including sheets of typewriter paper, beer bottles, and an overturned chair. The Westcott's should have known better than to ask a young co-ed to watch the property. Even a few good references didn't necessarily root out irresponsibility. Upon the homeowners return, Mrs. Schuster would make it her first order of business to give them the name of her magna cum laude grand-niece who (poor dear) didn't attract many boys, and thankfully was also allergic to alcohol. She was a sure bet for the job.

In the end, no one was happy with the deal. On the pled-down charges of Aggravated Assault 1 and Battery, Burglary and Grand Larceny, the agreement was fifteen years suspended after seven with ten years probation. The families of the guilty cried racism. The parents of the victim were appalled that anything less than life was considered in light of the attempted murder of their daughter. Hughes didn't sleep for nights after the convicted were led off to the high-security Max. In fact, he never slept the same again after this crime.

#

I read the police report through a second time while the detective sipped lousy, muddy-looking coffee from a stained thermos. The details lost their clarity and were gradually caught in a swirl of pixilated color. The plot line was thin. The story became more fantasy than non-fiction. I felt sorry for the main character but I couldn't get too emotionally attached to her. For all the noise I had made in order to get my hands on this original, the ending left me empty. I handed the document back to the plain-clothes policeman who stood solemnly at the bed rail.

"Was that hard on you?" he asked. His eyes were kind, but heavy with weariness and over-use.

"No," I said blankly. "Just slow going." He seemed to understand as I gestured feebly at the bulky bandage which blocked any vision on the right side.

"Did it stir up anything? Any details come to mind?" he asked. "Even the smallest one can help." he added. I regarded him with curious detachment. He was definitely younger than my father by a lot, but he carried himself with the same kind of assurance that pushing through challenges adds to man's stature. They were men who seemed taller and more powerful than they really were.

"What did you say your name was again?" I asked.

"Detective Hughes, honey," he answered. His jaw clenched with tension and he kept dropping his head side to side to shake out cricks in his neck. He appeared far more shaken up by this unorthodox reading of a story he must have known by heart.

"You're the one that wrote this?" I asked.

"Yes, I was the first officer on the scene."

"Did the girl live?" I asked.

"Lissa, you're…" he started to speak, and then changed his mind, perhaps reconsidering the logic of trying to re-orient a patient with fleeting delusions and narcotic overload. He pressed his lips together tightly and produced a terse smile.

"Yes, you did. You are one remarkably strong young lady," he added.

"Thank God!" I sighed and leaned back into the rubbery pillow that was propped behind my neck. There was a crackling, raspy sound in my ear. It was the patient in the far bed, an ancient woman sucking tiny drabs of air through her toothless mouth and releasing it regretfully back into circulation.

"How long will I be here?" I asked my visitor.

"You'll be going to Gaylord soon. That's the flagship of rehabilitation facilities. They're going to fine-tune you back into mint condition." He spoke cheerily, but his countenance relayed the gravity of a man who had seen far too much sadness. "Can you think of anyone who would have wanted to hurt you?" he asked.

"No," I said. No name came surfaced to fill in the blank.

"Take another look at the photographs and see if any of them look familiar," urged Detective Hughes. He produced ten wallet-size pictures of various men and spread them out in a grid across my tray table. I peered down at them, squinting against the glare of glossy paper. Who was I looking for in the rows of look-alike faces? I used to be really good at this game of Concentration. I scanned the photos again, hesitated, tapped one and then a second with my left hand.

"These two?" he asked excitedly. "You think you've seen them?"

"No, silly! They match."

"Okay, sweetie. You've done well. I'll be back and we can talk some more, okay?" Hughes replied, politely laying his hand on my forearm. I nodded and smiled.

"Can you bring me something else to read next time?" I asked.

"Sure thing," he said.

After he left, I watched a redwing blackbird hop furiously back and forth from ground to branch trying to find a stable platform for its nest. A jingle of some sort started up in my head: *the nest on the branch and the branch on the tree and the tree in the hole and the hole in the ground and the green grass growing all around, all around, and the green grass growing all around*. The sawing slumber in the next bed dwindled down to a wheeze and finally fizzled into dead silence. When the bosomy aide came an hour later to get the old woman up for a spin, turned out she no longer had any reason to walk on this earth. Heather removed the identifying name card from the plastic holder at the foot of the bed, folded up the walker and placed it on my side of the room, hoping it would get more use over here.

Some people claim they have memories as early as infants and have registered powerful events in their lives lying in a cradle. While we curl in our fetal tuck and suck our thumbs, important things happen that wake us, but we can't recall the details. My second infancy was spent in a crib with hospital rails where I startled awake almost hourly to a vivid voice and immutable face that was the focal point to everything that would shape me. This person demanded notice. Someone had abducted the sleeping baby of my former innocence and whisked her out of sight. But though I searched the dimly lit avenues of my past, I could not remember why or when or who.

The sequence of days and the hours became an interesting code of hash marks which the nurse on duty crossed off on the Boston Bruins calendar at the end of every shift. The scratched out squares started on the page with Wade Campbell and continued on over to the flip side. I lost count of how many days had passed. There's little way to mark time. No sun-dial slant of light to gauge day from night, just the ever-burning overhead light. The bed faced the door so staff could easily observe patients from a tour through the hallway, so the goings-on of the rest of the world played out behind me and beyond the drawn blinds. Rotating shifts merged into an endless parade of name tags and green smocks, all exaggerated by the hypnotic effect of my pain medication. I started over from the beginning, scanning each row and mentally marking the number of cubes at the end of every Saturday. If my calculations were right, today was number twenty-nine.

Detective Hughes returned and as promised, brought some new reading material. He arrived in the early morning when the nurses were doing their reports and the corridor got thick with the aroma of coffee. I could tell he was just coming off late shift by the sweat circles and abundant creases bunching up the back of his light blue Oxford shirt. Unlike other cops, he had spared the clippers and left his hair in an arrangement of sweeping brown curls.

"Morning, pumpkin," he said cheerily, an odd endearment coming from a straight-laced law enforcement official. He took a seat in the chair to my left and as he settled his weight onto the frame, the unforgiving plastic cushion squealed its resistance. He crossed one ankle over his knee, causing the hem of his khaki trouser to ride up and reveal a sockless ankle.

"I brought you a treat." Hughes produced a small stack of *Life* magazines from a shopping bag. He held up one that featured a dark-haired woman wearing a denim shirt and blue suspenders. His broad hand covered the caption.

"Are you married?" I asked abruptly. The detective looked flustered for a moment. My out-of-context question seemed to catch him off-guard. Words just blurted from my lips, tumbled and fell stiffly between us. Hughes obliged, despite his self-consciousness

"Yes. Been together almost as long as you've been alive," Hughes answered. I had under-estimated his age.

"Happily, though?"

"Yes, of course!" He raised the magazine back up to eye level and waved it slightly. He had to shake it a bit to keep it from draping over on itself. Age had worn the paper down to the luster of silk.

"Kids, too?" I persisted.

"Uh, no! Not now, anyway," he stammered. It was a non-answer of sorts, a shield thrown up to protect old pain. I knew enough to stop there.

"So, do you recognize her?" he asked. I peered at the Jewish-looking lady and squinted hard. I certainly didn't want to disappoint him. "This was the edition that came out just before your injury. Any recollection?"

"New York," I replied. Hughes smiled.

"Her name?" he asked cautiously. I shook my head. Nothing.

"Gilda Radner, this came out in March. Okay, let's back up." His blue eyes intently scanned through the pictures of another periodical. This one had a collage of snapshots on the cover. He hesitated on a particular page.

"How about this one?" he asked, "Look familiar?" He swiveled the page around so I could see a prone body and a girl on her knees, hand raised, beseeching the skies for mercy. For a miracle. For peace. Something stirred in my memory. Flowers in gun barrels.

"Kent State," I said.

"Wow! Amazing. How 'bout this one? Who's this?" he said. He flipped to a black and white photograph of a small boy in a wool coat saluting a casket.

"John-John."

"Fabulous, girl! Alright, now tell me about this photograph" he said. A white farmhouse with dark green gingerbread overhangs on the porch and a brooding maroon barn at the far end of a string of sheds and outbuildings. A woman stood the dirt driveway in a long, blue farmer's dress. I shook my head.

"Nothing familiar about it?" he asked.

"No," I concluded.

"Interesting. This is your home in Maine. And that's your grandmother, Helen." I shrugged indifferently. Might as well have been the first woman on the moon.

"Seems the closer we get to your personal circle, the more your brain throws up the blinds. We're going to try something a little different next time. You game?" he asked, kindly pulling back a few strands of stray damp hair that had drifted into my mouth.

"Yes, goddamnit," I said.

The expletive was not a typical go-to in my vocabulary. Hughes tried not to show his amusement, but a slight grin tugged at his cheek.

#

Two men walked into my room just as the speech pathologist was leaving. I rotated my head upwards by degrees and checked with my hockey buddies on the wall calendar. It seemed like weeks since he had last pressed the call button and in a trumped-up growl demanded that the Jamaican aide bring me some Ativan to help silence the squall of panic blowing in on the heels of his interrogation. Five more squares had been vandalized with black ink. I double-checked my bearings on the large digital clock on the night stand. The hands formed a backwards 'L.' Nine o'clock après minuit.

"Good morning, Lissa," Hughes said. "This is Dr. Brown. He works with our department but he's a licensed therapist. Remember I mentioned trying something a bit out of the box? Well, I'm hoping you will allow him to perform a little forensic hypnosis. It's a process used to lead you back to the time of the event. I'll let him explain more fully, but are you open to that?"

"Yes," I replied. It had never been done to me. The closest I'd come was at the Bangor County Fair one year when my best friend Bonnie was coaxed onto stage by Darlene the Hypno-Chick who had this incurably shy girl dancing like a chicken across the stage. There was something sketchy about the spinning watch and snap of the fingers and the robotic reaction of the volunteers but if Detective Hughes was a supporter of this method, I was willing. Any chance to escape the polarity play in my mind and all its accompanying drama was welcome relief. Dr. Brown stepped forward closer to the foot of the bed and adjusted his position to a few degrees to the left so I could see him. A stout man in his middle-age with wire-rimmed bifocals hooked over his ears.

"Hello, Lissa. I won't confuse you with too much information, but the purpose of this exercise is to enhance recall. We use the ECI approach, or what is known as Enhanced Cognitive Interview. If nothing else, we know that simple techniques like eye closure and relaxation increase our ability to look inside and remove the distractions that cause normal distortion in memory. I do need to ask you in advance, though, whether you are willing to let the prosecutors use any of the information you provide us in court?" asked Dr. Brown.

"Shit, yeah," I said, without meaning to add the shit at the beginning. He smiled benevolently and pulled the side chair up around to my left side. Nothing about this scene seemed to faze him; after all, he spent his working days peering down the convoluted alleys of the criminal mind. This must have been a refreshing detour. Once seated, he flipped open a tablet of notebook paper and rested it on his lap.

"Most importantly, just relax and forget that we are here. Okay then, you can close your eyes and use your ears as your guide. Ready?" asked Dr. Brown. "Follow me," he coaxed soothingly. He was a brave man, I thought, daring enough to accompany me back to a night that had been dead to memory for seventeen weeks now. A bloody corpse of hours buried in its own stench that no digging had exhumed.

"It's the afternoon of March seventeenth. You have just finished an errand and are walking back up Fountain Street. It's after six, actually closer to seven o'clock. You arrive at the Welton's home and are standing on the patio. What do you see as you enter the back door? Is anyone around? What are you wearing?" The questions rolled in like a gentle tide, lapping, lapping at my feet then tugging softly to pull me in. Like a game of Connect Four, my brain was now fixated on dropping red hot clues into place to form a straight line; but each time I set up for a win, a competing thought obstructed the flow. The balls flushed out the bottom and we started over again. My recall resembled the game's plastic framework machine-punched with holes. It was designed to hold a flashback only fleetingly, just long enough to convince me that might win.

'Now, concentrate. You're waiting for someone. You hear him walking through the kitchen. What do you see?"

My mind backtracked in a slow creep down a pitch-black path following the voice that led me. I stepped by instinct; all other senses were dead to use. I was fully detached from the conscious present by a batting of dark velvet that seemed to buffer out the fear and hold me safely, gently in suspense. I felt myself slip more fully into neutral, coasting, allowing the time machine to move me closer to the terrible truth.

"Tell me, what is happening. Who is there with you?" asked a faraway voice. My memory circled round looking for a place to make a soft landing but being the novice pilot that I was, I overshot the target zone by six years and crashed into a distant past.

I am sixteen, driving towards a motel with a seedy sign where an eager boy awaits. Premeditating sex was a lot like cruising south along Interstate 95 towards the Carolina border. Wondering as you spot the first sign announcing: South of the Border, 106 miles. Then sometimes later you see it again with gaudy tacos and inverted sombreros splashed in vivid color. South of the Border, 80 miles to go. Then it crops up every few miles with different gimmicks attached. On and on, always the constant reminder that the attraction lies up ahead. And then finally when the exit for South of the Border rolls around and presents itself, you either pull off to see what the suspense is all about or pass on to clear sailing, curiosity behind you now. I'd been coasting along for years, knowing from the start that I would turn down that ramp the first chance I got.

"Someone is waiting for me. It's a young man," I heard myself mumble.

"Alright now. Do you see him? Does he touch you?"

The motel is the kind with two stories of concrete balconies like low-slung tiers with door after locked door. The manager is leading me towards the far end to the room reserved for me. He tells me that I can make only one phone call. I realize that I have no way to leave. I am here for the next nine months with other guilty people. I try to tell him he has the wrong person but he unlocks the door and gestures for me to enter. My eyes can't adjust quickly to the shade inside.

"I'll be there soon. This will be fun, trust me," says a voice from behind the bathroom door. I sit on the edge of the flimsy mattress. This is what I've been waiting for and wanting, isn't it? Why do I feel so ill at ease? Someone steps into the room. The steam from behind the cheap shower curtain hugs his profile. It's like Jesus coming in the clouds. I lift my arms out to receive him. Two other figures emerge from the sauna cloud. This room is only for virgins, they say. You were not invited. I struggle to get up but the bed is so soft that I sink into the foam and can't get a firm grip on the frame. I lose my sense of balance.

I opened my eyes. It took a handful of seconds to come clear, those moments when subconscious is replaced by reality. I was in my patient room with two middle-aged law enforcement officials who were both peering curiously at me. The seated gentleman, I'd forgotten his name, had a notebook filled with marks like primitive etchings. The other I immediately recognized. Detective Hughes smiled encouragingly.

"You did well, my friend. Today was a good practice run. A few more tries and we'll get things really flowing."

"Wait! I remember. He was supposed to visit that night. He had something to give me. I was waiting for him," I blurted out spontaneously. "It was near seven-thirty at night. The door blew open, but it wasn't him."

The professional note-taker jotted a final statement and stood up. He wore the shoes of an academic and the bowed slouch of a humble man. He was someone I could trust. Dr Brown reached to shake my hand but realized he was perched on the bad side with significant paralysis and patted my shoulder instead.

"Excellent. I'll come back next week. We'll try this again, Miss Braum," he said. It was hard to tell if he was pleased or disappointed with the sketchy shorthand that he tucked inside his satchel.

"Okay," I said reluctantly. I didn't want my friends to leave. Detective Hughes sensed the anxiety in my half-hearted response. He grasped my foot through the thin linen blanket and squeezed it with reassurance.

"I'll see you before then, kiddo," he said. The two men strolled out into the anonymity of the public hallway. Within seconds their distinct footsteps were lost among the generic foot traffic on this wing. Visiting hours were concluding. After he was gone, I worried if I'd ever see him again. Hughes was the author of this mystery. With his help, the prologue to my story could be translated into fact and could tie this whole mess into a cohesive story that might just lead to a happy ending. Without him, it was just a bad read. I prayed he wouldn't lose interest in it yet.

#

Nine more dark squares had been blocked out in my primitive paper timekeeper. Dr. Brown was back. He dimmed the overhead lights and pulled the flimsy drapes to block out the somber sky. The kind clinician assumed the same position in the visitor's chair and began a litany of hushed instructions that worked like a lullaby, sending me into a half-conscious slumber. Dr. Brown had a precise idea of what direction he was headed in but unknowingly, he led me back to obscure clues and portends of future unhappiness that had gone into hiding.

"You're standing in the hallway of the house. You're walking towards the kitchen. What do you see? Think hard. Focus."

Pictures. Photos. People from other places. Something's wrong. Don't touch. I slip into a nebulous synthetic sleep-state.

I'm sitting on my bed cutting up National Geographic magazines. We were not allowed to destroy these keepsakes. The rule was that they were to be kept as references. Places we could admire but never go to. I had broken the rule. Had cut out pictures of Bataan and Calcutta and spread them on my quilt. The master bedroom is backed up to my headboard. There is a disturbing sound coming from in there. One not heard in this part of the house before. Mom is crying while Dad is trying to talk sense through her hysteria. Why are they so unhappy? They don't know I'm in here listening. They think I'm dead. Paralyzed by this realization, I sit listening to their voices choke and swell until my mother's rises a whole octave. A splintering crash shoots us from our beds. I tumble out of my sheets completely naked. There is blood on the floor. I spot the back of

Dad's bathrobe flapping down the stairs and out the front door into the night. Not a shower robe but an over-sized navy windbreaker with a hood. The dressing mirror has shattered, reflecting my face in a thousand different grimaces. Women are somehow attracted to broken parts, things that are not whole. I kneel down in the mess, collecting up the fragments, as if I can somehow mother even glass back into shape.

"When you're done, scrub off good." he says. It's my brother. Sounds like him, but I don't see his face, only his arms. He must be sick though. Like leprosy, patches of white skin spatter in three distinct patterns down one arm as he reaches down to touch me.

Once again, I awoke. First came the dream then the interpretation. Dr. Brown shared the facts that I had given him in my deep stupor. They are scrawled on his pad.

National Geographic. Photographs from travels all over the world. India, Africa. Darkness. Black. Like the men in the kitchen. Hoods, not turbans. Tension. Something smashed. Glass on the floor. Typing pages. Papers with lots of words on them. Letters on skin. Three of them.

"He has a birthmark. On his right arm," I said confidently. Detective Hughes beamed with approval.

#

Dr. Brown set up for session three with a bit less enthusiasm. He'd begun to doubt the therapy would prove fruitful in regards to solving any mystery here. It was obvious that he was a bit disappointed, if not bored by the random tangents my memory was traveling down. Like narrow tributaries that thread off the main flow of riverbed, they were of great intrigue to a mind lost in loops of same-looking rushes, but they weren't getting us anywhere.

"Let's give it one last try," Dr. Brown said as we prepared my descent into sleep. His time must have come at a premium rate unless he owed Detective Hughes a favor. Hughes for his part remained hopeful and encouraging. We started down the muddled path that was the access road to the intangible.

My Dad and I are in the car. The big red Ford sedan. We are going to get something we were out of. He had bent down, looked into the refrigerator, bumping off a few magnets on the door with his head as he straightened back up. Beer, was it? Yes, and cigarettes. But Dad didn't smoke. We were on our way back from the country market when it occurred to me.

"You forgot the beer," I said.

"Oh, did I?" he replied, pushing the orange flare of a match up to his cigarette. Ashes flitted by his chin like fireflies. He let the smoke ride up his temples. The pack was on the seat. Camels, no filters. Half a mile from home, he laid the smoking paper in the ashtray and left it there. As we cruised up over the slight incline, the house came into view. Mom was out in the garden with her trowel to the dirt. In that rock-infested soil, she had to dig deep for even a simple crop. She worked in her bra and shorts in the hot sun and the skin between her shoulder blades had toughened like cowhide. She persisted, not even bothering to turn her head when we circled up by the barn.

"Don't tell your mother," he said. "Or someone's going to get hurt." I turned in alarm. Dad was wearing a Giants hat. But he was a Patriots man, always had been. He grinned, mouth open wide in an insincere way I'd never seen before. Four of the teeth on the right side of his mouth were missing. There was nothing but gum there.

"He smokes Camels. And has missing teeth," I announced upon awaking. Dr. Brown slid his notebook into his brown briefcase and stood up. He gave Detective Hughes a professional handshake and nodded at me obligingly.

"It's not an exact science, but we may have something to go on here. Now, your job is to get well, young lady. It's been delightful to get to know you," he concluded. Translation: We are at a dead end. The insubstantial little tips you've given me describe a million random people. This guy's getting off scot-free or else he never existed in the first place.

In the following weeks depending on my ability to both concentrate and stay awake, Hughes came to sit and read short bursts of news headings. If I seemed able to absorb it, he'd read the entire article. Hughes was a wingless angel with a sidearm and a radio. Divine appointment had brought us together; it would take hell's all-out fury to scorch that bond. Why he came back over and over, I had no idea; but I never questioned the fact that he would. My parents visited faithfully, but brought with them the dragged-out look of worry and doubt. They had no voice for playful stories. Fear stuck in their throats so they could only watch and wait. For his part, Detective Hughes' presence engendered a sense of calm. He walked comfortably among the dirty wrecks of people's lives on the daily and stepped over tragedy like it was little more than a tumbling piece of litter on the sidewalk; an unavoidable by-product of messy human beings that needed to be cleaned up after. He understood the trauma of transitions, how to stubbornly wait out the change of mood from weighty midnight to thin day. He'd spent a pension's worth of nights sipping cold coffee, fretting over other people's losses, finally throwing off his vest and firearm and reaching for his overcoat as grey bands of dawn littered the streets with gradual illumination. These hours he dedicated to easing me from the retreating darkness into the safe light of day were what solidified my success, and convinced me that I could do it. I would learn how to purely exist and exhale the shallow gasps of panic through forged patience, firm in the knowledge that peace was always and again attainable. It was as certain as the weather that unfailingly crested over the horizon in all its predictable imperfection.

#

A shaft of sun fell directly across the television screen. The Sylvania set had poor reception to begin with and now the picture was all but lost. Grace, the paraplegic, was the first to complain in a howl that sounded like an Arctic moose caught in an ice jam. The other patients soon took up the call. Marlene, the black orderly finally ambled in and yanked the daisy-pattern curtains closed.

"Satisfied now?" she said, scowling at poor Grace who immediately settled back into her secret sing-song. Poor thing! Her car had been herded off a rural roadway by a stampede of dairy cows and she had crashed her brain against a massive culvert drain. The injury had left her with a tongue that perpetually lolled out the side of her mouth and a singular obsession for daytime soap operas with the sound off. But she didn't know any different and unless something obscured her view of the television and sent her bawling, she was content. I would have gladly traded places with her. I didn't care a whit for the nonsense that was taking place on that tube. In my opinion, it was nothing but a bunch of cheap talk and white noise to lull us into a daytime stupor. But despite my objections, Marlene knew best and insisted on setting my wheelchair directly in front of the television. The parking brake was clamped on and my feeble grip could not release it. She knew that, I'm certain, which made it all the more fun to leave me there to fumble and figure it out. *Nasty nigger!* The sting of that word startled me. Where had that come from? It was not a term I had ever used or entertained, yet here it was blinking across my brain. Black people. Suddenly, something clicked. I had been on my way to find them, get to know them. Out of white Maine. To the city. My heart throbbed.

"Nurse?" I yelled. Like shrill macaws, a couple of the elderly female patients mimicked the cry. We all knew it would be a wait. To my left was a large bookshelf made from knotty pine with intricate whorls of ancient pitch. It was an impressive art piece. Depending on the time of day, the rings morphed into winking eyeballs or strange beetles. A bouquet of magnificent day lilies crowded a crystal vase perched on top. A grossly sweet fragrance saturated the day room, but an erratic, jerking journey in my wheelchair to closer inspect the floral arrangement turned up the truth. They were one hundred percent plastic. The sweet odor that permeated the sitting room actually drifted from an air freshener tucked behind the pot. I was fascinated by the collection of paperbacks on the top shelf, mostly Jackie Collins and Danielle Steele books with forgettable titles. In the entire time I'd been here, which was anybody's guess, not one patient had bothered to take one down and lift the cover. The arrangement of dust on the spines of these useless novelettes remained intact. Our brains were less tuned to romance and far more focused on keeping both eyeballs open. The wear-and- tear these books had endured must have been done in secret at the hands of the lazy nurse's aides. They sat and talked and sat some more. They knew their careers were going nowhere. On the outside, everyone was on the move. The motion of people living their lives and doing their damndest to keep out of depressing rehab facilities like this one. I sorted them out by the throttle of their engines, the drone of a Cessna banking in flight, the thunder of a Boeing making descent or the vibrato of a news chopper hovering above the commuters on their way home. Once in awhile, an irritating siren pealed through the darkness, held its breath and shrieked again. Someone was either dying or fighting hard to live.

"Would you look at that!" remarked Annie Mae, RN. She had finally left the comfort of the nurse's station and meandered the short distance to the day room. At her encouragement, I swiveled my neck slowly back to the breaking news update on Channel 5. Everything seemed so distant and distorted. Little miniature cars and trucks were jammed along a freeway. Dump trucks, sports cars and cement mixers with animated drivers bobbing up and down inside their cabs; what appeared to be a parade of every Matchbox model ever made by Universal Toys all lined up in pretty profile. Squinting hard, I tried to make out the mayhem on the monitor. More staff was tuned in to the story now than on their assigned patients. One bored orderly yawned. I looked to her for a clue.

"Boston's biggest traffic jam in over thirty years. Thank God I take public transportation," she said.

Minutes later, the programming returned to the talk shows in progress. At mid-day, a news spot featuring the faces of two black men flashed up on the screen. One looked like a tiger with ragged teeth and dead-set eyes; the other had dark glasses, a frizzy ponytail, thin mustache and a brilliant smile. Good men or bad? It was hard to tell. The first appeared to thrive off punching bloodied swollen faces and dropping bodies down to the mat. The other swayed and smiled, hoping to sing in the White House. The audio coverage was gibberish. Though my ears were acutely tuned and sensitive to vibration and sound, that's what it remained; just auditory disruptions in one eardrum that bounced too quickly down the tubes. Tyson and Wonder - the names meant nothing. Whenever I fell asleep, these images all returned and intertwined in a bizarre assortment of scenarios interrupted by the face of a man who held huge importance in the plot, but was a stranger to me. It all revolved into a repeating series of mug shots, class photos, horror flicks and love stories.

In the morning, the cycle started up all over again. The volunteers rolled us into the day room after breakfast claiming that visual stimulation helped to reorient the confused. In truth, it was a cheap babysitter that allowed them an extra hour of chit-chat in the smoking lounge. Part of my aversion to television might have been passed down from parents who despised the invasion of this 'idiot box' and rarely turned it on except to watch Cronkite deliver his stately evening address. Now Brokaw's tight-lipped monotone joined the new parade of faces. Movie stars hawking products. Housewives scrubbing shower tiles, people making fun of people, the peeks at and giggles over pretend lives. But to its credit, that piece of electronic crap motivated me more than anything else; better than the pulleys, bars, squeeze balls, adapted spoons and special grip pencils. I feared the life it promised me unless I worked harder to escape it. So inch by inch, I figured out how to reach downwards to pull the brake handle and turn the rubber wheel with one hand, jerking fore and aft to make minute progress and not end up in a full circle facing front again. The charge nurse always found me in the hallway, near the water fountain, down by the elevator and *cluck, clucked* her tongue at the breach in care plan. Thanks to Winnie Cooper and Kevin Arnold, Barbara Walters, Luke and Laura's absurd General Hospital dysfunction and the dysfunction of hospitals in general, I cancelled my short-lived run as a trauma patient at Gaylord Hospital after nine weeks and went on to star in a more challenging but obscure role. The debut of my new-normal life.

#

The white farmhouse appeared, papered with streamers and balloons all bumping madly in the breeze. The lawn was lost under the feet of many people all crowded together in suspense waiting for a chrome bumper to come glinting through the stand of forest. When they finally spied it, they waved and clapped and let out a huge hurrah that echoed against the big firs at the edge of the clearing.

"What's this all for?" I asked numbly. "Did somebody graduate?"

"In a sense, yes. It's all for you, Princess," Dad said. I turned and looked at him with sincere shock.

"They all know what happened to me?" I asked, dumbfounded.

"Of course, this is your town. Your home," he announced with a wide flourish of his hand. Home. We'd been wending our way for hours past tobacco barns, sluggish rivers, antique flea markets, empty fish traps and singing bridges to just that place. There was a girl who had left here just a little less than four short years ago, her white Corolla packed to the roof with hangers and lamps and a red valise with black leather piping full of love letters that would ground her to where and whom she belonged. The laminated luggage tag was a dead give-away should she ever forget. A cold panic erupted in my belly. I began to frantically claw at the door handle. That girl was gone. People would be asking questions with answers only she would know. I had to get out of here. *Goddamn piece of Japanese shit!* The door handle sprung back with resistance.

"Baby girl, what the heck are you doing?" my father cried out with one arm thrown across my torso to still the thrashing.

"Let me out! Let me go!" I hissed, battling the buttons on the inner door panel.

"Calm down, honey. You'll be fine," he insisted.

"No, I'm not!" I wailed. Dad slammed the old forest green Subaru into park, jumped out, ran around to the passenger side and swung the tinny door open. It creaked with the effort of age. An air of unease seeped in through the open door. The crowd of people sucked in their breath in one collective inhale of suspense. What would they see? How would they react? Would their horror be apparent? Everyone wants to peer at the face of near-death. Murder is intriguing, sensational even. It causes people to gape in fascination and look away in repulsion when they've had enough, but no one wants to lift the dirty veil of shame on a rape victim. It is a matter to be whispered about behind cupped hands and closed doors. People examine you, their eyes dart and flit without censure as if this is some kind of figure drawing class and their assignment is to sketch out the tilt of pelvis, the slope of lean thigh and the lift of dense breast. *Is she a brash girl with a Brazilian, I wonder?* And from there, their imagination leaps into overdrive. *Did she scream? Maybe she liked it even so.* Suddenly, my extremities went dead on me. The limbs that had responded so well to all those months of physical therapy reverted back to the rubbery uselessness of a baby.

"I can't," I mumbled.

"C'mon, don't be shy," my father said. "They've been expecting you." My father leaned in and offered his elbow as a prop. He helped maneuver my thin legs on the warm leather until I could scoot over to the edge of the seat and tip forwards. He used that momentum to pull me upright.

"Now, look who's here!" he announced proudly. I took my maiden steps on home soil like a wounded warrior back from battle; a hero, but a damaged one that no longer knew the lay of the land beneath the feet. Aaron took up an escort position on my left and with the help of my chaperones, I executed a pigeon-toed waltz that left the crowd cheering for more. The reaction overwhelmed me. I could have done anything or nothing at all. It was unconditional love at second sight for the girl whose face had put Gust Harbor on the media map, not only local channel WBGT but also Associated Press articles in newspapers as far away as New Jersey and Chicago. My story had even hit the submission desk of America's Most Wanted, though it never aired. A special mutual funds account had been opened up at Bangor Savings to take in the bake and book sale profits, as well as a flood of incoming donations with all proceeds going to the Braum family medical fund.

"You look beautiful, honey," cooed Mary Murphy. I smiled. *Phony bitch!* I reeled that unpleasant, unspoken remark in tighter. I hadn't meant to think such a thing about my former Brownies pack leader. *Where did that come from?* Small waves of pressure began to pulsate behind my eyes. I turned to the next guest.

"We've been praying for you," said Bud Grant, longest-living deacon at the Evangelical Baptist Church. *Drunken bastard!* The judgment leapt to life of its own accord. I was instantly appalled at my brain's indiscretion and politely grasped the knotted hand that had been rinsing out tiny plastic communion cups stained with grape juice since before my birth announcement was posted in the Sunday bulletin. A shimmering wave of floaters cascaded into my line of vision. I blinked repeatedly. With Aaron's steady encouragement, I made the slow procession through the greeting line that had formed around the open yard of chapped grass. The attention lured me on. I tugged my arm free from my boyfriend's gentle grip and took a confident stride unassisted. Aaron looked hurt but stepped ahead to clear a safe path as I paraded about like regal Lady Di herself, minus the nifty wardrobe. The reflection tossed back from one of the barn windows told the truth and the spell was broken. It was a sham. The imposter was revealed for what she was, a pauper girl yearning to be lifted out of her rotten circumstances. The tottering young woman was a ghastly excuse for a royal, her tiara no more than a studded headband to hide the scars and patches of barren follicles. Her newly-sprouted hair had been swept into an awkward bob; one delicate hand clenched in useless palsy at her side. Worse, the prince who tagged behind her didn't have the balls to tell her the real reason he was doing it. It wasn't about passion but pity.

"I think you should rest, now. Let's take a break," said Aaron. He tried to steer me over to the old apple sprayer with the rusted seat.

"It's my party!" I shouted, much too loudly. Dad was kibitzing with Rolf Clark, but turned mid-sentence with concern at the shrill sound of agitation.

"I'm just looking after your well-being," Aaron replied.

"I don't need a fucking babysitter!" I shouted. The sound ricocheted off the bare wall of Ty-Vek insulation that bolstered up the weathered tool shed. A shard of pain speared through my temples and fizzled into descending pulses deep in the brain somewhere. Aaron looked nervously around to see which guests might have overhead and be growing alarmed.

"Shhh. Lissa, stop! Trust me, everyone here is your friend." *Trust me...trust me...* I was instantly appalled at the nasty language that had skittered out my mouth like stealthy beetles unearthed from their darkness.

"Nosy cunts!" I hissed, brushing off his handhold on my arm.

"Jesus, girl. Come with me," he ordered. I gave in and allowed him to lead me to the piece of old farm equipment. He grasped my waist carefully, lifted me slightly and helped settle me on the solid bench seat of the old tractor. "I'll get you something to drink. Wait here. I'll be right back," Aaron said kindly. He hustled off in the direction of the refreshment table that was obscured by a bustle of bodies. I waited patiently, watching the party-goers buzz and cackle. The people of this community all belonged to a familiar landscape where normal things happened. They couldn't possibly comprehend the tragic figure in their midst. They had turned out to my debut to compare sandals and handbags and thank their good Lord on the drive home that the worst problem their daughters had was which hair style to get next. I was the oddity here. The niceties had been replaced by nasty comments about Ruth Bassett's weight gain and the way Greg Thorsen kept his eyes trained on the breasts of his toddler's teenaged babysitter. Suddenly, the ladies congregated at the picnic table all swiveled their attention in my direction. Mom waved to me. A community-sized cake dazzled on and dwarfed the old wagon-train platter. It was her homemade recipe with field blueberries and hand-whipped cream.

"Come do the honors, Lissa," she sang.

"Speech, speech," echoed the guests. The princess-girl heaved a sigh of relief. *Finally! It's time for me to shine.* With graceful balance, she swung her legs over side-saddle and prepared to dismount the carriage. Prince Aaron came striding out of the masses to claim his love. The pauper girl knew better and sputtered in embarrassment. The back of my throat and tongue had been suddenly robbed of its moisture. My chest began to rise and fall in a rush of baby breaths. It felt like a heavy weight was tipping my skull over backwards. I had to get out of there! I propelled myself off the rusted seat but with no stabilizing surface to guide me, my body freewheeled in space for a span of about four feet. After what felt like long minutes, my chin touched down where my feet should have landed.

"Daddy! Daddy," I sobbed. Blood eked out over my bottom lip along with a shard of enamel from the chipped tooth up front. I had taken a good knock to the breastbone. From there it went all downhill. I couldn't stop crying, nor seemed to have the strength to roll up out of the dirt. People came running. A variety of footwear approached at eye level. Someone grabbed at my elbow. It was Aaron. He extended his palm towards me with gentle fingers pressing against my throbbing lip.

"Leave me alone!" I shrieked. The partygoers stood in an awkward semi-circle sensing a crisis. No one knew how to help the fallen princess until Dad's strong chapped hands brought me upright.

"It's okay, sweetie. You'll be fine. Just a little cut," he said, soothingly. I huddled up against his broad shirt front and refused to look back at the crowd.

"Get me out of here, please," I begged. My father hesitated momentarily. Being the magnanimous host that he was, he wondered what he should do? Disappointed guests on one side, a hysterical daughter on the other and his wife staring in stony disbelief from the fringe of the circle. He took it all in and came up with a magnanimous apology that appeased everyone.

"Too much excitement for one day. That's understandable," Dad said. "Excuse us, if you don't mind." He needn't have worried. His invitees had gotten more their money's worth. A real show with Cinderella transformed into a bundle of ashen nerves within the hour. My Mom dropped in beside us as he escorted me into the cool interior of the house. I realized I hadn't even made it inside before I was sucked into all the festivities underway. While my brothers took up the task of excusing the company early, my parents ushered me towards the safety of the back wing.

"Maybe we were a little premature on the party idea. You weren't up to so much company. We should have thought that through," Dad said. He squeezed my shoulders with regret.

"I'm sorry. I ruined it," I mumbled.

"We did what we thought was best. What's done is done, "said my mother. Life's recent ills had bred a new strain of skepticism that had taken firm root in her garden of faith. She swung open the door. "Well, do you like it? Doesn't it look just the same?" she asked.

The first floor parlor had been hoed out and overhauled, dusted and painted in a green pear and dusty rose décor. Apparently my upstairs bedroom had been recreated down to the smallest detail possible. The room faced westward with a view over the yellow field grass to the logging road dappled in weak sunlight before it disappeared quickly into darkness. This wasn't mine. I would move back upstairs as soon as I could manage the slippery steps.

Mel and Russ had just driven for over seven hours to bring me back to a homecoming celebration that had fallen miserably short of their expectations. They had mistakenly assumed that the sight of the familiar would welcome their vacant daughter back to wholeness; unfortunately, she was only partially occupied, blinking on and then off in erratic inconsistency like a motel signboard in a big wind.

"It's very nice," I said. It was unsettling being in some girl's bedroom with her collection of Bremer horses and Madame Alexander dolls perched on royal blue shelves exactly where she had deserted them, but without their owner present to introduce us. We eyed one another with detached curiosity; and then since I was the newcomer, I decided to break the impasse with a civil but silent greeting. *Buenos Dias*! To Miss Argentina with her brightly colored striped petticoat and a cool wink to Miss Russia in her red and white peasant apron and shiny black braids wound tight to her scalp. *Shalom*! to Miss Israel with her six-point star earrings and a subtle nod to Miss Cambodia in pink kimono, straw hat tied down tight to shield her eyes. Each one had the same beautiful face disguised in the dress of her native country. They stared at their new foster mom with global disinterest, batting their hard plastic eyelids and pursing perfect red lips.

"Are you tired, dear? Would you like to nap?" Mel asked.

"Yes, I think I'll rest for a bit," I said. She kindly turned down the quilt that was needed here in Maine even on a late summer afternoon.

"There are fresh towels in the basket and a new robe if you would like to change," she said. I saw her sniff the air for any trace of the medicinal smell that follows the sick.

"Thank you. I can manage," I said stiffly. She left then, turning on the window fan and closing the door quietly behind her. I was not going to sleep in that bed. The twin frame had been lowered closer to the floor and fitted with handrails. A bed for a sick person. It was their little girl's bed and I did not want to be caught sleeping in it when she came back. I yanked the comforter off with pinched fingers and dropped it on the floor, and then one by one took the dolls off their stiff perch and assembled them on the bed. We all needed to get along and it was nice to have their company closer. Or if in the case anyone acted up, they were within reach of a spanking.

\#

Overnight and with no warning like the fickle weather that sneaks up on the Bay, a batting of haze descended on my brain. High pressure one minute followed by a descent into socked-in fog. Peeks at fair atmosphere would arrive but invariably the gloom of amnesia would settle back in place. Bipolar, said one doctor. Borderline Personality Disorder warned another. Post-Traumatic Stress Disorder with psychotic features confirmed a third. I bounced back and forth to Bangor's loony bin for outpatient treatment. Individual therapy went nowhere. How was I to talk about a childhood that had been pulled apart and scattered like the sticks and spokes of a Tinker toy? I was a storm within my own skin. Sweet Russ drove me back and forth to each appointment without complaint. When I fell quiet with disappointment in the wake of failed medication trials or a lousy session of he said/she psychoanalysis, my father carried enough hope for the both of us.

"Trust me," he said. Why those two simple words caused such a feeling of dread, I wasn't sure; but pad by pad like a big cat sliding on its dusty belly, anxiety stalked in closer. Sleep skittered farther out of range. One moved forward; the other hop-tailed out of reach until the white flag of retreat went up and bounded out of sight. Panic pursued on a full-blown run until I conceded and collapsed tongue lolling. The bad days became more frequent. Dark moods like scudding clouds came rippling out of nowhere and refused to lift. Day terrors left me paralyzed on the bed with shocks of electrical charge buzzing though my body, eyes wide open but seeing only as a third-person observer. My mind screamed to try and wake me out of a dream I was fully aware was real. Sometimes it took hours to wrestle my consciousness out of the hands of the illogical and finally startle to a full-blown panic attack; after which I was so exhausted, I would fall back asleep to another round of torturous mind games.

Despite all the pharmaceutical and psychological intervention, I still couldn't recall a single thing about the attack or retain any detail that preceded it. There was only darkness and then there was me. Let there be light, God said, and when the sun exploded onto the scene, it revealed a creation that held little likeness to the image of what he had in mind. This version had a shorn head, dissected skull, sutured face, and skin completely sloughed off contorted limbs. A wealth of darkness stretched out over the early years. A first peek revealed nothing but an opaque net thrown over my life that had trapped whole days, weeks and months underneath it. I knew there was a teeming mass of stuff concealed beneath; important things that needed to come to light. While I didn't understand the scientific mechanics behind the changes, the trauma had altered my visual field so that daily life played out in only black and white. Once in awhile, tiny shreds of enlightenment burst through in shrieks of brilliant color. I tried to catch them like brightly-hued moths on a barn door without brushing off the fragile beauty or destroying them altogether.

My newly diagnosed symptoms of OCD evolved into a singular determination to sort through the myriad of clues and find what was missing. Like elderly folks that sit in front of one thousand tiny cut-out shapes and spend precious days of their waning lives looking for that one lone piece that will lock the border into a straight edge, I searched and discarded. This was no longer child's play; I was up against a monumental challenge. The vast majority of jagged clues were entirely black so I had to work by instinct rather than sight. Piece by tedious piece, I gathered up interlocking clues and slowly snapped the perimeter into place. The final answer was trapped among the incongruous empty space in the middle. .

The final tag was tacked on almost as an afterthought. Seizure disorder, announced the expert out of Johns Hopkins whose one-hour consultation fee cost more than the Hertz sedan and the gasoline to run it down to Baltimore and back. I now had four diagnoses and eight medications, but even I knew that healing would only come when I stopped searching for answers to old questions and began asking new ones.

#

My clothes were laid out on the guest bed the night before like a chalk outline of a body on sidewalk. The button-down shirt, cotton cardigan, painter's pants, and low-top sneakers all placed in ready position for the morning drill. The physical therapist had instructed my caregivers not to assist me no matter how much time it took. The trial and error repetitions would increase my dexterity and eye-hand coordination by degrees; but more importantly, this perseverance quotient was designed to have significant therapeutic value in strengthening my ability to stay on task and not give up.

The process was going smoothly. I had already mastered the zipper and blouse buttons with minimal delay. At this rate, I'd make it to the breakfast table in less than thirty minutes. I bent down to once again tackle the shoelaces that kept slithering through my fingers like thin grass snakes. I made a second attempt and then another. Suddenly the gravity caused my eyes to rhythmically throb and a dark halo rimmed the upper quadrant of both pupils. I immediately straightened up and grasped the corner of the desk for support. Fragments of prisms spun by like shattered stained glass.

Gradually, the visual horizon brightened in intense bands of color like the Aurora Borealis that shimmers in atmospheric prisms of raging light. Maybe it was just another optical migraine coming on. My hands became fumbling mitts and a sweep of heat broiled underneath my cheeks.

"Goddamn it! You mother-fucker!" I shouted.

"Lissa! Careful now! Your brothers are downstairs" said my father. "Now, try again." The top button had come loose; the middle one was altogether unfastened. "Start with the bottom first then work your way up like they showed you."

"I can't do this shit!" I cried, exasperated. Using my teeth to grip the cuff, I peeled the cabled sleeve off my arm and let the sweater fly. Foul language was a symptom of a tic, the uninhibited sounds of a brain abnormality, not unlike Tourette's syndrome; but in a family of church-goers, the new vocabulary was a harsh reminder that the sweet chorus girl had been abducted by demons.

"Give it a rest. We'll practice again later," Dad said.

"This is kid crap. I'm not retarded if that's what everyone thinks!" I yelled. "I know what the story is. It's a set-up for failure. That way, you can all feel better about putting me in the nursing home for good!"

"No. No, Lissa. That's wrong. We are all committed to your success," said my Dad, shaking his head at each irrational outcry. "Listen to me! You can't trust your instincts here. Not yet. You aren't able to see this from an objective point of view. Part of your brain is firing off on impulse, not rational thought. You know that's what is happening here, right?" I struggled briefly against his grip on my upper arm, then tears started up and the energy left me.

"Sit, sit," my father said as he patted the edge of the mattress and helped me lower by degrees to a seated position on the bed. It was not the first time this had happened, this display of polar moods; it was becoming a pattern. First a righteous red flare, followed by a spontaneous tantrum and then a flood of instant fatigue that operated independently of my wishes, especially the tears that were foreign and frustratingly frequent. But the tears served a purpose; they were what brought the rest of the world running to forgive the flawed young woman who kept fucking up through no fault of her own.

"Honey, remember what the doctors said? They distinctly told you that the fine motor skills are more challenging to master. It will take lots of practice. That's why they want you to do it on your own without us jumping in to make it easier. Right?" he asked. I nodded in passive agreement. He kissed the top of my damp head.

"I'll be back by week's end. Want to have a rematch on some backgammon?" he asked.

"Yes. And I won't cheat this time," I confessed with a sudden grin.

"Deal! See ya, sweet girl."

I heard him go down and then out through the kitchen, the hollow knob rattling as the draft automatically slammed the old door. I crossed to the window. Once outside, he hesitated for a moment on the brick walk, watching the younger boys kick up a sand fight out back by the pond. Then Russ stepped out into the tinsel shine of morning grass and carefully pressed down a piece of sod that had been gouged up in the run of summer play. He wasn't the least bit worried about things. When he got home in five days' time, that bare patch we were in might hardly be noticeable any more.

CHAPTER 7
LOSING GRIP

July 2014

Rev was an entitled kid. It's obvious by the smug turn of his lips and his utter disregard of others. His presence is both ingratiating and dismissive at the same time. He acts as if he's truly listening, but everyone knows there is only enough room in his brain for his own opinions. When someone else is talking, Rev's just waiting for the right moment to insert himself into the conversation and from there, he takes over. There is no denying that he is smart and crafty with persuasion as most preachers are. The real problem with Rev is that he is an asshole but doesn't know it. He doesn't have to say anything to make others instantly defensive; although he never misses an opportunity to say more than anybody wants to hear. Speaking is his self-ordained gift, but the rest of the world can't figure out who appointed him lord over others. Each time he steps into the classroom, he deliberately pauses in front of my desk waiting to be acknowledged.

It is twelve-forty when he finally arrives for group. We are already a good ten minutes into the discussion. I nod in his direction but continue to focus my attention on Euclid who had suddenly found his voice and lost his inhibition about using it.

"Good afternoon, Counselor," Rev announces loudly. I raise an open hand to indicate that he should put the brakes on his mouth but the pedal to his feet and take his seat. He doesn't budge.

"It's not my fault I'm tardy," he says.

"Gotcha," I whisper. But he still stands there, obstructing my view of the speaker. He clearly wants an acknowledgement like a salute, a bow or a round of applause but he gets what everyone else does, a plain old check mark in the attendance roster.

"So, you were saying.., one of your daughters took her own life and you lost another child to violence. And then something snapped inside you," I continue. Euclid's blurting admission of personal history has been a long time coming, especially given the verbal warning shot he fired on the first day when he made it clear that I was to back off and give him space. With wild eyes rolling, he drew the battle lines and told me that there were going to be days when it was too much being cooped up in a room with all those questions, too many questions, and that he might have to just bolt and leave or God knows what would happen. I had asked him to tell me when he felt that anti-social vibe coming on, even though it was obvious by the way he skittered into the room, fingers tugging at his oily black curls. On those days, I was glad that he was seated in the corner seat by the empty file cabinet, as far away as he could be in linear feet. He'd fold his arms across his thin tee shirt that only partially masked the tribal tattoos underneath and fidget unbearably, run his frenzied hands up and down his nervous thighs to calm himself. On several occasions, I excused him from the class when I noticed his fungus-covered tongue foaming up like a dog with disease. It's a calculated gamble any time a resident from the Mental Health unit is included on the attendance roster since they are often either so medicated or so agitated they can't comprehend the material. Plus, the teacher must allow for the fact that a psychotic break might send the guy into four-point restraints. But despite all the inherent deficits, Euclid has hung in and is on the verge of self-discovery. I'd be damned if some egotist was going to taint that moment.

"So continue, please, "I repeat. "You were talking about your family."

"Si," he says. "My mama no treat me nice. Say I'm too young to be raising babies. I don't like the way it made me feel. She got in my face. Kept nagging. Too close. Do something fast, she tells me. Fix this." He is wrestling around in his chair, then leans forwards with hands bouncing up and down on his knees, extends his legs and shakes out his arms, flicking his wrists as if the blood flow had been stopped and his extremities had gone to sleep. It makes me wonder about the blood flow to his head. He has old gashes on his arms and one horribly-disfigured lower leg that he drags a bit with a frightening patch of skin graft that is only visible at the ankle when he hikes up his pants. It is an injury he created with gasoline and a candle when he was much younger.

"And what did you do?" I ask.

"I stab her. Five times," he adds, one eye straying wildly to the right and over my head.

"How old were you when this happened?"

"Twelve," he answers. Horrific child abuse, premature fatherhood and paranoid schizophrenia had descended on this young man before he was even a true teenager.

"Was that when you were first institutionalized?" I ask gingerly. Each question is a risk, what might turn out to be the one-too-many that may push him over his limit.

"No, my mama not die. I come to America. She stay behind. I have big family here now. Twenty-seven kids," he boasts. No one in the room says anything. This could just as easily be truth as a delusion. Nothing surprises me anymore.

"Good job, Mr. Euclid."

"It's good I come to this class. I am a very violent man," he says. Whether this is a simple acknowledgement or an over-arching warning is unclear. What is obvious is the collective sigh of relief that is exhaled anytime we dismiss the group with Euclid smiling.

"Hey, Bud. Stick around for a minute. Will ya?" I say. Mr. Bowman comes to a halt. His feet stop moving and his long arms swing in suspension, eventually coming to rest at his side. I can imagine him in his natural element wearing Converse sneakers with no laces, long plaid shorts cuffed below the knee and a Cradle of Filth shirt with skulls scattered across it. He is always one of the last to shuffle slowly from the room. The rest of the guys have been dismissed and have already gone on ahead. This way he won't feel singled out in public. Bowman drops his languid body into a chair and his chin in his hands, but does not look up.

"You said you wanted to ask me something. What is it?" I ask gently.

"Yeah, I wanted to know if I get in a fight with someone, will I lose all of my good time?"

"Well, you've just been sentenced so you've only earned three days so far. A ticket for fighting would cost you twenty. So if that should happen, you'd owe us days," I answer. Bowman smirks and squints his eye. Some kind of calculating is going on inside his head.

"Might be worth it," he mumbles.

"What's going on with you?" I ask. He has uttered only a few sparse words in our time together. It's not like there's any history to build on here. "If you don't feel comfortable talking to me, I can send you to someone else."

"These Spanish people keep getting up in my face and chilling near my bunk, getting all loud and when I'm trying to sleep, they start pulling some sneaky shit on the low. I'm not here to get hassled. I'm not in the mood for their shit," Bowman says. His forthrightness is surprising. I didn't expect more than a grumble or a terse refusal.

"Not to change the subject, but I get the feeling you're not too pleased about having to sit in my class. Maybe a little hostile even?"

"True," he mumbles.

"You seem very uncomfortable in a group setting. Am I right?"

"Yeah," he admits. "I guess so. Don't see the point in listening to everyone else piss and moan. We all got our problems. Big deal!"

"So you don't think that your contribution can help others or that the wisdom of other people's experiences might benefit you?"

"Naw! Who the hell cares?" blurts Bowman, nearly snorting out his distaste for his fellow man.

"Any particular reason why you feel so strongly?" I persist. Bowman finally lifts his faded blue eyes to meet mine with a hollow stare. He is tolerating me out of some curt code of basic manners, but he is not at all pleased that I have pressed my thumb down hard on the snarl in his attitude.

"Just one. I hate people," says our resident anti-socialite. "Plus this place really makes it worse. I can't do anything I enjoy."

"Is this a recent change?" I ask.

"No, I've pretty much hated everyone since I was ten," he confesses.

"Did you just wake up one day feeling the disdain for others or was there an event of some significance in your childhood that made you distrust people?"

"I suppose so," he says, still apparently unwilling to divulge more than a cryptic word or two. I stay silent. The space between us fills with an awkward pause. Bowman coughs tentatively, then clears his throat and finally stretches his fidgeting neck side to side. I don't rescue him from his discomfort.

"Fine!" he blurts out as if I've got his arm twisted up behind him and am muscling the bloody truth out. "It's pretty simple, okay? I don't need a shrink to tell me what's wrong, if that's what you're thinking. My parents were both killed in a car accident two minutes after dropping me off at a friend's house. They were headed to work and a dump truck plowed them into a guardrail. I was an instant orphan. I spent the rest of my days in foster homes."

"My, God! That is tragic. Have you gotten any professional help to deal with this loss?"

"They tried, but I hate therapists and shrinks even more."

"Do you think you may need or want to talk to Mental Health?" I ask gingerly. "Maybe there's a medication that might help with the depression."

"I've already tried Remeron but I heard if you take it for too long, you can grow tits so I stopped."

"Let me ask you. In your free time, is there anything you draw pleasure from?" My question is a welcome relief. Bowman perks up at the switch in subject.

"Music for one," he replies. "And oh, video games, of course!" he adds. There isn't much outlet for the young gamer in a house of corrections. Deprivation and disallowed are the verbs of choice in a discipline-driven environment. The Department of 'Collections' is quick to confiscate and discourage all the ingenious ways prisoners crafted pastimes out of unapproved materials, which were usually stripped away and thrown out.

"Do you play music or just like listening to it?" I ask.

"I play bass guitar," says Bowman. He picks at a scab, stares down at the dirty tiles and scuffs his heel at a small shred of paper. I notice then the marks, silvery disfigurations on his lower arms. Old cuttings with a fresh gouge on his lower wrist that looks septic. This is worrisome.

"And what are you always scribbling on during our group? Artwork?" Bowman shakes his head and guiltily retrieves a creased piece of printer paper from his pants. It is folded over a dozen or more times. He painstakingly unwraps it into one contiguous piece without tearing the worn edges and spreads out in front of me. I examine the strange pattern of hieroglyphics and look up, puzzled.

"Dungeons and Dragons. This is our game board, so to speak, but it's almost impossible to decipher now. I have a form from a catalog that we could use. I've asked the counselor in our block to make copies, but he's a douche and won't give me the time of day."

"Who needs a game board to play Dungeons and Dragons in here? You're living it every day. What's that activity called, when people role play knights and minstrels and Renaissance type crap?" I ask.

"Larping," he says, with a weird but real grin.

"Yeah, that's it. That's what's I'm talking about. We're all in one big interactive play here." I take a closer look at the intricate design. It's quite a piece of handiwork. "Do me a favor. On Tuesday, bring me the form you're talking about and plan to stay after class for a few minutes."

Bowman takes the mysterious score sheet and carefully folds it back into his waistband. He has brightened noticeably and when he walks out, I can see he is moving at a markedly faster pace.

#

Two days later, Bowman's back and loiters around after class is dismissed. Once the other inmates are out of sight, he offers me the grid of elaborate mazes. He's certifiably animated now and beams when I peer at the diagram, looking mighty confused. I'm in his territory now, a world of imagination where men and beasts devour and destroy one another, where death is distributed gleefully and liberally until finally game over and you start again. Pain is not permanent.

"It's very complex. The average person wouldn't understand," he says proudly.

"That's me," I tease. "I will copy this for you as long as you can swear up and down that there is no cryptic gang code hidden in here." Bowman nods enthusiastically indicating that he is on the up-and-up. The young man is virtually dancing in place. His imagination has just gotten a big assist from an old-school champion of board games like Clue and Chutes & Ladders, games that could also come in handy in prison with the advantage being on the subordinate's side.

"Walk with me. I want to introduce you to someone," I say. Bowman follows along with a snappy new lift to his steps. He hums some discordant song and rarely looks up to see who is around him. I stop in front of the chapel wing. Bowman grows suspicious and clams up. I rattle the gate and the rover comes meandering by to let us through.

"I hate God too, Miss," says Bowman.

"That won't be a problem, I don't think," I reply. Immediately the sound of an upbeat jam fills the corridor. The melody lifts and swells as we approach the main auditorium-size room that serves all faiths equally. Pastor Fargo greets us at the entrance and waves us inside. His long silver braid dwindles to a meager point at his belt line. Today it is the Protestants who are ruling the roost here. A weekly praise service will be commencing after evening chow. Along the wall is a larger-than-life mural that depicts various religions, nations, and tribes rendered in a collage of portraits by many gifted hands. These are the faces of the inmates who have confessed and converted, worshipped and died as members of this incongruous congregation. It's an impressive tribute to the universal fact of faith under fire. Speaking of which, a pungent smoke permeates the religious services area.

"They're smudging today. Our sweat lodge ceremony," says Pastor Fargo.

"Native American?" asks Bowman. The Pastor nods.

"Chippewa," he states. We have a place for you…," says the spiritual man. "In our praise band and in our fellowship of believers."

"Passamaquoddy," replies Bowman.

"Brothers all," replies his new mentor. The two shake hands and Bowman follows him to the platform in front where a collection of diverse souls are playing their hearts out to the Spirit-Maker, whomever he or she may be. An empty chair with an electric bass has been arranged for him. It's just like heaven where our Father goes and prepares a room with our name on it the day we are born, just in case we take a wrong turn and end up there earlier than He expected.

#

Death, the great game-changer. The first time it arrives like a train wreck, knocking out power, throwing people off their feet, upsetting the entire landscape with the force of a cowcatcher snagging soft flesh. The worst part is the knowledge that comes afterwards, the undeniable fact that our perfect world has been irreparably plowed over.

My dad died instantly behind the wheel of his oil truck when it ran top speed into a grove of birches. The explosion immediately engulfed the scene. He was cremated spontaneously in a pyre of diesel fuel and all that was left to denote the spot where his feet left this earth was his grease-stained Aroostook Oil Service cap. Russell Braum would have turned fifty-eight the following week still palming the wheel over the rugged hills of lupine and down through valleys of hemlock singing his Randy Travis tunes and spitting out the hulls of sunflower seeds with no thought of retirement on his mind. We would have played that rematch of backgammon I planned to win fair and square; instead the game chips were flung deep into the dug well where they would lie cashed in for eternity.

Within days of his passing, Dad's things were gone, half the house removed in a four-hour operation. Like surgery, gaping holes and missing parts were what glared back in the aftermath. A creamy square on the wainscoting where age had greyed around the now-displaced dry sink that went to his brother; a length of pine shelving without a single World War II book on it, all his periodicals packed and given to the VFW hall. The queen box spring and mattress were dragged through the gravel and dropped in the dirt like an old bleached bone. Mom settled into an economical-size twin bed, guaranteeing there was no possibility of ever sharing it with anyone else. Our good years were pulled out by the corners and seams and shuttered away in taped cartons from Cutter's dry goods store. February 23, 1991, the date we stalled, the exact moment I plowed headlong into the realization that if I was ever to outlive the wreck of my life, I had to go it alone right then and crawl as fast and furiously away from the scene of my own accident as I could. Crippled as I was, I knew I'd eventually need to rise to my feet and toddle towards the rescue light before the unbearable heat of defeat consumed me.

I can empathize with Bowman. I am an orphan-girl of grown-up proportions.

#

I e-mail Dr. Brennerman, the therapist who runs the sex treatment program to ask for his help. I know him only as the bespectacled man in a sweater vest who rounds the pedophiles up into a cozy semi-circle twice a week, turns the lights down, has them shut their eyes and practice meditation. A year or so ago, a brand-new, very attractive intern had tried the same routine with a slight variation. Being young and enthused about her new assignment, she eagerly joined the men in the exercise and closed her own eyes as the sounds of the sea tide washed back and forth, back and forth from her CD player. At the end of the session, she opened her eyes to find three of the offenders masturbating. To be sure, those men left that group more relaxed than they'd been in years, but the female worker was so traumatized, she never returned. It's a rare person who's cut out for that type of work.

Brennerman is an oddity in this environment, one who dismisses the blatant hatred levied against sex offenders and plods onward into the murky swamp water of this mutated species. He's a different sort, socially skittish and dry as cork but I sense that behind his academic aloofness, the man has real compassion. So I'm not altogether surprised when he agrees to meet with me and take the time to listen to the plight of Mr. Willis who has been mandated to complete his program but is fighting fiercely to have that stigma removed.

"You must understand, as convoluted as it sounds, the treatment is voluntary on the part of these offenders with the caveat that if they reject the need for it, they will be put in the Denier's track. This then places them under intense scrutiny and maximum supervision both in and outside the walls. Not only that, it limits their housing options, their earning capacity in the employment world and guarantees a lengthy stay on the electronic monitoring bracelet," he patiently explains.

"So, what you're saying is, they really don't have a choice."

"In all truth, no. Not if they have been convicted of a sexual crime," Brennerman clarifies with a sigh of protest. He is soft spoken in presentation, but firm with the assurance of someone who knows what he's talking about.

"Mr. Willis is not a Denier. He is innocent," I explain.

"Well, if you believe that, I am willing to look over the folder of documents you've got there. I promise to call Mr. Willis in and speak with him in person."

"Well, I will rest better tonight, knowing I have done my part in putting this issue into the care of someone with the expert eye to decipher it. Thank you," I add, shaking his mealy hand with genuine enthusiasm. Brennerman squints and grimaces, his version of a tense smile.

\#

Two days later, Brennerman flags me down in the corridor just outside my office. I retreat back into the room and wave him over to join me. He sits down on the blue plastic chair, his turkey eyes aglow with information.

"I want to tell you how very impressed I am with Mr. Willis's comportment. He did an impressive job of representing himself. I think he has real cause here."

"Does that mean we can we get his score removed?" I ask.

"I am going to bring Ms. Dalton in from the Harvard School of Psychiatry. She's our consulting expert. After she assesses him, we would have to go before a Special Review Board. I also spoke with the Director of Population Management. They have requested all the original testimonies and the pre-sentence investigation records. As cynical and hard-ass as he can be, he agreed there's a chance this kid got royally screwed over. I can't promise Mr. Willis anything but I can make sure he gets a fair shake."

"Thank you for this good news. We'll see where it goes. It will be up to Mr. Willis to convince them," I say. Dr. Brennerman and I have more in common than a first glance would reveal. Beyond the fringe of unkempt beard that creeps in a haphazard trail down the side of his neck and the tiny globule of dried spit that rests at the corner of his cracked lip, he has a handsome soul that shares a kindred spirit of advocacy.

Willis continues to come to class, humbly taking his seat among the others and acting as if the private conversation never happened. For my part, I make no move to open the discussion again. There's always the chance that this is part of a master plan, a manipulation to undermine the overlord. I know this game. The grooming starts early; the formula is pat and proven. Look for the new kid, the rookie, one of the probationary cops whose naiveté makes them particularly malleable. Or perhaps a plain middle-aged woman who finds herself especially lonely in this age of shrinking fertility. Once the weak link is discovered, trust is ferreted out. I'm special, thinks the target host, the first and ultimately fatal step of their undoing. But at the end of the day, every day, I answer to my own conscience. I am no duck and I've got my sources. There's always someone willing to talk if he thinks he might win extra points. From what I hear, Willis spends his free time in the cell writing various public officials, magistrates and politicians in both Massachusetts and Washington. His requests come back with patronizing instructions to follow the chain of command and start at the bottom with his correctional counselor, which of course, he has.

I put it off as part of my job. If I did it for one, I'd do it for all. But is that the truth? Was this a select move born from a special spark? Naw, not a chance. Most offenders expect to be granted a ready platform for their cries of mistreatment. Many are litigious and just waiting for the right circumstance so they can snap the trap on the State. Fewer still accept the blame and take their lumps in stride. But every so often, along comes someone like Terran Willis who'd been roped in, hog-tied and then hobbled by a faulty system. Willis was not blameless by any stretch. His rap sheet contained fourteen arrests with a total of twenty-one convictions running the gamut from petty larceny all the way up to Robbery First. Sprinkled into the mix were numerous assaults, firearms and narcotics charges. It was a pedigree any hardened perpetrator would be proud of. But the shady facts of the purported crime that had launched him on his criminal bent in the first place, these were sealed in his Youthful Offender file. Arrest Zero, the one that never appeared on public record had become the catalyst for all others; and on this one false claim, the system had hedged their bets and played their hand.

It occurs to me how damaging the separate sexes can be, particularly in youth when hormones are the logic that precedes all action. Whether in love or hate, how easily we can undo one another and how hopelessly impossible it is to find repair.

#

"It's time!" Dale says dryly with a rasp of resistance as if his esophagus is ready to cough up a piece of stale biscuit. But very little comes up. It's like peristalsis trying to work the resentment down, forcing him to digest it, along with all the other shit he's had to swallow because of me. He doesn't have to say it; none of them do. My big brother was good up front with fists cocked stepping ahead of his pretty sister to ward off the horny boys, but when danger circumvented that strut and struck her down, all the fight went out of him. He dropped his hands and never picked them up in my defense again. My other siblings were staunchly polite but once the damage was done, they too gave up and went to find pretty girls of their own. All the sons turned their attention back to the mother matriarch who had lost track of them during the years of our family crisis and was now suddenly alone in her clapboard cave. We no longer talked about our own stories and only reluctantly shared excerpts from the ongoing history that joined us, my mother's tale of stoic denial. Everyone was keeping an arm's length away from the God's honest truth that none us knew how to fix things anymore.

"Time for what?" I ask, perplexed.

"A surprise. Here, hold on," he says. The receiver is fumbled in the hand-off. I can hear pillows being plumped and the hum of the hydraulics that raise the head of the bed.

"It's your mother," Mel says faintly.

"Finally! It's been forever, Mom. How are you feeling?" I ask. A nervous laugh of relief fills the gap.

"I will be fine," she answers matter-of-factly.

"I know it," I say.

"I want you to promise me something," Mel says with a rush of breath.

"Of course," I reply.

"When you come up in August, I want you to keep a good eye on your brothers, especially Brock. His blood pressure is up and ever since Dolly left him, there's no one around to oversee his medications. He's working the boat most of the day but if he's not likely to cook up anything fresh at the end of a long day. It'll be fried clams or cheeseburgers, neither of which he needs. So, there are two chest freezers full of our garden harvest from last year and a dozen roasters all quartered and ready to cook." Her words come out in choppy exhales riding the outgoing tide, broken only by short gasps of backwash as she pools up energy for another. All this focus on food when the poor woman couldn't stomach more than a ladle of applesauce.

"I'm on it. He'll be in the best possible hands. Second to yours, of course."

"You still like your job, honey?" she asks, switching subjects. It takes me off-guard, this sudden interest in my adult life. Very rarely has she ever wanted to talk about what I do in an environment she believes is toxic for any civilized female. If conversations come up about politics or religion, Mel is firmly entrenched in the discussion. These are the big-box storehouses of generic fact and general opinion that anyone could safely enter into. But if it involved her family or her feelings, she simply got busy in the pantry.

"I've got a great group going right now. I see some real signs of change taking place," I say.

"That's nice," she replies, her courteous way of curtailing things. "I'm getting awfully tired. Let's talk again soon," she adds. I want her to say something else though I don't know what. Maybe a rant of frustration or a bellowing yell against the fact that her monotonous circle of safety became utter mayhem against her will. She could demand credit for all the heart-wrenching hours she stood by watching me crawl hand over fist on a gym mat or tolerating the sickening specter of her intelligent baby reduced to mouthing vowels like an infant. What was her faith telling her now? Was it still the consoling whisper that believed God was perfectly capable of miraculous intervention but if He withheld it, then He had something else in mind that was far better? Or had it changed its tune into an anguished hiss, hollering out, 'Jesus, woman! Wake up and see how many levels of fucked-up this is. Cancel your reservation in the upcoming rapture.'

"Let me speak to Dale again, okay?" I say. The phone is passed back.

"Yep…?"

"I'd like to come surprise her this weekend. What do you think?" I suggest.

"You know Mom. She doesn't want anyone to see her in this state. Once she's through the chemo and out of the hospital, you can come up," he mumbles. Reluctantly, I cave in to his wishes or more accurately, hers. Mom knows she's not coming back home. Why else would she have Dale and family all moved into the house? He's subbed out his lobster traps to his oldest son and has taken on the farm chores. If the hospital can't keep her when her condition becomes chronic, she'll be transferred over to a nursing home, at least until they can pump her with liquid nutrition and manage her pain. Dale is the only one she allows in to visit. He's probably bringing in Egg Fu Yung and watching Animal Planet with his dirty corduroys thrown up across the thin porous blanket that's come loose at the end of her bed. That'll drive her crazy; not the muddy farm boots on clean linens but the top sheet she can't reach and tuck into neat hospital corners like she's always done at home. *Screw my brother's conservatism.* I try to patch a call through to the nurse's station several times over the ensuing days, but I'm told she is getting washed up or having her vitals taken. The mold of silence has steepened and is cast like plaster. There's little hope of breaking through now.

#

"So, run that theory by me again. Methinks I can punch some holes it," I tease. The lemon drop martini is just a puddle of liquid in the bottom-heavy glass. "Didn't I order another one of these?"

"That is the other one you ordered," laughs James. He cranes his neck, peers down the length of the massive oak bar and spots our bartender holding the remote aloft at the far end. The channel switches from Rory McElroy in bright red pants to Big Papi spitting and smacking his red batting gloves. You can't drink in a Boston swill-house and not be caught booing P.K. Subban or tossing curses at the Yankees. The city thrives on rivalries and racism. But the Stanley Cup is done; the Bruins are back in their den hibernating for a season. All attention has turned back to Fenway even if the team stats are as soggy as the tarp-covered field.

"Finally! Real men don't wear red pants and leprechaun jackets," I say.

"Unless they're Irish," James says. He's gotten the bar maid's attention, orders another extra dirty, dirty martini, which amounts to a handful of engorged olives floating in a salty brine of vodka, and a blueberry basil martini special for me. Buckman Tavern is an eclectic mix of New England history and West Coast cuisine, a salute to Paul Revere and a high five to the French Laundry menu. The tables are boxed in elbow to elbow with no standing room. This part of the North End is a squeeze at best, its cobblestone alleyways so narrow that one grandmother can reach out her second-story window and snip dead pansies on the neighbor's rooftop garden.

"I believe we were designed to love many people in the course of our lives. There are multiple dimensions to love that can't possibly be discovered with just one person," he repeats. I cock my head slightly, fold my leg under my rump and lean forward excitedly.

"So in essence, what you're saying is that men were never created to be monogamous? Am I right?" I tease. "Quel surprise!" The front of my navy blue cocktail dress buckles and dips down in the middle revealing a crease of cleavage. I instinctively grab my linen napkin and tuck it in front like a bib. James smirks.

"I want you to concentrate, that's all. This is important shit," I say. James is amused and keeps his eyes trained on my face as he throws back his drink. I flip my hair over my shoulder and wait for his answer.

"Why limit ourselves at such a young age when we're given a lifetime?" he asks.

"So, why did you? You're the one that's married," I reply.

"I think marriage is a cultural concept that came about to promote control. The rules that govern marriage were drafted up by priests because they weren't getting any."

"What I'm hearing is that you are in an unhappy marriage and are trying to justify relationships outside of it. This isn't a new concept, Hastings. Nearly every guy in the Department already subscribes to this rationalization."

"You're drunk," he says with a smile.

"So be it!" I say a bit defensively, but it's true. My last 'excuse me/ pardon me' wobble to the ladies room had me thinking these old Revolutionary-era floors were warped with age; but come to find out, it was my off-kilter footing knocking purses off of chair backs.

"Let's keep it real, as they say. Tell me, then. Are you happily married?" I ask.

"I don't honestly know. I guess," he answers.

"But...?

"But we don't really connect on any important level anymore. Maybe we never did."

"How long have you been married, James?" I grasp the stem of my glass and swish its contents in small concentric circles before downing the last of it.

"Eleven years. I was twenty-six when we tied the knot."

"Maybe it's unrealistic to expect the male species to be faithful for life. I mean, whose big idea was that anyhow? Betty Crocker? The Pope?" I stammer. He's clearly getting a kick out of my irreverent lack of filter.

"You think that only applies to men?" he asks.

"Yes. I've been with my significant other since I was twenty-two. Practically forever. We're inseparable," I profess. "Here, let me introduce you two." James looks nervously over his shoulder as if he can feel the torch eye of a laser burning through his spinal column and knows he's in the range of a jealous boyfriend. He turns back, puzzled when I hold out my right hand.

"Well, say hello!" I giggle. He's clearly confused for a few seconds and then it dawns on him and he bangs on the bar and spits alcohol on his shirt. This genuine, stress-releasing laughter is a side of James I rarely have a chance to observe. He clears his throat, takes the cocktail napkin, sponges off the spot on his front and orders another round.

"I didn't expect that to come out of such a classy gal," he says. Two mint mojitos arrive and disappear in short order. The conversation wends its way to sports. I am surprised to learn that he doesn't know crap about tennis. He can't believe that I still can regularly rack up a 186 on the ten-pin lane. He's afraid of rip tides and can't stand the feel of dried salt on his skin. He doesn't believe that I can barefoot ski over surf and have snorkeled with barracudas. He is an only child from a stuffed-shirt family in Westchester County, New York. I claim bragging rights to my roots as a red-neck clam-digger whose closest neighbor lived in a refurbished school bus. He adheres to a strict diet of high-quality meat and vegetables. No sugars, dairy or carbohydrates. I say, Why do you think God put potato chips on the earth? He can run a 5k in twenty-two minutes. I can throw a perfect spiral about sixty yards. He swears by a John Deere ride-on and I say it does a shit job compared to a push mower. He thinks Obama is a "high-yeller" catering to the old, white Republicans. I say he's a great orator but I don't believe in the two-party system. James doesn't believe in God. I do. We have absolutely nothing in common, which is the instant glue that keeps us bantering and debating for another few hours before he grabs my hand and says, let's go. We take a cab from Beacon Street to a club with dueling pianos and Dee-jays and a throng of young people dancing in groups. The girls sport towering heels and short skirts with hems that just clear the last wrinkle of flesh on their rear-ends. God forbid one of them drops her lipstick and has to bend over to retrieve it. I suddenly feel a bit dated, but James reads my reluctance and draws me in towards the crowd.

We dance to Drake, separating to improvise a little freelance footwork then waltzing back to the middle to do a dirty little bump and grind. In between sets we reclaim our bar stools, fan the sweat from our necks with menus and take shots of Patron. At two o'clock a.m., we stumble out the door and flag a cab to South Station. My date looks out the left-side window. There's a space of seat between us but the constant jostling of the taxi over rough asphalt and neglected frost heaves works us by inches towards the middle. At one particularly bad break in the pavement, James throws out a palm to steady his balance and grabs my knee instead. Or is it an intended breach in etiquette to get the ball rolling? Either way, I don't ask him to move it. Once on the train, the steady metronome of the rails lulls us into a silence. My head rests on his chest; his arm is thrown around my shoulder. We both stare sleepily at the row houses and the dark parks and the flat marshes that tick by. James is suddenly tapping my arm to rouse me.

"It's our stop, Elise. C'mon, gal," he urges. I struggle up from my nap and follow his lead down the steps and out of the steamy heat of the coach. There is something so adolescent and touching about his rough hand encircling mine as we walk back towards the two lone vehicles left in the commuter lot, both cozied up by the corner of the dumpster. I turn to thank him, assuming we are parting ways.

"Uh-uh. There's no way you're in any condition to drive, Elise," he says, admonishing my foolhardy attempt to force my trunk key into the driver's side door.

"Neither are you," I say.

"Yeah, true. But I have a badge and a gun that can talk us out of trouble should we get pulled over. C'mon. I'll take you home and we'll get your car tomorrow." I accept the leg-up onto the saddle of this work horse Ford. My flowing gauze skirt gets wrapped around the gearshift momentarily. James carefully disengages the fabric and tucks it back under my thigh but leaves his warm hand tucked beneath as he drives judiciously by way of back roads to Brigham. I don't question his sense of direction, but then it occurs to me that he seems to know where he's going.

"How do you know where I live?" I mumble.

"There's a lot I know about you that you don't know I know," he replies.

"That sentence was all screwed up. Or maybe I am. Anyway, I had such a good time tonight, James. Thank you for the wonderful evening and for paying for my hangover." He smiles, withdraws his hand from its nesting place and lays it on the top of my thigh.

"My pleasure, beautiful," he whispers. "You lean back and relax. I promise to get you home safely." The next thing I recall is being lifted up by a very strong man and carried to the front steps of my house, then set down so he can fumble through my purse for a house key. The dogs are throwing themselves against the door. My mind clears instantly and the fog of this fantasy dissipates. As he unlocks the dead-bolt, I step around him and in the door first so I can calm the animals with a quick command. They drop to the rug in an ever-ready crouch with their keen eyes tracing every move this stranger makes.

"I'd like to give you a goodnight kiss without an audience. May I?" James asks, almost shyly. I laugh, open the side door and usher his antagonists out onto the screened porch.

"Here," I say, lifting onto the balls of my feet with the intention of planting a kiss on my date's chin. That's as high as I can reach, but I've miscalculated the physics of passion that are already at play. The velocity of his desire has brought his mouth down to the dip at the base of my throat. I start to topple backwards, but James reaches out quickly and pulls me against him

"Wait!" I whisper. "You didn't specify what kind of kiss."

"Whatever kind you're offering," he says coyly.

"This kind," I reply. My tongue is quickly and fully entwined with his. I have a clear sensation of déjà vu though this scene has never been played out before and certainly not with this man. He begins to slip his hands up the curve of my waist.

"Hold on, James. I don't want to cause trouble in your family. You know I'm not that kind of person, right?" As expected, the introduction of reality tempers the impulses and dampens the dream. He releases me and drops his head.

"I do know that, Elise. Neither am I."

"Okay, then can I trust you to put me to bed?" I say. "I think all that liquid courage has got the best of me." James leads me back to the bedroom where he very gently helps me slide my fully-clothed body under the cotton bedspread. He hands me a tumbler of water to drink and tenderly lifts the hairbrush from the night stand and runs it through my damp, tangled hair. I drink deeply and place the glass on the table.

"Don't misunderstand. I like you, James," I say, reaching up to trace the line of his jaw from cheek to temple. The look in his eyes has shifted like a dog whose initial crazy abandon at first sight has settled into the calm reassurance that its owner won't be leaving again soon. He responds by touching his finger to the faded crease that mars the surface skin of my cheek and ends in a dimpled lump at the corner of my mouth.

"Childhood accident, huh? Bike maybe?"

"Something like that," I reply, hoping he'll be content with the mystery in this ambiguous response.

"Poor girl," he whispers. "I think I love you."

"Don't be silly. You're drunk, my good man."

"Which if true, means I'm probably telling the truth," he says, grinning.

"Or you're just another scuz-ball talking up a good line."

"I don't want to talk at all," he replies.

"Then you may kiss me just once. As a friend, of course," I tease.

Delight courses through his body as I reach up and pull him firmly down on the mattress beside me. His hands stay above-board, running over the bulky outline of the bed linens like a blind man who must imagine the shape of the curves and crevices with his fingertips. Our mouths connect and explore one another cautiously. The act of restraint is intensely exciting, as if I am once again a lusty teen in the grip of arousal on the straw mattress in the top shed with my parents only steps away from discovery.

When I awake an hour later, James is still there rocking me slightly back and forth like a child he doesn't want to wake or ever see grow up. The next time I open my eyes, it is to a powerful hunger and a full sun spreading across the pine board floors. And he is gone.

CHAPTER 8
STAND CHOW

It's not a job most would volunteer for. I mean, who wants to watch two hundred men at a time file in and out of a cafeteria room for a twenty-minute feeding? Much like a livestock auction, the specimens are paraded by. Staff including counselors, teachers, even the elderly principal line the walls along the mainline with arms folded and feet splayed in a ready stance. Most of them are shooting the crap about the past weekend's antics and paying little mind to the various breeds on display. For their part, the prisoners assume a multitude of poses as they ramble on. Some hang their heads, look straight down and shuffle nervous feet; others stare and throw their heads back in defiance. A little balking is tolerated but straight-up disobedience will earn them a prod from the cap stun dispenser. A few stop to impress the counselors with their newfound conversion which overtook them in Sunday chapel, the same salvation they accepted last bid and the one before. Nobody's buying. Some of the best looking men I've ever seen walk these corridors. Sometimes I think *maybe in another time, under different circumstances* but then I quickly squash that notion. You never know what you're getting until the deal is done and you lead the rangy buckskin out of the corral on a knotted rope only to discover he's got foot thrush and strangles. Each man makes his way to the stainless steel counter, accepts his tray of slimy mystery meat and metallic-tasting macaroni salad, and then quickly claims a seat with arms huddled over his plate like a mutt guarding his bowl. Any time there is mass movement, the element of danger increases. The chow hall poses a particular problem for officers despite the effort to limit the mix of multiple units. Time and efficiency dictate that the two adjacent cafeterias be filled to capacity and cleared out in a systematic manner. The inmates are wary. Chow is one of the best times to carry out a hit or exact a quick shot of retaliation. The officers are outnumbered thirty to one at best. The bustle of big bodies getting up and down gives inmates ample time to pass kites of cryptic code messages from one gang member to another. Though no one likes to admit it, the only reason we get to leave here and go home to our families at the end of a shift is because the inmates allow us to. It would be nothing for them to take over a block.

The counselors are staggered along the four walls at intervals. We've been recruited by the Warden to join our brethren in blue as extra sets of seeing eyes. So we watch and wait and the inmates watch us. Like a middle-school staring contest, each one waits for the other to blink. Last year a mouthy counselor who regularly insulted the men in his caseload was sitting on top of one of the chrome tables with hands in his pockets gabbing with his boys. Minutes after E-block was ushered into the chow hall, an inmate with a grudge punched him violently off his perch and repeatedly pounded his head against the concrete wall. While the seriously injured staff member was heralded as a hero when he returned to work, everyone knew that it was premeditated payback on an asshole.

I claim my spot along the inside wall facing the windows to the north. The floors are a peculiar manure brown tile (a shade that was likely discontinued before I was born) and carry a film of grease that cannot be dispelled. We keep a special watch out for the 'slip-and-fall' inmates who fake an injury and instantly run to the phone to call their attorneys. A steel railing runs parallel to the walls and effectively forms a cattle chute that separates the animals from the herders. I nod and say an occasional hello, more to separate myself from the overtly hostile majority than to be courteous. If shit goes down in here, I'm betting on the fact that these guys in their hurry for revenge may just brush by those who have been decent to them.

The meal is uneventful for the first fifteen minutes; but suddenly there is an explosion of raised voices on the far side of the room. Two officers make a run in that direction and a scuffle begins. I leave my posted position and hurry over as a secondary responder. As I draw nearer, I recognize the irate convict. It's Mr. Noble-I-Am on a full head of steam. He apparently has thrown down his tray and splattered another man's trouser leg with a clump of spaghetti and meatballs. The guy on the receiving end of the assaultive pasta has squared off in a boxing stance and is ready to go. I approach the skirmish.

"I got it. I got this one," I announce loudly. "What's the problem here, Mr. Noble?" The man is a bull on a tether, inflamed by rage and intending to charge.

"I said no fucking meatballs," he yells.

"Okay, okay. No meatballs," I say, trying to placate him.

"I don't eat fucking pork. I'm a Muslim," he seethes.

"Muslim, my ass," says his sparring partner. "I seen you eating pork rinds on your bunk."

"Fuck you, man!" shouts Noble, shaking off the officers who are trying to pin his arms in an escort position. "I asked for goddamn common fare. I'm a vegetarian. And they give me this shit!'

"This can be corrected. Back down, Mr. Noble," I order firmly. A code has been called in to Control. I can hear the crackling signal reception on the radio.

"Hey brother, you're good," announces a fellow seated at the table to our far right. Mr. Zimmer is leaning back, assessing the situation with a quizzical grin. "These aren't meatballs, anyway. It's TVP. Textured vegetable protein. You don't think the government would feed us real meat, do you?"

"Huh?" Noble pauses to consider this information. His distrust of the system is greater than his distaste for the food. The slight moment of hesitation gives one guard time to pin him up against the wall and mace him before he regains the momentum to overpower them. He continues to thrash and cough, then quietly succumbs to their orders as the mucus begins to flow from his eyes, nostrils and mouth. They cuff him and begin a rough pat-down in case he has any crudely-fashioned weapon in his pocket. Out comes an apple, two slices of bread, and a fistful of sugar packets. Bingo! They've got him now. Caught red-handed stealing the ingredients needed to ferment a batch of Pruno in his foot locker. In ten days' time, they would have had a drunken brawl on their hands. As Noble continues to struggle, his shirt pulls out from under his elastic waist and out rolls a suspicious plastic cylinder. A rookie officer jumps to the rescue, believing he has just confiscated the rudimentary barrel of an intended bomb. He snaps up the object but stands foolishly holding a container of Adobo, the garlic-salt that can be ordered off commissary and is routinely shoved down prison briefs and bras in order to season the tasteless food.

"Can I have that?" asks Zimmer. "These meatballs taste like shit."

The sheepish officer throws him the spice. Although Noble is the kind of guy that is on every teacher's least wanted list, still it is sad to watch him get dragged from the room. This infraction will likely keep him sequestered in segregation long enough to miss out on the remaining groups. But in prison, nothing is guaranteed. Things can turn bad quickly. A promising morning can become a deadly day. It's pass or fail and not much in between.

#

Wednesday is money day. The inmates start forming a pecking order around the time the sun makes its first attempt to squeeze through the rectangular slats of impenetrable glass. They need to make certain that Auntie So-and-So was fed enough guilt to go wire in some Western Union cash. Since they are not allowed to congregate near the officer's post, they create an informal numbering system like a deli counter. This is serious business and any guy with balls big enough to circumvent the line might possibly get his cut. The name, Inmate Trust Account implies that some bleeding-heart philanthropist or wealthy relative bequeathed a large sum of money to their unfortunate kin. Ironically, there is absolutely no trust in the system they believe is shortchanging them for a pack of beef jerky or a bag of Skittles. It is pure capitalism within an undemocratic society. Those who have something have some clout. Money buys commissary and commissary equates to leveraging power. Guys with a full trunk of crap can buy friends and favors. Those that have next-to-nothing are indebted to everyone else. And just like our national welfare system, the indigent (or those who scam to be) are rewarded with free stuff and a shoe-in to a job. The one-dollar-and-thirty-five-cents-a-day salary bumps them quickly up the economic ladder. With that new position comes power and with power comes the entitlement to belittle those below. It's the American way on the inside too.

I bring up the computerized query and load the printer with paper. Next I print off a sizable stack of postage-free envelopes and hide them in my drawer. I check the bucket to see if there is an ample supply of courtesy care packages, the dollar-store freezer bag variety with pro bono products including deodorant that smells like oven cleaner, hotel-size shampoo, toothpaste, toothbrush and bar of soap. Something akin to the novelty samples provided at medium-fee hotels except these cosmetics are much more versatile as proven by the ingenious ways they can be used as ingredients in making art materials, illegal tender, sex toys and deadly weapons.

The work call sounds at eight o'clock which is the Wall Street signal inside the walls. The men drag plastic chairs from their cubes and slam them into place outside my door like a game of musical chairs on crack. First out of the blocks is Barrios, an illegal from Honduras. I usher him in and punch in his number. He has zero. Since he cannot understand English, I form a rounded circle with my fingers. Thumbs up from him. Out he goes with his envelopes and goodie bag. Next a new entry from the city jail. He hasn't yet established a steady residence where his people can send money. Our second winner. On the heels of his departure comes the blush-cheeked, red-haired country boy who's been in and out of my office the past four weeks with not a penny to show. His grandmother in Montana had promised to mail in a check, but to date, the well is still dry.

"Please, can I put in a call to my grandma?" he begs. He is super jittery and doesn't want to leave the room too quickly.

"Like I've told you, we're not approved to place personal calls. I can give you one envelope so you can write to her."

"You don't understand, Miss. I'm in debt. I owe some guys who lent me stuff." Problem is, I do understand. A kid like this is neck-deep in a barter system. He obviously has not been schooled in prison-style finance. There are no gifts in jail and absolutely nothing is for free. Eventually, the debt will be called in; if not in like currency, then it is exacted in flesh. I feel scared for him.

"What's your grandmother's name and number?" I ask. "Just in case she calls." I scribble the information he provides on a sticky note and send the terrified kid back out to the loan sharks with a few sheets of crisp new lined paper. Maybe that will buy him some time. When office hours are over, I'll call up Norma Braxton from Lodge Grass and encourage her to pass along an early birthday check.

"Morning, Mr. Wilson. Here to find out if you won the Mega Millions yet?" He smiles. "Let's see…."

"I've got nothing, right?" guesses the good-natured convict who's scrambled up ingenious ways to live on less than a dollar by stitching soap pouches out of cut-off sleeves and making picture frames from the foil lining of potato chip bags. In many ways, he's richer than most.

"No, it's better than that. You've got thirteen cents," I say cheerily. The joke's on him.

"Have a good day, Miss A," he replies amicably and sidles out of the stuffy office already getting thick with body heat. Just as the door swings shut, it flies back open in a fury. Tommy Pisano barges in huffing and puffing. He's bypassed the wait list, which can be enough to trigger a riot.

"I heard that Irish kid that was working for you left yesterday. I want his job," he demands. I consider my approach. Is it feasible to try and reason with him? Too many words will confound his simple mind but a brush-off is equally unwise.

"Mr. Pisano, I think there were others ahead of you," I say in an even-keeled tone. Tommy flings himself into the inmate chair and rubs a rough hand over his bald head. I can see little nicks where the barber pressed too hard. There is one noteworthy dent in the top of his skull and a bulging purple vein running on the bias across his temple.

"Fuck 'em. I need to talk you worser than they do," he insists. His ears begin to heat up to a hot pink.

"But it is my job to make sure everyone gets a turn to be heard," I reply. The rumbles of discontent are building towards an eventual crescendo.

"I need that job," he says.

"Mr. Pisano, you have two-hundred and seventy-seven dollars and fifty-nine cents in your account." I hand him a print-out as proof.

"That ain't dick," he squawks. I try to explain that the jobs are divvied out with certain criteria in mind; for example, if someone has been waiting a long time and if that person is broke. And whether that person is black or white or some other color. We can't have eight slots all filled by white people, it has to be racially balanced. Tommy doesn't make the cut on any of the three.

"That ain't fuckin' right. I'm a US of A citizen. These people aren't even from here," he fumes. Tommy's eyes are beginning to bulge and one knee jerks up and down in rapid-fire succession. His fuse is lit.

"Let's do this. I'll get you in the running for a dorm job. I believe we may have an opening in the bathroom next week," I suggest with a smile. I'm ready to take the next customer, but Tommy has blown a gasket. His first victim is the blue plastic chair that skitters onto its side as he bolts upright.

"I KNOW you don't like me," he screams. Froth bubbles from the corner of his chapped lips. "You think I'm good for nothing but mopping up piss? You think I can't figure out how to hand out mail better than that fuck-tard? You expect me to live out there with all those freaks and jerk-offs and be happy doin' nuthin'? I want to go back to a Level Four. If I stay here, I'll pound someone and..."

"I never said I didn't like you, Mr. Pisano," I say softly, interrupting his rant. "Ever hear the saying, Get angry and you'll make the best speech you'll ever regret?"

"Huh?"

"Never mind. How would you like to give me a little help in my class?"

"I can't sit in a room with a bunch of other dudes. You know that by now. It fucks up my nerves."

"You don't have to attend the class. Just help me out before and after handing out papers and collecting homework. You can erase the board, sharpen pencils, and help me move the TV. Stuff like that."

Tommy looks at me, dumbfounded. He sticks a thick finger in one ear and swabs it around as if a clump of earwax has distorted his hearing. He swipes his mouth with his sleeve. He leans a shoulder up against the wall, crosses one leg over the other, bites his lip and takes stock of the situation as if he's got a million other offers on the table.

"I can't pay you for that, though. It would be strictly as a peer mentor." He squints his eyes and looks suspicious. "You know, a volunteer," I add.

"Yeah, I'd do that," agrees Tommy.

"Alright. I'll add you to the list. You can start on Wednesday."

"Thank you, Miss A. You think I could have a few envelopes?" he asks sweetly.

"Tommy, you have almost three hundred dollars in your account. You think you could order some next time around?" His face screws up with irritation and I can see another storm brewing. "Okay, raise your right hand!" He looks at me as if I'm the one that's got impulse control disorder.

"Just do it!" I repeat. "Pretend we're in court." Tommy lifts his hand up, palm forward.

"Repeat after me. I promise I will order envelopes and not harass my counselor anymore." He repeats the pledge word for word with a comical grin on his face.

"Okay. I'm hooking you up this one last time. We're good then?" I look over his shoulder at the sound of the milling crowd outside the door, a subtle social cue that he has been dismissed.

"One thing, Ms Abrams. If this was real court, I would have spit on you like I did to my public defender last time I was in the trap." I am tempted to laugh, but he's telling the God's honest truth. He's in this bid for assault on his attorney.

"I'm plenty impressed, Mr. Pisano. Case closed." I say. He likes the analogy and slaps the bookcase with hearty approval. A stack of visiting applications slips off the top shelf and slides to the floor in a randomly collated pile of Spanish and English versions.

"Fuck me," he says, but the new Tommy drops down on his knees and gathers them in a bunch.

#

This isn't like regular jury duty. There will be no judge. Noble has named me as his disciplinary advocate and also a first-hand witness to the incident that led to his ticket and pending sanctions. I am required to offer him an objective interview during which he can relate his version of the story and make a plea. This must be done within forty-eight hours of notification. Better to get it over and done with. In my limited experience, a face-to-face with Mr. I-AM is not something you look forward to.

The RHU, or Restricted Housing Unit, is sealed off from General Pop by a double set of jailhouse gates and an impenetrable locked door. Two officers escort me into the corridor that is a narrow squeeze along open-faced cells with heavy iron bars. Inmates wear bright red jumpsuits to distinguish their level of danger. Some are sprawled on the concrete floor so they can stretch their skin out on the cool concrete. Others look blankly up from flimsy-thin cot mattresses stripped of sheets. The heat is stifling in here. The interview room, which is down on the right hand side directly across from the Disciplinary Office, contains only two beat-up chairs and a table. Officer One ushers me into the seat closest to the door.

"You never want to be backed into the corner if shit goes down in here," he says matter-of-factly. He's just hoping that some shit will go off so he can practice the new defense moves he learned in behavior management training. I put my notepad and pen on the table and smile weakly.

"We'll go get the shitbag," says Officer Two and disappears out the door. I wait in the eerie silence. I expect guys down in the hole to be shouting crazy demands to have the governor brought in for a face-to-face chat or to be busy spackling the wall with feces in a do-it-yourself redecorating project. That's what happens in all the prison movies, but not so here. There's a palpable sense that everyone has just given up, laid down the fight and is curled around their own hopelessness A good ten minutes passes before there is the sound of scuffed slippers and the smooth shuffle of chain. Noble steps into the doorway, wrists cuffed and ankles shackled to another cumbersome chain that restricts the distance between hands and feet. Movement is difficult. A man this size is forced to hunch over at the shoulders and cow before his captors. They could twist Noble into a contorted human braid, padlock him limb to limb and still nothing would bend his pride.

"Take your seat!" orders Officer One. Noble lowers himself into the plastic chair.

"Drop your hands!" barks Officer Two. Noble complies and the hostile guard undoes the bottom end of the connecting chain and fastens the last link to an iron loop on the floor. The two guards step out and grant his right to privacy with counsel, but it's a formality, really. The verdict is already stamped in the minds of the State before any proceedings take place. Noble looks weary. Who knows what torment he's endured or inflicted in the darkness of this closed kennel?

"How are you faring?" I ask.

"I've been down here before," he replies.

"We miss you in class," I tell him. Noble regards me with a curious indifference. The resentment he carries is like slow-burning acid that etches holes from the inside out. Whatever good medicinal tonic is poured into this man seems to leach out through his pores.

"Do you want to stay in the group?" I ask. Noble shrugs. He doesn't expect me to care; in fact, he assumes he's already a black mark drawn in a straight line across my attendance sheet.

"I'm dead serious. I want to know what you want."

"I thought this meeting was about my ticket. Aren't you supposed to be trying to get me out of here? You're my advocate," he snarls. Noble lowers his head in defense, visibly bristling like a Tibetan Mastiff that's held on a short length of heavy-duty chain and for good reason.

"Yes, I am. I am building an argument on your behalf," I reply.

"So, are you going to tell them I'm not guilty?"

"No and neither are you. You're guilty as shit. If you cry innocent, they're going to slap you with the maximum loss of privileges. You know that. So you're going to plead guilty because that's owning up to your actions and at the same time, it makes them feel justified in what they did."

"And how does that help me?" Noble hisses. He's probably regretting his choice of legal representation about now. He's thinking that even the shitty public defender that cost him his case would have summoned up more false concern.

"I'm going to write a strong recommendation that you be moved out of here and into the ticket block contingent on the stipulation that you complete my program and an additional session of Cage Your Rage. My argument is simply this: Further restrictions and confinement without providing opportunity for rehabilitation will put you at greater risk of violent outbursts and is therefore a liability in terms of staff safety."

"What the fuck does all that mean?" he demands.

"In other words, they need to cover their own asses and show that we as a Department took positive steps towards addressing your anger problem. Otherwise, if you blow off out there and someone gets seriously hurt or killed, the public is going to demand an answer. And the first thing that happens is that they'll trace your history right back here to Hazen, pull your file and see who was to blame for not addressing the issue. Does that make sense?"

"Sort of, "Noble says. "Cover your ass, right?"

"Pretty much. So tell me. Are you serious about getting anything out of the class?"

"I'll keep it one hunnit. I'm only there because I have to be, but I have learned a lot by listening to the others."

"Will you commit to participate if I can get you back in? You are an intelligent man with a lot of wisdom to offer. In here, street smarts count over book smarts. You've got forty-three years of living behind you. You must have learned something along the way."

"Yeah, but I fucked up most of that," he admits. That's the closest thing to a confession that will ever come from this formidable man.

"Listen, figuring out what you *don't* want in life is equally as important as knowing what you *do* want. If you can eliminate the wrong decisions, then you're that much closer to answering what is right. Mistakes have a long memory." He looks confused. I decide not to press the philosophical points here. "Then, are we good? You'll plead guilty and I'll write up my report that will be read at your hearing."

"Yeah, we straight," he replies. There can be no gentleman's handshake here but we both know that a man's honor rides on his credibility, especially in the street where going back on one's word might mean a bullet in the back. Noble has given me his pledge. I will hold him to it.

"All set!" I wave to the officers who immediately come to free the accused and maneuver his big body out the door, one at each elbow in a slow tango back to his cell.

#

The following Tuesday, Noble is back in his seat, the fourth desk down on the far side of the room. The other guys give him fist bumps and shoulder slaps. In their limited assessment of the situation, it appears that another one of their own has beaten the system. He and I exchange a knowing look, one that contains gratitude and complicity. The thirty day loss of phone, visits and commissary are worth the measure of a man. He gets to keep his Rec time; I get to keep his respect.

CHAPTER 9
CRAZY BITCHES

"Good morning, gentlemen. Today we are on lesson ten. We're going to talk about where anger comes from. Is it through nature or nurture? In other words, are we born with it or do we learn it through our environment? Are people predisposed to hate or do they acquire it as they grow up and are rooted in bitterness? What factors contribute to....." and just then the Locke mower fires up right underneath the classroom window. A barrel of gasoline smoke drifts in as the engine throttles. The grounds crew begins its sweep of the lawns between the chapel and the school wing. With a whole hundred acres of state property to be hacked down, I wonder how imperative it is to carve up the perimeter of mealy weeds along the wall where the teachers are just beginning their lessons. It's meditated sabotage, a more devious way to try and silence a message the custody staff does not subscribe to. 'Hugging thugs' is not the Hazen way, though ironically the agency's stated mission promotes enthusiastic and successful reintegration of its offenders. I stop trying to talk above the background noise while the machine idles just outside our room. Finally the piece of lawn equipment jerks into gear, takes up forward momentum and crawls down the length of the building, eventually carving out a right-angle turn before it heads out over open ground towards the fence line.

"As I was saying, what factors contribute to us resorting to anger as a way to solve problems?" I ask.

"We're born with it," says Serge. "Think about it. Babies are selfish people. If left alone to raise themselves, they'd be ruthless little bastards. That's why we gotta discipline kids to get them to conform to society's way of thinking." Mr. Magrini speaks from experience. He was thoroughly schooled in the violent culture of organized crime. By the age of ten, a succession of backhands to the head had primed him. At fifteen, he had wholeheartedly subscribed to a charter of violence and lifetime loyalty.

"I agree, man. I friend of mine was brought up all Christiany and shit. His Pops was a pastor. None of those kids were allowed to do nuthin'. It was like, Get up, we got to go to church. They had no choice. They'd probably be running after money and cars and girls like men do. And check this out. One of 'em doin' base now and two are incarcerated. I mean, what the fuck? Maybe their Pop was a hot-ass when he was younger. He gotta be cuz he had two kids outside his own family. He sure ain't perfect," Ortega says.

"Don't drag religion into this. The church wasn't at fault. It was the sins of the father," Rev states coldly.

"Lissen, he's keeping it real. Even religious people have fucked-up kids," says Euclid. The men from the islands, the Dominicans and Puerto Ricans who have never heard of Hillary Clinton already understand it takes more than a village to raise a child. It takes a barrio full.

"If I got in trouble at school, the principal would whoop me and send me home," Euclid said. He tells the class how in San Juan, discipline was everyone's business. As he walked home in shame after being suspended, the aunt got the first whack in and then her cousin followed by an unemployed uncle or two. The fiercest barrage was dealt by the dominant grandmother who whipped him with a ficus switch until her fatty underarms were sore and then made him kneel on beds of rice with buckets of water suspended in his hands. And finally, when Moms arrived home from market, she dealt the final blows. The women were the ones that wielded the stick. But for all that corporal suffering, once the lamps were wicked out and the door to his bedroom locked, young Ortega was out the window and into the streets again.

"Did you come away from that experience feeling that it was discipline to help shape you or did it feel like abuse? Let me clarify, I'm not bashing anyone's parents here. No judgment, but I'm curious to know how you feel about it now you're looking back."

"Sure it was abusive, but our moms did it out of love. That's all they knew." I can visualize these stocky women in black scarves wading through a herd of milking goats to get at the little scoundrel. My heart breaks for the little boys who thought the welts from flailing extension cords were the norm, along with the beatings for truancy that followed a week long absence from school while they were kept out waiting for their bruises to simmer down.

"Miss, you come from an abusive home?" Ortega asks. As a rule, I never reveal anything about my personal life. The true answer to his question is so out of context, it would be ridiculous to even suggest that non-communication and a flick on the bare thigh with a plastic flyswatter could fall in the same category. I smile and shake my head. As hard it is, we keep going, wading deeper into the murky world where violence evolves like a tadpole out of mud, sprouting limbs and becoming an angry man. It is a process prompted by genes and chromosomes and spurred to completion by a defective environment. If that half-formed creature had sucked up out of the rocky ground in Gust Harbor, Maine rather than a ratty quarter-acre of dusty sand worn down by pit bulls on chains, the worst he might have endured was the loss of a couple dollars allowance.

Tommy has had his hand raised for the past five minutes. My guess is that Tommy never progressed much farther than grammar school, but at least he had come away with one of its basic principles. He is the only one in the group who has grasped hold of this elementary courtesy; that is at least until someone pushes his trigger and that hand drops like a boom on their skulls. He doesn't show up to class every session and he doesn't always stay the full ninety minutes. It's an impressive fact that Mr. Pisano has the desire to come at all without any mandate to do so and given his heightened levels of anxiety and agitation.

"Yes, please. Go ahead," I say, acknowledging his adherence to etiquette.

"If you axe me, the first thing a baby gets is a heapin' whack on the ass and it starts hollerin' back. The doctor's the first person made him mad. And then baby goes on home and he don't get what he needs, he's pissed as hell and figgers out that pipin' up loud gets people to pay him notice."

The conversation that ropes around the room is priceless. Here are grown men, many of whom have fathered batches of kids with who-knows-who, trying to describe the miracle of parenthood from their far-removed perspective. For many, it boils down to two roles in this fathering act. The first as the initial fertilizer spreader that often requires a paternity stamp of approval since there is more than reasonable doubt on the source of the seed. And in the second act, he becomes the collections-dodger when the child support enforcement paperwork starts streaming in. Yet deep in their hearts they mean well. It's not all bullshit and bluffing. There often is genuine attachment to the idea of being the father they have never been or had. It is a badge of manhood to produce as many children as possible regardless of relationship status. Part of their purpose is to impregnate women who welcome another swollen uterus and crying mouth to feed. It ties them together as "family." She now has the right to demand that he come to her bed periodically and bring money for the kids, and he has created a network of stopovers where he can escape nagging bitches or the police. It is an extended web of loosely-affiliated parents legitimized not by town hall or a Justice of the Peace, but by the church of conjugal union.

"Me and my baby mama make sure the kids is sleeping in the other room when we fight. That way, they don't hear nuthin'," Dent pipes up. He is visibly proud of the good psychology he is practicing on his offspring. Ten kids in a kitty-littered, TV-besieged three-decker apartment all crammed into the back bedroom when he starts throwing the Rent-A-Center dining set against the sheetrock walls.

"Don't be so sure about that," I reply. "Do you really think kids sleep through all that yelling and chaos? They probably have their ears to the wall, don't you think?" Dent reconsiders his statement.

"When we watched a horror flick, we used to make Serge Junior sit behind the couch and cover his eyes so he didn't watch shit he shouldn't see," says Serge Senior. A noble move he believes until I draw the pyramid diagram on the chalkboard and divide it up into thirds in order to illustrate how children absorb data. The tip-top sliver, the smallest portion represents what children see; the medium–sized segment in the middle is the amount that they hear and the remaining base of the figure, the majority of space, indicates what kids sense by awareness. This graphic always seems to work. It hadn't occurred to them that what is out of sight is not necessarily out of mind.

"Listen, your kid behind the couch is hearing horrible shrieking and monstrous noises. He can't see what's going on so his brain imagines it. And what his brain is picturing may be far more disturbing than what's actually happening. Kids are very tuned in to their environment. They are aware of a lot. Don't underestimate them," I urge.

For a brief moment, Serge analyzes his parental techniques based on this new knowledge; but then recalls his son is now twenty-seven years old and whatever he eavesdropped on from behind that mangy couch, be it chainsaw massacres, bloody shoot-outs or perhaps even bump-and-grind sex; well, it is too late. He can't know for sure, since his son doesn't speak to him anymore but he'd have to remember to make an extra confession for that now. The room is heavy with serious thought. Not even Zimmer dares to break the mood with his dry comedy. Finally, Serge raises a hand. I give him a nod. Our indelible talking stick has long been missing, lost to thieves or looted by stingy teachers.

"I just want to say, I'm not going to blame my parents anymore. They did what they thought was right. I'm the piece of shit. I physically put my hands on my girl. I was the one that let my anger sink in. I chose to hurt her."

"I respect your honesty, Serge. Thank you for sharing."

It's like giving one child a Tootsie-Pop in front of all the others who then instantly reach with hands out. They want what he got and will scramble harder and faster next time to get it. Whether the motive is the reward of respect or a better report card, the result is the same.

#

"There ain't any good women left in the world. They're all crazy bitches. Excuse my language, Miss A," says Dent. He should know. He's been embroiled in four marriages already.

"That's why the only bitch in my life is my pup, Cricket," laughs Zimmer. This part of the curriculum is usually where the pot gets stirred and emotions heat up. These embattled souls launch a weak defense of their gender as we begin to dabble in the area of healthy relationships. According to their claims, every female in greater Boston is bi-polar, which if validated by a clinical study, is information that should be passed on to the makers of Lithium and Lamictal. Cries of foul play go up on every front.

"Yeah, she called the cops and had my car towed." Willis insists.

"She threw all my shit out the window into the snow and made me go pick it up," Zimmer whines.

"She wigged out and slashed my tires," Euclid reports.

"She bugged and stole my crack," Noble hisses. One would think these she-devils possess supernatural power that can be beamed across miles and through concrete walls to make tough men with spines of steel do things they never would have if *she* hadn't made them; including going back to her over and over despite the torment. Of course, the offenders see no harm in the fact that they were sleeping with their sisters-in-law and wife's best friend or lounging on their other baby mama's couch. Cheating is what men do when pushed by bad women. Samsung and Apple must be delighted with all the relationship dysfunction out there. One wrong text message or nude selfie and suddenly, the mobile devices are skidding across highways, getting stomped, flushed, and flung. Followed by an order for a new phone. Conflict resolution is without question the most sorely lacking skill in this socio-economic group.

"So, I don't get it. Why are you with this woman if she is so bad to you?"

"I got with her cuz she like to eat and I figured she was a good cook and all, and I'd come home off the streets hungry as hell expecting a meal on the table and she'd have ordered up Burger King and shit. Dumb broad! I told her, it's your fault. You didn't go to the gym and now you're all fat," Tommy shouts.

"Okay, tell me if I'm wrong," I say. "You come home from working real hard all shift and your girl is sitting there waiting. You ask that harmless question: How are you? And off she goes about her bad day. Talk, talk, talk. After awhile, it's not even about the original issue. Now she's blabbering about her family, her girlfriends, her bad hair and chipped nail polish and on and on and on. Am I right?" Heads are bobbing in universal agreement.

"And you're sitting there thinking, I don't care about all these details. Just cut to the chase and give me the bottom line," I continue.

"Yes, true story. All's we want is for her to hurry up and tell us what's broken so we can figure how to fix the fucking problem and get back to our game of cards," Dent states.

"Okay, have any of you ever heard of the book *Men are from Mars, Women are from Venus*? It's an old-school self help book from the 90's but some of the truths in there are really good. It's about how men and women each look at the world and approach their problems from different angles. Neither one is right or wrong; it's just different perspectives. Let me give you an example. The husband comes home and asks his wife what's wrong. And she says she had a shitty day. She then proceeds to list all the things that irritated her over the past eight hours. Her spouse is thinking, How can I fix that and possibly make her happier? He needs to go think this over so he heads into that mental man-cave to sort things out. The wife thinks all he wants to do is get away from me. He's not talking so he's not listening and doesn't care. She follows on his heels, nipping and nagging and saying, We need to talk about this. Sound familiar to any of you?"

"Right on the money. That's my life exactly. She just won't drop it. After awhile, I block it out and all I hear is blasé, blasé, blah," Willis says.

"So, here's my point. Men need to realize that talking is a woman's therapy. She needs to vent her anxieties and frustrations with him, with her mother, with her sister and anyone else within earshot. This is how she makes herself feel better. On the other hand, a woman needs to recognize that her man is generally much more black and white. Tell me what's broken and I'll fix it. He needs to go off and ponder his options in the privacy of his own mind. This is not him rejecting her or keeping her at arm's length. It is just his natural way of tackling problems."

"That's so true. But I can't figger these broads out for nuthin.' Seems we always end up in each other's faces yellin' and shit,'" says Ortega.

"So let's move on to arguments. Are they part of every relationship? Should they be? Is it good for a couple to have fights, do you think?"

"Well, we men think from the hip down, ya feel me? Them arguments be good for some great make-up sex," says Noble. I pretend I didn't hear that comment and keep pressing onward.

"So what's the difference between a discussion, a debate, an argument or a fight? How would you define these terms? Or are they same?" This interactive dialogue lights up their interest. The men begin to debate over the definition and their voices elevate up a notch.

"A debate is an argument. Like what lawyers or politicians do," says Bowman.

"Nah, it's the same thing," insists Dent.

"No, man. They be different. An argument is like a fight," yells Serge. And pretty soon they are arguing over what a fight is. They catch me smiling and realize they've fallen into the trap. They are role players in a human drama.

"Okay, since we can't agree, give me some rules for a fair fight," I say. "Just call some out if you can think of any."

"Don't interrupt," Rev says, the king of intruding into other people's conversations.

"Don't talk over the other person," Bowman says. Willis and Serge are busy in a conversation of their own in the corner.

"Guys, hold up a minute. Give some respect here," I demand. The two men swing back around to full attention.

"Sorry, Mizz Abrams," they say in unison, as if their apology was choreographed in case they got caught.

"Don't call each other names?" Serge guesses. I nod in approval. Dent lets out a prolonged and deliberate belch before the older man has finished his sentence. "Say excuse me, you ass clown!" says Serge. Dent smirks and says nothing. He's obviously well pleased with getting the attention his poor manners aroused.

"Yes, what else?" I ask, trying to steer the two back to the topic.

"Take a time out," Zimmer suggests.

"Use 'I' statements," says Gemini.

"Agree to disagree." They know this stuff already.

"I try to walk away but she won't let me," says Dent. "She stands in front of the door and throws shit at me."

"Then who's the real pussy?" mumbles Noble, hoping to keep his comment out of range from the teacher's ears. I choose to ignore it. Pick your battles is another item on the list yet to be mentioned. It just isn't worth tangling over this one little remark.

"Okay, so then what? How did you handle that interference?" I ask Mr. Dent.

"I push her out of the way. It's her fault if any shit goes down after that."

I've got them roiling around like carp in shallow water, all flipping and folding over each other in a slippery struggle to feed on the morsels of bread, the manna I'm about to drop. Time to yank up the net.

"Has it ever occurred to you that maybe you're with the wrong person? That your relationship is totally toxic? Some things are just not worth fixing. You guys deserve to be treated better and so does your intimate partner. I'm talking to you all now. We only have this side of the story and that's the only one I want to focus on from this moment forwards. Time to man up now. You were men when you did your crimes; no crying like little girls now. I don't care if she pushed your buttons to the point of sheer madness, you have control over what you do. I want you to go back to your cells and write about your part in the violence and the abuse and what you could have done differently. And what you will do differently when you go back out. I don't care if it takes five hundred words or five sentences. I want you to put your heart into this."

The men sit quietly for a moment. I've caught them off-guard. They realize now that they took the bait without thinking and ran with it. And I popped the reel open and let them go just far enough until they were snagged on their own fibs. Too puny still, I drop them back into the undercurrent of blame to see who will sink and who will flutter momentarily and then set about swimming upright again.

#

Brennerman falls into step a few paces behind me after I pass by the supply closet where he lingers and then pulls up gradually alongside with his monologue well underway. One might mistake him for a stalker or a former creeper if they had never taken the time to stop and listen to the fine thoughts inside this nebbish little man's brain.

"Hey, Doctor," I say cordially once his battered loafers come into view on my right.

"Greetings, Counselor Abrams. Have you heard the update?" he asks.

"No! Any good news?" I ask.

"Two weeks after our initial conversation, Mr. Willis was seen by the Chief Psychiatrist and then his case was passed on to the Special Assessment Review Board. Their recommendation corroborated our belief that nine-year old Terran was unfairly processed and pressured by police. Nowhere on record was there any solid evidence of a sexual crime. So they concluded that it was both illogical and illegal to arrest a man for failure to register as a sex offender when he clearly wasn't one. While his controlling offense stands and there is no intent to erase any of his past charges, the Hearing Review Board removed the onus of this particularly heinous label and lowered his Sex Treatment score from a 3 to a 1. In all my thirty-five years of practice here within the DOC, I have never seen this kind of retraction. This is a testament to Mr. Willis's character and composure, and his patient pursuit to right a grievous wrong. I commend him for the excellence with which he handled himself," he gushes.

"I am so pleased. It gives me hope and restored belief in a system that can acknowledge making a mistake and then correct it. It's rare in here to see an injustice rectified," I reply. The victory is his; the reward is mine.

#

As expected, no one volunteers to go first. I look around the room and see that each man, except Zimmer and Bowman, has several sheets of notebook paper on the desk in front of him. The quantity is there, but the quality of the content is yet to be revealed.

"So, who's gonna lead off?" I repeat. Mr. Monopoly spots his opening and jumps up. Rev is in his early forties, a man of medium height and build with charismatic hazel-colored eyes and short cropped brown hair with streaks of white. He might even have been considered good-looking if it wasn't for the wedge-like, rodent shape to his face which started wide at the ears and ran a narrow angle down to a blunt snout. His bristling, aggressive approach is reminiscent of a badger. His limbs are stringy, his movements jumpy. No doubt his mind is brilliant but it comes with the cunning of his species.

"Allow me," he says in that ingratiating whine. Bowman shrugs in frustration. Zimmer rolls his eyes. They've heard this unsolicited tale twice before, we all have, about the woes and pressure of having to care for a terminally ill spouse and the post-traumatic stress from his exposure to the military as both the son of a veteran and a soldier himself. That hard line of tough love proved to be the tipping point; after which the depression settled in and curbed his activities to laps paced around his living room. The drawn blinds and fistfuls of tranquilizers helped to calm his nerves. Though he claims to never have laid a hand on his wife of twenty-eight years, Rev now sees in retrospect how his tight rein on his home and his angry mouth had caused real upset in his family. Once the cries of bullshit and liar go up and challenge his truthfulness, Rev's tune changes slightly and then it's swear-to-God only that single slap one time. After all, he loves his wife. It is all nicely packaged in the past tense as the man he used to be.

"You, too can change, my friends. I took this class voluntarily because I knew I could improve. This is my fourth time going through this program and each time, I learn more about myself and how I can help others with my story," he says, gesturing earnestly at the band of Neanderthals that strike their women as habit. The men are neither fooled nor convinced by his sermon. They are doubters, skeptics. Most of all, they find him irritating as hell.

Dent is the next to man to take to his feet and run his play pattern. Humor is his tactic and his unique delivery is personified in the ridiculous.

His belly swells above the elastic waistline of the baggy pants that fall short of his ankles by six inches. A stubble of reddish hair ranges in erratic patches on his scalp, cheekbones and double chin. His blue eyes sparkle with good nature but his words describe actions that are very dark. He recounts how he was convinced that his third wife was cheating on him with the garbage collector, so he went down to the guy's house, abducted him at gunpoint, and drove him down to the salvage yard. Though the man pleaded for mercy, Dent forced him in the back of one of the garbage trucks with the hydraulic gate that lowers down, pulls up all the refuse and dumps it into the well where it is crushed. Dent had his hand on the lever, lowering it inch by inch, demanding that the guy confess his guilt and apologize. Say seven Sweet Mary, mother of Gods and when his slow torture had exacted an adequate confession, he stopped the mechanism but left the man trapped in the garbage overnight. The sanitation crew found him there the next morning covered in coffee grinds and grapefruit peels, but alive. Dent was not a bit remorseful for what he had done and if given the same circumstances, he would do it over again. The difference being, next time he'd use one of the newer, efficient compacters and never push the kill switch.

"I respect your honesty," I say.

"No prob, Mizz A. I tell is like it is," says Dent proudly.

Gemini sashays to the front of the classroom and distributes his weight to one side so that the line of his hips is more noticeable. He pushes back a few strands of hair that have fallen out of his bun. His tale is long-winded and circuitous, much like that of a woman who thinks in a circle rather than a straight line like his peers. He truly is a beautiful she-boy with a sensual, theatrical quality. Gemini catches a lot of flak for the sexual confusion his presence engenders, but he also catches a lot of action back in the block. He articulates about how needy he was as a young man, how the neglect of his family drove him to prostitution and drugs and the bitch-slap, drag-out fights he had with his lover. While sad and true, his story lacks the requisite brutality that his long sentence would indicate.

Serge has his assignment in hand but prefers to just talk straight from his heart and memory. This man looms above his peers by a good seven inches or so. He has a curly shock of coarse hair and a thick build honed down to pure knotted muscle. His head is large but the circumference seems to have outpaced the size of the brain it conceals. The thought of being the object of this man's rage is more than sobering. Serge details the night of his incident when he and his girlfriend were arguing and drinking. She pulled a knife and stabbed him in the shoulder which made him stumble back and put his hand through the glass pane on the door. The sight of his own blood and the searing pain made him see red. After that, he remembers beating her first with his fists and then a wooden walking stick, pulling the whole china closet down on top of her, and finally dragging her out into the slushy snow where he dropped her bloodied, huddled form on the driveway. Serge had his key in the ignition of his SUV and fully intended to run her over, but a passing snow plow sent up a shower of sparks that illuminated her unconscious body. The emergency call was made and the ambulance whisked away a critically injured patient. Initial triage confirmed two fractured orbital sockets, broken cheekbones, nose and jaw, multiple rib fractures, a punctured lung, ruptured spleen and dislocated shoulder. He had stopped just short of killing her and that one measure of self-control was the difference between fourteen years and the rest of his life behind bars. His confession was a brutal forthcoming without excuses.

"Well done, Serge. I'm sure that was difficult to do," I say. My stomach bubbles with slight queasiness. Not much shocks me these days but this story is particularly disturbing.

"It's taken me over twelve years to be able to put this incident into words," Serge says.

"Amen," says Willis.

"Would you like to share yours, Mr. Willis?" I ask.

"If you don't mind, Miss Abrams, I'd rather hand this in and have you read it in private," he replies.

"The purpose of this exercise is to share it with the others. Everyone is equally vulnerable. If you can't do it here in safety, how are you to make any kind of real amends to others?" I ask. Willis has never struck me as a self-conscious type, but he continues to shake his head and digs in.

"Believe it or not, I was the deathly-shy girl in school who would rather take an "F" on an oral report than speak in front of others. I'd be in the girls' lav about to be piss my pants, I was so nervous."

"No shit. For real, Mizz Abrams?"

"True story, Mr. Ortega. So it isn't my natural style to force others to do what they're not comfortable doing. I get it. There's a lot to risk by revealing oneself in here. But if I let one guy off the hook, I'd have to do the same for the rest."

"No, Mizz Abrams. I can't. You gotta trust me on this," says Willis. Rather than bog down the others, I choose to move on.

"Who else?" I ask. Bowman and Ortega each blurt out a handful of half-hearted sentences that sound awfully alike. The two youngest members of the group are still playing the blame-game and offer cliché claims on how they want to change their lives without any convincing substance behind them.

"Good enough. We have time for one more. Mr. Zimmer? You always love to tell a story. What do you have for us?" The elder shrugs and pulls a little standing wheelie with his chair. The men applaud.

"I'm not angry and I've never been violent. I ran a little scam with prescription drugs. Passed bad checks and did quite well by it. I've got all the shit. You know flat screen TV, Bose sound system, Nintendo, a tablet. Cricket has more bling than any rapper on the block. I'm pretty bad-ass for an old fart and maybe by the next class, I'll show you my moon-walk, if I can get out of this bitch."

The first bell goes off for recall. The class across the way begins to file out into the hall, cursing and creating a real distraction to our heart-to-heart. A horizontal tear of lightning streaks across the dark sky and deepens in bold contrast to the white watch tower on the hill.

"Listen, whoever didn't read their paper or felt they couldn't, please make sure your name is on it and hand them in. As I said on day one, you will be evaluated on participation, written work, attitude, attendance and your credibility in taking responsibility for your actions."

"What if we were willing to tell our stories out loud to you in private, but not in front of the group?" asks Euclid

"I would entertain that idea. Time permitting."

"Counselor, that stack of papers in front of you, are those our certificates?"

"No, we still have two more sessions before you are finished. These are your police reports," I answer.

"We're fucked," announces Dent. Instantly, some of the men grow pale and shudder. Their versions don't even remotely sound like the facts; instead, they've submitted some sensational tales that make good fodder for Lifetime movie scripts.

"Hey, Mizz. I just realized there's a lot of spelling errors on mine. And I crossed out a lot of words. It's pretty messy. Can I re-do it and hand it in tomorrow?"

"Sure, Ortega." I hand the writing papers back to him. What a man won't do for a little gold star on an otherwise black report card.

#

Business is slow today. I've called for at least six guys from the bottom tier who are out roaming the first level for inside recreation, but not a one has showed.

"Damnit, I've got to get this shit signed," I say out loud. "What the devil is the hold-up?" I step out onto the tier and look both ways for oncoming foot traffic. No one in sight. Down below on the bottom floor there seems to be a jam by the stairs. Tommy's got his big bulk planted on the first step and has created an effective wedge. He's jawing at the other inmates who are trying to make their way up to the counselor's cubicle. *What did I do?* In my haste to help, I've created an even bigger browbeater. My nod of confidence to Tommy Pisano gave him the attention he'd been hammering for but not the diplomacy to handle it. In a brain that is chemically wired to be borderline, paranoid, antisocial and delusional all in a span of a few hours, the absence of an official title left the door wide open for his own interpretation. Tommy had appointed himself as watchman, body guard, advisor, intelligence agent, bouncer, deal closer and BFF depending on what he saw fit at the moment. Obviously he had made it his business to keep an eagle eye on the comings and goings in the counselor's office and he wasn't in the mood to play nice or let anyone else play at all. I'd have to deal with him later.

A healthy portion of the inmates were herded outside to do planks, dips off the weight stand or solitary laps around the pavement court with headphones on. Many of those remaining in the unit are resting or waiting for the return to work call. I lift my radio and buzz a signal to Boozer who is on duty at the desk. I can see him from the small opening in the door. He takes his sweet time, swinging his jackboots down off the desk and reaching around to push the call button on radio 36.

"What up?" he says casually.

"Can you pop Mr. Willis? Cell 215, please."

"Anything you want, sweetheart!" he says, the same line he uses on every female he encounters, be it young or old, homely or hot. As long as the female parts are proportionately in place, Boozer will hit on it. It takes much longer than it should to walk to the panel and jimmy the levers that disengage the cell door. Willis finally emerges in the doorway. The whole process has taken a good fifteen minutes which is just fine with the officer who doesn't give a good goddamn if the inmate ever makes it there at all. It's just another complication to his otherwise mind-numbing routine of sitting and sitting some more.

"Come in," I offer. "I thought this might be a good time to do your presentation. I should have told you to bring it along when I called you down." I'm always struck by how well African-Americans age. Willis's face is devoid of creases or wrinkles. The lack of sun exposure over years of being kept indoors is a better remedy than any Botox injection. He would be readily carded at a liquor store. I know his true age by the information on the offender face sheet. He's just shy of three years older than I am. All of the demographics are within easy touch on a computer screen such as height, weight, age, race, and religion, all the data that categorizes and distinguishes us one from another.

"I don't need to refer to my paper. I can just speak from the heart" he says. Humility is a rare virtue in a place where pride equates to power and protection. I can see it in this man, in the slope of his shoulders and the angle of his body as he adjusts his size into a more comfortable position. He's humble; not a broken man, but one who has bent of his own accord. Willis folds his over-sized hands in his lap and looks me directly without blinking or looking away.

"That's fine," I say.

"Well, Ms. Abrams, I am not here to talk about what I've been convicted of and punished for. I've done my time for those charges. To the best of my ability, I have tried to make restitution to those I have harmed. Some of that still remains to be done when I am released, but I've been trying for years. Mostly reaching out to those who will still communicate. Many of the bridges are too far burned, but I made peace with my God when I hit a dead-end." *Not another one*, I think. If I had a dollar for every crook turned theologian, I could have erected a small church in Haiti for future Jesus freaks.

"So tell me a little about what brought you here," I reply.

"Unlawful Restraint and Risk of Injury," Willis states.

"Yes, but I'm more interested in the why's and what- ifs involved."

"It's not really what it appears like on paper. My wife knew what I was up to as far as selling dope, but I kept her out of my work on the streets. Didn't tell her what I was up to on the daily. I'd just go out and take care of business and bring home the money. She knew there was a gun in a shoebox and another stuffed with cash in the closet. She was well taken care of, she and her kids. But one day she gets sick of the life and wants me out. Goes to the police for a restraining order claiming I been threatening her and abusing our kids. All of a sudden, I can't even come back to the place I been paying for. All the money I have saved is in that shoe box so one day when she should be at work, I go by to get what's mine. I had no idea she'd be home sick. Once she comes to the door, I tell her I'm there to collect up my belongings and go but she runs to the closet, grabs both boxes and says she's gonna dump this shit outside. I tell her to give me back the stuff and start thinking with some sense. She's crying and won't put the gun down. I grab her so she'll calm down and she starts bugging, so I pin her down on the carpet so she won't hurt herself. I've got my hands on her shoulders, you know but she's struggling hard and they slip up near her neck. I keep saying, gimme my gun back, but she won't let go. We're in a tussle, wrestling and her night dress gets ripped. By then, she's screamin' like she's gone bat-shit and my oldest daughter who's walked in sees me on top of her mama and calls the police. I'm hit. The State got me on all kinds of charges – attempted burglary, possession of a firearm, strangulation, assault third and risk of injury to minor. My lawyer got it pled down to violation of a protective order, unlawful restraint and risk of injury."

"You aren't going back to this woman, are you?"

"No, we're divorced now. Can't fix stupid," he says with a particular sting of nastiness. Willis corrects himself immediately. 'I don't mean it to sound like that. I forgave her."

"And do you have a plan? Where are you going to live if you can't go back there?" I ask.

"I'm gonna stay with a friend. She's got a place in Roxbury and wants me to come there. I can help her out cause there's no man in the picture right now."

"I don't understand, Mr. Willis. What was so hard about telling that? Your story isn't much different than anyone else's in the class. Why couldn't you share it with the others?"

"You know me, Counselor. What happened to me as a kid. I don't trust anyone but you. I'm not just another criminal crying wolf. This is serious business to me. I want to leave this place with a clean record."

"Well, you must know it's very difficult to get your record expunged. It can be done, but there is a five-year wait period from the time of conviction and the Board of Pardons looks closely at what productive steps the person has made since that time. You may have a very good chance if you do all the right things in the meantime."

"I don't mean on paper, Mizz Abrams. I mean I want to leave this life with a clear conscience. What's troubling me are things I've done that I never was caught for. The things a man carries around in his own soul."

"We all have dark spots in our souls, Mr. Willis. And we must try and scrub them clean if we are lucky enough to. That's where church and religion can play a part. Perhaps a priest or the chaplain might be helpful in purging your conscience."

"I'm not spilling my guts to a bunch of guys. Some of them are homos, even. Their opinions don't matter to me."

"I'd expect you to be more tolerant than that. I mean, you've been dealt a pretty fair hand in all of this." Willis retracts his claws and makes nice purring sounds again.

'I don't mean it like that. But bad men don't handle the truth like a good woman would. Not even clergy. At the end of the day, they're just as guilty and dirty as the rest. I need to hand this shit over to someone who cares and can tell me that it'll be okay. That's my good Lord Savior and you, Counselor."

"Alright. I prize confidentiality and will honor it. People need to feel they are safe with someone before they can expose these flaws. But you need to know that if you tell me you've hurt a child or something that endangers someone's safety, I am a mandated reporter."

Willis's eyes swim with liquid. His eyeballs have yellowed and have fine threads of capillaries streaking across like bloody little meteor showers. He swallows, coughs and then looks off into the distance. Whatever is troubling him is somewhere far enough away where he has to reach way back and grope hard to catch a thread tail of it. It's not something he really wants to touch.

"When I told you that I never sexually violated that girl, I was telling the God's-honest truth. But…." He pauses, and then continues with a cracking voice. "When I was older, in my twenties maybe, I was a very angry young man. I got caught up in violent crimes like robberies and assaults. Bad shit. People got hurt. Three women…" He stops, puts the sounds together to form the distasteful word he needs to spit from this mouth. "were raped and beaten. Bad." Willis falters but forces the truth that burns like emesis and bile on its way up. "One of them might have died. I never knew for sure because I took off down south to Kentucky and hid out with my cousins. I was sure someone would show up looking for me, but the case was pled out and the other guys who were caught never gave my name up. I came back home since no one was lookin' for me. But it troubles me deeply now that I have become a mature man and given up self to my Jesus. If we confess our sins, he will cleanse us from all unrighteousness. Isn't that what the Word says?"

The purging seems to have eased his discomfort. Like nausea, the worst of it is right before the inevitable release.

"Yes, how long ago was this, Mr. Willis?" I ask. Willis appears distracted and even

"A long, long ways back now. I don't want to say too much and put you in a predicament."

"You're not under any obligation to tell me anything. The best way I can help you is to pass you along to Legal Assistance or at least provide you with the information related to the laws."

"I came back when the trial was over but there was nothing worth coming back to. I lost my Momma to her heart attack while I was down in the Juvie. All the stress and strain of my life killed her with worry. I can't ever make that right."

"That is tragic and sad. I'm sorry," I say.

Willis reaches down and pulls up the cuff of his over shirt. Up close, the contrast between the vitiligo and the dark complexion is even more vivid. Like a Beardsley print of swirling patterns, it melds into a collage of linear ink and uneven margins. The first three letters of a faded tattoo fall within the range of the skin discoloration. B E R.

"That's her name. Berea. Named after the town she was raised in."

"Lovely. What does it mean?"

"It was a city in the Bible. It means heavy, weighty," says Willis. "It's a sad word," he adds. We have much more in common than he knows. I know this word. It's related to the term bereavement. Its synonym is bereft;

to be left desolate or alone especially after death. Grief. He knows that I too have been formed out of the same gritty substance; not the dry dust that issues under happy running feet but the muddy clay that forms from the mire and builds in layers, piling up, hardening over time into brittle strength.

"In order to truly make this right, you would have to admit to your actions. But the statute of limitations on assault, rape or even intent to rape may have run out already. Each state is different. You may be a free man in Kentucky."

"This happened in a different state."

"Oh, that might make a difference. Which state?" I ask innocuously.

"Massachusetts. This state we're in," says Willis. A bleed of dazzling light flashes and fizzles in the outer corner of my right eye. A hazy film obscures the view like spent fireworks drifting downwards in a misty rain.

"I'm not sure I'm comfortable with this. I'm not the right person. I have to go, Mr. Willis," I announce abruptly and stand up.

"But I ain't done yet, Mizz Abrams. Please," begs Willis.

"Tell it to your Jesus. He's got a stronger stomach than I do," I answer as I half-trip over his big boots in my hurry to depart the confines of the boxy room and get out into clarifying air.

#

On the drive home, my temples start to ache. Little auras begin to hover around the street lamps like migrating bacteria in a Petri dish. Before long, minnows are swimming around the sun. Damn! Feels like the precursor to a migraine or worse, a seizure. I've got to tell my shrink that I don't like the side effects of this new mix of meds, Effexor and Topamax. Suddenly, my vision in one eye fractures into the gaily colored triangles of a kid's kaleidoscope. Startled, I flick on my blinker and pull over into the parking lot of the farmer's credit union. I turn off the motor, lock my doors and lower the driver's seat to a reclining position. Nausea begins to bubble in my gut. I put my hand on my cell phone in case I need to call for an emergency crew. I keep my finger on the speed dial and swallow first one Xanax, then another. While I wait for the medicine to take effect, I try to distract myself. With what? Tomorrow's lesson plan. This week's grocery list. Count backwards. No forwards. One…two…three.. Shit. A cold sweat rolls over my back. My memory begins to flutter and skip like a flash book.

Three letters on a wrist. Rape. Trust me. Might be dead. Long time ago. Massachusetts. Clues. The series of flipping pages clump in awkward, random order and then speed up, smoothing out a cohesive string of frames into a story that finally begins to make sense. *Long time ago. Massachusetts girl. Raped. Might be dead. Letters on a wrist. B – E – R. Missing person.*

I sit bolt upright out of my haze and fumble briefly with the handle, flinging the door wide open just in time to retch on the gravel. I can't tell if the rushing pulse in my ears is my brain in revolt or moving traffic. I vomit once, then again but it does nothing to relieve the awful sickness of dawning truth. My eyesight is still so badly occluded I can't decipher if the concerned motorist who has stopped to help me is male or female. Friend or foe. Either way, I shove back, fighting to free myself. No one is going to fuck with me. Not ever again.

CHAPTER 10
COMING CLEAN

"So any word on your parole hearing date?" I ask. *Keep everything neutral and objective.* My stomach is jumping with apprehension. Willis lingers after class as requested and drops into a seat close to my desk. He is not at all suspicious of my intent. And why should he be? A teacher has a right to single out special students who may require extra help.

"Yes, I got my date. August 7th. Two weeks from now," he answers confidently.

"You must be as overwhelmed as you are excited."

"It's been a long time coming, but I'm ready. As you know," Willis replies.

"So, you'll go back to Boston where you're from?" I ask. I've chosen wide open-ended questions that circumvent any suspicion. There is more than one way that leads to the right answer.

"What? No! My people are from Kentucky, remember?"

"I apologize. Where on earth did I come up with Boston?" I reply.

"The few years I was drifting on the streets there going between aunts and cousins. Remember when I told you that?"

"That's right. You did say that. My memory is shot. I'm old, you know." Willis laughs. His face is visibly relaxed, prepared now to break into an easy smile as he heads down that final lap. He can afford to let down his guard and coast the rest of the way in.

"Then I'm ancient, Miss A, cuz you can't be a day over thirty." Somewhere else under different circumstances, this would be the opening line that cracks reluctance and extracts a coquettish smile. We might laugh off our unease and take this awkward courtship to a new level. But not here; not us. Not ever.

"Where did you end up settling then?" I ask as I innocently map the trajectory of his life.

"I left town and the state and headed down south. I was on the run but everything was on the down-low. No one knew what I'd done or where I'd gone to." Two pieces snap together.

"That had to be torturous. Living with the knowledge of what you'd done but being the person you truly are. Knowing the world at large would never understand or care to hear your version." Willis wavers. He is considering it, but chooses only to nod in agreement.

"Tell me about those young women. Only if you want to, of course." Willis shows signs of discomfort as the memory is being shoved in front of him to recount or to recant.

"I couldn't give you names even if I knew them. There were three girls in all. Two separate incidents.' His voice begins to falter and his sentence trails off into stiff silence.

"I imagine it's hard to move forward with your new life until you are reconciled with your past. It's almost impossible to do so without looking at the hard stuff straight on. You want to give it another try?"

"I couldn't make steps in a positive direction for a long time. Not until I came here on this last bid and God got a hold of me. I could finally lay those sins out in daylight and let them be seen and cleansed."

"You firmly believe that you are forgiven for those murders?" I ask, searchingly. His eyes flick up to my face in alarm. Willis becomes instantly defensive.

"Who said anything about *murders*? They were assaults." Snap.

"Oh, I apologize, Mr. Willis. I thought you told me last time that one of the girls was badly beaten and died in the hospital."

"Lord Almighty. I've never talked about this to a single soul except my Maker. But you understand my background and what happened to me as a child. And you are the only one who had the courage to speak for a fuck-up like me. I trust you."

"I'm glad," I reply. "Everyone needs to have that one person in their life. In addition to their God," I add. Willis's voice cracks and falters.

"Two of them were roommates at Boston College. They were scared to death and threatened into keeping quiet. We took their address books and the family photos off the walls and told them that if they went to the police, their people were goners."

"We...?"

"Yes, I was with two other guys. Older than me." Snap.

"And what about the other woman, the third one? Was she raped too?"

"Not by me. But..." Willis pauses. I can see the Adam's apple in this throat bumping up and down as he fights to swallow back the distaste in his mouth. A single swell of moisture blossoms in the corner of his eye and lights off down his cheekbone. Another follows a duplicate path. "I didn't stop them. Something just went off in my head. Seeing these white bitches, forgive my language, parading their asses by us like we're good for nuthin' shitbags. All I could see was that skunk-mouthed little whore who ruined me at an early age just for fun. I made up a lie right then and there that I kept tellin' myself, that someone had to pay for all the shit that happened to me. But I got carried away and took it too far."

"Do you know for sure, though? You may have been running away from something that never actually happened." I'm turning the tables now, playing to the other side. The devil's advocate.

"It was in all the local papers and on television. She went to the hospital and was in a coma for a long time. And then she disappeared from the news altogether. There was no obituary in the paper but I'm pretty sure she died." Snap.

"God, Willis! That's a lot to bear. But you yourself just said you didn't sexually assault anyone, so you don't need to carry the blame for that."

"No, but I did put my hands on her."

"Was she in the same college dorm as the others?" He shakes his head.

"No, she was living in a house. A nice neighborhood just up from the projects where we hung out," he answers. Something tells me to push harder.

"How do you know she was a college student then?" I ask, pressing this one resistant piece against the adjoining ones, hoping for a fit.

"Because she had school books and research papers and shit. Plus the article in the Globe said she was in the last semester of her senior year." Snap. Snap. Snap. Finally, a few of the convoluted clues scattered across my life lock down into place, revealing a partial image of a very dark landscape.

"Did the other guys go down for the crime? Or did they get off too?" I ask. Willis is growing tired of the interrogation, however much it is cloaked in friend's clothing.

"They did time but not for the rape. In a way, they are the lucky ones because they paid their price up front. I still have to settle up on mine. That's what I mean to do when I get out. I don't yet have a plan as to how I'm gonna make it right, but my goal is to try."

The puzzle pieces are now linked in one contiguous and inescapable picture. I have what I need.

"Well, I hope this has helped. You need to be of a clear mind when you go before the Board. I wish you my best with that."

"You have done so much for me, Mizz Abrams. I am grateful for everything. Just so you know, I tell everyone that you are the best fuckin' counselor in this whole place. Maybe even the country!"

"Now that's stretching it a bit. I'll settle for just New England." We smile at one another in a truce built on trust. I have been tested and proven to be worthy.

#

Surprisingly, Detective Hughes is not all that hard to find.

He had kept up with our family long after the court transcripts were filed and the keys thrown. He visited regularly during my eight months at Gaylord, always with questions and the subtle hope that a glimmer of a clue might bubble up out of the mud of my memory. I had very little to offer. He was one of those cops who had photographs of murdered wives and missing daughters pinned to the bulletin board beside his desk. Long after everyone else had moved on, he kept them alive in his mind. Bereaved families flocked to him to help them find peace for their loved ones. It was this spirit of perseverance that brought his little Datsun to our Gust Harbor dooryard the day that inmates Carson and Turner were released to halfway houses having completed eighty-five percent of their eight year sentences. That was two-thousand four hundred and eighty-two days apiece, enough time to either repent or relapse.

Turner lasted three months as a free man before being remanded back to custody on a technical violation for dirty urine. Carson, on the other hand, finished out his remaining time under supervision and enrolled in tractor-trailer school for a commercial driver's license. That was the last thing any of us heard about these men until a newspaper clipping from the Boston Register arrived in my parents' postal box ten years later. Carson was one of two men gunned down in a drive-by outside the Magic Lady strip club in an apparent turf war between rival Blood sets. Turner had long since disappeared from the state altogether and a run of his rap sheet pulled up no further arrests.

I was amazed that this Detective would use his own time to come all the way up to meet with us in person. I believe he would have even if his wife's family didn't own property up on Chebeague Island where they planned to retire when he reached the age of pension eligibility. It was an antique fixer-upper that required multiple summers' worth of hours cracking out ribs of lathe and horsehair plaster, shoring up rotten sills and tacking down tarpaper. It was a therapeutic change from spending his working hours trying to extract truth from old bones and rotten hearts. At least when you he worked on wood, the results were obvious. Hughes dropped in for a handful of visits over the years, a cup of coffee or a plate of apple crisp and a visual check on a former 'client.'

I don't think Hughes ever stopped seeing me as that twenty-something-year-old. When it came to me, his time clock had run out of battery power. We had bonded in a co-dependent sort of way. Back then, he was like the lead dog in a harness pulling my sled across slick ice and black drifts when I was unable to do anything but hold on for dear life, hoping that we would eventually crest up over the snow cap to clear blue light. I was the symbol of his cause, a living unsolved mystery that cracked his reserve and brought passion back to his profession. Unlike my parents who never lowered the bar and believed with enough cheerleading, I could rally and reach the peak again; Hughes knew that I was unalterably changed and met me there at the juncture of helpless and hurting. He accepted my deficits as beautiful tributes of endurance and embraced the unpredictable in me as proof of the purposeful madness that causes a victim to march headstrong and headlong back into the face of evil.

I'm certain he never planned to be an accomplice; though his role in the drama was minor. When the phone rang that hot August night, Hughes had already brushed his teeth with Pepsodent, slipped into his cotton pajama pants and was watching heat lightning sputter over the treetops. He did his absolute best to introduce calm to the hysteria on the other end of the line; but in fairness to him, there wasn't much a middle-aged man could do with a broken down girl sobbing over his sentences. When I threatened to hang up and hitch-hike to Canada, he changed his mind and promised to come, but only if I stayed put and agreed to hear him out before I made any drastic decisions. His wife was used to him dashing out into the dark to investigate crime scenes, so she didn't bat a sleepy eye when he headed north impulsively. He drove straight to the old fire road just past the small pond, left his truck in hiding behind the big pines and walked in from there. Since I had no ability to lift anything, I had decided to toss my belongings piecemeal out the window and ask for his help in collecting them. Together we hobbled through the wet, hip-high field grass to his waiting vehicle. Ten miles down the road he pulled over at Fanny and Gramp's diner and insisted that we discuss my desertion over a meal of runny eggs and grilled muffins. The vinyl booths had been recently sprayed with lemon soap that smelled like bug repellent. The older waitress looked askance when we walked in, but kept chatting to the fisherman in waders on the stool in front of her. Finally, she yawned, ambled over and poured us each a mug of steaming coffee. People were watching me; I had to keep my shit together here. Hughes knew what he was doing. How many teen runaways had he coaxed into going back to their miserable little lives? I wasn't to be one of them.

"Jesus, Elise. This will be rough on your mother. Have you considered that?" he asked.

"I'm smothering here," I replied flatly.

"What about your boyfriend, Aaron, right? What does he want you to do?"

"I didn't tell him. It's not fair. I'll explain it to him later when I can make better sense of things. Besides, he has a future."

"And you don't, is that what you're saying?"

"Not if I stay. I'll die here as nothing but the disabled girl everybody felt sorry for. They'll always compare me to Lissa, the golden girl of promise. I need to go where no one expects me to reach back up," I said.

"I'll take you back to the farmhouse before they even miss you. If need be, I'll explain everything to your mother."

"Just get me back to Boston. I'll figure it out from there," I begged.

"Are you sure this is what you must do?" he asked.

"Yes, and I will with or without your help. I'm going," I said. And he never asked that question again.

The Hughes home was a cramped three-bedroom bungalow in Jamaica Plains that he shared with his wife and two small kids. He shoved a cot in the corner of the sun porch and made room, thinking it was only for a night or two until I relented of this madness, saw reason and took the Trailways bus back to Portland. That never happened. I enrolled at Boston College under the Americans with Disabilities provision and began the painstaking process of completing my degree. With the help of his connections, I was hooked up as an intern to a forensic psychologist at the Boston Police Precinct. The decision to join the incoming class of recruits at the Massachusetts Department of Correction took everyone by surprise, Hughes included. In the absence of a father, he did his part, put up initial resistance and gave me a heart-to-heart on the hazards of the profession, particularly for a young female. But it was with a salute and a petition to Saint Maria Goretti that he dropped me off at the gates of the Academy as I was ushered into a sea of blue uniforms.

#

With a small fee to one of those data-collecting web sites, I am able to come up with both the phone number and address to his homestead in Waldoboro County. His adult daughter tells me that her father, now in his thirty-fifth year in law enforcement, is still working full-time in Massachusetts. Hughes is a man who will die on the job. His tenacious drive to round up the last of the worst will be the cause of death. I can visualize him clutching his heart and slumping forward with his face in a file. I dial up the direct extension she has given me.

"Detective, it's me, Elise. The Braum's daughter."

"Get out! What a surprise," he says with genuine excitement. His voice has not aged in timber or tone; though by quick calculation, he must be close to sixty now. When he knelt over my near-corpse and took stock of the grave situation, he was a clean-shaven, bright-eyed study of a young Woody Harrelson. Both intense and intuitive. Of course I didn't register that until many weeks later and by then, the stress of my case had sprouted stubble on his chin, creased his brow and upped his habit to a pack and a half a day.

"How are you feeling, honey?" he asks genuinely.

"Very well, Detective. How's Mrs. Hughes?" I ask.

"Healthy! At this age, that's the first and last thing you give thanks for each day."

"You heard about my Dad, then?"

"Yes, we received a note. What a tragedy. So unfair. Your family has already more than paid their dues. But I'm not naïve enough to expect that life is just. Seen too much over the years, you know?"

"I want to hire you to do a little side project for me," I say, switching the subject.

"I don't moonlight as a private investigator so tracking cheaters is out," he teases. "What kind of work?"

"I need you to get some evidence out of the closed storage. I pray to God it's still there."

"I assume you're referring to your own case?"

"Yes," I reply. Hughes and I share one very strong characteristic - our hunches. He had always been willing to disregard logical obstacles and put aside convention to chase down that one nagging thought. I know he had put that box away in the back room with great reluctance.

"What is it you're interested in? I'm guessing the biological material? If I recall there were multiple pieces of evidence."

"You do hold on to that stuff, don't you? I know it's been a long time and space must be an issue. I want to know if it's still accessible," I ask.

"Let me answer you in a professional sense. It's often an arbitrary call made by prosecutors and evidence technicians. In the case of biological evidence or DNA, there's a standard rule. When the evidence has been fully tested and belongs to the defendant who's been convicted, there is no need to keep it. The statute governing the holding of DNA mandates the longest holding time and for good reason. Technology, which is ever changing, allows us to re-examine and link the evidence to a suspect. That's why this type of evidence should be maintained until *all* uncertainty is gone. That's a pretty technical, long-winded answer but I want you to be clear on the laws. In layman's terms, that kind of DNA is kept around for a long, long time if it's proven that it does *not* belong to the person who was convicted. This was the situation in our case. I mean yours."

"So, if I understand you correctly, no motion was ever made to have it destroyed?" I ask.

"Not to my knowledge," he replies.

"But it could have been done, unbeknownst to you?" I ask.

"It's possible, but not likely. A notice to destroy evidence has to be submitted to the defendant, his attorney and the convicting court. Any or all of these parties can object. If no one does, than the prosecutor can ask that it be destroyed. But remember, honey, no one was ever charged or convicted on the sexual assault because the material on the mattress pad and the nightgown could never be conclusively matched to the two bastards in hand." He chooses the generic term, *material,* which is a kind attempt to protect my sensitivities.

"But we're light-years down the road now in terms of DNA testing. Can this material be re-tested and matched against current DNA samples?" I persist.

"For what purpose?" he asks.

"To identify the invisible man. Our third guy," I state.

"I don't want to know what you've got in mind. Let me answer your question by saying yes, there are new techniques that use evaporation to lift prints off materials. And these results are virtually indisputable. That all did not exist when we were looking at your case."

"And can't we link into the national database and fingerprint files and stuff like that?" I ask.

"There's definitely more information available to us now," he admits.

"So, if I send you a new sample, can you have it tested and compared to the material in the evidence file? Please, there must be a way. Someone you can ask. I just need to know."

"You know I would do anything to cremate the bastards that did this to you, but ethically, I have to do what's within my scope. You know, you're in criminal justice too. We can't risk our careers doing anything illegal but...."

"But what? Are you saying you won't do it?" I ask point-blank. Another thing that Hughes and I have in common is that new addition to our vocabulary, a small but useful conjunction that we've learned to kick into a jam: *but*: 'an introduction to something contrasting with what has already been mentioned. Despite that; in spite of; nonetheless.' Hughes coughs, and fumbles with the phone.

"You'll do it, then?" I ask. There's another prolonged pause while he wrestles with his conscience, trying to justify the small breaches in protocol he'll have to take to accommodate me.

I hold my breath.

"Shit. Okay!" he says finally. "You know I can't turn you down, Elise. Never was good at saying no to a pretty girl. Send me what you have. I'll give you my home address. Make sure the sample is properly handled. It can't be compromised or contaminated. Bag it up, seal it and send it overnight express. Give me a couple weeks to see what I can find out. And make sure you say a big hello to your mother for me."

"Bless you, Detective!" I gush. He likes it when I address him by his title. It makes a man feel powerful and protective. He knows I need him and I know he needs me too. What he'd never admit to is the inexplicable feeling that I was his soul mate, that person in his life to whom a connection was grafted before the beginning of time and the Big Bang migration of continental plates. It was that deep. We had never been lovers in the typical sense. It had been years since we had seen one another; but the tragic force that drew us together bonded us in some intense and unbreakable way. We were life partners in our mutual quest to right this wrongful world. Cop and co-ed joined in a consensual cause. Women are wildly intuitive and I believe that the moment he laid eyes on my battered bare body, he hoped that someday he would see it again healed and radiant and offered up to him in act of pure sacrifice. Circumstances seem to disprove this theory since his amicable marriage to a loving woman whose simple pleasure is using her silver coins for a Buy-Two-Get-Three-Free deal at Big Y is still solid and going strong. But underneath his apparent satisfaction, I wonder if he yearns to be harnessed up with another restless soul. I'd bet my Christmas bonus on this - that after I'd left that musty daybed on his sun-drenched porch where I'd camped for months, and before the bed linens were stripped and laundered, that he lifted the sheets to his face to inhale my fragrance, looked up at the dim city stars and made a wish. A wish he never said out loud.

#

The video we are watching today is a grainy copy of a pirated documentary burned in someone's basement during a desperate budget crisis. The audio stutters; the picture is blurred and jumpy. It shows a woman who after being raped repeatedly had her arms severed completely and was tossed in the desert to die. She wills herself to walk with bloody stumps held heavenward; knowing that succumbing to the pull of gravity on her exhausted shoulder muscles will kill her. The men are sickened by what they see. Some drop their heads; others wince and cover their eyes.

"What the fuck?" murmurs Willis. He looks away.

The next segment features an interview with a former USFL football player, a stand-up guy until he stabbed and killed his wife over a text message. He is speaking from inside prison and telling his audience, 'You don't know what you are capable of doing and *will* do under the right set of circumstances.' The men are drawn in by his gutsy testimony. 'A wise man learns from his mistakes. I say a wiser man learns from the mistakes of others. I already made that mistake. It's done. You don't need to repeat it,' says our reformed athlete. 'By the grace of God, I only got twenty-three years. You do what I do now and you're finished. *Finished!*' he emphasizes.

"Twenty-three years? Shit, that might as well be life," Gemini whines while preening the tendrils of frayed threads on his worn shirt.

The video switches to a woman, bird-like in appearance with a tight twisted beak of a face, eyes pulled to slits, her neck taut with bands of shiny, convoluted scar tissue. She lifts her arms to show the third-degree burns that etched away over eighty-percent of her flesh after she was bludgeoned with a hammer and set on fire by her husband. I swear Serge is crying. He stares in open-faced horror at the screen shaking his large cranium back and forth in disbelief. Rev keeps glancing away and looking back, both horrified and captivated at what he is seeing. Bowman raises his hand and asks if he can be excused to go to the bathroom in the hall.

"Everyone stays until the end," I state firmly. When the film clip is over, there is utter silence in the room. Zimmer forgets his whole cripple act, gets out of the wheelchair and walks up to the front to turn off the DVD player.

"Anything jump out at you?" I ask.

"That's so fucked-up," says Noble.

"How could anyone do shit like that to another person?" asks Dent incredulously.

"Believe it or not, that's what you guys are capable of," I say in a neutral voice.

"How can you say *us* guys, Miss Abrams? Those are extreme cases," says Rev defensively.

"Listen. Here's the deal. No more second person, *she*. It's *I* or *me* from now on. Understand?" The men are taken aback by my uncharacteristic abruptness. I can guess what they're thinking. Counselor Abrams is bi-polar or else it's that time of the month. Or maybe she's in a fight with her husband and brought that shit to work. They feel defensive, even a bit antagonized by this hormonal shift, but isn't that just like a female to change colors? The blame game has started.

"I already know. It's the probations officer's fault because she had it out for you from the get-go. And the cops who need to make so many arrests per month to meet their quota. It's a business, this prison thing, and we keep our jobs if you keep coming in. Of course the state makes all kinds of money off your sorry asses. And, oh yeah, your woman cried wolf and turned you in so she can cheat on you. And wait a minute, it's bigger than all that. It's a friggin' hate crime too because you are black or Hispanic or just goddamn poor. Am I right? Did I cover them all?"

'Jesus, Mizz A. We thought you was on our side," Ortega mumbles, clearly hurt.

'I am. That's the whole point. The sooner you guys starting owning your shit, the quicker I can help you become the men you were meant to be."

They need time to mull this one over. It's the same with every class. I turn my back on them and pop the video out of the player, collect up the dry markers and the eraser. A quiet conversation starts up in one corner of the room. I ignore them and get busy rustling homework papers into my briefcase. In the reflection of the corner mirror, I can see several huddling together in earnest discussion. A few others are leaning in over the table top, gesturing with their hands and getting heated. Only two appear to be totally disengaged. Crespo is watching an earwig beetle creep slowly up the pull cord to the blinds and Bowman is doodling anime figures on the cover of a Daily Bread devotional he picked up off the floor. The volume of voices gets louder; more opinions are being thrown into the debate and are being hashed around. A small grass-roots revolt is brewing, one that will froth and foment and eventually be quelled by a lone voice of reason from the one guy who is brave enough to use it. I still don't turn around or acknowledge them.

"Let's face it. We must love this place an awful lot," says Dent finally. "Hell, we have to cuz we keep coming back over and over. It's like my grandma said, 'What's wrong with you? You got a prison wife or something? Why else do you keep going back to live with men?'

"Yeah, we're good at telling what our shorty's done wrong. But we must have done something first to push 'er to that point,' Ortega says with conviction. They have entered a new phase of this purifying process when as peers, they begin flushing out the fakes.

"Let's knock off the bullshit. I could've killed my ex. I almost did," admits Serge. "Four minutes of rage is all it took to ruin a life."

I notice that Willis has his big body half-turned and is looking out the window towards the small driveway where transport vans race by shuttling inmates to and from court at unsafe speeds. The passengers in leg irons and jumpsuits are not in any danger of ejection, they are bolted tight in place.

"What did you think, Mr. Willis?" I ask.

"I really can't say," he answers. He seems unusually distracted and reserved.

"Did what you watched bother you?" I press for some type of reaction. He's pulling back, detaching himself from whatever gut reaction prompts this sudden aloofness. Willis shrugs but doesn't respond. I decide to take a different tact.

"Most of you guys are addicts, right? And I'm assuming that the majority of you have been through the 12-step program at some point. Does anyone recall the fourth step?" I ask. The attention swings back to the front as the topic changes.

"Take a fearless moral inventory," says Rev.

"You're right. This is one of my favorite challenges because it asks each of us to stare into the mirror of self-reflection and be honest about what we see. It's such a vital step in recovery. So tell me, guys, if you take a good hard look inside, what do you see?" The question goes to the group as a whole and is meant to hit each man where he sits squirming in his own discomfort or denial.

"I feel nothing but disgust," admits Willis suddenly.

"That's wonderful," I say. I don't mean it to be sarcastic. The brooding man snaps out of his slouch and gives me the full force of his intimidating stare.

"Hold up! Hear me out. That feeling of self-disgust is your heart sending a signal. It means that it knows you can do better and that you are capable of different choices and better outcomes. Self-disgust is one of the best motivators if you are ready to make a change. If all you see is self-pity, than you're helpless and stuck in your own misery."

This is the point where the tide turns like the salty inlet that whittles its way inland from Frenchman's Bay. The high water surges forward and spills headlong into the fresh flow of the Jordan River heading back out to sea. For brief moments, there is the optical magic of reversing currents as the force of colliding elements turns tail and retreats. Some of these men will continue to pound stubbornly upstream; others will meet resistance and fall back. But chances are a few will allow themselves to be diverted like a brackish mix of rain and brine and will settle into transparent pools of true reflection.

"Thirty seconds is all it took for that linebacker to go from zero to sixty and kill his old lady. Just like that," Euclid says, snapping his fingers. His bewilderment is clearly evident. Something has touched a nerve.

I would never dare tell them that the trauma of my attempted murder has made me kin. I am more comfortable among the damaged. I can visualize Euclid as the little boy stripped of his dignity and drawers, hands duct-taped as he was forced to eat cat food. And Ortega too, made to sit in a warm bath for an hour before his pink, turgid skin is flailed with extension cords. I don't feel pity, not a bit. It is pure disgust, a retching wave of repulsion against adults who will reach for iron, steel or flame as a means to their end, which is nothing more than a puny helping of quivering fear in return. My heart has empathy for those little sniveling boys throttled into becoming these grown-up mimics. I am neck-deep in this struggle for understanding along with them. Each of us is floundering for solid rock to get a toe-hold on; all of us are grabbing for a fistful of stabilizing root so that we can lift one another to safety.

If I ever sit with a therapist for longer than a med change visit, I will ask him or her why it is that I have chosen to sit among murderers, thieves and fraudulent men. Jesus did that too and he was safe among them until his blessed luck ran out and they took a whole Old Testament's worth of wrath out on him. But his Father had willed it to be so. Perhaps my lot was cast in the same mold.

#

The young woman on the other end of the line is distraught. Calls like these are never easy. Weddings, deaths and holidays all drag up the freshness of the loss though their missing person is alive and listed on a locator card in the prison's master file. Regardless of where he is, the loved one who is absent from the table, the cemetery or the hospital has just walked out on them all over again. The calls come in and the cries go up: *Please, miss, we need him home… I'm sick with cancer. My son is all I got*; as if I hold the instant get-out-of-jail card in my desk drawer and can walk the inmate out the front gate in time for the family cookout. This girl is sobbing and begging me to please do something. I switch the phone to my better ear and ask for her name again.

"Crystal," she says, choking out the words.

"And which inmate are you calling about?" I ask. It's a courtesy to even entertain the call. We counselors never know who is on the other end of the line. With no proof of identity, we are hobbled when it comes to providing any information beyond what the public information website reveals. This young woman persists in her hysteria and I can't disconnect.

"Owens. He's the father of my daughter," she sobs. The mention of the child throws her into an inconsolable state that lasts for several more minutes.

"What are you calling about?" I ask.

"Our baby just died," she gasps. "She was one month old on Sunday. I went in to wake her this morning. She wasn't breathing." Her cries turn into howls of agony.

"Oh, I'm very sorry to hear this. Does the father know yet?" I ask.

"No, I need to tell him. Oh please, he can't do this alone," she cries. A siren erupts in the background.

"What was the cause of death?" I ask.

"The autopsy didn't show anything." Sounds like SIDS. *Poor thing.*

"It's my first child. And I need him to be with me. I can't go through this by myself." I hear the shrill wailing of other females in the background.

"Who's with you now, honey?" I ask.

"My sister, my aunt and my mother-in-law, but this is her first grand-baby so she's no good for helping anyone."

"I understand," I tell her, whether or not I can fully comprehend the magnitude of a mother's sorrow. I take down the name and address of the funeral home and ask her to call back when the arrangements have been made. This is the difficult part of the job, trying to tailor real-world events to fit an environment that has little room for compassion. The best I can hope for is to get him escorted by two officers for a fifteen minute private viewing before the public convenes for the service.

"Let me call him in so I can break the news," I say and gently hang up. I ring the officer's station and he gives a bellowing shout for the inmate who claims Bed 14-C. Within minutes, Owens rounds the doorway and I wave him to sit down. He's new to the unit. I've spotted him in the chow line but have not yet engaged him in any conversation. The boy looks pretty young to me.

"Mr. Owens, I just spoke with your fiancée who called to let you know that your baby daughter passed in her sleep this morning. I'm very sorry to have to tell you this," I announce as gently as I can. Getting bad news when one is already penned up can be particularly risky. A helpless man is a desperate one. Owens drops his head in his hands and nods up and down. He doesn't speak. When he finally looks back up, it is with a longing that defies interpretation.

"I've never held my baby daughter. I only saw her in pictures. That's all," he says.

"What's her name?" I ask him.

"Kali. I never got to name her neither. But it's a beautiful name," he says.

"How old are you, Owens?" I ask him.

"Twenty-one," he replies proudly. He likely had no idea what the demands of fatherhood were going to be, but he had in theory already stepped up to embrace it. Unlike many other procreators whose names were omitted from the birth certificate so the moms could collect welfare assistance, this guy was blissfully prepared to claim the signature line on that document.

"I'm going to try and get you approved to go see your infant before burial. We're still waiting on the details of the service. You understand that you can't be there when anyone else is, including family members."

"I know that," he says meekly.

"Your girlfriend wants to come see you. I noticed she's not on your visiting list though. Why not?"

"She was in trouble with the law once, but that was a long time ago," he answers.

"I see. Well, I'll check it out. You want to speak to Mental Health?" I ask. Standard fare for unexpected news in jail. He shakes his head. "How about Religious Services?" A priest or chaplain might offer some eternal solace. Again, he declines. I dial up Crystal's phone number and give him the requisite thirty seconds during which he mumbles, "Babe, babe, babe" over her moans as if they were dubbing a soundtrack for a heartbreaking love story. When he is forced to hang up, he settles his shoulders and clears his throat. Tears begin to well up in his eyes so I allow him extra time in the office with me until he has purged himself of his initial shock.

"I'll see what I can do on my end. I'm very sorry, Mr. Owens."

"Thank you, Counselor," he says and walks back out into General Population. I must remember to document the encounter in the officer's log book so that our respective asses are covered in case this young man gets suicidal or aggressive later.

#

Two days' worth of scrambling has paid off. I have the approved paperwork in hand. Miss Crystal is on probation for drug charges, which under normal circumstances excludes her from visiting anyone in prison; but the powers-that-be have made a special exception and will allow the young couple ten minutes of no-contact time here in the visiting room. In addition, a very sympathetic probation officer not only granted permission for her client to come inside the facility but sent a social worker up to our front door with birth documents. Without those, we cannot prove Mr. Owens's identity as the biological father and risk sending him to the wake of another man's baby. After it is signed and notarized, Owens holds the yellow duplicate in his hands and reads the name out loud, Kali Tanaya Owens. The social worker informs him that he has sixty days in which to rescind his claim to being the father and request a DNA test.

"That won't happen, ma'am," he says, clutching the proof that will send his legitimate daughter to Paradise with bragging rights — his last name. The Warden followed suit on the heels of this good deed and signed off on the funeral trip despite his reservations about this kid's possible ties to former gang activity. It is a step of good faith made by an institution that rarely budges.

"You doing better?" I ask Mr. Owens when he is summoned to my office again.

"Yeah, a little. When the guys in the unit found out, they had a moment of silence for Kali and they made a card for me. The officer let us stand in a circle and the Indians prayed for her. They gave me the feather to put in the coffin so I mailed it home," he says.

"They're going to allow you to see your daughter, Mr. Owens," I say. He displays a genuine smile, the first of its kind in the short time I've known him and it doesn't quit. Even when he clenches the corners of his mouth, his lips quiver and pull back from his teeth in a reflex of unspeakable joy.

"Thank you. Thank everyone who helped me," he says with reverence.

"There are good people on both sides of this fence. I would like to think that at the end of the day, and no matter what roles we assume, we all are human beings with heart when it counts," I say. "I'm happy it worked out for you."

#

On Friday morning, I stop at the window near the Admitting/Processing Unit and watch as Mr. Owens is brought out the side door. He's dressed in a flagrant red jumpsuit, handcuffed and shackled in leg irons with his hair neatly edged by the barber's razor. The C.O.s give him an elbow-up into the white court van. Within the hour, he will be leaning over the miniature casket where his infant is displayed in her pink dress and tiny lace socks. Because there are imperfect people with decent hearts, this father will say goodbye to his perfect little baby with his hands tied but his grief set free.

As I walk back towards the housing units, I hear the thrum of a bass and a chanting melody. I follow the mounting vibrations that emanate from the rear of the school wing. Outside the corridor there is a small courtyard hedged in by smooth block walls on all four sides. The space is inviting, a tease in the midst of functional concrete; but it's rarely ever used. During the summer, top-heavy sunflowers thrust up between the granite stones and then topple over with the weight and lay their petals down. Today, several rows of plastic chairs have been arranged facing towards a music stand. To the side of the instrument ensemble is a blue tarp rigged up on a metal stand and filled with water. A baptism is underway. Several men are dedicating their lives to their newfound God. Killers and con artists dip their heads into the makeshift pool like they are bobbing for fruit with Adam's evil apple stuck in their throats, hoping when they rise up from the brink, they will gulp down new refreshment.

The inmate praise band is in full tilt with front man Cordona on the rhythm guitar. Nineteen years ago this man killed another in a jealous rage by slamming the skull of his competitor repeatedly against the curb and then fleeing. Now he's banging out some mean chords. Bowman is to the right on electric bass. He's got the tempo down body and soul, his knees bent in a perpetual sway. Six other black men make up the vocals. They swivel back and forth on loose feet with their hands lifted. The audience of two dozen or so inmates is standing, clapping enthusiastically, their voices joining in on the chorus. *I'm trading my sorrows, I'm trading my shame, I'm laying them down for the joy of the Lord. Yes Lord, yes Lord, yes, yes Lord. Amen!* I find myself caught up in the spirit of the moment though we are separated by a thick barrier of bullet-proof glass. Cordona looks up and an ethereal radiance has overtaken his face. It's then I notice Willis in the half-shadows with his head bowed and his strong hands folded. His lips are moving in a devotional meditation of sorts. He's praying. *Say your prayers.* Suddenly I recall the question I posed to my Mr. X before he struck the first crippling blow. I asked if he was Christian because he would need to repent for the sins he was about to commit. And what did he say to me in return? *Think, think…. I know!* 'No, bitch, why?' was his answer. Never say never. If this is him, then here he is in a genuflection of faith, but is it real or rehearsed? That's for God to sort out. I sure wouldn't want His job. The chorus repeats and lifts in volume. *I'm pressed but not crushed, I'm persecuted but not abandoned, struck down but not destroyed,* they sing, but that is my song too. Willis looks up and catches me standing in the window. His eyes acknowledge my presence but he looks beyond and through me as if I don't matter and never did. I duck my head and turn away.

What a strange world unites us —death and life intermingled, joy and grief harmonized in a house of unlikely worship. On this glorious morning, Baby Owens will be christened for her entrance to heaven and these convicts sprinkled with divine forgiveness and spared from their momentary hell. For all who are fortunate enough to be held captive in the blazing sunlight of this tiny walled tomb, the only way out is up.

#

"So you seem at peace this week. Have you reached some resolution? Things more settled in your mind?" I ask.

Willis takes the chair he's been offered and stretches out his legs. The noise of bodies milling around by the shower area is distracting, so I stand up and step over to shut the door. I wave to the officer through the small window indicating the closed door is at my discretion and all is well. The guards don't like to have anything barring their view, particularly in the instance of a female staff member in a closed room with a male offender. I sit back down and continue eating from the plastic take-out container on my desk

"I don't want to interrupt your meal, Mizz. I can come back another time."

"No, no. I set aside this time. Not to worry. Have you been to chow yet?"

"No ma'am. I don't mind missing it," Willis says.

"I saved you the trouble. I asked the kitchen to send me two feedback trays." I produce two blue Solo cups from my bottom desk drawer and a half-gallon jug of cold Arnold Palmer mix from my thermal bag. I pour one for each of us.

"I wouldn't want to drink that blue jungle juice either. Sorry, no ice cubes." I slide him the other clamshell container with a plastic fork and napkin. "So, you talked to the chaplain?"

"Yes. Not in specifics, but in the area of forgiveness."

"And did he offer you good counsel?"

"He gave me a verse that spoke to my heart," answers Willis.

"Which one?"

"If we confess our sins, He is faithful and just to forgive us our sins …"

"…and cleanse us from all unrighteousness," I say. Willis is momentarily taken aback. "I went to Sunday School growing up. We had to memorize a lot of Scripture to be graduated into Junior Church," I add, smiling.

"So you know about this stuff, Mizz Abrams, So then, what is your view of forgiveness? Do you believe that God can overlook even the worst of our wrongs?"

"I think our failings are equally disappointing but also equally human. According to the Bible you believe in, not only does God choose not to see them, He removes them as far as the east is from the west. Which if you think about it means totally out of sight."

"Do you personally believe that?" he asks again.

"A lack of forgiveness festers and becomes resentment. It's like you taking a swig of poison and waiting for the other person to die. If we refuse to purge it, the other person holds power over us. So to answer your question, I don't think we can forgive *and* forget; or should. Because the memory of the wrong keeps us on track. It's like a signpost to remind us of where not to go. What turn not to take."

"Mizz Abrams, you have a gift. Men like me, we need to hear these things. People just don't care. You don't treat us based on what we've done. You see us as the people we are or could be."

"I see a lot of very gifted, bright, talented people with tons of potential

that needs to be tapped into. You're a good example of that, Mr. Willis."
He smiles, a quick flash of brilliant teeth.

"Here, let me illustrate the concept with a story I use in my anger management class. Alright, so there was a boy who was angry all the time. His father told him to drive a nail into the fence each time he lost his temper. Within a few weeks, the fence was riddled with nails. Then the father told his son, each time you control your anger, I want you to pull a nail out. And so little by little, the boy learned to hold his temper and each time he did, he removed a spike. One day the son came back to the father and said, come see. Every single nail had been pulled from the fencepost. You've done well, said the father. But tell me what do you see? The boy took a good look at the fence post and said, Lots and lots of deep holes. It's the same with the wrongs that we've done. You can ask forgiveness but the wounds are never gone. The holes are there as testimony to the past."

The intercom announces time for recall, which means twenty minutes until count time. Willis dutifully stands up and instinctively reaches to collect his garbage. I put a hand on the container.

"Leave the evidence here. We don't need the others thinking this is the new fast food joint in town," I say, winking at him.

"True enough. They'll be whining like little bitches."

"Have a good afternoon," I say, opening the door and closing it quickly behind him. I yank a pair of blue Latex gloves from the box in the back of my desk drawer. In there are the mandatory supplies for contact with any potentially contaminated inmate, especially in the case of fresh blood. The collapsible CPR face mask is tucked beside it, a device provided to all staff for saving the lives of people the public could care less about. It's our choice if we want to waste our precious breath in exchange for an HIV or MRSA exposure. I put on the sterile gloves, carefully grasp his drinking cup by the base and drop it in the clear freezer pouch. Touching only the tip end of the used fork, I place the plastic utensil in a separate sandwich baggie, seal the strip and drop it into the larger bag. Just as I am about to double-bag both specimens again, the door to my office swings briskly door open and lieutenant steps in. In his hand is a roll of rope, a radio and a notebook.

"What's your name, Counselor?" he asks.

"Abrams, sir."

"Well, Counselor Abrams, we're going to be spending some time together today. We've got a simulated Code Yellow about to happen and you've been randomly selected to be my hostage. Don't worry. I'll go easy on you," he jokes. As Lieutenant Ford sets up operations in the tiny airless space, I quickly drop what looks like garbage into the bucket of soap bars and shampoos. He gets on the phone to Main Control and then the code is announced.

"We'll see how these schmucks react," he says. "Here, give me your hands. Just pretend the rope is knotted real tight and all. What's the first thing you would do?"

"Try to discreetly dislodge the receiver. Remove all identifying equipment or parts of uniform associated with authority and make myself appear as a civilian."

"Good! What else?"

"Comply with the hostage-taker's requests. Don't resist. Keep a conversation running if possible. That will keep us on more of a personal level."

"Excellent! Okay, I'm going to try and place an outside call to the television station. Make some demands." He dials out on the '9' extension and is able to reach the receptionist at WBBB. Ford hangs up, irritated. He then rings up the adjacent housing unit.

"Fuller, what the fuck? This line should be dead." He hangs up and patches through to Main Control. "Watch this," Ford says to me, grinning. "Listen, assholes. I'm serious in here. I want a helicopter on site in twenty minutes or this girl gets it. You read me? Twenty minutes!" He slams the phone down, sits down and offers me one of the apples from his bag. "Let's see what these goons do." Nothing happens. No sign of any response. Ten minutes clicks by. Lt. Ford picks up the phone again. "Jesus Christ, it's still working. The first thing they should have done is cut the lines." He dials back up front. "I'm getting pissed in here. You think I'm fucking around? You got ten more minutes to show me some good faith." Phone slams down again.

"So how long have you been in this block?" Ford asks me.

"Eight months, roughly."

"You look to be about my age. You almost winding up on your twenty?" he asks.

"Not quite. I started a little later."

"Me? I've got five months to go. I can't wait to get out of this fucking dump." The phone rings.

"What? What?" he answers excitedly. The game is heating up. He looks over at me. "Yeah, she's alright. I haven't done anything yet. You got that helicopter?" He pauses, pretending to listen intently. "What? More time? Fuck that! What?" Pause. "Okay, I'll show you the girl. Then you get me that plane and ten thousand dollars. That's my best offer."

He slings the rope around my neck, slowly raises the blinds on the glass door and we take a peek. I am stunned to see a battalion of uniforms with shields and mace canisters stationed in the main hallway outside the locked unit.

"Okay, just a few steps out. Far enough where they can see you. Give them a little wave, then right back in," orders my captor.

They have the wrong girl for this job, but I do as he says. There is a commotion of activity as another wing of officers begins a strategic assault on the door that is a bolted fire exit to the outside yard. Lt Ford yanks me backwards, waving his butter knife and shouting obscenities. This war game has become a real competition in his mind. He hops up on the office chair, throws a rope over the plumbing pipes near the ceiling and cinches it in a slipknot. Then back on the phone.

"Time's up," he shouts to the appointed commander at the staging area. "If you don't have what I want in three minutes, she's dead. No more talking." He indicates that I should stand in the middle of the room just beneath the noose. He tugs it down and sets in gently around my shoulders just for a visual effect. We both wait in silence half-expecting to hear the harried descent of a chopper on the roof. Nothing happens. Ten, maybe fifteen minutes pass. Ford tosses another apple core in the trash can. Suddenly the door to the office blows open with the force of a swat team behind it. Boots pounding, shields up. I am knocked off my feet into the bookcase. The blunt end of the extraction shield catches my elbow before pinning my captor's face to the cold concrete wall.

There's one C.O. on each limb now as they subdue their target. In the commotion, some over-eager cadet-in-training sets off the cap-stun spray and the room quickly fills with the acrid agent. An officer grabs my arm and escorts me through the fog to safety. Even so, my airway constricts and a spell of violent coughing comes on. Mucus streams from my mouth and nose as I bend over letting the fluids drip out.

Within fifteen minutes, we are all rounded up and directed to the large visiting room where the Warden debriefs us. Apparently the entire operation failed on several fronts. The perimeter crew was far too slow in getting to the live weapon arsenal. Some staff did not respond to the proper staging area designated for such an emergency. The state police had come on cue, but were unable to get an accurate face-to-face count of all staff using the hostage cards that were kept on file in the Admin wing. A swat team had not gotten to the alternate access area in sufficient time. Main Control failed to cut the connection to the outside which left the suspect with access to the media and accomplices at will. Finally, the Warden turns his attention to me.

"And just so you know, you would have been dead three times over." *Good to know.*

We are dismissed back to our posts with a reprimand and the threat of a repeat in the near future. My office is in complete disarray. These guys took their orders seriously and left no stone unturned and little standing. My stack of files is curdled with a layer of yellow foam. Pages from the lesson manual are sifted all over the floor and the contents of my wastebasket dumped and scattered. *Shit!* The bagged evidence is among the mess. The eating utensil and drinking cup are still inside but the bag itself is curdled with the toxic film. *Fuck!* I zip it into my thermal lunch bag and lock up. I'm not one-hundred percent certain of its integrity, but I can't go back on my promise to myself. Otherwise, I have no credibility at all.

PART THREE

CHAPTER 11
EMPATHY

"I always be good to the ladies. Treat 'em real well. They come to me and I take care of them. I'm not from here. Miami is my home. I only came to jail because I turned myself in," says Ortega. He's just plain slimy like some reptilian creature that coils over and around on itself with darting eyes and a forked tongue. Ortega shifts his wiry frame, puts one foot on the desk and slouches to the side.

"Don't do that!" I say. If he persists, it's a write-up for flagrant disobedience. "So what are you going to do when you leave here?"

"I'm going to college and get a psychology degree. Prove to all these mother-fuckers in here that look down on me that I can outsmart them."

"You're full of shit!" Serge shouts suddenly. I focus my attention on our resident mobster. This is no Godfather stereotype. Serge is regal in height unlike his swarthy Sicilian relatives back in the old country. His towering presence commands immediate attention. He is a man of silent intimidation until someone presses his button, which has unfortunately happened innumerable times in his life; and once he's turned on, watch out! Someone's going to bloody well pay. Unless you are fortunate like I have been to catch him in private. Then, and only then, is the soft side of this criminal displayed. I know Serge's secret. He is a man who has begun the process of change. For the first time in his thirty-year career of crime, he has something that he has never had before — hope. He is finally ready to retire from the street. I am surprised then to hear such virulent hostility in his voice. Ortega shoots him a greasy smile.

"No, I mean it. This guy is really pissing me off, Miss Abrams," Serge says, raising his voice. He is speaking to me but has not taken his eyes off Ortega. Before I can intervene to determine what has triggered his irritation, Serge stands up and moves his towering frame around his desk. He's staring down the Cuban on the far side of the room. The other participants feel the tension but do nothing. Ortega is alone in this. He has alienated all the others with his not-so-subtle habit of telling the teacher exactly what she wants to hear. Everyone knows he is just here to collect his certificate.

"What's bothering you here, Serge? Each person has their own story and the right to tell it," I ask. The big Italian balls up his fists that are twitching with anticipation.

"Yeah, but his is total bullshit. Can't you hear it? He says one thing here in class but I know him from back in the block. He's all about manipulating everyone," rants Serge. Ortega is squirming in his seat but does his best to maintain face in front of the opposition. He nudges Crespo with his elbow and nods in the direction of the irate mobster.

"Can you believe this shit?" he says nonchalantly. "The guy just don't like Spanish people chillin' in the same space as he do." His Latino neighbor immediately flies into stream of Spanish chatter. Both men nod and smirk. Ortega looks back at me. "I'm just sayin' I didn't have to come to jail. It was my choice. I had a good life in Miami. Money, cars, women. Gave it up to do the right thing."

"You're tallkin' crap out the side of your mouth, man. I see you in the unit. You're a pussy, always whining like a little bitch. You don't know how to do your time," Serge hisses.

"I don't know why you gotta be such a hot-ass right now," Ortega spits back. "Maybe that's how you see it cuz you're older than shit. But it's a new generation now. Our time. It's not the old-school way of doing things in here anymore."

"You little fuck. You want to sound like a big man? You're no pimp, you're a punk," shouts Serge. Ortega's dark eyes open wider, his deep lashes flutter with pretend piety as he looks imploringly at his tolerant teacher.

"Miss, I know my life was wrong and seen that I needed to change. I'm taking care of me first now, cuz at the end of the day, if we don't love ourselves, we can't love anyone else," he says. Serge is bristling now. No one is egging him on, certainly Rev, not his closest ally, who is absent today. Serge is propelled by some inner voice that tells him to take a few steps farther out into the middle of the room. He points his finger at Ortega who is tilting back in his seat now, eyeing the crowd.

"Shut the fuck up, asshole!" Serge says with cold-blooded calm. I grab the phone and dial up the officer on post.

"Can you give me a hand down here, please?" I whisper. No need to spell it out. A lift of the receiver is automatically interpreted as a summons for help unless clarified otherwise. If the guard is on point, he will be out of his chair and on his way down the hall now. Right on cue, Officer Madden darkens the doorway in less than a minute. His hand is on his utility belt like a cop fondling the handle of his revolver as he steps warily into an unsecured crime scene. Unfortunately, Madden's only available tools are a set of handcuffs and a pair of purple latex gloves tucked in a pouch.

"Everyone playing nice in the sandbox today?" he asks almost sweetly, masking his air of superiority with slick sarcasm.

"Would you please escort Mr., Magrini and Mr. Ortega back to E-block West?" I ask.

"I'd love to," says Office Madden, grinning. In his mind, he's thinking this could be good for a little sideshow entertainment if either of the inmates get mouthy on the way down. Even though he's outnumbered two to one, there's no risk involved. A literal army of back-ups are easily summoned out of the officer's mess and at least a handful of his buddies will be chatting it up by the hall keeper's desk as he and the troublemakers cruise by.

"Let's go, gentlemen," he says. Both men leave willingly under the watchful eye of their uniformed escort. Before they exit the room, Serge lets one more threat fly.

"I'll see you at tier Rec this afternoon. We'll settle this man to man," he hisses. Both Ortega and Officer Madden act as if they didn't hear the threat.

"Shit, dudes. I thought Ortega was going to get his ass beat down," says Dent with disappointment after they are gone. He was looking forward to a show.

"Naw. Pop's all talk. He's not gonna mess up his own shit over some greasy Spic. I mean, Spanish dude," says Noble. He speaks with the assurance and authority of one who knows his customers well, fully aware that no one will challenge his resume of experience. The remaining members begin to break out into separate conversations and choose sides.

"Guys! Hold up! I want to hear your take on what happened here today. We've been talking about conflict resolution and what it means to be assertive versus aggressive when addressing issues. Unfortunately, we just witnessed a hostile encounter between two individuals. Any comments on whether you thought it was handled properly or not? Maybe suggestions about what might have been improved in this interaction?" I ask.

"Serge over-stepped his boundaries. He should not have threatened that kid," says Zimmer.

"But Counselor, that kid is a punk. He talks mad shit. All he's doing is trying to win points with you so he can make parole," adds Bowman.

"Trust me. I didn't start this job yesterday. You guys assume whoever talks the most in class or reels off more paragraphs on his homework will get an automatic gold star on his report card. Not so! I look at many things such as attitude and initiative." I note a few blank stares in the crowd. "You all know what initiative means, right? That extra effort and determination to improve. But the biggest piece of the pie is the degree of responsibility you all assume. By that, I don't mean paying child support or getting a job. I mean taking responsibility for your actions as a real man should."

The group is totally silent. Each man is busy trying to figure out where he falls on my human integrity scale, hoping like hell that my assessment has not tossed him in the poor category. "Ortega didn't do anything wrong. He's irritating as fuck but he didn't do anything to provoke that reaction," Bowman says.

"Agree or disagree?" I ask the rest of the participants. Most of the men nod in the affirmative.

"Just so you know, based on his poor attitude and absences, I could have kicked our friend Ortega out of this group a long time ago. In fact, I did remove him from my morning session where he was a major disruption to the younger guys who were actually making real progress. It's my job as a group facilitator to preserve the greater good. You've probably heard this expression before. One bad apple can spoil the whole bunch, right?"

"Yeah, Michael Jackson said that," says Euclid.

"No, douche. He said 'one bad apple don't spoil the whole bunch, girl,'" replies Dent.

"Apples don't come in bunches. They are in bushels or pecks," Zimmer adds.

"Fuck off, old man," mumbles Dent. All this negative energy makes me wish the Rev was here today. Even though it's fake and syrupy as shit, his words do have a way of lulling these guys into complacency. Or maybe it's boredom.

"Okay, stop! Now! It doesn't matter about the apples. You've gotten way off the track here. What I'm saying is that one person should not be allowed to spoil the experience for the entire group. So I switched Mr. Ortega to this class because there are more mature students in here who can model better behavior for him. I decided not to kick him out for one other very important reason. Because he *needs* it. Maybe more than anyone in here. He's still far from admitting his part in the mess he's made of his life. Now, anything else?"

"I think Serge took it personally and he shouldn't have. He was pissed because that kid reminded him of his own cockiness when he was young," Zimmer responds.

"Excellent point. That's something we have discussed. Sometimes anger is triggered by internal factors such as our own personal interpretation of the facts. Maybe it struck a bad chord with him because he wasn't able to see it from an objective point of view. So what could have been done differently here?"

"He could have ignored him," Dent says. I nod in agreement.

"He could have fallen back and waited until he cooled down. Then maybe axed him 'bout it," suggests Noble. I'm nodding furiously now. We're getting closer.

"He could have tried to understand where Ortega is coming from. Heard him out," Willis replies.

"Good. Good. And what's that called?" I lean in and urge them on with an enthusiastic expression of anticipation. We are on the brink of something big here.

"Empathy," announces Bowman. I turn to look at the somber kid who speaks without looking up. *Bingo!* I extend my arms in his direction encircling him in a hypothetical hug. "Brilliant! Extra points to you!" I say enthusiastically. "Coming to the table to resolve an issue is not about winning. It is about arriving at a conclusion as swiftly as possible. Solving a problem or making a decision. Not dragging it out, but putting the matter to rest."

"Compromise," someone shouts. I look out at this motley collection of broken souls and I see the little boys they were or might have been, bouncing on their bottoms with an eager hand raised, hoping to be the one the teacher called on for the right answer and announcing it slowly, clearly, with a pound of pride; then basking in the beaming smile they are rewarded with from the proud lady up front. She will be remembered in their daydreams as someone who cared enough, cared too much perhaps; but the one who told them to tuck in their shirts, stand up straight and put their best foot forward.

#

"Miss Abrams. Can I be excused to go to the bathroom?" Gemini asks. He's been fidgeting in his seat and tugging at the fine wisps of long hair that frame his face with an interesting color rendered from a homemade paste of coffee grounds and orange juice.

"Yes, you may, Gemini. You know the deal," I say. They all do. The rule is one at a time and no longer than five minutes before the whistle is blown and someone goes looking. Gemini drops his folder on the desk and hustles out the door. We move on in the material without him. Many minutes go by before I notice an inmate from an adjacent class is standing outside our room waving to get my attention. I go to the door and crack it open enough to hear him.

"One of your students needs help in the bathroom. He's asking for you," he says.

I can't leave the group unattended so I lift the phone and summon the school officer who is posted at the entrance to the unit. He agrees to walk down and supervise the men so I can "make a personal trip to the ladies room." There is a staff bathroom that serves both men and women but I bypass that door and head around the corner to the toilet area by the entrance to the library. This restroom has a door that is always partially ajar for security and safety reasons; an aperture I usually avoid peering into since only a half-wall stands between the urinals and the sink area. I can immediately see a man's body half-slumped against the far wall.

"Oh, Jesus Christ! Gemini?" I shout. Without checking to see if there is anyone else in the room, I rush over to where he is crouched. There is a fist-sized hole in the plaster just above the radiator and a film of white powdery debris and insulation paper on the floor underneath. A clutter of broken egg shells with dark gray yokes sit atop his lap. I can't fathom what has happened. I lean in and peer more closely at the scrambled mess, which turns out to be the tiny deceased bodies of nearly-formed baby birds still tucked down in their incubators with wings glued tight to their sides. Gemini is holding a pen which he used to pry open the nesting place hoping to rescue the brood that had somehow become trapped inside the wall. Birds fly through this old ark of a building all the time, flapping up in the bowers of the high hallways and chittering from wire perches; but how any grackle could have gotten in here and chosen that tiny niche for a nursery is an unsolvable riddle. There are six dead and dehydrated fledglings on his lap and a seventh baby in his right hand. Its eyes bulge from its bald face. Its beak slowly opens and closes, opening again and snapping shut as it looks to his rescuer for life-saving support. Tears are running down Gemini's face and his big breasts jiggle from the force of his sobs.

"Oh, this is so sad. How on earth do you think they got in here? And how did you find them?" I ask. His grief is so great he can't answer. I put my ungloved hand on his shoulder, ignoring the Universal Precaution of avoiding exposure to HIV or MRSA or any other infectious diseases that run rampant here.

"You did your best to try and save them all. They would thank you for that! Give me the little guy and we'll give him a decent chance." I take the dying bird from his hand and wrap it in a few layers of paper towels. Gemini stands to his feet and wipes his face with the heel of his hand. I'd like to know what brand of foundation he's wearing since not a single blotch of it has smeared during this breakdown.

"I nominate you for a special humanitarian award and induct you into the Audubon Society's Hall of Famers," I say. Gemini sniffs and then giggles. His perfect doll-shaped lips reveal lovely white teeth. "I'll give you some more alone time. If the officer comes by and gives you any hassle, tell him to come see me. Alright?"

He nods, grateful not to be dragged back in the room with a bunch of homophobes who detest weakness and who react to tears like sharks to blood.

#

Serge is immediately wary when his name is bellowed out from the officer's post and his cell is popped. A summons like this can be either good news like a visit or bad news in the case of a disciplinary investigation. But when he sees the friendly face of his counselor, Serge brightens considerably and gladly joins me in the tiny concrete cubicle tucked beneath the upper tier. He is visibly remorseful and immediately apologetic.

"I'm sorry for my behavior, Miss Abrams. I really am serious about changing my ways. But I have a bad temper and a lifetime of acting a certain way is a hard habit to break."

"I understand. That's why I'm here," I reply. "I saw that in you from the first day."

"I'm so pissed at myself. I know better. I shouldn't have treated that kid like that but he reminded me of my own self at that age. An insincere piece of shit. His ignorance just set me off."

"I'm sure there were people that were patient with you when you were at his stage in life."

"I didn't get much time to grow up. I was always bouncing between New York and Danbury, Connecticut. My mom was in the suburbs and my Dad was into organized crime. I'm not a good person, Counselor. I ran clubs where women dance. You know, strippers. And I feel awful now about these young girls that looked to me to lead them. I was twice their age and I took some of them in. But it was always about what we could get out of one another like drugs and sex. I'm tired of that life. I can't do it anymore. Thirty years behind bars is enough. I'm fifty-three years old for Christ sake."

This tough guy sits in front of me with more gun fights, beer brawls, drug busts and money handling than the number of Hollywood blockbusters made in my lifetime and yet he is beginning to cry. He drops his head in his hands in the posture of a truly contrite man. In any other world, I would reach out and brace his shoulder or offer him a tissue but I am kept away by edicts that categorize us as human beings in different stations of life. It's always been that way. People looking for what separates us, always herding the sheep away from the goats, the wheat from the tares, and the good from the bad. All I can see is what binds us together, the remorse of being born with flaws that crack under pressure and send us splintering.

"I've lost the respect of my son and his mother. I have no one left to call family. Last time I was released, I had just enough money to get myself an apartment and hook myself up with some video games and a TV. I never left the place. I was too afraid because there was no one out there who cared. I had no purpose other than dabbling in fantasy games and watching reality shows about other people's lives. I couldn't stand the loneliness." A few minutes later, he shakes back his head and wipes his cheek with his sleeve.

"Do you want to come back to group?" I ask. He nods his head and then straightens up to full height. Stripped of his temper and the terrible past that has created a permanent scowl, he is quite a handsome man. *Shame on you for thinking that, Elise. He's a ruthless and persistent offender just like all the rest of these shitheels.*

"I do," he says emphatically. "Don't give up on me yet."

"No chance," I say with confidence. "It's time for chow. I'll see you tomorrow, Serge."

As I depart the unit, a cat call of hoots and whistles goes up. Men are waving papers through the bars and banging to get my attention. It's like a dog pound in here, loud and reeking of urine. Not many unfamiliar faces come through this place so all vie for a look, a handshake or a scrap of a kind word, each one hoping that they'll be the one chosen to go to a new home.

#

On Tuesday, Zimmer is missing from the class. His handicapped spot closest to the door is empty. Though he's skinny as a matchstick, he demands a double space the width of two desks to fit Bertha, his wheelchair bitch in. Without him, the atmosphere is noticeably different. There is less levity in the air and no snappy side cracks to keep everyone at ease. Whether or not he knows it, Zimmer is a pivotal player in this twelve-act production; maybe not the lead role, but the guy who keeps the action moving and the audience entertained. He has a knack for filling in the blank spaces with improvised monologue. The other men have come to really appreciate his wry insights.

"Anyone know where Zimmer is at?" I ask. The call down to the officer in the old-timer's unit turns up a snippy, three-word explanation. 'In the hospital.'

I know more than I can tell. Zimmer is a decoy of sorts planted voluntarily in the marsh to make the real targets feel comfortable enough to land next to him. He has no domestic violence in his history. Arguments with his long-ago wife never amounted to more than a few short words, but he unwittingly ruined another happy marriage. Somebody else's wife was plowed under by the wayward steer of Zimmer's big white Caddy which he was driving while drunk. That car was both his home and a means to a livelihood. His last known residence was in Tent City under the railroad bridge spanning Waltham River. He peddled his produce from the trunk of that beauty; Spice, K2, Meth, and Puppy Chow, fatal drugs with flirty names that caught the eye of high-schoolers; but Zimmer had a conscience. His own son was barely twenty years old and was now running loose with no home-sweet-home since his ex-wife's house had literally gone up in smoke during a five-alarm insurance scam. But the true tragedy, the gut-ripping heartbreak that placed this whole man's spirit in lockdown, was the chapter that he edited out of his daily monologue. He had a freight train-sized load of guilt over his daughter who in his prolonged absence was taken in as ward of the State and then committed to the Merrimack Institute. Desperate to be with her boyfriend, she leapt from a third-story window and suffered severe head injuries as a result. For the past two years, Juliana had existed in the nebulous world of brain injury, unable to speak or walk or move except two fingers on one hand. Up until his motor vehicle accident, her father, Ezra Zimmer, had been her unflagging advocate and nightly bedside companion. Whether drunk or sober, arriving as a hitch-hiker or pedestrian, he never missed a single day. Her mother was unaccounted for, her boyfriend had bailed and fair-weather friends had moved on but Zimmer stayed. In a tragic turn of events, this horrific catastrophe had finally defined his purpose on this planet. He knew without a doubt that he was meant to be the caregiver to his only daughter. But then he fucked up and went weaving down the roadway going too fast. He missed the intersection. Frustrated at his oversight, Zimmer navigated a wobbly U-turn, adjusted the wheel recklessly and gunned the accelerator. Next thing he knew he found himself strapped upside down in his seat gaping at a wall of crushed metal. On the far side of the twisted hood was a knotted red and black chassis with unhinged doors and shredded rubber all braided together into a deathtrap. The rest was a blur of ambulances, police and then jail. He didn't know until day afterwards that there had been a woman trapped inside.

When her father ceased to come, Juliana Zimmer languished in her routine. She stopped eating, cooperating, and responding. It was clear she was holding out for him. Zimmer thought of every calculated move he could make to get his sentence reduced or commuted. He even considered jumping out one of the windows to join her, but being that he was housed in a maximum security prison, that plan had been thwarted from the building's conception. He tried to get his sentence modified and his parole date moved up, but nothing doing. He requested a hardship transfer closer to the location of her rehab hospital. Negative. His latest scheme was the disability scam he had concocted to earn him a settlement pay out from the State, which he would then use to leverage a court-ordered early release. Time would tell, but time was running out. In another eight years, a reunion between father and daughter was highly unlikely. One or both of them would be dead.

After class, I walk to the sour-smelling hospital wing and find Zimmer corralled in a large holding pen waiting on his name to be read from the sick call roster. His injury is a hoax, but his pain is real enough. His liver is pickled, blanched white and rubbery like the texture of firm tofu from two pints of straight Majorska a day. His endocrine system is giving out. Zimmer looks jaundiced. A yellowish hue has overtaken his dry skin, mellowing the sharp contrast of flashing dark eyes and his baby-pale epidermis. He is tired, not from age but the un-ending string of escape plans that plays out in his head. He doesn't mind coming back to prison, once his daughter is better and he has found an apartment where he can have a hospital bed set up and has sufficient capital to pay for twenty-four hour care. That's what he was in the business of doing when everything fell apart. His pug, Cricket, has been displaced from her royal purple princess bed with plush velvet padding. He's afraid the other dead-beats under the train trestle have stolen the little mutt's diamond-studded collar and hawked her bling for booze. No one knows about the unauthorized call I had placed to the chronic care floor at his daughter's rehab hospital. What a sweet sight it was to witness this broken-down man humming nursery-rhymes into the receiver, and joy of all joys! just before we had to hang up, seeing his face when the nurse told him that Juliana's index and pointer fingers had twitched to life at the sound of his scratchy lullabies.

I wait with Zimmer until the disgruntled nurse shouts out his number. He has to keep up the artifice, the faux limp and excruciating discomfort. This is just a required check-in to keep his grievance at the forefront of the litigation pile.

"I hope you find a way to be with your daughter," I say as the nurse repeats his name in a pissed-off curtain call.

"Thank you, dear," he says to me. His hands wobble on the rubber wheels as he starts to roll in her direction.

"You got my martini ready, hon?" he replies. The battle-axe gives him a stink-eye glance as he glides over the threshold into the dirty exam room.

#

Ten more minutes to recall. I sense the group is drifting today. Perhaps it's because of the brilliant sun and shimmering sky that teases through the panes. Twenty-three hours of confinement is bad enough, but there's always the possibility that that one precious hour of recreation could be yanked away for any number of reasons such as a staff shortage, rainy weather, icy walkways, lock-downs or just because. When that happens, the twenty-fourth hour is spent circulating around the perimeter of the windowless gym with numbing headphones on, imagining the bustling breeze that is winnowing the acorn hulls from leaves deadened by drought. I decide to wind things up a few minutes early and allow them to enjoy the fresh scent of cut field grass and sweet corn fodder that's come streaking in the windows.

Suddenly our shared calm is shattered by sounds of distress. A woman is shrieking. My gut goes instantly cold.

"Go, go. All of you can go!" I yell. I flush them out ahead of me forsaking my duty to secure those under my charge. If there is any error to my alarm, it is on behalf of the unidentified victim who is screaming in terror. I rush blindly forward with my ears wide open to her alarm.

"Stop it! Stop it! Stop!" she screams repeatedly, her voice shrill with panic. The terrifying cries come from a classroom on the opposite side of the hall. The teacher in there is a petty middle-aged woman who, despite being unpredictably bitchy, has a big heart for these guys. I am the first staff member on the scene. Several inmates are milling about in the doorway staring at whatever grisly scene is playing out in the room. I push past the big bodies that block the door and they give way under my frantic hands. Mrs. Frank is still standing, red in the face, shaken and hoarse but apparently unhurt.

"I should have called a code, shouldn't I? I'm not doing the right thing. I was just trying to get them to stop!" she wails.

An inert inmate is face down on the floor with his arms at right angles to his body. Papers are scattered around and underneath him. Large splotches of blood have dripped all over the hand-outs and the folder that neatly contained them before this whirlwind blew in and upset everything. One desk is overturned and other nearby ones have been kicked out of the way. My first instinct is to run to the fallen man who is dazed and rolling side to side trying to get his bearings. Apparently he was knocked out cold either by a hit to the temple or the fall. A deep gash below his eyebrow is pumping blood down his cheek.

"Stay Down! Stay down!" I tell him. A small utility sink and a dispenser of paper towels are at the back of the classroom. I grab a handful, run them quick under the faucet and force them into his hand.

"Put pressure on it. You've got a good wound there," I urge him. The injured inmate continues to try and sit up, despite the fact that there are several officers and teaching personnel now on the scene encouraging him to lie flat. They tell him medical is on the way, but no one comes closer than a healthy ten foot distance away. I keep putting the batch of towels back in his hand and lifting his arm up towards his face. He finally responds by dabbing at the laceration and wincing.

"Thank you, Miss!" he mumbles, bewildered. After the medical team arrives and kneels down to assess the damage, I turn and focus my attention on the harried teacher.

"Are you alright?" I ask. My nerves are pulsing wildly.

"Yes. Just scared to death," Mrs. Frank answers. While all hazardous duty staff is well trained to anticipate fights, it is still terrifying to be on the front line when brutality erupts. We walk on tiptoe with our steel-toe boots knotted tight and sharpened pencils clenched in our fists. Always ready but never prepared.

"Who did this?" I ask.

"It was Pisano, the newest school worker. He completely flipped out," she blabbers. *No, not Tommy. He's done so well.* My compassion goes out to the rattled woman in her petite lemon blazer and black pumps. Her knotted hands are shaking and perspiration has dampened her fringe of bangs. She looks like someone's grandmother. This is not a place for ladies.

"Out of the blue, you mean?" I ask. It's not beyond Tommy to do such a thing, but the new man that has been on display for the past few weeks seems genuine.

"Well, after I fired him and told him to leave my room immediately," Mrs. Frank adds.

"What did he do? Or not do?"

"He was in here putting the audio-visual cart back in the closet and all of a sudden he blurts out. 'Hey, did you see who won *The Voice*?' I'm shaking my head and put my hand up to stop him from spilling the ending. And just as I'm telling him to keep quiet and not spoil things, he announces the name just like that. Like it's no big deal. And I say, 'Are you *serious*? I've been waiting an entire season for this finale. It's all recorded just waiting for Friday night when I can sit down to watch it. Can you believe it? This idiot just blurts it out. So I ripped him a new one and kicked him out.'"

I want to slap her, standing there all self-righteousness with her foul-mouth flapping and a man's future riding on her small-mindedness. *A goddamn television show. Are you kidding me? You're the shallow bitch that should be groveling on the gritty tiles.* Did I say that out loud, I wonder?

"So he didn't really do anything serious then, you're saying. Nothing that would warrant a termination from his job," I state.

She looks at me dumbfounded. I see the territorial lines being drawn like the heavy window treatments that hang from thick rods and are yanked by ropes over the wall of glass to close out sunlight and winter cold. It's teacher against counselor and I'm on her turf now.

"I dunno about that," she says. "It's damn serious business to me. Besides, I gave him a direct order and he disobeyed it."

"Mr. Pisano can't take a lot of over-stimulation like excessive noise or someone shouting at him. It's a known fact. You can't bombard his senses all at once. You have to come at him slowly and patiently." She scowls her disapproval, turns her back on me and begins to straighten up the disheveled piles of paper.

"I don't have time to pussy-foot with these guys. This isn't summer camp, you know?" she snips. Not a thank you for the heroic hustle to ward off an attack and spare her post-menopausal skin.

"I still don't understand, though. You and Tommy Pisano had a beef. How did this gentleman got involved?" I ask.

"My peer mentors were still in the room cleaning up when this exchange happened. Mr. Eaton here, he said something to Mr. Pisano about being crazy like, 'All your chairs ain't pushed up to the table'. And Pisano punched him twice in the head so hard it took him off his feet and he fell onto the desk. He was ready to stomp his head to pieces if the others hadn't pulled him off. Before I could call anybody, he ran off down the hall."

I want to doubt her. After all, there is no evidence to prove anything and no suspect; but I don't need eyewitnesses to confirm his guilt. Tommy has been demanding for weeks that he be moved back up to a Level 4 facility where he can be housed alone, not surrounded by a dormitory full of douche bags. What else is a feeble-minded, enraged simpleton supposed to do when the world gangs up and hands you a bogus deal? Pisano has two speeds: *on* and *more on*. Mr. Pisano's outbursts are predictable and ironically endearing much like a naughty child that needs to be hugged and spanked at the same time. He simply wasn't organically equipped to live in close quarters with his fellow human beings.

Sadly, Pisano has just gotten his wish. If the system wouldn't listen to his cries for help, then he'd help himself up out of here the best way he knew how. The dead silence awaiting him in the solitary lock-up will suit him just fine. People were the problem, people like this dim-witted shrew that didn't have the smarts or the interest to try and understand his limitations and chose to come at him like he was some primitive brute to be chained and humiliated. People like her were half the reason that this man would eventually blast off and bludgeon someone. I accept the fact that prison is the only outcome for someone like Pisano who does not have the skills to live outside the walls for long. If he does leave, it is only a matter of time before he's back in Admitting & Processing bagging up his empty wallet and shoe strings and heading to the showers again.

#

Later, I sit at my desk and try to define the measure of sadness that seems to have seeped in to my being. People keep leaving my life without those vital words of closure, no final I wish-you-wells. Pisano is just one more name on the list of people I have vested myself in that will drop off into oblivion. Columbus screwed up somewhere. The world must be flat because one step out over my horizon and they are completely gone. There is no coming back. It's a persistent feeling with me, this longing for the missing. It started way back when young Lissa Braum abruptly departed while I slept, leaving me to befriend her imposter. Though we'd learned to get comfortable with one another over time, neither one of us trusted the other.

"What's wrong with you?"

James steps into to the small office. His head almost brushes the bottom of the mounted wall fan that's gyrating on loose screws and blowing hot air down his back. He has not given up on trying to maximize the *friend* definition, redefining and stretching it to get the most mileage out of our relationship as he possibly can. We've seen each other a few more time since the evening I repaid his favor with a healthy round of kisses. It's been safe things like taking a walk on a dusky park trail and coffee in a late afternoon café, benign activities that sidestep the slippery slope of commitment.

"I'm okay," I reply solemnly.

"Heard about the fight down at the school," he says. "I'm not surprised you were the first to lend aid to the other guy. Being the kind hug-a-thug that you are."

I look up from my keyboard and smile. No matter how hard he tries to convert me to his agnostic ways, I will remain my convicted self.

"You're telling me you wouldn't help a person who is down and injured? Isn't that a normal reaction we all should have?" I ask him.

"Not if it was an inmate. And certainly not without gloves on. You should have had yours with you, Elise. You could catch a host of diseases doing that. I worry about you, you know that. I hope you washed up well and sanitized your hands."

"I promise to be careful. When a crisis hits, my mind just jumps into auto-pilot. Instincts take over, you know what I mean? I can't help it," I confess.

James crosses the few feet between the doorway and my desk. A tall bookcase filled with curriculum manuals hugs the corner wall by the bulky air conditioner that leaks air out in the summer and in during the winter. There is little room to navigate in this tight space that already holds two desks, two chairs, two printers, a pair of waste baskets and boxes for shredding. Add in the solitary scanner and it's pretty apparent that this spot was not designed for social calls from a six-foot two-inch friend.

"I wouldn't want you to be any other way. Your sweetness came as a complete surprise to skeptical me. I have come to believe that like you, reality can be surprisingly beautiful."

A flush radiates down the sides and front of my neck. My scalp prickles with heat. An ill-defined longing creates an ache in my core. James reads something in my hesitancy to respond and places his warm hand on my wrist.

"What's wrong, Elise?" he asks with concern. I shake my head as tears well into view. The sight of blood, the shrieks for help and the pitiful treatment of human beings one to another is all too much. People say this prison has a unique darkness. Even when the sun is out and flooding the nearby fields, it shines differently on this place, as if the walls suck in all the vitamin sunshine and reflect only a yawning weariness. Souls have departed here; not just the sick and elderly prisoners who perish waiting for parole or a pardon, but others who have sat in the hot seat or had hell's potion injected into their bloodstream. A sense of anguish and gloom is ever present. The sucking need and the overload of negative gravity that can break men down. The weightiness of it all is just too much at this moment.

"Hey, how about tonight?" he asks. "Can I come be with you?"

"What did you decide at home?" I whisper. My voice is feeble and hoarse.

"I work a double today. I'll swing by after second shift and you can tell me what is bothering you. Okay?"

I nod ever so slightly without looking him directly in the eyes. My brain is trying to overrule a heart gone haywire, but it is still feeble in its formation of systematic stop-gaps. A trembling ripples out from the middle like a seismic quake moving old plates of soil and a layered past, building in intensity as it moves away from the original schism that parted my soul into two disjointed fragments – the before and after me.

CHAPTER 12
ARM'S LENGTH

James steps tentatively into the foyer and carefully wipes the soles of his boots on the mat by the door, as if he can scrape away the filth of the last sixteen hours that still clings to him. He looks tired and hasn't had time to change.

"Would you like something to eat or drink?" I ask.

"Thanks, I'm all set. I took my dinner break on the late side," James replies.

"Well, come in then," I say and wave him in towards the interior. He smiles sheepishly, scoots around me and takes a safe seat in the solitary captain's chair in the dining room. He's still wearing his utility belt with cuffs and chits that rattles against the wooden slats as he stands back up and reaches to undo the cumbersome buckle. An unfamiliar awkwardness arrived at the door with him. This unease is not resolved in words. We both know he didn't come here to talk.

The belt slides to the floor with the weight of its accessories. James leans down to pick it up but my hand on the top button of his trousers stops him. He looks up at me puzzled, trying to decipher any mixed messages. The tug and purr of his zipper being lowered ever so slowly makes it very clear. No time for indecision or change of heart. He stumbles slightly as I take his hand and start to lead him back towards the comfort of my room. His pants begin to slide down but he hooks a belt loop with his free hand and does a little shuffle and slide down the hardwood floor in the hallway. Once seated on the edge of the queen bed, he reacts quickly and frees his feet from the clumsy work boots that are holding up everything

248

else. He strips down to his bulging briefs and extends his arms in an eager invitation.

I shed my shirt and any former apprehension about committing cardinal sins along with it. The silk blouse slithers off my arms and onto the floor. I step closer. James reaches around behind my back and deftly unhooks the bra, pushing the buckled undergarment up over my sternum in his eagerness to mold and form the breasts under his cupped hands. They are fuller and rounder than he imagined, I'll bet. He whips back the quilted covers, pulls me onto the sheets beside him and smothers me with his teen boy body. His mouth covers mine, tongue parting and then prying open tight teeth. He touches everything, everywhere like a child set loose in a novelty store, so many alluring playthings that he wants but can't choose from. His fists are in my hair gently smoothing and tugging. He licks my earlobes and my cheeks. A consuming weight of warmth presses me down and wraps me up. I reach up to embrace him but he pushes my hands away, pinning my arms back down. My pulse takes off at a gallop. I can only catch shallow little gulps of air. *Flight or fight. Free yourself,* screams my adrenal gland. I take a deep breath and resist the impulse to tag out and flee. James seems to sense the internal tension building below. He takes it as a sign to continue with more fervor. *Calm down! This is your choice.* There is no going back now and neither of us wants to.

He means to ravish me completely and attends to this purpose with a maniacal attention to detail. I lie still and allow the physical worship to continue uninterrupted. James is up on his elbows now with his feet close together like a human tripod. The protrusion in his briefs presses with increased determination and force against the fabric of my panties. Someone is moaning. Someone else is breathing in rapid gasps. He lowers back down and moves with his mouth, leaving a trail of slick saliva as he migrates slowly southward over smooth terrain. At certain stops, he lingers. He is an experienced traveler that knows where he is headed and how to pace his movements. Finally his cheek comes to rest on my left thigh and his legs ensnarl with my feet. Again I reach down to touch him and he again he pushes my advances away, intent on pitching camp without distraction. I rest my palm on the top of his head and comb my fingers through his curls. *Relax. Don't flinch. Hold still.* He toys with the elastic that holds my panties tight in the crease between thigh and pelvis. He defies the resistant nylon and lifts my bikini bottom up and slightly over. The peek at pink flesh excites him. He pushes the panties to one side by increased increments until there is nothing left to cover the budding rose petals underneath. Beyond them, a wet steaming playground where he rushes to play with abandon and then takes me along with him, pushing me higher and higher until I launch up and out with limbs splayed and mouth wide open. There's that one split-second sensation in the drop of my stomach and then I'm falling feet first into a perfect landing; again and then once more until we're both too tired to play a minute more.

"Why are you crying, sweetie?" James asks. He is confused by this response to his lovemaking.

"Don't worry. It's all good," I say, reassuringly. I'm weeping over nothing, over everything but it is only healthy feelings springing back to life. The destructed nerves have been partially fused back together. I cannot find an explanation to accompany these emotions as he might want me to. Those words are buried so deep no man will ever find them. Only one man ever did. James doesn't ask again; instead, he draws me against his side and rocks me ever so gently.

"I loved that," James says sleepily. The energy has gone out of him. I can feel his muscles slack and jerk as he succumbs to the sleep he so badly needs. There are questions pressing into my view, thoughts of a worried wife burning up their family minutes trying to track him down. *Am I a mistress? Is this an affair? Does it matter?* I have staked my claim. He is with me now. I listen to him take shallow sips of air and then release it in lengthy drawls. I hold my breath waiting for something to go wrong, but the night carries on with the subtle trill of peepers and the rustle of poplars in the breeze. The thoughts I am happiest about having are the ones that come to me in contented silence and are never spoken. Better that the heart be without words than my words lack heart like the 'I (almost) love you' that stays cuddled in my craw for another time and place.

"Time to say goodbye to this greasy fat fuck," announces Dent. He looks ten pounds lighter today though he claims no change in his honey-bun diet. It suddenly occurs to me what the difference is. The weight of oppression has just been lifted. A man stands far taller when he's facing freedom.

"What up, man?" asks Noble. "You bouncin'?"

"I e.o.s. tomorrow," replies Dent. End of sentence. Finit. As of midnight he will officially be on Ex-Offender Status.

"Congrats, man," says Serge with the slight reservation that those who must remain behind always feel. For some, the sight of a bunkie heading to Property for his departing photo is often just too much. It's not uncommon for envy to erupt into a provocation to fight as a feeble attempt to sabotage their comrade.

"What about you, dude?" asks Dent. "You gonna get outta here any time soon or are they rollin' you out in the casket?" Zimmer laughs his dry wheeze and self-deprecating chuckle.

"They want to send me to inpatient. But how the hell am I gonna get my hands on some real chicken parm in rehab?" he says.

"You like Italian food?" asks Serge.

"Shit, yeah," answers Zimmer.

"You come see me, my friend. Down in Manhattan. We'll hook you up with the best pollo cazzo in New York. The country for that matter."

"Pollo cazzo. Does that have red or white sauce?" asks Zimmer.

"Translation: best fucking chicken, my friend. Family recipe."

"You mean family as in your Mamma or as in Mafia? You wrapped up in organized crime, hit men and all that Godfather shit?" says Zimmer.

"Let's just say, ladies, I was *involved*," Sergio confesses with a wink.

#

I keep looking at the clock and wondering what's going on in the airtight conference room in the back of the visiting room where the parole hearings are held. It's been over two hours now and no sign of our resident gadabout. I'd know it if he'd come back to the unit; a buzz of chatter follows him everywhere. This morning he was up at daybreak fixing his limp hair and penciling in his eyebrows with a nub of charcoal pencil. Despite several postponements, Gemini finally has his chance to sit before the Board. After twelve long years of preparation, he's beyond ready. The man has been voracious in digesting every sweet opportunity to add to positives accomplishments to his portfolio. And in truth, all of what it contains is pure fact.

I'm busy printing off time sheets when Gemini stamps back into the block, flings his pass on the floor, storms down the steps and into his cell, demanding that the officer lock him up immediately.

"Don't lock it yet," I yell the block officer as I hustle down after him.

By the time I reach his bottom cell, Gemini is already face down on the bunk blubbering. He has the privilege of a single cell given his sexual vulnerability, so crying is definitely an option in here

"What happened? Gemini, tell me what happened in there," I say. "C'mon, hon. Get up and talk to me."

He finally obliges, rolls off the mattress pad and comes to the doorway. His face is blotchy and flushed pink. One of his flamboyant eyebrows has been wiped off on the pillowcase.

"I showed them everything, Counselor. All my certificates, program completions and the college degree. Not only that, I told them all about the volunteer time I've put in. You think it counted for anything? No fucking way."

"What about the other thing?" I ask. And yes, he had saved the best proof for last, pulling out the meritorious award he received for saving the life of his vocational instructor when the maintenance supervisor inadvertently came into contact with a live wire and was being electrocuted. Gemini used a broom to knock the man down, breaking the current that had paralyzed his muscles and rendered him unconscious, then performed chest compressions until help arrived.

The Board members listened carefully while rifling through the copies they had in front of them for review. Mrs. Tilton, the chair of the proceedings was an elegant but aloof white woman who seemed to take special interest in his story. When the interview was over, she asked Gemini to leave the room so that they could confer on their decision. Forty-five minutes later, he was summoned back in.

"Mr. Briggs. We have come to a conclusion on the matter of your Parole," announced Mrs. Tilton with perfect diction. "And I will allow you…" There was a significant pause, during which Gemini crossed and uncrossed his legs, wet his lips and leaned forward with anticipation. "…to serve out the remainder of your sentence within the Hazen penitentiary." The words were sharp and snapped with indifference. It took him several minutes to comprehend what she had just said and the cruelty of it. Jumping to his feet, Gemini looked the Parole Chairman in the eye and gave his own closing statement.

"Well, Mizz Prick, I will allow you….," he said, holding his tongue for a few seconds to let the suspense build "to suck my ass through a sippy straw 'til your lips turn juju brown." The woman and her constituents were of course horrified. This was definitely what *not* to say to the people who hold the future in their hands.

"You are dismissed, Mr. Briggs," said Mrs. Tilton. "You may leave the room now. You will not be heard again," she said, her voice empty of any emotion.

"You're goddamn right I'm leaving this fucking charade," he yelled. Gemini kicked his chair a few feet and tossed the personal file he had brought along with him. Sheaths of paper waffled and wended their way to the feet of the self-proclaimed judge who had just relegated him to six more years of hard time.

"And that's it, Miss Abrams. My whole life the last dozen years flushed down the crapper," moans Gemini. There's not much I can say to encourage him.

"You're a bigger person that she is by far," I say. "And much prettier too." A flicker of a smile flashes and fades. He bats his wet lashes and sniffles.

"Yeah, fuck her! She couldn't dress her way out of a paper bag. You should have seen the crap she tried to pass for business professional. And, she lightens her own hair with some cheap box of peroxide from Wally World," he says. "Looks like buffalo piss."

"Atta boy," I reply. Inside I curse the woman whose indifference might be the last straw that ultimately costs him his life. With his identity already swinging so precariously between genders and his self-esteem so dangerously low, it wouldn't take much to push him into hanging up.

#

I open the curriculum manual to our current lesson: Session 11. We are nearing the end of our odyssey. Eleven men and one woman slated to cover decades of dry ground and arrive at the finish line in less than two months' time. It's an amazing race of fortitude that few excel at. There is no million-dollar prize at the end of this short season to egg us on; just the hope that one or two among us will emerge stubborn enough to grasp and hold on to a new way of life. The proof of change is tricky. Like love, it is measured not in time but in the amount of transformation. One can be moving on a continuum over decades and have accumulated little growth or distance; and in an instant, another can make a leap that clears a lifetime of cheap talk.

"Malcolm X believed that second to college, prison was the place for a man to do his best thinking. If a man wanted to change, this is where he can start. Why do you think he said this? What do you guys have in here that people on the outside lack?"

"Time," answers Ortega.

"You got it! You all have an abundance of time to reflect and analyze and plan. Do it now before you get out. The world is waiting for you and you'll be consumed by bills and making a living and children and all those things. Most people on the outside never stop to question their lives. They don't have the luxury of time to do so. They are too busy just living. Put the thought in now while you have opportunity. You have to start caring about your lives more than others do. That being said, I disagree with Malcolm X," I propose confidently.

Noble immediately tenses his shoulders and starts to mouth an indignant protest. More than likely, there is a tome of philosophical differences between the black Islamic activist and my white self; and without question, Mr. I AM and Ms I'm- Not have had our differences. I sense he is getting ready to throw the race card at me.

"Hold up! Before you say anything, let me one up Mr. X by suggesting that prison is an even *better* place than college to do your best thinking," I add. "Why would I think so?"

"Because of all the distractions at college?" asks Bowman.

"Exactly! Temptations like drinking, women, sports, and socializing. Besides a hand-held Game Boy or a small TV with poor reception, a prisoner has his books and his solitude. Anyone who comes to prison will be smarter than he was before. Guaranteed. If you want to learn to be a better criminal, here's the place to do it; but if you want to learn to be a better man, now's your opportunity. And on this one point, Malcolm and I agree. If he is motivated, no one can change more completely than the man at the bottom."

"There's some real evil dudes in here that ain't ever gonna be different, Miss Abrams. No matter how bad you want them to. They spend their time planning how to pick up where they left off. Soon as they get out, they're going back to the streets. You can't stop a man from doing what he's gonna do," Ortega warns.

The reality of the statistics makes me sigh with weariness. Eight of the eleven will be back within the first twelve months, most of them on technical violations of probation or parole rather than a new charge. The three lucky souls who make it to the magical three-years-free mark might just stay out but they are far from free men. The drug addiction has pickled their senses; the emasculation behind bars soured their sensibilities. Their forwarding address may well be the parking lot behind the old train station. They are still handicapped by inferior educations, hounded by child support enforcement, aspiring to be sandwich makers at a sub shop for marginal pay if they are fortunate to have the manager overlook their criminal record. *What if I I'm wasting my time? What else should I be doing?* If I stopped to question my part in this human drama, I'd be doomed as well.

"I realize that. It's up to each individual to make peace with this idea. The system can't force people to change," I admit.

"Why do they got to punish me for what another man does? I mean, I served my time. That's what they wanted, right? And then some other mother fucker gets out and shoots a dude in a gas station and out comes this new law. I shouldn't have to pay for his fuck-up. I can't know what he's gonna do."

"Listen, you have to remember that public safety is the number one priority, not only for law enforcement but for the citizens they swear to protect. This is what propels politicians towards drafting up public acts," I say. Euclid is right to a point. God Himself must be taken aback when one of his first draft picks falls miserably short of expectations and ends up buffing the locker room floor instead of mopping up the other team.

"But that's just human nature, my man. People judge us all as a group. That's never gonna change," Noble says.

"You just hit on a very good point. None of us can ever know what is in a man's heart. He might act like a model citizen on paper and be capable of incredible evil. Some of the guys who have left here and gone on to do heinous crimes looked great on paper. They were ideal inmates, supposedly."

"They tryin' to cover their asses, that's all. If something should happen. The Governor makes some dumb-ass decision that affects us all." Crespo is talking out of turn and off the cuff, but at least he's talking. However, he couldn't point us in the direction of his native Puerto Rico even with the help of a compass and he sure can't steer his conscience minus a moral compass. He has not a clue about politics, except the clearly-delineated party lines between one gang's turf and another's.

"In part, that is true because they pay attention to what goes on in their towns and cities. They listen to what is important to the citizens that vote for them. That is what drives the laws. When an ex-offender goes out and commits a horrific act, people are scared. And you can't blame then. The community puts pressure on the politicians to do something. Then the legislators meet and deliberate and try to come up with some new policy that will address that issue. Are others sometimes unfairly caught in these laws? Sure," I conclude. "But what's the alternative?"

"Enforcing laws or making up new ones is not going to change anything," Bowman argues.

"So, let me ask you guys. If not laws, then what will?" No one appears to have an answer for this question. Dead quiet ensues as each man ponders this question privately. The bell rings for recall. Noble immediately stands and starts walking towards the door.

"Hold on a minute. Thursday is our last class. I want each of you to spend some time thinking hard about what you have gained, either through the material in the hand-outs or from something someone has said here. And I'm asking each of you to bring in a piece of wisdom to share whether it be a in the form of a quote, a poem, a rap or an original thought. Does that make sense to everyone?"

"Miss. Miss. Will we get our certificates then?" asks Ortega.

"Here's the deal. You bring me the 'cash' and I'll hand over the goods. Fair deal?" I ask. There is a choir of discordant yes's, for sure's and no doubts.

"Will you bring the ice cream and cake?" asks Zimmer.

"Yeah, sure," I reply. "You're responsible for the entertainment. "

"Let's kick some ballistics. I don't wanna ever come back here and I never wanna be reminded of this place. Lots of dudes will say they're gonna go work with kids. Stop 'em from getting into trouble and shit like that. I'm not going out there and try to save the world. That's your job," Crespo says, looking straight at me with unwavering honesty. Amazingly, his near-perfect English has come back to him at this final hour.

"Yeah, Miss Abrams. That's your job!" they all echo.

"Well, looks like I'm doing a great job at screwing that up," I say. "You all are proof of that." The class erupts in good-natured laughter.

"Yeah, we're not changed men. We're just re-circulated personnel," says Zimmer.

CHAPTER 13
CRACKDOWN

Ready. Set. Go! As planned, the inmates are not expecting the army of staff that comes marching into the unit. The cons are milling about the officer's station and lounging on their bunks with their sneakers untied when we descend like a swarm. As ordered, counselors each choose a cube and man it up front as the residents are recalled. I keep an eye on the eight men under my watch as they grumble and dress, observing each movement, checking to see if an inmate tosses anything in the garbage so we can retrieve it. Two guys are acting suspiciously. One tucks small papers in the pages of his Koran and the other has produced a roll of Scotch tape and is wrapping it madly around a pen barrel. Whatever use it is intended for, tape is contraband and must be removed. A tall African-American seems disinterested in the whole show, props his mirror up against the plastic coffee cup and dabs pimple cream on his face. Another fellow is flushed out of the showers and comes skidding over, hopping on one foot in order to shed his shorts. I discreetly look down at the floor for the few seconds he is sans boxers. These guys are no different than women. Having unexpected company has prompted many of them to pull styling gel from their lockers to comb through their scalps. Bed C lumbers down from the top bunk in a lackadaisical crawl, slips his feet into untied kicks and scowls. A sleek, black German shepherd lunges against his leash whenever any inmate makes a sudden move or looks him in the eyes. His handler is enjoying the show of bravado. This half-grown pup will make a keen officer in another six months.

"That dog hates black people," mumbles bed A.

"He hates anyone wearing tan," says his bunkie.

"Like I said."

"Listen up, everyone. Off your bunks, now! You need to be in full tans only," barks the Captain. "No sweatpants or shorts. Have your ID's and shoes on. No headphones or electronics. We're shaking down this dorm. You'll be led out in groups of fours, strip searched and sent to the gym. Let's go!"

The Intelligence unit has learned that there is a cell phone in the facility, apparently in the hands of several gang members who are running game and orchestrating business with it. The mandate has been issued: Find that phone as soon as possible. The cell device reportedly has magnets attached so that it can cling up under anything metal. The Security Division has garnered details down to the make and suspected location of the phone, but we are not privy to the exact source of its signal. During our search we are to remove all disallowed items, anything deemed a fire hazard and any excess supplies above and beyond what is allowed on their personal matrix. Once the room is clear of inmates, we are underway.

I sift through grocery bags gorged with jelly-filled pastries, cupcakes with artificial cream centers, squeezable pouches of sandwich spread, bags of yellow, salty popcorn which smell much the same as the old socks and Converse knock-offs tucked beneath the metal bed. Packets of sweetener are crammed into Styrofoam cups along with denture cream and plastic combs. It's amazing how a life can be reduced down to a ragged envelope of letters, both love and legal. I roll the mattress end over end and search the frame underneath. Then I force a gloved hand deep into the shoes and boots, feeling for any pockets or opening in the lining where drugs can be stashed. The K-9 has pulled up short and squatted near a bottom bunk.

"Good girl!" exclaims her handler. She has rooted out the bag of heroin he planted there as a training tool. Some guards get a primal thrill out of looting through another man's possessions with the permission to decipher at will, tossing and tearing and leaving an ungodly mess behind. We work in pairs, two sets of eyes on the same territory. I'm teamed up with an officer who has done this routine a thousand times and scans robotically over the same old, same old. It is a filthy task. As worthless as these possessions appear, it is all a man has here. I try to respect the time it took for the inmate to fold his shirts and align his devotionals but for most, it is a free-for-all. A growing number of questionable items have been handed over in marked bags to the Captain, but still no cell phone.

"Take your time. I want you all to dig in and do a good job. We're in no hurry. We've got five days to take this place apart," shouts the Lieutenant.

The task of sifting through photographs is tedious but can often turn up vital information for gang Intel. I discover a pile of photos that chronicle a life of clubs, cookouts, cars and more stacks of cash than the local teller has in her drawer, but nothing noteworthy. My counterpart has pulled a bundle of papers out of a Federal Express envelope and left them strewn on the bunk. Pages torn from rapper magazines and Christianity Today, multiple years' worth of birthday cards, car catalogs, scorecards for gambling bets, journal entries of workout repetitions and newspaper clippings from Sunday inserts all manhandled and badly shredded in the hunt. I toss them on the floor to be swept up with all the other refuse. Several obituaries have been carefully creased and clipped together. So many young men lost to this make-believe war on the streets, like this handsome buck glowing up at me from his memorial prayer card. Poor Alix Carson, 1973-1998. *Carson*. Instantly my gut turns ice cold. I scan the short article for clues, perusing the lengthy list of survivors that in addition to his mother includes a sizable extended family of aunts, uncles, half-siblings and cousins. No cause of death noted.

Carson is one of three names on the short list of those who had the greatest impact on my life. The mention of it had the profound effect of stopping me in my tracks with the fearful reverence one has for something that has the power to kill and nearly had. I never saw the man in person. I'm not certain I would have attended the trial had there been one, even if I was well enough to get to the court house. But the plea proceedings took place in the privacy of the District Attorney's office and Carson disappeared into the crowd of thirteen thousand prisoners before we ever got a good look at him. All I had was a flash portrait like a profile in a quick strobe light, a shape moving in a jumpy dance away from me. The dynamics of our ill-fated encounter were spoiled from the start. I was his victim; therefore I was nothing to him. But for a time, he was everything to me. I received the victim notification call when they transferred Mr. Carson to a lower-level facility three years into his bid. When I sat at the parole hearing, he chose not to look at me. My only recourse was to read the impact statement that I hoped would sting his soul. Based on the lesser charges that he pled guilty to, the Board decided to release him after eighty-five percent of his sentence was served just shy of seven years. The final courtesy call came to inform me that Carson had just suited up in civilian clothing and was walking free. His co-defendant Turner followed a similar track but the onus of the crime fell on the first man as the instigator. Carson resumed his life pretty much where he left off. As for me, I was forced to recreate myself. What drove me to throw myself headlong into the mud of mankind was the need to find common ground where I could eventually look these men in the eyes; not up from the vantage point of a pitiful patient and not down at them from a distance of denial. No, straight on as a human being they could not ignore.

But what did this dead man have to do with the inmate who slept in this bunk? There is not time to formulate a plan. No materials can be carried out by a staff member. The only way to spare this item from the garbage is to declare it contraband and have it catalogued for removal and possible reprimand; but nothing about this benign pile of papers warrants this action, I need to find something else. Quickly, I rummage through the locker where his cosmetics are stuffed in Pringles containers. I dump out the Q-tips, nail clippers and strips of state-issued pills in a roll of serrated strips. Nothing suspect. And then it comes to me. I can use the potato chip canister. If they aren't storing food in them, these containers can be tossed. I grab the envelope of clippings off the bed, roll it in a cylinder and push the wad down into the tube. I mark it with the cube and bunk number and drop it in the trash.

There are more folders to go through but my partner is back to wind up this cubicle and move on. Even rooting out sexually-explicit material or gang codes is not enough to keep anyone here past shift change.

"All set?" he asks. Most of the other teams have snapped off their latex gloves and are sitting at the inmate tables tossing checkers at each other.

"Sure. Let's do it," I reply. Together we sweep up the debris on the floor and dump it in the waiting bins. We high-five one another. My heart is palpitating wildly, either from uncontrolled tachycardia or another full-blown anxiety attack approaching. I can tell everyone is looking at me, wondering why that counselor is walking stiff as a wooden Indian. My steps are out of sequence and bring me up short and breathless in front of the officer's staging platform.

"Can I have a locator sheet please? We're done in our cube. Oh, and a marker, too?"

"Help yourself," says the harried officer. I pull a copy from the stack and lift a pen from the officer's desk. On it we record the findings of the day and account for each man. Bunk 4D. Who lives there? Without my reading glasses, it's hard to make out the fine print. I run a finger down the left-hand column of the graph and stop at the designated coordinate, tracing across for the name and number. Terran Willis, # 99012. I quickly walk back over to the cube, bend down and collect the remaining pile of papers from the dumped envelope and place them at the top of the near-to-overflowing garbage bag closest to me. These will be dragged through a trail of laundry crystals and powdered creamer out to the hallway and taken en masse to the loading area. Already there must be thirty to forty huge bundles waiting there. Using the permanent marker, I make a large 'X' and label it 4D. I move with deliberate intent, but I have no clear plan yet on how to locate this bag and retrieve the rest of the suspicious evidence contained within?

Carson had stepped in front of the Final Judgment Seat and taken his knocks. That was justice, right? But hours after the shakedown was complete when I am home sipping a glass of Moscato and contemplating the soft snowing of white pollen from the sycamore tree, I realize it is nearly impossible to manufacture hatred towards a corpse. By now, my rapist is a bundle of bones in a casket stained with mold and black rot, and all I feel is disappointment that I have missed the annual joy of spitting on his grave.

#

Planning a crime is not a simple matter of putting on a ski mask or stealing a credit card. In order to achieve success, the smart criminal does not focus on what he hopes will go right, but rather what he knows will go wrong. He subscribes to Murphy's Law starting at the worst possible outcome, which of course is getting apprehended, and backing it up from there to the moment he decided to do such a thing. By calculating the pratfalls, our offender can pinpoint these areas of weakness and trouble-shoot them in advance of any action and thereby eliminate the obstacles to success. If the number of people that are involved is limited, the chances of getting away with the crime are proportionately increased. Every man has his price. Someone always sings in the end, so best not to let your right hand know what your left is up to.

Some are born with this genius of evil-doing. It stems from a mutated thread of DNA which creates clones of crazy cells that form a criminal brain. Everything about that person's perspective is skewed through a deviated lens. Others learn how to be aberrant as young toddlers bumping around their cribs, unaware that they are slowly being indoctrinated into the wayward choices of their caregivers. Fighting, lying, and cheating become as normal a routine as the bottle of Enfamil or the pacifier between their gums. They grow up in it. And then there is a third, much smaller subgroup of folks like me who must forcibly push aside past principles if they want to get the job done. As it turns out, none of us are above becoming evil especially when it's in the name of good.

I lie here thinking of what it must be like to know that not only are you capable of doing such a thing, but that you are *going* to do it. All of the cases on *Forensic Files* are eerily similar in one respect. These were average people who sat at the supper table every evening calmly sharing beef stew with their spouse as if nothing irritated them in the slightest, just as they had every other night until that one second when something tipped them off-center and they took that first step in a calculated plan. Where would one even begin?

I am intrigued by the evolution that takes a harmless housewife from mousy discontent to the blazing defiance of a killer in the courtroom dock. This episode is fascinating and features two wicked wives who used chemicals as a means to the end. Women can't handle a full dose of premeditated hatred. They choose to dilute it down instead which apparently makes the idea of taking someone out more palatable. I guess it assuages some of the guilt if you dish it out in little dainty measuring cups. In this particular case, the spurned woman chose ethylene glycol. Common antifreeze, we learn, is syrupy, odorless and sweet-tasting, making it easy to mix into coffee, tea, soda or juice drinks undetected. Antifreeze tastes pretty darn good for something that can kill you and it doesn't set off any alarms. Less than one-third of a cup can severely maim. It affects the central nervous system causing initial headaches, dizziness, slurred speech, vertigo, vomiting and eventually kidney failure. A preferred choice for poisoning.

Damnit! My show is interrupted by a call on my cell phone. I ignore it so I can watch the final ten minutes when the dead marine's wife is found guilty of poisoning him so she can collect a quarter-million dollars and use it for breast implants. Five years it took for them to pin her for the crime. It is amazing what little regard one person can have for the life of another. I switch off the television and check to see who called. There is a voicemail on my phone from my detective friend. I try to interpret the tone of his voice which sounds neither victorious nor gloomy. It's a generic request for me to call him back at my convenience. My heart beats wildly. I've been waiting my whole life for the answer to this question. Convenience is not in the equation. I dial him up instantly and after several rings, he is on the line.

"I got your message," I say breathlessly.

"Hi, honey," Hughes replies.

"Well...?"

"I want to preface this by saying that you need to think very clearly about what action you may or may not want to take. Information can be a dangerous thing. And there are repercussions that..." begins Hughes.

"Do you have the results?" I interrupt.

"Hold up. You sure are an impatient girl." He catches himself on that remark and retracts it. "I don't mean it like that. What I'm saying is just slow down and think before you react."

"Yes, yes. I understand. I've been thinking for twenty-six years, remember?"

"You've got that fiery Cooke spirit in you. But I shouldn't expect anything different. Okay. I ran the samples you sent me through the lab and checked against the National Database system. We know definitively who raped you, Elise."

Process of elimination hadn't worked when the case was fresh. Three men, two distinct DNA profiles but no proof. At the time of the trial, the seminal slides were little more than a cloudy pool of confusion that was ruled inconclusive and unreliable. Tell that to the parents of a daughter whose lower intestinal tract was ruptured and riddled with the human papilloma virus, a sexually transmitted disease, in a port of exit that hurriedly was converted to a welcome entrance for the depraved. Ask those parents to keep that knowledge to themselves since their daughter couldn't even decipher the menu or retain what she ate the meal before.

"Tell me," I say without hesitation.

"It was the two men, Carson and Turner. Just as we thought."

"No one else?" I asked.

"Absolutely not," Hughes confirmed.

"What about the fingerprints on the ropes and the pillowcase? Everyone agreed, the defense and the prosecution, that there was definitely a third set from another man. The one who tried to kill me," I insist. I can visualize him rolling his eyes like they all do at the mention of my invisible nemesis, the same way parents do to a child who has outgrown the stage of having imaginary friends but still sets a plate at the table for him and demands that he be buckled into a car seat.

"We can't prove that, honey. Even if we know it to be true. The technology that we have available is called decent but it too is limited. Forensics in this state relies on what's called Vacuum Thermal Evaporation where lab techs use intense heat to isolate the DNA on materials. There were partial fingerprints there that looked to be different, but it was not enough to match it or identify the person. We know they belong to a male but that's all I have, Elise."

"So you're giving up, is that it?" I ask accusingly.

"Listen, we can still go after Turner with what we have here. We may have a case within the statute of limitations. I would have to take this to the District Attorney to see if it's something they can re-open. The case never went to trial and the charges of sexual assault never lodged. I would have to see what contractual agreement was made between the attorney and the state when they drafted up the plea bargain. But it is possible that there is a loophole that we can slip through to hang this guy."

"Do you know where he is?" I ask.

"I'm an investigator," he says. "I always do my homework first. Hold on…" he says. I can hear the dead pause of a phone on hold. A minute later he is back on.

"Listen, I've got an urgent call on the line. I will ring you back as soon as I can and give you the few facts I have on this guy. In the meantime, let your gut lead you. Often our instincts are our best guide, okay? Love you, honey," says Detective Hughes before patching back over to his waiting distress call on line one.

#

"Miss Abrams. I'm only telling you because you're a good lady. There's nuthin' in it for me. Willis in 2-B's been on the phone with his 'boy.' Telling him the second he gets out, he's gonna go find his bitch ex, tie her up and throw her in the closet. Make her sit in her own piss and eat dog shit for trying to leave him. Then maybe clean 'er up and have some fun with her. I'm only sayin' this cuz he's bragging about it in the blocks. You need to know he's playin' choir boy in your class."

A snitch has a certain M.O. about him. He's overly friendly behind closed doors and openly defiant when he's on show with his peers. He offers others up willingly but his services aren't free. He tries too hard to groom favor with those in authority but really only cares about himself. I squint my eyes as if filtering some of the artificial light will make my vision clearer so I can spot the holes in his story. Would this mealy-faced manipulator have any reason to lie to me? What's in it for him?

"I appreciate your concern. I'll keep it in mind," I say cautiously.

"I'm not shittin' ya," replies Mr. Clancey. "He's always braggin' 'bout what he's done to these chicks. Tuned 'em up when they needed it. I've done my fair share of shit, don't get me wrong, but I'd never put my hands on a female. And if I had, I wouldn't be proud of it. I've got sisters and I sure don't want some dude treating 'em like that."

"I know the code in here," I reply. "It's risky to come to me. Thank you for looking out for others," I say. I rise to my feet and reach to pull the keys off my clip so I can let him back out into the henhouse.

"There's one more thing," Clancey says. I hesitate then, allowing him another minute more of privacy before he is absorbed back into the mass of drama that's milling about his bunk.

"Yes…?"

"Willis has been talking on the low the past two days. How he's going to find a way to get alone with you and mess your shit up."

There's a slight delay as I process what he has just told me. This Maine girl has to take in a shred of street jargon, turn it over end to end, spin it around and translate it into something that makes sense to a middle-aged Yankee who's straddling two worlds. Take for example, 'mess your shit up.' As in 'make an advance' or 'take what is mine and destroy it?' Is it open to interpretation or is there no other way to receive this but as an indirect threat? Is Willis playing me now knowing full well who I am? Or is this just opportunistic evil with its mind set on the next random victim? Either way, a female stuck in a six-by-six foot office space that was originally half of a shower room is a sitting duck.

"Would you be willing to repeat this to the Lieutenant if asked?"

"Yes, ma'am," he replies. "This guy's a tickin' time bomb. One of these days, he's gonna end up doin" some real damage."

I question his motives for speaking up. Clancey has no reason to lie, but then again, it's not his habit to be Joe Boy Scout. Either it's a false accusation to take a man down or a fact that will win him some favor. It's up to me to figure out which.

"We're done here," I say stiffly. Clancey looks as if he's expecting a pay-off for his services. He hesitates for a brief second and when I make no further move, he retreats, crestfallen. His fifteen minutes of fame are over.

#

The chairs are lined up in a ragged row like a low-income walk-in clinic. The officer on duty tells me they've been waiting in formation since six o'clock this morning. Mondays are always intense. These guys have had two whole days to sit and think what they can ask the counselor for when she returns. I am their information highway and they don't mind driving full speed and running me down in the process. I've decided that inmates are the most self-absorbed people I've ever met. With nothing but hours on end of idle time to dwell on themselves, why wouldn't they be? I am their mandated audience. All one-hundred-and-sixteen of them, each stunned when I pause for a moment to recall the issue he left me with seventy-two hours ago. 'You know the thing I asked you for.' 'You forgot, didn't you?' 'Did you look into that for me?' As if there's something wrong with me that he isn't the first thing on my list that day.

I step into the unit braced and ready with briefcase on one shoulder, water bottle in the other hand, keys dangling precariously from two fingers until I can find the right one and force it into the lock. It's stiff and won't turn without a second hand to stabilize the door. The officer is completely oblivious to my plight and has his head down. It's the tail end of his double shift. The floor is filthy with millions of bacteria from fecal matter and urine. It's an unsafe surface to lay anything down on; even flies would be put off by the conditions. I drop the water bottle into the briefcase and use my elbow to prop the door ajar. Water leaks into the paperwork. The guys sit and stare. No one is willing to give up their seat to help a lady out. I swing the door open and push it quickly shut behind me. I sit and listen to the jawing and haggling outside the office, a mounting impatience that is palpable. By nine o'clock, I typically unlock the door from the inside and stuff a wad of paper towels into the top corner to keep it hinged open. It's a tough reach for a woman of average height. If the janitor's dustpan is anywhere within sight, I often opt to jam it near the hinges on the bottom. It's growing louder in the unit. I'm still sitting at my desk paralyzed by some unwillingness to let them in. A wave of warmth radiates across my back and up my neck. There's no air in here. I want to go home. Not feeling up to it today, but I'm trapped by my own signature on a contract. Can't risk another unauthorized excuse to run out of here. *Calm down!* That clicking sound is driving me crazy. The small desk fan is struggling to keep its motor running. I realize it's been on since Friday. What if it had short-circuited and burned down the whole prison? So what if it had? I switch it off and swallow a good gulp of water. Someone's kicking the far side of the wall. The inmate phone is mounted there in that corner. Could be a restless habit or retaliation for my long delay. Finally, I stand up on my feet. *Time's up!*

First man in the door needs a sentence modification. Didn't get my jail credit, he complains. Second man wants me to place a call to his wife. Hasn't talked to her in three weeks. No money on my account,' he insists. *I am not a goddamn switchboard operator.* This is prison. You don't get to make social calls. Third man has a grievance. His house keys and cell phone were lost in transit when he was transferred and are not in the prison property room. *So what, I'm supposed to crawl on hands and knees to look for your crap after you stripped an innocent man of his credit cards and cash and threatened to blow a hole though his spine as you ordered him to walk away?* I can see in the reflecting mirror that more than one man has slipped into the hall area between the two doors. There are three of them now congregated on the other side of the wall. A dangerous scenario. "Wait outside!" I yell. You'd think the officer would notice the jam up and police the door. There's further unrest out in the main room as the stragglers file back and resume the front of the line. Fourth man wants a bar of soap. Claims he has no money. "You have thirty-six dollars on your account, Mr. Green. Look at the print-out in your hand." He won't back down. Claims he needs it to wash his clothes since the liquid detergent does such a shit job. His shirts are scratchy. "I'm sorry," these supplies are for the indigent. I pay taxes, he says. And you're telling me that you won't give me one bar of lousy soap? I glance at the paper bag of hygiene supplies. I have a slip of six bars in there. "It's not about me; it's state policy." My family pays taxes, he argues, so that should entitle me to soap. "I'm pleased your family is sharing the burden with the rest of us who work, but we all still buy our own soap," I tell him. So you're not going to give me the soap? he asks. "That's what I said," I repeat firmly. I don't fuckin' believe this, he whines. "You have a problem with that?" No, I have a problem with you, he rants. "You can leave," I tell him. He stubbornly stands there unmoving. "You need to leave," I repeat. I don't believe this. "Just go! Now!" I order loudly. No sooner has he turned the corner when in comes another. My heart has started skipping beats. Too much. Too many. They keep coming, same questions as yesterday. Can I have a statement of my account? "Last names A- L today. Let's give every man his due turn." I just need a quick balance. It will only take a minute. "What's your last name?" Rodriguez. "You're a Wednesday guy," I correct him. "Come back then." Are you serious? That's what the sign says. I keep at it, waiting for recall. Even as I close the door, they are shouting out demands. One more thing. Counselor, can I just have...? I slam the door despite the protests. Relentless. It pisses me off. The more I give, the more they expect.

A stack of requests rests on my desk with return answers to be distributed to the men. I can't go back out there and face them. I should sign the logbook and tour the unit, but I don't want to be harassed. I decide to wait until they clear out for chow and then run the requests to their bunks. I listen for the radio dispatch as they stagger the units by sending fifty first, then the remaining men at fifteen- minute- intervals. The volume of voices decreases and fades. I think they're gone now but as soon as I step out into the common area, I see that only half the unit has been dismissed. I begin the rounds anyway looking straight ahead, refusing to engage them. I'm on a mission to make it through all fifteen cubes and get this mail handed out. One guy steps up and begins to explain his predicament. I need to keep going, I tell myself. Another one blocks my way, disappointed that I won't dawdle to hear his tale. "You need to step back, sir. You're too close." Others have come back in the unit and the floor is beginning to fill with bodies milling around me. One figure approaches at a diagonal. My senses go on alert.

"I'm doing my tour now. You can drop a note to me in the box," I say. I take the defensive route.

"Did you call my girlfriend and let her know about my GED graduation?" this young man asks, ignoring my tactful approach.

"That's a matter to take up with the school. I don't make personal calls," I reply and continue walking around the perimeter.

"You said you were gonna. Don't say you're gonna if you know you're not."

"Are you telling me how to do my job?" I ask, gritting my teeth but without looking back at the insolent young buck.

"You lied," he hisses, seething mad now. I stop dead in my tracks, turn and look at this cagey, young black man. He's both defiant and derisive. I see the evil that compels him to hate me without provocation. I glance at his compatriots who stand blank-faced waiting to see what will happen. Not one of them intervenes on my behalf. These are not my friends. They never were.

"You need to step away, Mr. .?"

"Baker!" he spits out, as if I should automatically know who he is.

"Mr. Baker. We're done here," I add. "All of you. Back down!"

As I turn away to continue the mail drop, I hear him say it under his breath. You fucking bitch, that's what he says with utter distaste. I have two choices. I could ignore it and pretend I didn't hear anything, shut the door on his brash action and leave him to swelter in his own nasty attitude. But suddenly I see red. I could be anywhere but here, stressing myself out on a daily to mother these bastards and clean up the mess of their lives. They expect me to, and once they drain me to the point of collapse, they'll step over my hapless form to get to the next fool.

"Fuck you, you ungrateful little shit!" I hiss. It comes out with a vengeance that surprises even me. Mr. Baker looks like he's been shot in the gut. One hand jerks up and clutches his stomach. His eyes widen with alarm. Dozens have witnessed this encounter including the guard on his post who has been rattled awake by the commotion. Baker starts to spool off an explanation in the officer's direction when he sees me heading towards the desk.

"She lied. I never did nuthin'," he whines. The same smokescreen of excuses he's thrown in the face of the police, the judge, and the warden all along his dishonest little life. He is not allowed to make any contact with his baby mama so this was his round-about scam to get to her and jam me up. His girlfriend is his victim, but I will not be.

"Chapman, bag him up!" I shout. The others pull back and away from the female who has transformed in front of their eyes.

"Don't fuck up a good thing, asshole!" someone shouts at Baker.

"Done," answers Officer Chapman who needed some kind of adrenaline to get his second wind. He calls Main Control and then directs Baker to his bunk that will now be stripped down and assigned to one of the inmates in the overflow population on the gym floor. I sit at the desk in plain view and write the ticket that will send Baker down to the hole. It feels good recounting the incident verbatim while it is still so fresh. ..." *And then I, CC (Correctional Counselor) Abrams felt threatened by Inmate Baker # 351972 when he said in a hostile tone and I quote: "You'll pay, you fucking bitch."* It was that easy. I had this bastard's balls in a mole wrench and I'd chosen to lock the grip down hard even if my aim was a slight bit off.

#

Twenty-eight percent is the going rate; in this case, the number of prisoners who will be able to desist from crime and fall off the law enforcement radar. There it is in fine print in the latest recidivism statistics. That means that only three and a half of the twelve men in my charge are slotted for success. A smidge down from what I had guessed last week. I'm no psychic. I make my predictions based on the depth of soul or the lack of one I see behind a man's eyes. All will graduate from the program but I scan the roster carefully to dredge up the winners. Bowman, Serge, Willis and the Rev are the candidates who get my vote for Most Likely to Succeed. That's forty percent; we're defying the odds here. Guys like Noble and Ortega have had the street handed down the generational ladder. Violence is so thick in their bloodstream, it circulates its viscous poison like a sluggish drug. They both have a few more bids left in them. Dent is an entertaining character but his limited reasoning skills and faulty trip switch will be his downfall. Anger is his only language. The pressure from multiple ex's, bawling babies and the money to keep them all quiet is just not in his favor. Zimmer's the guy that luck pisses on. No matter what he does and how affable he is, that man is doomed to come up short. Gemini will stamp, pout and cry but somewhere written in his genetic code is the name Victim and a future foreshortened by the wrath of ignorant people. Euclid will be shipped out to Rushfork, last stop for the criminally insane and hopefully before he accumulates any bodies. And who's left? Crespo, a fugitive and an unwanted encumbrance on our welfare dole. Perhaps if he made it back to his mother-land, he'd assimilate back into being a goat-herder or a pan flutist. Granted, if no drug lords or political coup have razed his herds or raped his women by then.

At times, it makes me want to gather them all in my arms say 'there, there,' and squeeze each with an it-will-get-better hug. *What are you, some kind of bleeding heart liberal? These are convicted killers, rapists. Let them hang.* I know. I know. But it won't get much better for most of them. Like sedimentary rock with its layers and layers of sludgy build-up, the deficits pile up one on top of the other: substance abuse, poverty, neglected educations, dysfunctional family groups, mental illness or marginal health. The crust grows and hardens. We treatment-minded folks pick away at solving the issues but it's like trying to dislodge diamonds encased in a mountain of trouble using a butter knife. Show me an inmate who has only *one* problem, the Commissioner stated in his challenge to the lawmakers. Not a single case was produced. No surprise, since among the twenty-eight thousand, six hundred and three offenders in the State system, not a single man or woman qualifies. That statistic alone is more than enough for some people to jump off the rehabilitation bandwagon and climb on board the anti-recidivism float. In the parade of politics, the latter one spouts harmonious music, gaily decorated banners and diverse participants waving grandly from its broad platform. It's a subtle shift in policy, but one that grants permission to correctional treatment workers to care only between the hours from eight o'clock a.m. to three fifteen. Seven hours and fifteen minutes of a paperwork chain that proves they did their job of keeping these bad people comfortable and safe until time's up. After that, it's anybody's guess what happens. The house of correction is in truth a hotel of contradiction. We can only help up to a point. We can publicize an altruistic mission statement that's no more than an advertising pitch to a reluctant public. We can give a prisoner a bar of soap but not expect him to clean up his act. We can temporarily house him with mediocre service, strip his bunk and toss his valuables in the trash. His identity matters not the least. If he returns, it's on him.

The blank evaluation forms are ready to be completed. I stare at the empty white comment box and neat series of squares aching for a checkmark. I want to be wrong. Maybe this will be the first class of matriculating magicians who disappear before our very eyes and reappear off-stage as real live fathers, sons and husbands.

#

There was a report on NPR about this split-brain thing and how schizophrenia frequently sets in at puberty. The study proposed that an afflicted person often outgrows the dueling personality disorder in middle age. What I'm wondering is, can someone grow into it? The fractures and hematomas on the right side of my head had caused intractable panic and neurological paralysis on the left side of the body. The two halves could no longer communicate in concert. They were always quibbling like a hard-of-hearing couple and the discordance in this cerebral dichotomy was getting worse. The lobe on the left keeps insisting: *Listen, linger, and learn. Let go.* This man has evolved. The former person, Mr. X is as good as dead, laid out on a silk lining six feet under or incinerated and left to the wind. The right shrieks in opposition. Terran Willis is a murderous deceit artist. He's run his game well to win over any doubters. A Bible-touting rapist with a carefully assembled tool kit of charm and accolades that will get him out of this pen better than any wire cutters. And once he strolls out with his two hundred dollars of gate money, he'll order up that first round of Patron and bag of White Rhino and toast the saps on the Parole Board who let him walk at sixty percent of sentence served. He had even duped her ass, the trusting counselor who like any other bitch could be played to get what he wanted.

Easy. Flunk the bastard. A failed program evaluation would jam him up and force him to discharge off his end of sentence. He would be automatically denied for early release. The assessment had five distinct areas of competence: attendance, initiative, productivity, attitude and responsibility. Poor! Poor! Poor! The frenzied checkmarks jump to life, cutting the small paper boxes with the force of the pen. I am in control now. Other counselors type a formula statement in the comment box, something to the effect of 'Inmate So-and–So has met the requirements of the program and successfully completed the group,' followed by a recommendation that the individual take advantage of voluntary resources in the future. It is one thing to make a generic pencil mark, there's nothing too difficult about that; turns out it is quite another to actually write out a lie in grammatically correct sentences. *Shit! Elise. Even I am surprised at what you might be capable of.* Total fabrication. No worse, it's slander and defamation of a man who has been a stellar student in all respects. Call it what it is — outright perjury on paper.

The truth is Willis hasn't missed a beat. His humble confidence has quietly encouraged his comrades to reach for better. He is the one student that asks for extra sheets of lined paper to attach to the hand-out instead of settling for a few bare-boned sentences. *I can't do it.* The paper flies into the shred box. Here's the problem. If I jam him up and he is denied early release, he stays here for the duration of his bid under the same roof with me. With his inherent craftiness and access to the legal library, he will have both the time and the know-how to plan a counter-attack with legitimate grievances of staff misconduct, appeals and formal litigation. Even more frightening is what he might do to sabotage me. More than any other living soul on earth, I know what this man is capable of if he is who I believe he is. Hell, just take a look at his criminogenic and hostility scores when he first landed in assessment. If provoked, there's no telling what his wrath might look like, especially if he realized who I really am to him. These prisoners have people on the outside who do their bidding. Hits are ordered from within the walls and executed on the outside. I would be at risk no matter where I went.

As inconsequential as it seems, I worry equally as much about what the fall-out will do to my reputation. My credibility is at stake. Talk seeps faster behind bars than the torrents of rain that tumble through the frail seams of caulking in this old ark of a structure. *Phenomenal* and *exceptional* are rare compliments in this dark place and yet these adjectives had been granted to me verbally in gloomy corridors or scribbled on the back of commissary slips. These are the evidence of respect gifted from men who pitted life and death on a reputation. It is praise that has been hard won over years of putting the brakes on impatience and pushing back against the heat and hatred. If I choose this act of vindication and then remain on the job, the tide will turn against me. The other inmates will hear his claims and know the truth. When push comes to shove, they are all in cahoots. I would be in danger. *Tan versus blue. Remember, Elise? Calm down. Breathe in through the nose, out through the mouth.* As the pulse of anger slows to a level beat, the words come reluctantly in terse phrases. One by one they add up to a written portrait of a man who appears to be the sum total of transformation. I examine the finished form. All the excellent boxes are now checked. Excellent is what he gets. In truth, though, there is a looming gap in his testimonial that has yet to be accounted for.

#

I call Willis down to the Interview room which is centrally located in the hallway down the main line with officers nearby and traffic on the move outside the door. It's a safer spot to confront difficult issues or individuals. The security camera leers from the left-hand corner where it is bolted out of reach of even the tallest of prisoners. Peering down from a height of ten feet or so, it blinks its watchful eye day and night and tattles its secrets on spools of videotape. These voyeuristic devices are everywhere in the facility. The chair is positioned just so. The desk pushed forward and angled so that my profile is what will be seen. No chance for a crafty lip-reader to get a full peek at our conversation.

Willis comes in and bends slightly as he always does in a common curtsy caused by the length and breadth of him. He has a written pass in hand and looks a bit confused at the nature of this visit.

"Sit down, please," I say, waving to the second chair in the room. Willis hesitates and then lowers down onto the blue plastic chair. I smile. He brings in the dusky smell of men who have been in close quarters together in a swamp of humidity. His skin shines with a mist of perspiration. I yank the string attached to the pull chain on the wall fan and it begins to swivel nervously. A flutter of air brushes across the table between us and freshens his face first, then mine. The motion repeats. He is grateful for the relief.

"I wanted to give you this in private. It's your evaluation which is one of the very few perfect scores I have ever given out. Usually I praise in public and critique in private, but I didn't want the others to feel slighted. And I added a little extra in the comment section specifically for Parole's eyes. Go ahead, read it."

Willis looks over the document thoroughly and beams. He appears to be a bit flushed with genuine self-consciousness.

"It's more than I ever expected. Or could have hoped for," he says finally.

"Go do something great out there, okay?" I say.

"You can bet on it," Willis says. "I don't know how to thank you for having my back in this way."

"The thanks is in the doing," I reply. "The world is waiting for your contribution."

"I've never met a woman like you," he replies. Something buzzes in one ear. Simple tinnitus or a warning? What sounds like a benign compliment echoes with an insidious ring. I look directly into Willis's eyes, something I just now realize I've been avoiding doing by always focusing just left of center. I wonder who I'm really looking at.

"There are good women out there. You need to find the one who has your best interests at heart. Anything's possible after that." Willis lowers his head for a moment, and then brings his gaze up to meet mine.

"You're one of those women, Mizz Abrams," he says, almost timidly. Rejection of any interest or advance is automatic. The book of my life is closed and padlocked here. I give them no clues, no hints. I wear a generic ring on the wrong finger and assume a vague title that reveals nothing about my marital status. I never let on what car I drive or which direction I come from. A rustle of shyness filters over my face.

"Good luck, Mr. Willis," I say, ending the telling pause between us. He interprets that remark as a dismissal and rises to his feet.

"I'd like to repay you for all your help. I probably shouldn't say this, but I'd like to invite you over and introduce you to my Moms. Are you on Facebook?" Willis says. A cold knot of indigestion roots in my belly. A flare of alarm sets off into circulation by this false pretense of a happy family seated around the Sunday dinner table when I know full well that he is alone in this world. Has he forgotten that he shared the sad tale of his mother, Berea's unfortunate heart failure when he was just a belligerent boy and that he has no siblings and his foster-aunt is also deceased?

"Do you think we could see one another outside of here when I'm free and clear? I would treat you like the true lady you are," he continues. He has crept over the boundary line with no warning shot from my side. There's a subtle smugness in his tone like he knows more about me than he lets on and that I should be flattered he has chosen me to set his aim on. *Did he just ask me out? If so, it's a pretty twisted reversal on the usual dating schematics. Rape, violate, and then date?*

"You know me better than that, Mr. Willis," I say, closing the folder in front of me, sliding it into my workbag and snapping the leather case shut. My back faces the interior wall. I must circumvent the bulky metal table to extricate myself from the room. A bad design I now note. Staff should always be nearest the exit. Willis stands motionless as I scoot around the cramped corner with briefcase bumping the cabinet and my portable cup tilted just enough to dribble coffee on the floor. In case of emergency, it would never be too difficult to track the whereabouts of Counselor Abrams. A signature spill-trail of medium cappuccino marks my movements from first stop at the ladies room to the Outer Control check-point at end of day. I bet the hallway janitors curse my comings and goings.

"I'll get that for you," Willis offers, reaching towards the door. As I pass, he rests his powerful hand on my shoulder and applies the slightest pressure. His touch is purposed, premeditated, and perhaps even predatory. Is it meant to catch my attention and cause me to swivel slightly towards him? Or does it stem from the need to circle back around to the scene of the kill just to reclaim it from other scavengers who might encroach? Does he even know who I am? "Thank you. Thank you so much," he says. Willis reaches out and down from his position of superior height and clasps me in a genuine hug. My overstuffed bag filled with paper supplies buckles against his side. The metal cup in my hand wobbles and tips, dribbling iced chai on my Skechers. Soft mocha-colored droplets blossom on ugly beige tile. *Get your hands off me, you prick! Don't you dare touch me!* Did I say that out loud? Willis doesn't seem to have noticed.

"I'm sorry. I couldn't help it. I just appreciate you so much." He releases his grip and I stagger backwards in an exaggerated stumble against the wall. "Oh, my apologies. I didn't mean for you to hurt yourself. Here," he adds, bending down to dab at my footwear with the paper towel he produced from his pocket. He swabs at the blotches on the floor and the tiny spatter that has marked the cuff of my linen pants. I knew from the get-go it was an asinine decision to choose off-white between mold, ink, dirty files and a possible misguided menstrual flow.

"No matter," I say. "It's fine." But it's not. The breach has happened and we both know it. He thinks he's got me, but I have him as well. We're each in a position to jam up the other. It's an impasse that can only cleared by breaking silence. Willis swings the door open and I step out ahead of him into the mass jam of human traffic on the mainline.

#

"Can you get access to camera footage?" I ask. Hastings is alone in the officer's mess hall when I approach him. He looks at me quizzically, trying to figure the angle on my line of questioning.

"I've got ways, but what are you fishing for, Elise?" he says. "I can't just stroll down and help myself. There is protocol in obtaining stuff from the Security Division."

"Well, let's just say that I had somewhat of an awkward encounter with an inmate. I was hoping to be able to take a look at it." My friend is instantly alarmed.

"He didn't hurt you, did he? I'll tune him up myself, that grimy bastard!"

"No, no. He came on to me," I reply. "Not a big deal."

"Forget the films. You report the guy and we'll deal with him from there. They'll check the cameras as evidence during any investigation, regardless. You can't taint it by getting your hands in the mix. Where did this happen?"

"The Interview room in the Main Hall," I say. His look of disappointment is immediately evident.

"You're fucked, then. That camera's been dead for years. The Administration figured it wasn't worth a line item on the budget since we have rovers stationed right outside the door and two direct phone lines to Main Control. So, who's the guy? We'll drum something up and get him shipped out."

"No, never mind. He's leaving soon anyway," I say.

"Elise, don't protect these assholes. If he crossed the line or threatened you, we'll cuff him and he's gone."

"No, it's alright. I'll handle it," I say. "I appreciate your support." The thwarted knight grins reluctantly as I pat his shoulder and smile. Hastings is a good man. He can be counted on to do the right thing and to step up for a friend. I give his taut triceps a playful squeeze and shoot him the grateful look of a damsel-in-distress who's been rescued from her own helplessness. He continues to stare long after I've left the break room and rounded the corner down the long hallway.

#

The original copy of Willis's evaluation is in the folder with the others. I scan them one by one into the desktop folder on my computer. From there, each is uploaded individually into the caseload system that can be accessed by the Board of Parole. Our community partners rely heavily on our insight and hands-on interaction with their clients who either walk out early or take it to the gate, based heavily on what is fed up through the pipeline. It's not a matter to be taken lightly. A generic pass or fail does the public no service. My recommendations are carefully rendered after weeks of intensive observation and mental notes. I am comfortable that I have done the best I can for the people who are out there blissfully barbecuing and have placed their trust in a system that will keep the monsters in the closet and risk at bay. I save Willis's for last, twirling it in my fingers, holding it to the artificial light as if might illuminate any glaring error. What is the right answer here? How does one measure a man's transformation in months or years? Is Willis truly a new man? Have a dozen years been enough to complete the conversion from core criminal to model citizen? Salvation is granted in a moment's repentance, but the path to perfection is a slow, sometimes endless road. Something isn't right. If this is the man who not only knowingly but willfully inflicted such horrors and havoc decades ago, what is enough? Studies say prison is beneficial only up to a certain point. For the man who has been genuinely rehabilitated, prolonged incarceration becomes detrimental and begins to have the reverse effect. But if it is him, doesn't the bastard deserve more time? Suddenly, the answer is perfectly clear. I deserve more time; time enough to be certain.

The evaluation sails smoothly through the shredder and bubbles out in ribbons below. I pull up a blank form and start retyping it. The checkmarks on the top portion snap the reader to attention like warning flags. Poor…poor…fair…poor. The remarks that spool out into the comment section are emphatic and undeniably convincing. The man is a threat, a risk, a manipulator, a persistent offender whose agenda has been covertly disguised behind a bright veneer. I write what I feel: Strongly recommend *Denial* based on extensive criminal history, severity of violence, lack of ownership, pernicious disregard for and damaging mistreatment of his victims. There. I've done my duty. Willis is probably still gloating and shoving that glowing evaluation in everyone's face as proof that he can come out on top again. Stupid bitch, he's probably saying. This ingenious *fuck you w*ill stay my little secret. And guess who he'll come running to when he gets the decision handed down to him? That's right! His oh-so sympathetic counselor.

CHAPTER 14
DISMISSED

Pictures don't lie. Right up there on the big screen monitor at the top of the fourth with the Sox up by two, the camera pans to the crowd and hesitates on a couple who seem oblivious to Big Brother. They are kissing deeply, lustily. Her auburn cascade of curls and his Ken-size build are unmistakable. It's James Hastings and Sharon Gaudette, the red-haired lieutenant on second shift getting hot and heavy; but then just as quickly, the lens zooms back on the umpire hunched over home plate and the couple is lost among thirty-seven thousand other fans in a collage of red shirts and waving white banners. The paralysis of shock stops me in my tracks. I'm used to being numb, but not this new sensation that comes on its heels, this royal rip of red-hot jealousy that shoots up through my veins and rattles my brain. This is something new.

"You damn bastard," I shout. The bowl of pretzels lifts off the table and is airborne. The books go next, landing heavily on the floor. The glass picture frames of loved ones follow. *He loves me. He loves me not. He loves me. He loves me not!* There goes boy Aaron, passive-aggressive prince who never asked me to marry him when he should have. Then another framed photograph of the man-version all grown up in his happy-family Christmas snapshot from Sears. The man who never returned to sweep me up to safety; even now, when he knows he wants to. *Fuck him!* The accompanying sound of shattering glass is a round of applause in my ears. I let the brothers fly against the brick fire wall. All five put together don't amount to a lick of shit. They couldn't see out of their incestuous small world to realize they had a big-picture sister who needed them. *Assholes all!* God forgive me, I didn't mean to but in the frenzy of rage, I get carried away and accidentally grab my prize photograph of Dad and me half-buried in a sand castle on the Cape. It takes off on its own and sifts downwards straight into the hot ash pan. The heat bubbles it immediately. The two of us grin, then grimace and finally huddle into a distorted heap. Now that I've ruined the one thing that's most valuable to me, I need to hurt myself a little more. I sweep all the Cooke family knick-knack china collectibles off the mantel in one motion. Useless things given out of guilt as replacements for words.

When I finally stop, I'm surprised at the extent of the damage. I don't remember toppling the plants out of their holders. It looks like one of the dogs might have gotten cut on the broken glass and traipsed through the clumps of potting soil and shredded photo album pages. Sadly, the quiet that comes after a riot is an incomplete peace. Despite the chaotic release of pent-up energy, the root cause remains untouched. I feel weakened, not stronger as I expected. *Fuck me!* I'll clean it up later. I sit back down and resume watching the game at the bottom of the fifth.

By the seventh inning stretch, I'm feeling very confused and less convinced it was him at all. My eyesight is far from perfect. I try to drum up the image of that snapshot again. *You could be mistaken. I mean, your memory isn't the best.* Goddamn-it! *No, go with your first instinct.* I've got to fight for what I want. Champions don't just relinquish their lead. The come-from-behind late in the season Red Sox know this all too well. Big Papi keeps at it, slapping his red gloves and kicking his bat and swinging hard each and every time. And eventually that clutch play comes when he sails a grand slam out to the Green Monster and claims his victory lap. By the bottom of the eighth, I am resolved to win. I sip my Sam Adams lager, take nibbles from the fist-sized microwave pretzel and find myself cheering for the underdog. Myself.

#

James comes when I call. He's eager and happy to be summoned. It's a Friday night and he's raring to get out for a little action. He dashes right over after the gym, his face radiant from endorphins and his skin fresh with the scent of Axe. He pulls me tight into an earnest embrace.

"What would you like to do? What are you in the mood for, my dear? Maybe some Thai food? A movie?" he asks. Then he notices the large suitcase and smaller duffle packed to the brim and pushed to the right of the open door.

"Oh, where are you off to?" he asks, jovially.

"We, you mean. Surprise! I made a reservation for the two of us at an inn near Pemaquid Point. I thought we could swing by so you could meet my family and then we can celebrate our newfound happiness for a couple days. There's a lobster festival going and a Renaissance fair near Camden. Maybe do a little jousting." My wink and beaming smile is quickly dimmed by his hesitancy to immediately sweep me up and spin me in a circle. Have I misjudged him? His awkward pause suddenly casts doubts on my impulsive move.

"That's a lovely idea, Elise. But I can't disappear like that. Unfortunately, I'm not that expendable at home."

"I knew I should have asked first, but I wanted it to be a surprise. I can still change the reservation and make it a day trip if that's better," I suggest.

"You're so thoughtful, love. Maybe down the road we could make this happen. Perhaps you misinterpreted me. It would be difficult to explain an extended absence away from home. You understand, right?" James reaches for my hand as if he's poised to waltz me back to the bedroom. "But we can still make the most of a couple hours tonight."

"Oh," I say. I sound like a pathetic adolescent girl who is stewing in her own disappointment. Even knowing this, I can't help the pout that turns down the corners of my lips.

"C'mon, pretty girl. Let's not focus on what we don't have, but rather the precious moments in hand." James steps up and kisses me eagerly. I lean back away from him.

"So, what you're really saying is it's too risky to be seen with me in broad daylight. Is that it?" I spit the words out with no polite introduction. He appears startled as I struggle out of his grip.

"What does that mean?" he asks. He peers at me intently trying to determine if this is one of the sarcastic teases that he likes to deflect.

"Listen, I'll cut to the chase and save you some trouble. I can accept the fact that you are married, but not that you would have other girlfriends, too. That's not what I signed on for."

"Now, hold on. What other girlfriends, Elise?" I eye him suspiciously. His face is flushed and he shifts his gaze to the right away from my fierce glare. He looks an awful lot like a cheater coming out a motel room; in this case, caught red-handed with a redhead.

"You and your flame at Fenway. Ring any bells with you?" I ask. James seems genuinely stunned by this accusation. He scrunches his brow and rubs his jaw, contemplating what tact he should take.

"You sound an awful lot like a jealous woman right now. That's not the girl I've come to admire and respect," he replies. "One of the wonderful things about you as a friend is that you are remarkably uncomplicated and understanding. There have never been demands and rules or the need to control one another."

"So, is that really all we are? Just friends?"

"Isn't that what you wanted? It's pretty much what we agreed on. Let me rephrase that. How about great friends with a multitude of benefits," he says sweetly. His faces relax into a gentle smile. "I think we're beyond the age where we have to post our status on Facebook. 'In a relationship with a married man' still isn't cool, even these days."

"I just don't know if I feel comfortable being one of many," I say. James pulls up taller and clenches his jaw.

"I don't know where the hell you got the idea that I'm a skirt chaser. I told you that I'm madly in love with you and I absolutely am. But that doesn't erase the rest of my life, the part that came before you and continues to be. It's not an all-or-nothing kind of thing. I have a different kind of love for my family which can co-exist with the way I feel for you."

"So I get my own special compartment in this big heart of yours. And how many others does it accommodate?"

"What are you talking about?" he demands.

"That skanky, slut-bucket Gaudette," I say. "She in there, too?" He bursts out with a laugh and then reaches out to pat my shoulder.

"Oh, now I get it. I don't need to explain myself. But I'm willing to, if it makes you feel better. The guys and I drag her along to the bar sometimes cause she's a hoot and a party girl and knows a helluva lot about baseball. Plus she's friends with my wife, but for Christ sakes, that's it, Elise. Now, will you drop it?"

"So you *were* with her at the game on Friday?"

"I was with my wife," James states firmly. He softens noticeably when he deciphers the look of confusion of my face. "Wait. You've never met Lynne, have you? They do look an awful lot alike. Feel better, now?" I should back off and calm down, but the guy and girl in the bleachers are still taunting me. *That stupid twit*, they say as they wrap their arms around each other. *Fooled her.* Instead of feeling reassured, I choke back a rush of repulsion and slap his hand off my shoulder.

"I don't understand. You got back together with your wife and didn't tell me? Don't you think that might have mattered before you jumped in bed with me?"

"I don't know where you got the idea that I my wife and are were separated. I never said that. Sure we have our spats and differences and things have been rockier lately, but that's a far cry from what you're saying."

In the past I could shut down the spigot in my gut and stop any welling of emotion with a conscious crimp in the piping. Something is different inside of me. The boiler is churning with compressed steam. The heat radiates up my chest.

"I've always been honest with you, sweetie. Remember when we very first connected? I told you that I believed we are created to love the special people who come across our path. Be it one or three or however many. You are one of those delights that I am lucky to have been gifted with. My hope is that we can enjoy a loving, special romance for as long as you are willing and feel the same about me."

"Yes, I heard you. One of possibly many."

"What's gotten into you all of a sudden? Are you having a hormone swing or something? You've never been clingy before. You're always so independent and self-sufficient."

I clam up. He's right. This is not at all like me.

"Elise, you knew exactly what you were doing the other night. In fact, one could honestly say that you seduced me. And Lord forgive me, I wanted you to. Badly. I have ever since I met you and would never have had the willpower to turn you away. I feel no remorse or guilt, but I still love my wife." I look at him incredulously. He doesn't see the problem with any of this.

"You love your wife but you make love to other women. How does that work?" I say flatly with a sting to my diction.

"Other women? You mean, you!"

"And don't forget Sharon. I can't imagine you were just sharing earned run averages with her."

"C'mon, Elise. Sharon's not smart enough to waste more than the price of a beer on."

"But she might be worth the cost of a condom though, right?" The crass statement sets sail before I can catch it. That's not what I had intended to say. Too late. He's mad now and sick of dealing with the petulance of an immature girl.

"I didn't come here to take a rasher of shit. I could stay home and get that. I'm going to go. Nothing good is going to come out of staying," James says. He turns decisively and puts his hand on the doorknob. "You're the one that called me, remember? Maybe it's best if we just cool things down for a little while. This obviously isn't working right now." He swings the door inwards and takes a first step forwards.

"Screw you! I'm not just some free-for-all, fuck-by-night. I took you at your word, Hastings. I believed that I was someone special to you." I fly at him from the rear, striking his broad back with my fists. As he twists around to face me, he catches a forceful palm strike on the soft skin of his neck.

"Jesus, Elise! What's wrong with you?" he yells. My frantic fingers claw and flail at his insensitive rejection. James whirls back around and assumes a practiced defensive stance. He clamps my right wrist with one strong hand, spins me off balance with one twisting yank and then presses his bulk up against me, effectively pinning my front to the wall. My attempts to thrash and struggle resemble puny twitches of a mouse in a glue trap, all desperation but no chance of breaking free. The sensation of being restrained brings on a burst of claustrophobia and an involuntary rush of a frantic flashback. The dull ache in the pinned wrist, the shallow respirations of a compressed chest, the panic of being led meekly to the precipice of my own demise and now, I've lost all control. In that compromised state, the terror of the past comes shrieking out of nowhere.

"Fuck off, you bastard! I hope you rot in flaming hell," I shriek. *There's no going back now, girl. You're in control.* James is flabbergasted and frightened by the power of the writhing convulsions that rattle in his grasp.

"Son-of-a-bitch! Let go of me!" I cry. My voice is frothy and pitched high with a fury dredged up from the deep. For my own safety as well as his, James stabilizes my epileptic-like struggles against a fixed surface as officers are taught to do when an irate inmate puts up major resistance. His grip is firm and non-negotiable. He says nothing; instead, he quietly waits for the fight to go out of me. When the inertia of emotional exhaustion overtakes my muscles, he relaxes his grip slightly and allows my arms to drop. Gravity restarts the circulation. Once he eases up, I slide my wilted spine down the wall and drop rump to floor. Now I am crying openly, uncontrollably. It is a unwanted reaction I have reserved and protected against my whole adult life, one that is not for public viewing. There's nothing else to do with this outburst but let it take its own unrelenting course. James doesn't crouch to comfort me. I don't reach out with remorse.

"I don't know what just happened here," he says finally. I shrug and stare out through the flickering floaters that spiral across my watery vision. My veins pulse hard with heightened pressure. My blood feels turgid and my limbs heavy.

"You want to explain it and help me understand?" he asks, dumbfounded.

"I can't," I mumble.

"You mean you won't," James says. I have no ready answer for that.

"I don't know if it's safe to leave you alone. Should I call a doctor or something?" he asks. I shake my head.

"You can go now," I reply blankly. The flare of spontaneous combustion has now dwindled and died. It's doubtful that it would trigger another flash fire.

"You sure?" he asks. I can tell by the tremor in his voice that he is anxious to separate himself from this scene. He just as soon leave than stay with a madwoman.

"Yes," I whisper.

"Can I check on you by phone tomorrow? I'm worried about you, Elise."

"Sure," I say in what rings as a feeble stab at a nonchalant response. My eardrums echo with a throbbing drumbeat. *So sorry…so sorry…so sorry* but I can't put the rhythm into words.

"Elise, we're at that age, you know. Maybe it's the female change, a hormone swing of some kind. Is it something serious?"

"I'm fine," I reply with an eerie calmness.

"You're freaking me out," James says. "I'm going to give your Mom a call."

"No, please don't. She can't take anymore worry. Not after everything that has happened. My mother's ill. We shouldn't trouble her."

"Stress can do a number on people. You're obviously under a lot of pressure at work and in your personal life. It can't be easy. Maybe you should consider taking some time off," he suggests.

"You're right," I say. "That's what I'm going to do. I'll take some extended time off."

"There you go. Put in for family medical leave," says James.

"Maybe I should just quit this game early," I reply. Shock replaces his previous state of confusion.

"Elise. You're making absolutely no sense. Nobody walks away from this retirement. That pension is the only reason any of us put up with this shit for so long. You're still a few years shy of your full payout. You'd be out of your mind to do that."

"My mind's never been my most reliable guide," I confess. James becomes suddenly tender, takes my hand and helps me to a standing position. He uses a thumb to rub at the streaked mascara on my cheek and smoothes my tangled hair with his left hand.

"You don't have to live with these demons forever. The best way to get rid of them is to talk about what happened. Whatever it was, it's not going to change things or scare me away. Do you believe that?" he asks.

It's so close I can almost grab on for dear life. The exquisite bridge that is slowly being built to connect us is nearly within reach but still only partially crafted. Will it be enough to support the dangling weight of such a burdensome past? I'm afraid to try, only to fall again. To date, no supports have held. *Forget about him. Men just screw you up.* It's so unfair, so frustrating to be caught in the middle of this competing conversation. All the voices saying, *Do this! No, don't do that! Let him go!* Tears of frustration bloom in my throat.

"Did you hear what I said? Please don't lock me out. You need to open up, Elise."

"I'm Lissa, goddamnit!" I blurt out impulsively. "Lissa Braum. Elise is the fucked-up person that took over my life. The one that you're seeing now. The one that can't love for shit. Who doesn't know how to get out of her own skin. Who wants to keep you but will ruin everything between us. You're better off not knowing her. Trust me." For a few brief moments, the filter is off and the cries that come from within are the primal howls of downed prey that can no longer stay on its feet or outrun the hunter. The swells of suppressed emotion take over in unleashed sobs that shake my ribcage with their power. James wraps me in his arms and holds on tight as if to protect me from hurting myself. When I finally grow still, he lets go and lifts my chin so I have no choice but to look him straight in the eye.

"I'm so sorry. Do you want to continue and tell me more?" he asks. I shake my head. That heated outburst of vulnerability has cooled back down into a guarded stubbornness. It was an accidental exposure. I've said too much already.

"I'm listening, sweetie. With all my being," James insists. "Are you sure?"

"I can't," I state. He doesn't push any further. Instead, he takes my hand and brings it tenderly to his chest.

"Do you want me to stay for a bit and just be near you? We don't have to talk at all."

"No, you should go. I'm exhausted. And you must be too," I reply.

"Well, that was a good start. A real important step. Whatever it is can wait. Get some sleep and call your doctor first thing Monday morning. I'm sure he'll sign off on that extended leave. Some quality time with your family could do wonders. You'll feel worlds different after a couple weeks away from all the madness. When you get back, we'll talk some more."

No matter what I do, it seems I always leave good men paddling in my wake. I try to tell them it's not worth it. I am damaged goods, guys. Hang on to those women who will have your crew socks rolled in a neat ball and your casserole stewing in the crock pot. Not me, not the person who can bring her best game to the lives of strangers, to mediocre men, mad men, even bad ones; but one who can't offer a healthy connection to the few good men who would willingly donate their entire strength to her cause.

"Okay," I say weakly. My throat and nasal passages are filled with congestion from all the tears. James smiles and gives me an affectionate pat on the head.

"Atta girl" he says.

"Don't forget your bag." I nod my head in the direction of the small duffle bag that holds the few remnants of his brief stay in my life.

#

The number on the incoming call is indicated as Blocked; perhaps a doctor or a lawyer or a former inmate who has used the public computer at city library to Google the counselor who had put her two cents recommendation into his future plan. I hesitate and let the call go to the automatic answering machine. It is Detective Hughes requesting I call him back as soon as possible. I feel a tingle of excitement at the sound of his voice trapped in the Radio Shack contraption. At the push of a button, I can make him come to life over and over. At the same time, a cold streak of dread settles in my core. Now or never, I tell myself. I dial him back.

"It's me. Anything new?" I ask, when he picks up after the second ring.

"We've got an interesting situation here. After the first test came back, I took it upon myself to send some evidence on up to Canada where they use a different technique to lift fingerprints. It is called VMD, or Vacuum Medal Disposition. We have something similar down here in the States that uses thermal technology, but it is not nearly as sophisticated or sensitive."

"Okay. Shoot!" I realize the cliché cop pun after it's fired off.

"The forensic expert up there, an old friend of mine, put the ligatures and the pillowcase through this process and he was able to lift two prints. A partial one from the ties and a full one from the piece of linen. He sent them back to me and I ran them through the AFIS system."

"And…?" I ask.

"And I got a hit," he announces. Neither of us says anything for several long seconds. For that one blissful moment, I am still in the dark, but he knows as well as I do that I can't dwell there any longer. He's got the trump card and it's time to play his hand.

"You can tell me now," I say.

"They belong to a man named Terran Willis. He's a registered felon and a repeat offender with multi-state offenses and more than a few incarcerations. He is our missing man, the one who tried to kill you. But you don't need to live in fear right now. He is currently in prison."

For years I'd practiced this moment in my head. I always imagined if and when that day ever came and my attempted-killer was introduced, I'd either freeze up in paralysis or collapse in a quadriplegic mess but nothing so dramatic happens. Perhaps too much time had elapsed waiting for the pivotal moment of the plot to be revealed. The suspense has been ruined. Or maybe it's because I already knew the ending.

"My long-lost Mr. X," I whisper.

"What?" Detective Hughes asks.

"Nothing," I answer quickly.

"Which facility did you say you're currently working at?" asks Hughes.

"Fowler," I reply quickly. The lie comes out more easily that it should have. The man shouldn't know that my enemy is right underfoot; not before I decide exactly what I'm going to do.

"The female prison, right? Good! That eliminates a huge concern then. Otherwise you'd need to go to the authorities and lodge a profile right away. You wouldn't want to be in the same prison with your attacker. So, he's open game, Elise. There is no statute of limitations on prosecuting an unsolved crime of this magnitude. We've got proof of Attempted Murder here." He hesitates and there is nothing but dead silence. What does one say in response to that?

"So what do you want to do?" Detective Hughes asks finally.

"I don't know," I reply.

"I understand this is a big deal and a psychological struggle. After all the time it took to put this behind you. You may not want to dredge it up. It's very difficult going to trial. I may be able to put a case together with the D.A. and push for a plea. That would spare such intense personal scrutiny and exposure to details that you might rather avoid."

"May I put some thought into this and then let you know my decision? There's a lot to consider and though I'm the one that pushed for the answer, the reality of knowing the truth is pretty overwhelming," I say.

"I'm not at all surprised. I think I cautioned you about this when you first asked me. But I wanted to finally get to the answer truth you deserve, and now you have it."

"Thank you, Detective for going the extra distance with this. A least the mystery is solved. I will think this over before we make any move. I'm not so comfortable playing God, you know?"

"Yes, I understand. I respect that. Get back to me when you feel ready."

After we hang up, I watch the rain strike the skylight with the force of small pellets shot from the pressurized barrel of a BB rifle. Hot humidity has been stalled over the East Coast for days and now tailgating cold air has slammed up the back of this idle mass of moisture. The lightning it produces causes an involuntary flinch. I am too big to hide in the linen closet or under the bed as I once did; but not too old to shut all the bedroom doors and create a little storm shelter within the walls of the hallway. As I cower there listening to the tropical wind threatening to upend the shingles, it occurs to me. I have been building a storm brake for nearly a quarter-century, following a careful emotional blueprint that has effectively sealed me off from any future catastrophe. My retreat was designed to keep enemies and the elements at bay and up until today, it had worked.

#

Every so often we're handed a gem, a small chip of diamond sifted out from the coarse sand of hard reality. The Records Specialist calls to tell me that there is a guy in my unit whose sentence time was miscalculated. Apparently he had jail credit that was overlooked and when it was applied to his docket made him a free man two weeks ago. The Department of Correction is holding him unlawfully. Of course, I don't plan on telling the inmate about this inadvertent blunder or we'll incur another lawsuit.

I take the discharge forms down to my office and ask the block officer to pop out Mr. Dailey in 8 Cube, B- bunk. He's housed back in the stuffy dorm where the un-sentenced guys are kept. Seven minutes pass by before a short, middle-aged man with a crew cut and striking blue eyes steps in the office. His arms are wrapped protectively around his chest and he looks puffy and disconcerted.

"Take a seat," I say. It sounds more like an order than an invitation. Mr. Dailey blinks rapidly and settles on the edge of the chair like he's back in middle school and has just been called to the Principal's office. His guilty conscience is hard at work.

"Apologies, ma'am. I was asleep," Dailey says. "I had a rough night."

"You just come in?"

"Yeah two nights ago from the County Jail but I've gotten no sleep since I've been here. Plus, I almost got into it with someone this morning."

"What happened?" I ask him. The precious release form burns a hole in my palm. My secret for now.

"I saw the laundry worker taking out the linens so I grabbed my tee shirts and threw them in to get cleaned. The dude on the bunk above calls me over a while later and says, 'You ever touch my stuff again, I'll beat the living shit out of you.' Apparently one of his shirts had fallen down and was wedged next to my mattress. I took it by accident. The guy was pushing for a reaction. I know myself and it was a big deal for me just to walk away," he says. Dailey shivers and yawns, though it is already getting very warm in here.

"Well, I guess you're being rewarded for your wise choice. You're leaving," I announce. He looks at me, startled.

"What do you mean? When?"

"Today. As soon as we can make transportation arrangements. You're gone," I repeat. A grin is seeping out my mouth. I can't help it. I see his whole countenance change. Dailey hugs himself, drops his head, runs his hand across his head, looks up, smiles, looks away, looks back and snaps to attention.

"You mean, today? Right now? For real? This can't be happening. I don't believe it. Pinch me," he says.

"Yes. We'll make a call to your family so someone can come pick you up. Seems you're today's lucky winner."

While I'm on the phone with his elderly father, Dailey continues to marvel over this piece of unexpected good fortune. Nice surprises just don't happen in jail.

"Okay, he'll be here in two hours. I suggest you go pack up your things and be ready," I say after hanging up the phone. Dailey stands to his feet, still amazed.

"You're an angel, that's all I gotta say."

"I had nothing to do with this. I'm just the messenger," I reply.

"Yeah, a messenger from heaven," he states. "An angel, like I said."

"Fine, I'll take it. You go get ready for your new life."

"You know what I'm going to do?" he asks. "I'm going to give that guy all my new shirts. The ones Property just gave me. I'll tell him, 'you need 'em more than me.' That'll make things right, you think?"

"I like it. Paying it forward instead of a payback. Nice move, Mr. Dailey. I like it a lot. He'll be wondering what prompted you to be so generous and you'll be long gone."

"Thank Jesus, I can get out of here and never have to do another night like that," he says. "Miss, I thank you. There is a God. No doubt now. And Miss, I'll never forget this. I swear!" he gushes. I walk Dailey to the door, unlock the bolt and release him back into the bull pen. If there is a God, my guess is He's an avid writer, one who enjoys crafting up a nice reversal and a surprise ending that leaves his reader breathless. It's moments like these that balance the massive weight that overburdens the scale on the glass-is-just-about-empty side of the house.

#

It isn't until the car is a quarter-mile down the road that what looks to be an errant leaf trapped under the arm of the windshield wiper turns out to be a slim strip of newspaper fluttering recklessly in a gust of summer wind. The bold strokes of penmanship can be seen. If the clouds let loose like they are threatening to do, the handwriting will be lost in the downpour. I flick on my right-hand signal and settle the car into park on the shoulder of the access road. The perimeter van slows to have a look. Any stopped vehicle on the state-owned driveway is suspect. I snap my badge off my belt and flash it for the concerned guard who is satisfied as to my identity. He waves then and eases down the slope of road that he's navigated a thousand times with his hand on the concealed shotgun riding just under his seat. A part of him is disappointed; he's been hoping and praying his whole career that one day he'll come across a lone runner in tan pants making a desperate break over the low stubble of dead grass so he can finally use the tactical weapon skills he's super-certified in. He's got more chance of hitting the Powerball jackpot than getting a pot shot off at an escapee. In Hazen's sixty-year history, only one inmate ever broke loose from custody but that was during a court transport in the days when officers routinely carried guns and were overpowered with one of their own firearms.

I roll down the window, reach around and snag the note off the windshield. I'm not sure if the dance in my gut is one of anticipation or apprehension. You just never know what crazed individual may have spotted the key fob on your belt clip, noted the make and model of the car you drive, or memorized what direction you walk in from every morning waiting for that day of opportunity when he discharges out into the same dull afternoon and leaves his first mark as a free man. A make-no-mistake reminder, I know who you are and where you go. But not this time, thank God! I recognize Hastings' sloppy script immediately. An exhale of relief comes involuntarily; a sigh of sadness follows.

Elise, I still believe that we were meant to be. I think we are each broken in our own way and perhaps that is part of the attraction, but I also believe we could find a fix together. Though I don't yet understand what's caused the painful hardness in you, I think in time you could feel safe enough to share it with me. If not, I'm willing to work around it or possibly even through it. Just as I hope you would do for me. I've learned that sometimes there is not just one right answer. For me, being in love with you is as right as fighting to keep my family together. What has come before is already in place but we can build our own separate future together. I hope this makes sense to you.

I stop reading for a moment. Everything about me is always past tense, past imperfect. I can't see ahead. Perhaps the future is a discretionary reward that God grants to those He deems able to handle it. He's got a big book of probability like the Classification manual used to pigeon-hole offenders and try and predict which ones will make the wardens look good at end-of-fiscal year. Those most likely to succeed and those who fall into the high risk category. God must be more than a little perplexed when it comes to my case. I never predicted this, He says, scratching his divine head. Not from her. Call it what it is. I'm a recidivist, a skid-bidder, a repeat offender who always returns to the start-point where things first went wrong. I get a pretty nice streak of momentum going but eventually it all circles back to the point of disaster. I am a statistic, one that good minds will puzzle over when it comes to sorting out the winners from the losers. I glance back at the note in my hands and slowly read the final sentences.

I guess I'm asking you to trust me and see where this can lead. If you are not able to make that leap, I forgive you and will always care about you. Love, James

A sluice of rainwater dumps down on the roof of the car and drains over the hood. In minutes, condensation swamps the interior of the vehicle and masks the landscape in a dreary film. The wild turkeys are caught in the onslaught and stand out in the open field like soldiers under siege, about to surrender. I watch the wipers whisk right to left, left to right in a manic race to clear the water away, succeeding for a second before the wash overcomes the glass again. Back and forth in ceaseless uncertainty like my mind's eye trying to open a long view to the horizon, spotting that one gasp of beauty before it all gets socked in with fog again.

I force myself for a moment to think of the others in his life. I acknowledge that he has a wife though I can get by that one with some justification. We're all adults here; all capable and culpable for our success or failures. But then there are those dear daughters sprouting up now into adolescent restlessness, eager to ask questions of a bigger, brighter world than the disillusioned banter that passes for conversation at home. They look to their father to promote these fantasies and fuel their flight up and away from mediocrity. It's so fucking obvious, it hurts. I could never harm the dreams of a child who is preparing to make a launch of faith from the solid platform her loving Dad has built. She needs to know that if all else fails, she can always go back to that one place of safety. It is not for me to rob her of that right.

If you are not able to make that leap, I forgive you, wrote James. I'm in the driver's seat now. Where I am going is no place for a reluctant passenger with baggage.

"Then forgive me," I say out loud as I put the car back into gear and slop forward through the forming puddles without looking back.

#

What was I expecting, really? Men dressed in tuxes taking the podium to deliver the speech of their lives? I mean, this isn't the Oscars. No doubt there are characters here that have played leading roles with great finesse. Others assumed cameo appearances in my seven-week production. There is no guild of critics or an audience poll to base the results on. I am simply a one-woman committee hired to discern who among the current cast had the most convincing auditions. Still it's an award of great import. Even with all the build-up, the last day turns out to be sorely anti-climactic

The guys want it over and done with. They've played the game, jumped through hoops and dragged their unmotivated carcasses out of their bunks to earn that twice-weekly checkmark. Now it's time for me to live up to my side of the bargain and hand over the goods.

"Will Parole get a copy of this?" Zimmer asks.

"Can our people on the outside write the Warden?" wonders Noble.

"How long will it take before my release package is approved?" whines Ortega.

Why am I surprised that no matter how it's worded, the pressing question that overrides all else is: When am I getting out of here? It's a damn prison after all. Put in the same circumstance, I'd be harping on the same point just as loudly.

"If you have any question about the assessment, come see me afterwards. Please sign the top copy and return it to me. You can keep the bottom one. Hold on to that one in case there's ever any question about your compliance. I will enter the completion code into the computer today and put these into your master file. It will be scanned into your Community Release case notes so everybody is on board."

The men file up and drop their last assignment in the metal homework bin on my desk. In exchange, I hand each man his prize. The only exception is Willis who was given his report one week ago. He has not bothered to come today. There are a few sincere thank-you's from the crowd but attention is elsewhere now. They've disengaged and have mentally moved on to tackling the next hurdle in this obstacle course at the end of which is freedom. A part of me is hurt, but why? This isn't a publicity party for Ms. Abrams. I am paid to present this approved curriculum in generic fashion to the dozen or so men in each incoming class. A robot could do this, though admittedly not as well. We complete the required exchange. They drop in their final questionnaire and eagerly accept the long-awaited stamp of approval.

After they are gone, I feel that familiar tinge of sadness. I've never been good with transitions. I collect up the final papers and begin to arrange them in alphabetical order. Mr. Euclid will be pleasantly surprised to see the last-minute scribble where I changed his participation from Fair to Very Good. His parting comments today impressed me. His troubled mind had actually processed far more than his wild flight of thoughts had indicated. Crespo is downright grateful to have been allowed to stay, nodding and smiling and clutching his certificate to his chest. I was tougher on Noble but then, he's been tough on me, holding me to task and pushing me with impatience, the tip of his pen ever poised above a grievance form. The Rev looked stunned that someone could view him as anything less than perfect. He took a hit on Attitude.

Mixed in with the homework assignment papers is a folded sheet of notebook paper, woven over and tucked under to form a perfect little origami pouch. At first I mistake it for a kite, the cryptic, coded notes that find their way around the facility riding in laundry bags until they reach their intended recipient, but this is a personal note addressed to me. I don't need the signature at the bottom to identify its author. The primitive block letters are created with so much force that the pencil point tears through the page in spots. Even on paper, Noble's intensity is hard to control.

Most people do this because it's their job. I can tell that you are not in this for the money. You treat us like human beings. Something not found in the DOC where we are judged by the color of our uniform. I thank you for all you did for me and for all of us. And for not giving up when anyone else in their right mind would have. You made the class a comfortable place where everyone's story could be told no matter how ugly or unimportant. My story is no different.

My first reaction is to run after him, grab the lousy evaluation back, erase the scores and rewrite the constructive criticism I had offered. But he's a big boy now. The honest words of one woman will not break him. We all want to be liked and as shallow and superficial as it sounds, I'm no different. Now here is my validation spelled out in black and white, scribbled with a stolen pencil nub on the back of an electronics order form.

Proof that there's something wrong with me. A real counselor would probably figure it out in the first five minutes of a therapy session. But I'm a special case, a complicated one. I am much like an empty bottle held to the wind. If tilted just so, the vessel emits a sing-song of haunting beauty, a story that forms within a vacuum of apparent emptiness and is brought to life by the friction of troubled souls blowing by me.

Hidden at the bottom of the pile, I discover a beautiful dream catcher disguised in a bundle of paper towels. The outer circle has been constructed from twisted cardboard likely stripped from toilet paper rolls and molded with toothpaste, then wrapped in yards of dental floss. The tips of the intricately knotted fringe have been either dipped in ink or more likely hand-colored with permanent marker. A painstaking process exacted under cover of night using tools that are stolen and hoarded as risky contraband. The gift is from Bowman, the hater. My new number one fan.

CHAPTER 15
TIPPING POINT

The final voice message comes through like a cryptic telegraph: *Not long now. No more pain. Come soon.* What she doesn't have the energy to say, my brother Dale explains in terse terms after he gently removes the phone from her trembling hand. Mom is actively dying though it's anybody's guess how many days it will take. It all depends on how much grit she's got left in her and whether or not she chooses to summon it for one last rally. What is known for certain is that it Mel Braum has made the decision to discontinue all treatment and forced feedings. Since she is of sound mind, the doctors are obligated to sign her living will into orders. All nutritional support will be withheld starting now. Morphine will be administered as palliative pain control and only at a minimal therapeutic dose per Mom's request. She wants to go out with her eyes open and her mind clear. She wants to see her Maker coming in the clouds. At my insistence, Dale holds up the receiver to her ear one last time.

"Anything you want to say to me?" I ask, terrified by the thought that she might actually have nothing for me or not answer at all. But at the same time, I'm frightened to death by what she might utter in her last moments of truth. She struggles to utter some distinct speech but the latest bolus of morphine has flooded her control center. Her language is slurred like a drunk but she is able to master one all-important word: 'Come.' There's no mistaking it.

"I'm on my way, Mom," I whisper. "I'm coming home. Two days. Give me two days. Okay?" I plead. I can hear the clicking gasp that indicates that not only has she heard and comprehended, she's agreed to wait.

#

The door slams behind me cutting off the clamor. Nothing stops these guys; not the normal social cues like turning off the light, locking the door or turning my back to the incessant jabber. Even after I dismiss them with an obvious nod to the guard who pops the door as I push past, they keep at it like a whooping throng of howlers dropping from the canopy. There is no stopping this shit-show of human commotion; not even the recall announcement that orders them back to their bunks for count. They take their sweet time and drag their feet, waiting for me to clear the stairs and appear on the second tier so they can continue to holler out their demands. I'd rather hang back and linger in the calm darkness of the cloistered stairwell but if I don't reappear shortly, the officers will come looking. As I round the first landing a wave of alarm hits me. A lone figure leans against the concrete wall partway down the stairs potentially blocking the way. All inmates should be back in their cells. The officers are all on deck. There are no windows in this area, no viewing point from above. *Shit!* The body alarm has slunk over to the backside of my belt. I'll have to put down my clipboard and water bottle to activate it. I press onwards so the loiterer doesn't sense my concern.

"Hey, Mizz Abrams! I want to thank you," Willis says. His voice breaks the stillness in the tight space.

"Jesus, Mary! You could have warned me," I say grasping my chest. He unfolds his body from the dim shadow and jogs down a couple steps in my direction.

"Why aren't you in your cell? You don't want to get hit with a ticket for being out of place, do you?" I ask.

"The C.O. on post asked me to deliver some supplies to the tier men."

My mouth is moving but my brain is racing ahead, thinking of how I can dodge him. The Parole hearing took place two days ago. I haven't seen the dispositions yet. He couldn't know about the switch I'd pulled with the paperwork, could he? Even if he had produced the glowing recommendation I had given him, it wouldn't have mattered. In his haste to thank me, Willis hadn't stopped to notice that the document I used was an outdated version and was missing the requisite signature that proved its validity. Inmates were always trying to pass off forged paperwork and get a newbie to put a copy in the master file. That's the reason that all communication that makes its way into the book of record never touches an offender's fingertips. My plan was foolproof. My colleagues at Parole wouldn't give him a duplicate of the form I submitted when they laid the bloody bad news on him. And even if they had made any reference to it, his objections would have fallen on deaf ears. Their decision is made long before they hold video court.

"I saw Parole on Tuesday," Willis says. His tone is measured and flat with absolutely no indication of the outcome.

"And...?"

"I know it's all because of you," he replies. My heart drops and the pit of stomach rushes up to meet it. This part wasn't in the original plan, getting caught face-to-face in a closed corridor with a man who has just had his freedom stolen away from him.

"There are a multitude of factors that go into the decision, you know," I stammer. "You can't really know which one carried the most weight with the committee."

"Oh but I do, though," he says. "It was yours." If I race back down the steps and flail against the door, perhaps the officers will have circled round the far perimeter and be within earshot to come to my rescue. I shift my weight slightly in anticipation of making a quick reversal; but before I can make my move, a surprising thing happens. Mr. Willis breaks into a huge, beaming smile and presses both hands in a gesture of prayer with his fingers pointing upwards like a steeple.

"I could never thank you enough for your help. I was approved! They granted me parole. My date is August 16th. That's next week, Mizz A! Can you believe that shit?" he gloats.

"No," I reply incredulously. "I can't."

"I know. Me either. Thank you mightily," Willis says. He jumps down to my level and extends his arms towards me. "May I?" I don't know if he means to hug me or dance with me. When I hesitate, he grins and lifts the bundle of papers from my hands. "C'mon, Elise. I'll walk you out," he adds, as if we are on some kind of date and he has the liberty to escort me safely to my car. He raps four times on the upper door in sharp succession and it swings open. Officer Weiss waves us through.

"Hey, Buddy! Take this roster on down to the Lieutenant's office and grab me a bag of chips from the hall keeper's desk on your way back, will ya?" he asks.

"No problem, Bud," laughs Willis.

So it's all fun and games and slaps on the back now that he's walking out into their community soon. Wait! Did I hear him correctly? Had he just called me by my first name? Willis bumps shoulders with Weiss, shoots a sidelong wink my way and takes some fancy steps out into the hallway.

"Take advantage of me now, bitches, cuz you won't be seeing me again after next week," he says with swagger. Or is it arrogance? I'm moving in slow motion as I follow behind. How could it be that with all the bad press I'd provided, he'd still been granted early release? Had the folks over at Parole lost their fucking minds? Had they failed to read the recommendation? Had they just blinked a lazy eye to it and made a choice of convenience since he was their last case of the day and they didn't want to leave late? Or had someone pulled a fast one and hooked him up? By the time I reach the sally port on my way to close up shop, I've run through the gamut of emotions and settled on a deep seething bitterness. After all the time I have put in and everything I have laid down and given up for this stinking agency, they had left me to hang. *Fuckers*! Did they realize who they were siding with? Better yet, did they know who they had chosen to side against? Didn't they give a good goddamn about going to bed with a clear conviction?

"Hey, Terran!" I call. The happy man interrupts the conversation he's having with one of the lieutenants and swings his head round to see who's looking for him.

"Trust me. I'll see you out there," I yell above the din.

He grins slightly and gives a sallow wave, unsure if he's interpreted the remark correctly above the roar of the gates that part and then shuttle back together, ushering thousands of men out to the streets and welcoming many of them back after a short run. I believe Willis when he says he won't be one of those repeats. He's too smart to get caught again.

#

Brennerman is equally flabbergasted to learn of Willis's good fortune in front of the Board. He had no idea that the words of recommendation on his psychological assessment would have carried so much clout.

"I asked Mrs. Tilton directly what most influenced their decision in his favor," says the therapist.

"And...?"

"She said without doubt it was because he was one of the very few in the system who had successfully defended his case for an overturn. The fact that his sexual misconduct charge had been dismissed and his sex score dropped played to their emotions. This was one of those 'make good' stories that everyone likes to get behind."

"'Unbelievable!" I say, resting the back of my hand against my forehead as if I was suddenly overtaken with a fever.

"I know! It sort of restores your faith in mankind, doesn't it?" Brennerman says with a rapid eye blink and twitch at the corner of his terse lips. I recognize this as his attempt at unsuppressed joy. It is the most animation I've ever seen out of this man. The greatest irony of all is the fact that I was the one who had propelled him right to the front door without even meaning to. I am my own worst enemy.

#

The neighborhood is middle-class on the whole. At one end, the street dwindles down to tiny bungalows and squat ranch houses but the majority of homes are solid little colonials stacked from red brick. The address was easy to pick off the release form that was faxed through to our Records office. Angelica Nunez comes to the door. She's looks to be in her thirties but it's anybody's guess. Spanish women age well compared to their withered white sisters. She wears a black halter top and leggings that swell at both hips and thighs. She's the type of woman who looks better with flashy makeup, the kind she likely started the day with before the sweltering humidity drained it from her face. Ms. Nunez does not hesitate to welcome me in. We have an appointment after all.

The living space is open and modern in contrast to the conservative exterior. It looks as though someone's hard-earned paycheck has been exhausted at the local home goods store. Everything is bright and chipper. A red enamel tea pot sparkles on its brass stand and beside it on the composite counter is a pewter tray with a set of ascending sized table spoons carefully laid out and linen napkins rolled up inside shiny seashell rings. It looks as if she is expecting the local women's auxiliary group to show up rather than hosting one nosy parole manager who's second-guessing her choice in men. She has a right to be questioning since she already had the paper in hand saying this is a home fit for a felon. A request for a second inspection is not a typical step in a process she is well familiar with. There's things she's not saying, but when you love a man who runs street, you gotta be willing to jump through the same hoops and do time along with him.

"Do you want to see the room?" she asks impatiently. When I nod, she walks ahead of me towards the back of the house. The nylon fabric of her leggings thins and shines with each stretch of her fleshy rump as it strains to gain momentum. She rambles slowly along on this impromptu tour, lifting her dimpled arms and flicking her hand half-heartedly at the major sights of interests, the clean but tiny galley kitchen and the cluttered half-bath with wet towels draped over the shower rod. I'm startled suddenly by the unexpected sound of happy children at play. It never occurred to me that there would be kids in the mix. I stop, fixated on the sing-song of muffled voices behind the closed door.

"My babies are playing dress-ups," explains Angelica. "Our bedroom is down here. As I told the other officer, there aren't any guns or alcohol round this place."

"You have how many daughters?" I ask.

"Three girls," she replies.

"How old?"

"Nine, twelve and thirteen," she answers, bored at having to repeat herself.

"May I meet them?" I ask. Angelica nods subserviently as if she has no say-so in the face of a badge, though mine holds no power on these premises. To her, all of us are cops. She's hesitant at first, but sees no good reason why she shouldn't open the door on the left hand side of the narrow hall. Two girls sit cross-legged on a twin bed. A heap of skirts and black velvet hangers decked with Juicy Couture tops swing off the footboard. Pink handbags and silver sandals are strewn in a haphazard trail from the louvered closet doors to the main event by the mirror. There, the teenaged sister is posed in front of the long looking-glass, her hands clamped at her waist. She casts a darting glance in the direction of the intruders and then resumes her modeling act, dipping one shoulder in and locking her hip to one side. The stretchy purple skirt waffles loosely around her pert bottom. In a year or so, the elastic grab of the fabric will be plumped out with the swell of hormones. Her breasts are poking playfully at the thin silk camisole she has forgotten to yank down over her pudgy belly. Her siblings squeal and clap. The show is still for them; no men allowed. Not yet. Something jolts through my memory. That color she is wearing, lavender, the shade of lilacs before they are deflowered and stripped of their beauty. A vision of me twirling in bare feet in front of a dressing mirror gauging the shape of my sex in a brand new lingerie set. A balmy night with the scent of warm earth through the open window. A storm door flung open. I shake my head to rouse my focus back to the present.

"These are his daughters? Mr. Willis's, I mean?"

"Yes, the two oldest," says their mother. The relationship between Terran and Angelica is not clear to me. She senses my confusion and stalls.

"Girls, y'all gotta wash up soon for supper!" she shouts, refusing now to engage, signaling with her indifference that unless I have any other mandatory points on my checklist, this little drill is over.

"How old are you, Angelica?" I ask directly.

"Twenty-nine," she replies defensively. As if she's not old enough to be a good mother. As if she hasn't made a good home here without a man.

"And Willis's date of birth is what again?"

"Uh, I don't know. March, I think," she mumbles.

"But he's your husband, right? How do you know when to get him a birthday card?" She's puzzled by this line of questioning and backs away with accusing eyes. I follow her, looking down at the folder I brought with me for added credibility.

"Let's see. It says here his birthday is August 18th, 1963. Wow! That makes him 51 this summer," I announce. Angelica sets out in a purposed line towards the front door intending to escort me out. I keep talking, hoping to distract her enough to catch her off balance and trip her up.

"You know what they say. You can't teach an old dog new tricks. You believe that's true, Angelica? Men are pretty set in their ways by that age, don't you think?"

"He's a reformed man," she states confidently, though there's nothing in her look that proves she believes it.

"How do you know he's changed?" I ask her.

"They told me. The people at Hazen. They said so," Angelica insists. She heads to the refrigerator and removes a slip of paper. Small ladybug magnets drop to the floor in her hurry. "See? It's from the jail. It says he's learned his lessons." She waves it my face, the bogus copy of the domestic violence program evaluation that I signed into life. Willis must have mailed it to her, proof that he was a good risk when he coerced her into taking him back. My stomach drops like it's on a swing seat that has just reached the highest apex and yanks backwards on its chains. I feel sick.

"You people get paid real good. I gotta believe y'all done a real good job of fixin' him."

"You need to stand up for yourself and protect these girls. You know what he's capable of and what he's done, don't you?" I push harder.

"Please, ma'am. Everything's okay as long as I don't stir the pot. This is an issue between spouses. Y'all don't need to get involved."

"Who is he to you, really? I know Mr. Willis's case in depth. In fact, I've read all of his police reports and pre-sentence investigations and there is no mention of you as his common-law wife or his victim." I flip open the folder in my hands. "It says here Vonnie Lugo is the party who filed a restraining order against Terran. Is Vonnie his real wife?

"His ex," says Angelica flatly. There is no spit in this statement. She's losing ground. It's become so tiresome protecting others from their own dysfunction.

"You know her then?" I ask, pressing into the wound that is nearly visible to those who have the insight and stomach to look for it. I know the scope and depth of that kind of injury by sense, by heart. Angelica finally buckles under.

"She's my mother," she whispers just loud enough to finally be heard without naming a name. His name. Angelica has kept the vow of silence that was exacted from her time and again by the man who was supposed to love her the way daddies do until it's time to give her away proper. But after he was done making her a woman, nobody else wanted her.

"What's on the line if you do speak up?" I ask. Her eyes dart quickly towards the girls' bedrooms and back to me. She can't say the words.

"And you trust him to keep his word? You believe that he won't harm your precious daughters? Are you certain that he hasn't already?"

"Stop, miss," Angelica pleads but she's cracking now. I know her youth just isn't strong enough to hold up all the lies. She's already dirt tired of keeping face and picking back up each and every time he knocks her down. Wouldn't be surprised at all if she's considered hooking up with women if she ever finds a way out. He's taken all the sex out of her; it's not that she worries about any longer. Next thing he's going to take is her life.

Click! I hear it go off in my head. Something is different. It sounds like the pop of a dial on a washing machine. The timer is still beating even after all action of the drum has been suspended. It circulates slowly until it comes to a peaceful stop. The small ticking pulse that wends down and no longer controls anything is just a reminder that time will soon run out and the cycle will come to an end. The restless churning of the cylinder inside my head always trying to wash things off, redistribute the weight, regain proper balance and slush off all the messy, clinging dirt is all hushed now.

"Don't worry, Angelica. Your destiny is not to be a victim. I'm sure of that," I tell her. She flashes a nervous smile as the youngest girl comes running and slaps her eager arms around her mother's fleshy waist.

"Come play with us, Mama," she whines.

"Shush, baby. Just a minute now. I'm talking to the nice lady, here."

"You go on and join them. I'll all through here," I say. She's still young enough to catch up on all that playing she never did.

#

"Feeding time at the zoo. All hands on deck," shouts our Unit Manager. Problem is it's the last dash of summer and the majority of counselors are off on jet skis or a Sailfish somewhere. The entire teaching department has been on break for the past month. That leaves only five of us grunts to do the dirty work of servicing two thousand customers. I knot the disposable plastic apron around my waist, don the throw-away hair net and begin sweating profusely. The temperature in the building is already up into the nineties. With a pair of roller skates, we could have dashed the trays from kitchen to customer windows and knocked out all the orders in less than two hours, but the tips would suck. I'm assigned to handle the three blocks on the east side of the main hall which includes my own. The officers in both I and J units accept the food carts at the door and are willing to take over door-to-door delivery from there. Must be the officer's mess was serving up 5-hour energy shots or an extra shot of something else. *There is a God after all,* I conclude.

I'm halfway down the corridor on my third run down to my own block when I feel a rippling wave of amplified heat crawl up my torso. Irritation prickles my skin. It's like a momentary out-of-body experience. For a split second, I see myself the way the world must at this moment. Look at her, the middle-aged cafeteria lady with a trail of perspiration crawling down her spine, a splotchy face with another sun spot planted front and center. You can tell her age by the leathery skin on the back of her hands. Yes, these are hands that have worked and feet that have more than paid their share. I hope they would feel sorry for me and think this decent-looking dame deserves better than plodding like a Percheron pulling a weighty load of gruel. She's too old to be doing this, they must think; but they need to understand it's far too soon to give up my grip on a career designed for young people, most of them retired well before the shaky world of peri-menopause descends. They are lucky enough to wage the battle against hormones while snipping rhubarb and trailing their painted toenails off pool floats, all because they were smart enough to sign up right after college. Not me. At that age, I was consumed with trying to thread shoelaces through stubborn eyelets and putting letters to a line that turned out to be a laughable stab at a rudimentary alphabet. Blame the man that sent me skidding backwards to relive my infantile crawl up through the Erickson's developmental stages. It's because of that bastard that I'm here in the first place. What irony! Here I am hustling hard to make sure he gets his adequate calories and is well fed before he walks out of here. In a matter of days, he will be gone and I will muddle on slogging this slop to other rapists and killers for years to come.

A rush of rage overtakes my senses. My lungs squeeze out thin oxygen in short, sharp pants. I can't think straight. *Goddamnit!* I unlock the interview room and wheel my rolling cart of aspartame beverages into the room. Two yanks of the pull chain and the oscillating fan begins a sweep back and forth. I close the door and stand still relishing the relief. We're into a scheduled shakedown, a seasonal house-cleaning that will last four more days. I despise the thought of it and I loathe the fact that it's taken me all of my lift to hate the man who robbed me of the emotional tools to conjure up such intensity of feeling, for good or bad. Instead, I've been a pegged marionette that jumped when people jerked and danced when people pulled; but when left to my own ability collapsed into a knot of balsa wood and string. I will never be any better than this, never less broken than right now. Try as we might, we can't help dragging the whole bloody mess of our past into our future. As it turns out, fate and faith are equally powerless to save us. It is time for this flawed puppet to step up on my own wooden feet. An alien sensation begins a slow crawl up my brain stem. For once in my adult life, a sweep of peace overtakes me. All the rattle and din of clanging voices and competing consciences stilled for one defining moment. Here in the peace of this private secret hideaway, I suddenly and unequivocally know what I need to do. Malcolm X was right.

This stark environment is the breeding ground for brilliant revelations. I agree with my late activist brother who might have spurned me for the shade of my skin but not for the color of my world. As he himself said so eloquently, 'I'm for truth, no matter who tells it. I'm for justice, no matter who it is for or against.'

I can't stay in here any longer. The men will be missing their meal and that could start a riot. I mop the back of my neck with a Kleenex, shut off the fan, and step back out into the hallway. One deep breath and it's back to the food frenzy. I make my way down to home turf, H-Block, pushing the awkward food cart and dragging the rolling plastic palette of Styrofoam juice cups behind me. The feeding station is arranged in a central position at the front of the unit. The officer pops out the tiers one at a time and the men shuffle by in steady formation. In a matter of minutes, high fructose corn syrup and the saccharine film of artificial orange drink have left a sticky residue on my forearms.

We have this down to a science. I stack a juice on top of a container and they reach for the combination while flipping their ID into full view. Low-sodium, high-protein, double portion designations stand out in bright stickers on the back of the laminated badge. The clamshell containers are marked in corresponding colors to ensure that the special-needs diets go to the right persons. The juice cups are standard and uniformly poured. The top shelf of the mobile food cart is filled with a couple dozen of the saccharine-sweet beverage cups. I dispense the orders efficiently, acknowledging the men I know by name and responding to their polite thank-you's with a nod and a smile.

"Mr. Tejada."

"Thank you, Miss."

"Here you go, Mr. Quinlan,"

"Ma'am."

"And one for you, Mr. Willis." I hand him his entrée and reach up into the compartment for one of the special drinks that is a hard to find flavor. I give him a wink. It's a myth, the notion that good parents never play favoritism with their children. Whether or not we are linked by a common genetic threat, some are people we would choose to be friends with. It's true for counselors and clients too. Each inmate gets the same treatment but there are those who touch us in a different way, who think in a similar vein, whose soul is deep and who see the world from the same plane we are standing on. A person we would strike up a lively discussion with over a mug of IPA or a chocolate martini and find ourselves still lingering with when the lights go up and the bar tops are being washed down. And while we must disguise the preferential attraction and restrain it, it's no secret to the ones who have found good graces with us. Terran Willis might have been one of those guys if things had been different.

"Gratitude, Counselor," he says and strolls off a happy man.

#

Sick call has been inundated with urgent requests. The hospital wing is already flooded to capacity and the medical team is just as quickly transporting the more seriously ill to area hospitals. Prisoners from multiple housing units have been affected. Initially it was thought to be the fallout from a bad batch of Pruno that had made its fermented rounds affecting the men in various states of intoxication. Efforts to locate the forbidden tonic were intensified but the officers on shakedown duty came up dry. Thirteen guys from H- Block have already been afflicted along with dozens more from other blocks. The stricken inmates first languished on their bunks with an ashy pallor, but within hours were clutching their bellies with faces contorted in pain. Severe nausea was quickly followed by persistent vomiting. At that point, the nursing staff had kicked into high gear and reached out to their contracted hospital facility. If the sickness was not caused by a sour mix, then the next best guess was that it might be E-coli breeding in rancid meat or produce. The summertime heat could have taken its toll on the compressors and fans in the refrigeration units; or it might be blamed on the indifferent food service workers who kept opening the doors to the walk-ins allowing warm air to raise the overall temperature in excess of the required 45 degrees. The Warden ordered his Food Service Supervisor to quickly get a read on the climate in there and narrow down the suspect food items.

I watch as two inmates are taken out by wheelchair. Several more roll by on stretchers. I'm helpless and unqualified to intervene in a medical emergency beyond extending reassurance to the other anxious prisoners who fear they will be next. I check the roster of names against the officer's list.

"So all of these guys are down in Medical?" I ask Boozer. He scans the sheet.

"Yep. All but a few are still down there being treated. Three others were shipped out to U-Mass yesterday," he answers. It's hard enough to keep regular count, let alone try and tally up the missing and mobile.

"Which ones?" I ask. He scours his pad and points to the names.

"McCloud, Clemens and Willis," announces the officer.

"Shit! They must be pretty critical then. Do we know what's wrong?" I ask. It seems as if we are suddenly under the white-hot heat of a searing magnifying glass whose focal point is bearing down, focusing in on the very spot where I stand wishing I was invisible.

"Naw, but it's not surprising given the crap they call food here. It's not like the State dishes up prime rib. My guess is it's from the rat shit in the kitchen. I've seen the little bastards running over the rubber mats and climbing into the dry goods." He wasn't lying. I'd seen plenty of rodents while slopping trays in there.

"So how does this all affect the facility shakedown?" I ask. Boozer shrugs and pulls out his crossword puzzle from the post log.

"We'll stay on lockdown indefinitely until they figure this out. The warden is dismissing all non-essential personnel in case this shit is contagious. He doesn't want staff in the blocks if they don't have to be. I'd head on back and check with your supervisor. See what he wants you to do."

"Hey. Bud. Thanks for the info. You take care, okay?" I say. He nods obligingly.

Back in the privacy of my office, I shut the door and dial up the Admitting Department at U-Mass Memorial Medical Center. After learning the nature of my call, the receptionist patches me up to the critical care unit. The call is answered quickly.

"This is Counselor Abrams. I am hoping to gain some information on my client, Mr. Terran Willis."

The receptionist on duty sounds both harried and young, two flaws that work to my advantage.

"No need, Counselor. Just a minute. I'll get the charge nurse on the line." A montage of recorded messages starts up. The first is an offer to anyone over eighteen years of age who is interested in joining a clinical study for bipolar depression. The following informational ad is a new clinical trial available to women or men who suffer with metastatic breast cancer and the last, a cheery announcement for a new baby class aimed at soothing potentially territorial big brother or sister. The message repeats twice before a live person comes on the line.

"Attorney Abrams? This is Helen, the ICU Charge Nurse. Mr. Willis is with us in the Intensive Care Unit and has been since early Sunday morning. It is difficult to give you a conclusive report. He came in with heart failure and complete disorientation. Before we could get any information from him directly, it appears he had a cerebral event and lapsed into a comatose state. We are running batteries of tests but at the moment, his condition is considered quite critical and he must be maintained on the respirator. We are trying to reach next of kin."

"Mr. Willis has no living or known family members that can be contacted," I reply authoritatively. Her misinterpretation of my title plays nicely into my overall plan.

"I'll note that here in his chart," she says. "May we forward you a Medical Release so you can provide us with some information that might be needed here?"

"Absolutely," I answer and provide her with the fax number to the records office at work. "When he is more stable, I plan to come in to visit if I can be put on his list of permitted guests," I suggest.

"Besides the officer that is posted here, there is no one else," she replies.

"Thank you so much, Nurse Helen," I reply reverently and hang up as softly as I can.

#

The hospital room is chilly and darkened except for a soft bulb over the sterile sink. Mom is resting comfortably with her head sunk back in a foam pillow, her mouth slightly agape, her thin hands crossed over her ribs. An alarm on the monitor is beeping, triggered by the angle of her wrist restraint which is cutting off the tubing. I reposition her arm flat at her side and retape the foam board that holds the arterial line steady at her wrist. As requested, the ICU resident orders the Dilaudid to be dialed back and slowly Mel rouses from her narcotic slumber. Eventually, she is alert enough to turn and regard the figure by her bedside.

"It's me, Mom. Lissa. I'm here to take you home."

Even on the verge of death, she has not forgotten the brilliant smudge of coral lipstick that is her signature style. Likely celibate Saint Peter himself will be forced to sneak a quick once-over as this striking woman passes by his gate. She pats the mattress weakly and I climb on board, stretching out at an awkward angle so we can continue to hold hands without causing any undue pressure on her riddled bones.

"Talk to me," she says. It is the sweetest order I've ever been given. For five long hours, I re-tell the story of my not-so-triumphant life and for most of that time she listens, truly listens, absorbing in all of what she couldn't stand still long enough to hear in health. At one point, she stops me with a raised hand.

'You were never a disappointment to me, honey. Your father and I both were always proud of you. It took great courage to choose the occupation that you did even if it was hard for us to understand why. We were just so worried and afraid for you. It's a parent's job to try and protect their little ones and head off disaster. It felt like we failed at that. Your suffering was so painful for me to watch. I really tried my best to handle it."

'Oh, Mom. You did. We all did."

'You have a real talent for inspiring others, Lissa. The world needs you, especially in that dark place. I will be happy knowing that you are where you belong. We only get one shot in this life. Or in your case, a second chance. Go make it matter."

Mel's words falter off after that and she closes her eyes and grows quiet. I keep talking hoping to revive her. While she doesn't speak, her responses are appropriate, tears at the tragedies and luxurious sighs when the romance enters; when I tell her that I will be having dinner sometime very soon with Aaron. The final thirty minutes we are quietly clutching hands allowing an exchange of deeper truths to come by osmosis. I hold on hard, absorbing the dignified strength of a woman who kept her love at a distance though it was always there. She squeezes and relaxes her grip intermittently pumping out a Morse code of *I love you's* that she could never quite bring to words. Stubborn we are, we women of Scots. Five minutes before her time, I kiss her profusely on the cheeks and tell her that I am taking my name back legally. I will finish out my time on earth as the baby daughter she christened forty-eight years prior in a snowstorm near Hamilton, New York. And as promised I, Lissa Cooke Braum, am there at the exact moment it comes for the angels of heaven to take her home.

#

There is something magically calming about picking through my mother's dresser drawers, a reassurance that she had had another life besides dusting and dishes. But it was some time ago, this other happiness. Her powder puff had crumbled into the chalk and the orange clip-ones hadn't been worn since their last public appearance in a family portrait, the six of us neatly arranged on a piano bench in front of Dad and Mom in her coral suit and swept-up hairdo. April 1974: Mel Cooke's expiration date. After children, she refused to adorn herself. Any of the gifts my father gave her were pressed back into their tissue paper and stacked in the closet. A soft rosebud nightgown from Sleeper's Department store and several velour slacks from the Calliope shop all carefully arranged in chronological order of rejection. Russ must have mistaken his wife for a larger woman. For years, he bought her size tens even though he knew better and she was forced to drag the packages back the day after Christmas to collect a dozen credit slips. Then there was the problem with color, the magenta and teals that he fancied. She would sigh at the sight of them. Dad always told her she could pick out something she liked better, hoping in his heart she would say no. But the very next day, she'd be standing at the sink in a brown cardigan with new tags on. In the years she might have accepted his gift, he didn't know her well enough to choose them. Later these arbitrary refusals got to be such a habit, she couldn't stop.

I see the trend now. One side of her jewelry drawer was for the junk and the other relegated into compartments of precious pieces; past and present separated by a wall of wood. On the hutch in the dining room are soup tureens and a crystal punch bowl that traveled in a covered wagon from Alberta to Bozeman at the turn of the century. They were there locked in that mausoleum and preserved for posterity. What was set out on the table each night was a collection of bank china we each accumulated plate by plate for every deposit over twenty-five bucks. I suddenly realized that everything in her life was delineated. The wisdom she had could have dispensed during our growing years was kept hidden behind a mound of housework and soiled towels. She had been saving up the good stuff for some later day that never came.

In black velvet bag tucked at the back of her top drawer is a slender silver bracelet with a Lakota design on the band. Three oblong pieces of old turquoise set in steps that rise in graduated increments that resemble the peaks of the Teton Range. The name *Lissa* is inscribed in old Lucinda script on the inside; what was my grandmother's name first and now mine. I slip the prized antique on my wrist. I will wear it for both; no, for all three of us. It is time to celebrate the strength of pioneer women who have persevered under avalanches of snow, icy silence and a flood of newly thawed courage.

#

The tiny post office shares half of its square footage with a bait worm shop. The odor of muck and tundra seeps into every parcel that is handed out over the dingy laminated counter. Even though the U.S. Postal Service finally granted permission for a mail route to be established down the dirt road to her farm, Mel still preferred to make the trek into town to collect her circulars and bills. It's my job to finally close down the antiquated mail slot.

I spin the combination on the dial and pull the knob on the small hinged door. Several days' worth of junk mail is crammed inside. A small envelope is nestled among the grocery flyers. On second glance, I'm surprised to see that it is addressed to me. I slit the envelope open with my car key. Folded neatly inside is a printer-generated copy of an article that appeared in the Boston Herald in June of 1988. The heading immediately sends electrifying signals through my nerve channels. *Bright Girl Faces Dark Future*. It is a piece of journalism I had banned from my reading list as soon as it came off the press. The chronicled account of my first crawl out of darkness was too brutal a tale to take in. This was one memoir I refuse to read and will incinerate as soon as I can strike a match. I stand near the out-of-town mail slot with the article shaking in my fingers. What cruel person would want to rub my face in this shitty ordeal all over again? And who on earth would be creepy enough to track my known whereabouts at a time like this? Whoever that person is has taken painstaking time to search my history under my former name and make the connection to my current alias. There are three photographs embedded in the text. The first snapshot is the crime scene record of a body down in a flood of blood; the second is a picture of Hughes by my bedrail in the wee hours of rehabilitation and the final one is my senior photo. In it, a glowing, animated seventeen-year-old girl perched on the apple sprayer and casting a *just dare me to* look to the world. It is Lissa Cooke Braum at her finest. I flip the two-sided piece over and discover a penned note at the conclusion. The page is rumpled and smeared. Whoever sent this has obviously read and reread its content.

No wonder, my poor dear. No words will suffice. But no more worries, my sweet girl.
I will show you how crazy I am about you. Always, James.

I can't help myself. Unfettered joy leaps through my being. I can't wait
to see what true love looks like.

#

Dale and I ride together in silence. I don't expect anything different. He's a
man that's been suffering on the inside so long that any emotion that is
trapped inside his formidable frame is caught and calcified before it can
find release. At the front of the promenade, a massive granite ledge drops
down to sea level. It's a bit of a tricky descent down through a patch of
angry raspberries and knotted bramble before the trail levels off. Of course
Mom would never choose the easiest route knowing that a little hardship
makes the reward that much more precious. Several cars are already lined
up along the sandy shoulder of Point Road with their tires dipping
dangerously close to the slope. Dale throws his old F-150 into park and we
make our way down the incline to where the small band of brothers stands
with hands folded and heads bowed. They've always lived on blind faith, all
of them short-sighted believers who would fail to pick up their heads to see
a miracle if and when it ever actually arrives. God incarnate could be
walking among us and they'd miss his appearance because they are too all-
consumed with the idea of prayer to look up for its answer. And in a way,
he is.

Aaron stands at the fringe of the small clearing shaded by the feathery
tamarack branches that have thinned from too much salt and lichen. A
shaft of sun cuts a diagonal across the crest of his silver-flecked hair runs
down the dark dress shirt and grey slacks and strikes gold on the toes of his
Timberland boots. Like the dove of peace descending on God's disciple, he
is blessed with the best light heaven has to offer streaking down through a
mixed bag of clouds and pre-autumn mist. It's been decades since we laid
eyes on one another. That first glance is tentative, cautious, the kind of
look that peels away age-progression in reverse, searching to find the
familiar young person that went missing years before. And in that stunned
moment of recognition he knows he's found the love of his life that was
buried alive and is still breathing. Beyond that, the chances of her survival
are unclear. I look away and focus on the cremation urn perched on a

square stand in front of us. This piece of furniture is actually the old card table with padded top on which we played Russian Solitaire and Gin Rummy, covered by a fine linen bedspread. Underneath the crocheted throw are blotches of model airplane paint and turpentine stains. The leg on the far right has been bent since the day Seth kicked the whole set-up over during a game of Stratego when his flag was captured by a lucky scout. The mess of red generals, blue soldiers and time bombs was scattered to the winds. Game over; battle lost. The crook in the table leg rusted into a permanent angle. Too much weight or commotion could be guaranteed to buckle it under. I hope the ashes are scattered by loving hands rather than a rogue wind.

After a few long moments of silence, Dale carries the funeral vase down the stone steps in the ledge rock. Summer bathers and local kids alike use this natural trail get access to the flattest skimming rocks in all of New England. I kick off my wedge sandals, lift the hem of my dress with one hand while I scoot on my rump and use my free hand as a brace against the rock formation. A tidal pool has formed in the lava fissure. I hesitate, trying to gauge the jump down. Seaweed and barnacles are unpredictable factors in the physics.

"May I?" The male voice comes from just behind my right shoulder. Startled, I turn my head only slightly for fear I will pitch off my perch. I know who it is anyway. Aaron does not wait for a reply. Instead he jumps down easily onto to the dry beach and turn with arms outstretched. I hesitate. Suddenly my equilibrium seems to tilt the horizon at a peculiar angle.

"'Go ahead. It's fine,' he urges. For some reason, my pulse seems to be pounding in my throat and my legs are suddenly skittish underneath me.

"C'mon," Aaron says gently. "You know you can trust me." *Trust me.* Those ill-fated words of deceit. I teeter with indecision. *He loves me…he loves me not.* Finally I tip forward and allow myself to drop into his grasp which is solid and steady as he lowers me down. I smile in gratitude. The rest of the men folk follow and together as a group we wade down to the water line where the highest roll of surf has just broken and retreated. Dale opens the container and gently shakes a helping of powder and bone fragments into our waiting hands. So this is it, the recipe of a life poured out; the dust of Adam passed through our fingers into the transparent sea. I watch the small clots of ash coalesce and then dissipate into sediment on the ocean floor. Without doubt, this is where my mother most loved to be, creasing rapid strokes in the frigid water and then huddled on her towel eating her peanut butter crackers and sipping grape juice. Her own holy communion. There's a long moment of silence during which no one cries or sniffles. The six Braum children stand like the stoics they were raised to be, chins up, heels dug in, determined not to disappoint. Mom would have been pleased at how well we've managed her passing. After another five minutes or so, my brothers wrap arms of solidarity around one another and agree to head back to the house for a supper of crab casserole and chowder.

"I'll join you soon," I say. "I want to spend a little more time here." Seth, the youngest, turns back concerned.

"It's going to fog in and you're not dressed for it. Plus you rode with Dale and your car is back at the house. C'mon, kid," he pleads teasingly.

"Listen, I'll wait at the wharf and then give her a lift home," offers Aaron. "Go on ahead and I'll swing her home when she's ready. "

"That works," I say, relieved. My baby brother shrugs and joins his siblings as they heard back up the slope in a pack.

"Can you hold on to this for me? Just put in your truck. Don't look inside, though. It's a surprise for later."

"Sure. Take your time," says Aaron. "I've got some phone calls to make so no hurry. I think the fresh air will do you some good." Aaron turns on his heels and follows slowly behind the gang. Not once does he turn back to see if I'm okay. But then why should he? It's wasn't his duty to rescue me back then and it isn't his job now. I'm on my own. I knew it was only a matter of time before I broke down and cried, but what triggers it finally is the realization that I never saw my mother weep in front of me. She had somehow stymied up the ductwork to her emotions and was able to face the biggest of life's trials with calculated and dry-eyed detachment. I am terrified that I am going to end up the same way.

I choose to take the route around the bold front of the Point slipping over fatally slick seaweed until I can ascend up over the giant boulders that nest in the shallows. It's death-by-dashed brains if one slips up. The cormorants dip and dive as fishing boats lumber noisily in the rough tide setting traps and snagging lines. At one spot, the ocean has eroded the cliff and pushes a full head of breakers under the overhanging trees. I am forced to climb a long flight of wooden stairs that lead up from a private dock in order to bypass the interruption and complete the journey around to the boat house. When I reach the wharf, I've pretty much exhausted my well of sorrow. I spy Aaron out on the float sprawled on the hull of one of the overturned rowboats. He waves as I walk out onto the pier, then springs up to meet me at the halfway point where the movable walkway can change angles from perpendicular to near parallel depending on the depth of the tide. Today it is a sloping forty-five degree hop, skip and a jump. When he comes closer and sees the crumpled expression and smeared eyeliner, Aaron instinctively pulls a tissue from his pants pocket. He dabs gently at the residue of dried tears and salt spray stuck to my face, a gesture so familiar it starts full-blown sobs all over again.

"Come here, Lissa," he says, pulling me against him. I let the shudders roll through my body. Aaron holds me and willingly absorbs each one of them. We stand pinned together like two consecutive pages in a torrid romance novel. My damp hair tangles around his wrist. The wear-and-tear of this world is gone from his face as the evening comes on and he is transformed into that boy in the faded blue Colby sweatshirt underneath the stadium bleachers where we crept to consummate our love at second sight.

"I'm ready to get better," I state finally. My voice is hoarse from crying.

"Oh, sweetie. It takes time, possibly even years before you get by a loss this big," he says reassuringly.

"No, this is not about my mother. I'm talking about me. I mean the mess of my life."

"You are miles and miles better," he replies, squeezing me with encouragement and admiration.

"In body, yes. But now it's time to heal the soul too," I whisper. Aaron takes a step back and holds me at arm's length so that there is no mistaking the expression on his face or the import to his pledge.

"I will do anything I can to help you accomplish that. You know that. Whatever you need, Lissa."

"It's taken a long, long time but I'm almost there," I say.

"That's wonderful to hear. It's all I want for you."

"I wish we could have that one night over again. The one that was taken from us," I say in a weepy mew. Aaron doesn't hesitate. All the logical reasons that overrule love are dismissed before they can object. We don't mention his wife. We don't talk about my history. We don't speak beyond a humming chant of our names meshed and married in a sing-song of regret.

Instead we hug each other with passionate regret for all the promises and pledges and plans we were never allowed to make or keep that night so long ago.

"C'mon. You're getting chilled. Let's go sit in the truck," he says. We walk back up the small incline. It's cold enough on these summer evenings in Maine to warrant a quick run of the heater. A plume of sea smoke is creeping around the backside of Beale Island. The horizon is cut off from view.

"Are you a happy man?" I ask eventually.

"Yes, I am. Now more than ever," Aaron replies.

"I want you to know you were never the cause for my restlessness," I say cautiously.

"I obviously wasn't a good enough reason for you to stay here. In Maine. I blamed myself, Lissa. For not being there to protect you in the first place and then for falling short in understanding what you needed."

"But you shouldn't have, Aaron. It was my choice. You never deserted me," I insist.

"It's hard to imagine that spending your days with criminals and your nights alone was preferable over being a wife and mother. I've always respected your intelligence but I had to question your judgment," Aaron replies.

How can I explain it to him, how I was stunned at the moment of impact when trauma struck? Stopped dead in my developmental tracks much like an alcoholic who floods his brain with pickling solution at a young age and never progresses beyond the immature coping skills he has saddled himself with. I learned how to attract boys and men with the flitting beauty of physical youth way before the substance that forms a woman had time to root and grow. I was struck down, held back, left with the inconsistencies of a brash teenager and the numbing fear of a little girl taunted within inches of her own life. I never really had a chance in the grown-up department. Since I couldn't fix myself, I helped others. Isn't that what martyrs do? Powerful men like Malcolm X who knew in his heart it was better to forfeit life as a mortal person in favor of a greater principle. He was a prophet that transformed from a street hustler to the black shining prince of his people, someone who unwittingly but willingly became a god-like inspiration to so many misguided men. We have more in common than I ever imagined. Me, the 'blue-eyed devil' and my fiery

Islamic brother were partners in walking the fine line between violence and justice. He ultimately reached his iconic status; my transcendent climb is only partway complete.

"It's hard to explain," I say.

"It's even tougher to grasp," Aaron replies with a shrug. His lack of resolution is understandable, but I know for certain that I did the right thing. I had protected him from my dangerous instability. He wasn't safe with me. I wonder now if that first longing look cast across the front seat of that old Plymouth Fury was truly love or just need. We hold on to what makes us feel good and project its power into all the shadowy, uncertain places on our trek to find an end to life's dark tunnel.

"I want to show you something," I say, sitting up. "I think it might help you understand why I did what I did."

"Not now. Just be here with me," says Aaron. At his urging, I lay back and rest against the seat. He tentatively slips a working man's arm around my shoulders. As he does, his wedding band snags briefly on the cotton fabric but it doesn't halt the motion. He lifts his free hand to my cheek and traces the irregular scar that runs from mouth to temple. Aaron leans in and plants the gentlest of kisses along its tangent. His fingers continue to search the crescent curve along my cheekbone and jaw line making new discoveries where the fullness of age has blended bone and flesh into new contours. I hold still, hoping that he can feel and sense the raw beauty that has taken hold now. I am no longer that emaciated girl with protruding collarbones and bony knees that could punch holes through cardboard.

"Just stay a little longer, please," he asks. I comply, moving closer and wrapping him up in a subtle, rolling motion. We cling fiercely together and rock ever so slightly in a synchronized sway. I burrow into the warm musk of his chest.

"I never stopped loving you," Aaron says. "And I never will." We lie quiet, still bound together and completely at peace like it was the very first time and knowing that it might very well be our last.

"You're a good man, Aaron Mitchell. You always have been," I say with conviction. I want nothing more than to have his respect.

"And you are a hero in my book, Lissa Braum. And always will be," he says. A small spattering of sun spots and moles cascade near his right temple His eyes are half shut as he mumbles and blinks the puffy eyelids trying to ward off exhaustion. He is after all a middle-aged man with a long work week behind him. I reach across the seat to find his warm thick hand and slip my fingers around his. We cuddle up on the musty cloth seat of his old pick-up. It feels like we are two teenagers holed up for the night and plotting our next move after a long day on the run. Truth is, we're headed in different directions.

"Wait. What is it that you wanted to show me?" he asks, fighting back the growing tide of fatigue. I glance over at the paper bag that holds the dream catcher and Noble's note. To anyone else it might seem like insignificant crap created by misguided men with too much time on their hands; but in my estimation, they are proof positive of my purpose on this wayward planet.

"I'll leave it here. You can look in the morning," I whisper.

In the morning, it turns out, Aaron will wake up and as promised, he will continue to love me. By then, I'll have left Maine far behind in a cloak of glowering clouds that have scuttled up over the horizon and are bustling with brilliant fuchsia streaks and scarlet underpinnings. *Red sky in the morning, sailors take warning.*

It is time to bury the past.

#

Sixteen weeks it takes, two-thousand six-hundred and eighty-seven hours before Mr. Willis opens his eyes and when he does, he is at totally blind, partially deaf and partly brain-damaged. His kidneys are shriveled and useless as dried beans. He is dependent on an artificial filtering system to remove the waste from his body. He has atrophied down to spidery bone and sinew. If he attempts to walk, he must depend on the kindness of his physical therapy aides, two at a time with a gait belt. He will soon complete his sentence and become a free man. Free to wander within a matrix of convoluted thought like a corn maze at night with vision obscured on all sides, movement hedged in by a monotony of stiff unyielding stalk. The only way out is by looking up at an azure sky and following the sun's compass towards home. But he has no more reliable memory to lead him. He will live with this dose of interminable torture with a mind clear enough to comprehend that he is damaged. The immensity of his incapacitation is staggering. Pity has no place here. This business is not for the faint of heart.

"Mr. Willis!" I shout to catch his attention. His hearing aid picks up the vibrations and relays them to the auditory nerve. He turns slowly in my direction, eyes like clouded marbles and bulging with expectation.

"Yes?" he answers, hopeful for a visitor.

"It's Lissa Braum," I say slowly and distinctly. Willis cocks his head and his eyes roll side to side sorting for some association.

"We met when I was twenty-two and you were twenty-five. Remember?"

He has no recall. His fingers turn the dial on his hearing aid and he waves for me to step closer.

"Were we friends?" he asks.

"No, we were strangers," I say slowly, enunciating every syllable clearly. A puzzled look fleets across his sallow face. His right shoulder flinches and relaxes several times. A tic.

"That's an eternity ago," he mumbles.

"An eternity it is," I reply.

"We met again. At Hazen."

Willis hesitates and begins picking through the faces framed in his mind. It is a lengthy line-up and he must concentrate extra hard to finger the right one. He scans again squinting down hard, honing in on the familiar. The voice is the most telling. Suddenly, he shoots up straight in his seat. A wave of recognition rolls over his confusion and for a moment, the ceaseless rocking in his mind is still.

"Could it be...Counselor?" he asks tentatively, putting the emphasis on the crisp consonants which are easier to mouth with tongue clucked in the back of his mouth. A wide smile breaks out. It has been a long time since one has been spontaneously forthcoming and not forced as a matter of practice by a speech pathologist.

"Yes. Mizz Abrams," I say. His hand leaps instantly in my direction as he gropes for a defining touch. He is leaning away from the not-so-distant past—what was— and reaching out into the near future—what still might be.

"Thank the Lord. I'm not forgotten. You came back."

"I didn't forget you for a minute. I told you I would see you on the outside, remember?" He nods and his head inclines in my direction.

"What happened? Do they know what made you so sick?" I ask.

Willis tries to muster up complete sentences but it's like juggling three batons successfully until the fourth is tossed into the mix and concentration is lost. His eyes wander in an incongruent stare as he searches for a way to reassemble his thoughts and his ears scan the auditory horizon for a sign that his visitor is still there with him. It's more difficult than I thought to stomach the sight of such suffering. *Too damn bad! The bastard deserves worse.* I swallow back a swell of indigestion.

Getting in the door of the Westerville Health Care Center turned out to be as easy as stepping through the pair of automated doors. Security was non-existent. Quite frankly, so few visitors ever came to this outpost that the staff was more than happy to welcome me in. No one questioned who I was or if I was kin. The badge at my waist spoke loudly enough.

"Do you know what time it is?" I ask. Willis shakes his head, ponders for a moment and takes a wild guess.

"Four o'clock, I think," he replies. "Maybe you could take me out for some fresh air?" he asks innocently.

"No, it's time to go to sleep. Now, you're gonna close your eyes, count to three and then start your praying. When you finish, I'll be gone." My words are purposed and sharp with diction. He hesitates. My former torturer is bewildered. In the pause of several minutes, I say nothing and do nothing. I let the realization sink in slowly in its own timing. Mr. X is suddenly agitated, flailing in thin air, overtaken by emotions I can well imagine like the sheer terror of realizing that his life has been wrenched from his own control and rests in the hands of the person who casts a shadow across his crouched frame. But unlike me, he will not get better.

"But before you nod off, take a good listen. You're in the presence of a legacy," I whisper. "Because what I do with the rest of my life will far outlast your shameless waste of time on this planet. And *nobody,* least of all you, can rob me of this right. Remember I predicted this? Years ago, I told you it would happen. Your existence would be erased from this earth's memory. There's not a single soul waiting outside this door to come visit you, now is there? Let's hope that when the time comes for you to meet your Almighty Maker that your measly name is jotted down in his Book of Life. And eternity is an awful long time to spend alone, my friend. Trust me," I add.

Willis sits bolt upright in his chair struck by a dawning awareness. I can guess what he must be thinking. *Could the compassionate woman who had seemingly taken genuine interest in his future be somehow connected to that college girl from long long ago?* Maybe he's remembering her bloodied face as the last on his horizon before he dashed off into the night on his fugitive run from justice. I can only hope that when karma brought this devastating illness to his door and silenced his final moments of clarity with concentric circles of confusion and darkness closing in, he was consumed by one thought and one only — that he was slowly and unequivocally dying. I know the feeling all too well. Willis thrashes in his chair and fumbles to find the call bell clipped to the front lapel of his robe.

"Nurse, nurse," he yells. Saliva dribbles down his right jowl. I lift the corner of the blue paper napkin clipped under his chin just like the ones at the dentist office. Willis balks by pulling his head back

"Open your mouth!" I order. It is the most beautiful imperative I have ever uttered. He is stuck. Victims know when it is time to bend to the will of their perpetrator. In his panicked state, he complies. There on the right side of his jaw is a line of pink, spongy gum with four spaces empty of enamel. Proof positive. This is the man who tried to take my life. And I am the young woman who wouldn't let him. We both know it.

"Thank you," I say, softly dabbing the spittle off his cheek. I put a calming hand to his shoulder. "Sweet dreams, lovely!"

"Please...sorry... don't..." he stammers in a voice shaken with remorse and fear. Before he is able to finish his sentence, I am out the door and back on the Turnpike heading home breezing past small boroughs lit with wood fires and warmed by happy families. Good people live out here in this good world, nestled in serene valleys brightened by a galaxy of glittering hope overhead.

#

"Here, Gemini. If you don't mind taking these lists and handing them out to the block officers, I'll go get the classroom open and aired out. God knows, it's going to be hot as a greenhouse in there with all this late-summer humidity. Maybe I can drum up a fan from the supply room."

"Sure thing, Mizz Abrams," he replies amicably. Gemini takes the papers from my hands and gives me an indulging wink. I swear his breasts have grown another cup size. The plus side of having a transgender clerk is that it's highly unlikely that either of us will be accused of granting sexual favors behind closed doors. There's no lack of takers who come to visit Gemini at all hours of the day and night. In a place where no man is your friend, I can count on this sweet she-boy to run interference on my behalf. Gemini sashays off down the mainline and I head into the off-limits corridor where the supply room is located. Two of the lifers are running buffers over the floors. Another older gent is on his knees scrubbing the baseboards with a frayed toothbrush.

"Welcome back, Counselor," he says cheerfully.

"Greetings, Mr. Davenport. What's new with you?"

"Still living the dream. Did you hear what happened while you were gone?"

"Big goings-on while I was away, huh?" I ask as nonchalantly as possible. "I heard quite a few of the inmates got food poisoning."

"True story. The Health Department shut us down for a spell. A batch of bad bird done it."

"Too bad we couldn't just open up a KFC franchise in here. You and I could make some serious bank on that extra crispy chicken."

"No doubt, Mizz A," agrees Davenport.

"But seriously, that was a bad scare. All those guys are fine now, aren't they?" I ask.

"Yes ma'am," agrees Davenport. "But that ain't the story I was getting at."

"Well, what's the dirt then?"

"That piece-of-shit Terran Willis had a major stroke and nearly died from an overdose. They saved him but I'm not sure that was a kindness. The man is ruined." I'm astounded by the caustic tone and uncharacteristic venom in his remark. This man is a self-professed born-again child of God now.

"An overdose of what, Mr. Davenport? Do they know?" I ask.

"They claim it was Suboxone. Don't make no sense, though. The man was a known dealer but never did the drug himself. A real professional never does. I hear they found a big stash in his cell."

"What?" I ask incredulously. "How'd he get his hands on that stuff?"

"Rumor has it that some C.O. planted it there and jammed him up just before he was due to get out."

"You don't sound convinced," I say.

"Between you and me, that's cuz I know different. Word is there was a batch of arsenic in Willis. That's more likely what nearly kilt him," says Davenport on the down-low. "I'm surprised we all ain't died from it, what with all the shit this old building throws off."

Arsenic. I know all about it. Atomic number 33, the forerunner in the family of malicious poisons. Its symbol is As in the periodic table. White arsenic, a toxic chemical that in acute overdose causes black water urine, cardiac failure, hemolysis, nerve damage, shock, delirium and death. Disguised as a harmless-looking powder, this poison is virtually undetectable in food or drink and can be quickly fatal in small doses. A near-perfect murder weapon according to those who have either studied the science behind it or those who have gotten got caught administering it. But even in my darkest dreams, I never considered using this deadly compound; nor, as it turns out, could I have followed through on it. Murder was never what I was after. In the end, it was just me and God left to choose how to make this bad thing better. I decided that the good Lord had way better perspective on things, looking down as He was from a dramatic height far enough removed from all the faulty workings and inconsistencies in human hearts; and with good men like my father by his side, advising him, He would know what to do.

"Are they saying who the dirty cop on the inside is?" I ask.

"They ain't sayin.' Truth be told, they don't care enough to find out. They'll conduct an investigation but they're just goin' through the motions. You know how that shit plays out here, Mizz Abrams. Nobody tolerates the guys who hurt women and little children. Most think he had it coming to him."

"You knew he was a sex offender?"

"Hell, everyone did, Counselor. The brothers were too afraid of him to take matters into their own hands, the way we used to handle things back in the old days. But like the Good Word says, 'vengeance is mine.' When justice comes round, it can be a real bitch."

"I don't know what to think," I say, stupefied.

"I say if a man puts his livelihood and his family on the line, he's either crazy or a better man than the rest of us. If Hastings did do it, then he had reason to do it."

"Did you say *Hastings?* Why would you think such a thing?"

"He and I have growed up together. After twenty years in this joint, you get to know a man, know what I mean? Enough to judge his character and figger out whether you can trust him or not."

Then in a blazing bolt of illumination, it all comes clear. I recall that arsenic is an ingredient found in household items like rat poison and weed killer. The veteran officer who is entrusted with every key to this kingdom also supervises the outside clearance crew on their landscape and garden duties. He has access to the lawn chemicals and the MSDS closet of hazardous materials. My friend and ally, James Hastings. My heart takes off on a wild run of adrenaline. I should act shocked like everyone else who can't equate what they see on the surface to the deeds that emanate from the heart, but I know better. What this wise old convict understands is pure wisdom. *The truth of what one says lies in what he does.* Hastings had kept his promise, stepped outside the circle of boys and took that big brave leap to manhood. I am awed and humbled by the overwhelming realization that I have finally looked into the face of true love in all its raw glory, and found favor.

"Who else knows, Davenport?"

"Only you, ma'am," he replies humbly. We exchange a knowing look that serves as my oath on a code of silence that neither of us will break.

"Stranger things have happened, you know," I reply.

"Sho' nuff," teases the old convict. When I don't answer, Davenport lifts his gaze.

"What's got into you, Mizz Abrams? You win the lottery or something while you be gone? Most folks round here don't start lookin' happy 'til it's close to shift change."

"I don't know, Davenport. You think all this effort is worth it? At the end of the day, do you think any of them will change?"

"I believe God can make saints out of sinners," he answers without hesitation.

"I believe that, too. Otherwise I couldn't walk in these doors every day and do what I do. Got a new class starting up today and it's going to be a challenging one. I'm expecting a bunch of very resistant guys. Anyway, I gotta run. We'll finish catching up soon," I add.

"Yes, ma'am. We sure got plenty of time. I'll be lookin' for that smile of yours come mornin."

"Lord willin' and the crick don't rise," I say.

Davenport grins, lowers his head and resumes his menial task. I leave him kneeling on the dirty floor and step confidently through the sally port. It's impossible to act like this is just another dull day in the land of outcasts where people walk robotically through the motions of maintaining sanity. *Can't they see it?* The beam of redemptive light that has just broken through the window struts overhead and anointed me? This is my end of sentence, my time to shine when the main gate jerks into motion, roll backs and I am released into the first day of the rest of my life.

THE END

ALSO AVAILABLE by Beth Harden

pissing match

beth harden

Small town New England has unique charm and a shared pride. It's a place where folks notice such things as strange cars and unfamiliar faces. Here, residents keep a close pulse and a protective eye on their neighbors, particularly if the newcomers are of a different culture or color that challenges the accepted mindset and jars the commonplace.

"Beth Harden has captured the essence of this American genre in her novel, *Pissing Match*. If it sounds familiar, it may well be. Those in her reading audience who hail from rural hamlets find themselves peering closer at a character that sounds an awful lot like them, or peeking up from the page to double-check names on road signs. Some have gotten completely stuck at the intersection where fact and fiction meet."

Harden is humored when asked if her book is based on real people or true happenings. "There's a little bit of all of us in here. It could be *any*, and is *every* small town. Human nature is not confined by boundary markers and stone walls," Harden says. "It's got folks talking and as we all know, word of mouth is what small towns thrive on." Press Release. 2013.

Made in the USA
Charleston, SC
04 November 2015